Evliyá Efend

Narrative of Travels in Europe, Asia and Africa in the Seventeenth Century
Volume 1

outlook

Evliyá Efendí

Narrative of Travels in Europe, Asia and Africa in the Seventeenth Century
Volume 1

1st Edition | ISBN: 978-3-75235-032-6

Place of Publication: Frankfurt am Main, Germany

Year of Publication: 2020

Outlook Verlag GmbH, Germany.

NARRATIVE OF TRAVELS

IN

EUROPE, ASIA, AND AFRICA,

IN

THE SEVENTEENTH CENTURY,

BY

EVLIYÁ EFENDÍ.

Part I

ADVERTISEMENT.

The narrative of an Asiatic traveller, enthusiastically fond of seeing foreign countries, and unwearied in his investigation of their history, condition, and institutions, is in itself so great a singularity, and so deserving of attention, that no apology seems requisite for thus presenting Evliyá Efendí in an English dress: and the name of the Ritter von Hammer, by whom this work was abridged and translated, is a sufficient voucher for its intrinsic merit and the accuracy of the version.

It is requisite to inform the reader, that throughout the work the Asiatic words and proper names are spelt according to the system of orthography adopted by Sir William Jones and Sir Charles Wilkins, which gives to the consonants the sound they have in our own, but to the vowels that which they have in the Italian and German languages; and by assigning to each Arabic character its appropriate Roman letter, enables the Oriental student to transfer the word at once from one mode of writing to the other.

London, 20th Jan. 1834.

BIOGRAPHICAL SKETCH OF THE AUTHOR.

Evliyá, the son of Dervísh Mohammed, chief of the goldsmiths of Constantinople, was born in the reign of Sultán Ahmed I., on the 10th of Moharrem 1020 (A.D. 1611). He records the building of the mosque of Sultán Ahmed, which was begun when he was six years old, and the gate of which was executed under the superintendance of his father, who in his youth had been standard-bearer to Sultán Suleïmán. His grandfather was standard-bearer at the conquest of Constantinople, by Sultán Mohammed, on which occasion the house within the *Un-kapán* (flour-market), on the ground attached to the mosque of Sághirjílar, was the portion of spoil allotted to him. On this spot he erected one hundred shops, the revenues of which he devoted to the mosque. The administration of the mosque, therefore, remained in the hands of the family. He mentions more than once, as one of his ancestors, the great Sheikh Ahmed Yesov, called the Turk of Turks, a resident of Khorásán, and who sent his disciple, the celebrated Hájí Bektásh,[1] to Sultán Orkhán. Evliyá's mother was an Abáza, and when a girl, had been sent along with her brother to Sultán Ahmed, who kept the boy as a page, and presented the girl to Mohammed Dervísh, the chief of the goldsmiths. The brother had, or received, the Sultán's name, with the sirname *Melek* (angel), and is mentioned in history as the Grand Vezír Melek Ahmed Pashá, in whose suite Evliyá performed a great part of his travels.

Evliyá attended the college of Hámid Efendí, in the quarter of the town called Fíl Yúkúshí, where for seven years he heard the lectures of Akhfash Efendí. His tutor in reading the Korán was Evliyá Mohammed, a learned man, after whom it appears our traveller was named. Distinguished by his acquirements, his melodious voice, and, as it seems, by a fine person, he performed the duty of Móazzin at Ayá Sófíya on the Lailat al Kadr of 1045 (1635), on which occasion, as he himself relates, he attracted the particular attention of Sultán Murád IV. He was then twenty-five years old; and under the care of his master had made such progress in the art of reading the Korán, that he could read the whole in seven hours, and was perfectly versed in the seven modes of reading. His uncle Melek Ahmed was at this time sword-bearer to the Sultán, and it seems that Evliyá was in some degree indebted to his interest for the favour of being immediately admitted as a page of the *Kílár-oda*. The Sultán was not less pleased with his melodious voice and his witty remarks, which evinced much information, than with his handsome person, in consequence of which he was initiated into all the profligacies of the royal pages, the relation of which, in more than one place, leaves a stain upon his writings. He, however, continued his studies in caligraphy, music, grammar, and the Korán, the latter still under the direction of Evliyá Mohammed, who was then imperial chaplain (*Khúnkár Imámí*).[2]

His stay in the imperial palace was, however, very short, as he was removed from it previously to the Persian expedition, undertaken the same year (1045) against Eriván, when he was enrolled among the Sipáhís, with a stipend of forty aspres *per diem*. Whatever importance Evliyá may have attached to the honour of having been for a short time an inmate of the seraglio, it seems to have produced no change in his life, which was that of a traveller all his days. To this vocation, he conceived he had a special call in a dream on the anniversary of his twenty-first birth-day (the 10th of Moharrem). He fancied himself in the mosque of Akhí-Chelebí, where the Prophet appeared to him in full glory, surrounded by all the saints of the Islám. When he wished to pray for the intercession (*shifáa't*) of the Prophet, by mistake he asked for travelling (*siyáhat*), which was granted to him, together with permission to kiss the hands of the Prophet, the four Imáms, and of the saints. His friends the Sheikhs, from whom he requested the interpretation of this dream, assured him that he should enjoy the favour of monarchs, and the good fortune of visiting in his travels the tombs of all the saints and great men whom he had seen. From this moment he formed the resolution of passing his life in travelling, and visiting the tombs of the saints; thus his name *Evliyá* (saints) became significant, as he was all his life *Mohibbi Evliyá*, that is, the friend of the saints. This circumstance accounts for the predilection he evinces in visiting the tombs and monuments of the saints, as he often dwells with particular pleasure on the description of places of pilgrimage. Evliyá (the friend of saints), Háfiz (knowing the Korán by heart), and Siyyáh (the traveller), are the names by which he styles himself, although he is more commonly known by the name of Evliyá Chelebí or Efendí; and his work is called *Siyyáh Námeh*, or the History of the Traveller.

Having received his call by a vision of the Prophet, he commenced his travels by excursions through Constantinople and its environs, his topographical descriptions of which, as to the latter, are perhaps the best extant, and occupy the whole of the first volume. The most valuable portion of it is that towards the end, in which he gives a detailed account of the various corporations of tradesmen, and the rank they held in the solemn processions.

He travelled, as he frequently mentions, for forty-one years, so that he must have completed his travels in the year 1081 (A.D. 1670), when he was sixty-one years of age, and he seems to have devoted the rest of his life to repose, and to the writing of his travels, which extended to all parts of the Ottoman empire, in Europe, Asia, and Africa, except Tunis, Algiers, and Tripolis, which he never visited, and which he therefore passes over in his statistical

4

account of the Ottoman empire. Besides travelling in Rumelia, Anatolia, Syria, and Egypt, he accompanied the Turkish Embassy to Vienna in 1664, as secretary, whence he proceeded to the Netherlands and Sweden, and returned by the Crimea. Though generally employed in diplomatic and financial missions, he was sometimes engaged in battles, and mentions having been present at twenty-two; the first of which was the expedition to Eriván, which took place the same year in which he entered and left the Seraglio (1645). His father, who had been standard-bearer at the siege of Siget (1564), and must at this time have been nearly ninety years of age, was ordered, together with some other veterans who had served under Sultán Suleïmán, to accompany the expedition in litters, merely to encourage the Janissaries. This was Evliyá's first campaign, but he has left no account of it.

His second journey was to Brousa, in 1640, with the account of which he commences his second volume. This journey he undertook, together with some friends, without his father's consent, and having visited all the baths, monuments, mosques, and public walks, he returned to Constantinople, where he was well received by his father.

In the beginning of Rebi-ul-evvel he set out on his third journey, which was to Nicomedia. On his return he visited the Princes' Islands, and arrived at Constantinople a month after he had left it.

Ketánjí Omar Páshá having been appointed to the government of Trebisonde, he made his old friend, Evliyá's father, his agent at Constantinople, and took Evliyá along with him. They left Constantinople in the beginning of Rebi-ul-ákhir, and proceeded to Trebisonde, coasting by Kefken, Heraclea, Amassera, Sinope, Samsún, and Kherson. From Trebisonde he was ordered to attend the *zemburukchís* (camel-artillery) of Gonia to the siege of Azov in 1051. He proceeded along the shores of the Black Sea through the country of the Abáza, the history and description of which form the most interesting part of Evliyá's travels. The fleet destined for Azov reached Anapa shortly after the arrival of Evliyá. He immediately waited upon the commander, Delí Husain Páshá, who received him into his suite, and placed him on board the galley of his kehiyá. They sailed for Azov on the 12th of Sha'bán. Evliyá was present at the siege, which being unsuccessful, was raised, and he accompanied the Tatár Khán's army, which returned to the Crimea by land. At Bálakláva he embarked for Constantinople, but was wrecked, and escaped with only two slaves out of the many whom he had collected in his travels through Abáza and Mingrelia. He was thrown on the coast of Kilyra, whence he proceeded to Constantinople.

In 1055 (1645) the fleet was fitted out, as was generally rumoured, for an expedition against Malta, and Evliyá embarked on board the ship of the

Capudán Páshá, Yúsuf Páshá, in the capacity of *Móazzin-báshí*.[3] The expedition, however, having touched at the Morea, suddenly turned upon Candia, where Evliyá was present at the reduction of the castle of St. Todero, and the siege of Canea; after which he attended several military excursions to Dalmatia and Sebenico.

On his return to Constantinople he made arrangements for his sixth journey, with Defterdár Zádeh Mohammed Páshá, who was at that time appointed governor of Erzerúm, and whom Evliyá accompanied as clerk of the custom-house at Erzerúm. Their route lay through Nicomedia, Sabanja, Bólí, Túsia, Amásia, Nígísár, and they reached Erzerúm, having made seventy stages. Shortly afterwards the Páshá sent him on a mission to the Khán of Tabríz, with a view to facilitate a commercial intercourse. This was Evliyá's first journey into Persia. On his way he visited Etchmiazin, Nakhchaván, and Merend; and returned by Aján, Erdebíl, Eriván, Bakú, Derbend, Kákht, the plain of Chaldirán, and the fortress of Akhíska. Ten days after he was again despatched to Eriván, on returning from which he resumed his duties at the custom-house. He was, however, scarcely settled, when the Páshá sent him on a mission to the governor of the Sanjaks of Jánja and Tortúm, in order to collect the troops which had been ordered by a *Khatt-i-sheríf*. With this commission he visited the towns of Baiburd, Jánja, Isper, Tortúm, Akchekala', and Gonia, of which latter the Cossacks had at that time taken possession. Evliyá witnessed its reduction, and was the first to proclaim on its walls the faith of the Islám.

The Mingrelians having revolted on the occasion of one of the Cossack inroads, a predatory expedition into Mingrelia was undertaken by Seidí Ahmed Páshá; and Evliyá having over-run the country with his plundering party, returned to Erzerúm, whence, on the 18th of Zilka'da, he set out on his return to Constantinople. His Páshá, Defterdár Zádeh Mohammed, having openly rebelled against the Porte, he followed him from Erzerúm through Kumákh, Erzenján, Shínkara-hisár, Ládík, Merzifún, Koprí, Gumish, Jorúm, and Tokát. He once fell into the hands of robbers, but fortunately effecting his escape, he followed his master to Angora. The inhabitants of this town not permitting the Páshá to shut himself up in the castle, he was again obliged to take the field. His great ally Várvár Páshá, on whose account he had rebelled, though he had beaten and made prisoners several Páshás (amongst whom was Kopreilí, afterwards celebrated as the first Grand Vezír of the family), was at last defeated, and killed by Ibshír Páshá. Defterdár Zádeh Mohammed Páshá, however, managed his affairs so well, that he obtained not only his pardon but a new appointment. Evliyá was with him at Begbázár, when he received the intelligence of his father's death, and that all his property had fallen to his step-mother and his sisters. On hearing this he took leave of Defterdár Zádeh, and proceeded by Turbelí, Taráklí, and Kíva, to Constantinople, where he arrived at the time of the great revolution, by which Sultán Selím was deposed, and Mohammed IV. raised to the throne. Evliyá's account of this revolution, and of the principal actors in it, is so much the more interesting, that the chief favourite of Ibrahím, the famous Jinjí Khoajeh, of whose ignorance he makes mention, had been Evliyá's school-fellow. Evliyá, however, had been well treated by him, and received as an old school-fellow, shortly before his own fall, and that of his royal master, Ibrahím, which happened in the year 1058 (1648).

Evliyá next attached himself to Silihdár Murtezá Páshá, who was appointed Governor of Damascus, as *Moazzin-báshí* (an office which, as before mentioned, he had held under Yúsuf Páshá, in the expedition against Canea), and as *Imám Mahmil*, or priest of the caravan of pilgrims to Mecca. He left Constantinople in the beginning of Sha'bán 1058 (1648).

The third volume commences with an account of his seventh great journey, which was to Damascus. He had scarcely arrived at this place when he was sent by Murtezá Páshá on a mission to Constantinople. This journey was performed very rapidly, and he gives no particular account of it, only mentioning that he met some of the robbers belonging to the party of Kátirjí Oghlí.

He returned with the same despatch to Damascus, whence he set out on his pilgrimage to Mecca, through Egypt. Of this pilgrimage no account is given in our manuscript copy, as it seems he died before he had completed the work. There is no question, however, as to the time at which it was undertaken, since in his account of the reign of Sultán Murád IV. he states that he was just in time, after his return from Mecca through Egypt, to share in the glory of the victory gained by Murtezá Páshá over the Druzes, in the year 1059. Now Evliyá's account of this expedition commences in the month of Moharrem 1059, from which it may be supposed that he had just returned from Mecca, where the annual ceremonies of the pilgrimage take place in Zilhijeh, the last month of the year.

Evliyá was employed by Murtezá on various missions, the object of which was to collect debts and exact money. On such errands he was sent to Mount Lebanon, Karak, Balbek, Akka, Yaffa, and Haleb, whence he took a journey to Rakka, Roha, Bális, Meraash, Kaisari, and over Mount Arjísh (Argaus) to Ak-seráï, Sívás, Díárbekr, and in the year 1060 (1650) returned to Constantinople by Ainehbázár, Merzifún, Kanghrí, Kastemúni, and Táshkoprí.

He now entered the service of his uncle, Melek Ahmed Páshá, who, after having been Grand Vezír for some time, was removed to the government of

Oczakov, and afterwards to that of Silistria, in the year 1061 (1651). Evliyá accompanied him, and this was his ninth journey, reckoning each journey by his return to Constantinople. He travelled over the whole of Rumelia, and made some stay at Adrianople, of which he gives a detailed account, and thus completes his description of the three Ottoman capitals, viz. Constantinople, Brousa, and Adrianople. He left Adrianople with his uncle and patron, Melek Ahmed, who was now raised to the rank of a Vezír of the Cupola at Constantinople; but being unable, notwithstanding his marriage to a Sultána, to maintain his credit in the Ottoman court during these revolutionary times, he was obliged to accept the government of Ván, to which he proceeded with great reluctance. Evliyá, who had been left behind, followed him a few days after, having been despatched by the Sultána, the lady of Melek Ahmed. He travelled through Sívás, Malátía, Díárbekr, Márdín, Sinjár, Míáfarakain, Bedlís, and Akhlát. A considerable portion of his narrative is devoted to the history of the warfare between Melek Ahmed Páshá and the Khán of Tiflís, the latter of whom was beaten and deposed; and his account of the Kurds, and their different tribes, is not less interesting than that in his second volume of the Abázas on the eastern coasts of the Black Sea.

Having already given proofs of his abilities in diplomatic affairs when employed by Defterdár Zádeh Mohammed Páshá, on missions to Tabríz and Eriván, and by Murtezá Páshá in his Syrian missions, Evliyá was now entrusted by Melek Ahmed with several missions to the Persian Kháns of Tabríz and Rúmia, with the view of reclaiming seventy thousand sheep, and the liberation of Murtezá Páshá, who was kept a prisoner by the Khán of Dembolí. From Tabríz he went through Hamadán to Baghdád, his description of which, and its environs, of Basra and of the ruins of Kúfa, contains some most important geographical notices. From Basra he travelled to Hormuz and the Persian Gulf, and returned to Baghdád by Basra, Váset, and Kala'i Hasan. In a second excursion he visited Háver, Arbíl, Sheherzor, Amadia, Jezín, Husnkeif, Nisibin, and returned to Baghdád by Hamíd, Mousul, and Tekrít. With the account of these the author concludes his fourth volume; and notwithstanding every endeavour, and the most careful search in all the markets and sales, no more of the work has been discovered. It may, therefore, be taken for granted that he never wrote any continuation of it. The fourth volume ends with the year 1066 (1655), and these four volumes embrace only a period of twenty-six years of the forty-one which Evliyá spent in travelling. Of the events of the remaining fifteen, the following notes may be collected from his own work.

In the year 1070 (1659) Evliyá accompanied the expedition into Moldavia, and assisted at the conquest of Waradin. The Ottoman armies extended their inroads as far as Orsova and Cronstadt in Transylvania, and Evliyá received twenty prisoners as his share of the booty. He then joined his uncle and patron, Melek Ahmed Páshá, then governor of Bosnia, who on the 12th of Rebi-ul-evvel 1071 (1660), was appointed governor of Rúmeili. With him, in the following year, Evliyá made the campaign into Transylvania, which was then disturbed by the pretenders to the crown, Kemeny and Apasty. He was at Saswár when the news arrived of the death of the Grand Vezír, Mohammed Kopreïlí, in 1071 (1660). After the battle of Forgaras he left Transylvania, and took up his winter quarters with Melek Ahmed Páshá at Belgrade. Melek Ahmed was shortly afterwards recalled to Constantinople in order to be married (his first Sultána having died) to Fátima, the daughter of Sultán Ahmed. He died after he had been a Vezír of the Cupola three months; and thus "poor Evliyá" (as he generally calls himself) was left without a protector. He, however, remained in the army, then engaged in the Hungarian war, till the year 1075 (1664), when Kara Mohammed Páshá was sent on an embassy to Vienna, and Evliyá, by the express command of the Sultán, was appointed secretary of the embassy. The ambassador returned in the ensuing year to Constantinople, as may be seen by his own report, published in the Ottoman Annals of Rashíd; but Evliyá having obtained an imperial patent, continued his travels through Germany and the Netherlands, as far as Dunkirk, through Holland, Denmark, and Sweden, and returned through Poland, by Cracovie and Danzig, to the Crimea, after a journey of three years and a half, thus finishing, on the frontiers of Russia, as he himself states, his travels through "the seven climates."

Although he repeatedly mentions his travels through Europe, it is doubtful whether he ever wrote them; from doing which he was probably prevented by death, when he had completed his fourth volume. It appears that after having travelled for forty years, he spent the remainder of his days in retirement at Adrianople, where he probably died, and where his tomb might be looked for. It also appears that the last ten years of his life were devoted to the writing of his travels, and that he died about the year 1090 at the age of seventy.

This supposition is borne out by his mentioning, in his historical account of the reign of Sultán Mohammed IV., the conquest of Candia which took place in 1089 (1678); and further by his speaking of his fifty years' experience since he commenced the world, which must refer to the year 1040, when, at the age of twenty, he entered upon his travels; during which he declares he saw the countries of eighteen monarchs, and heard one hundred and forty-seven different languages.

The motto on his seal, which he presented to a Persian Khán of his own name, was: "Evliyá hopes for the intercession of the chief of saints and prophets."[4]

Judging from the chronographs and verses which he inscribed on several

9

monuments, and the errors into which he frequently falls respecting ancient history, Evliyá must be considered as but an indifferent poet and historian. But in his descriptions of the countries which he visited he is most faithful, and his work must be allowed to be unequalled by any other hitherto known Oriental travels. Independent of the impression made upon him by his dream, that by the blessing of the Prophet he was to visit the tombs of all the saints whom he had seen in their glory, he found that his lot was to travel; and besides the name of *Háfiz* (knowing the Korán by heart), he well deserved *par excellence* that of *Siyyáh* or *the* traveller.

TRAVELS

EVLIYA EFENDÍ.

IN THE NAME OF GOD, THE ALL-CLEMENT, THE ALL-MERCIFUL!

To GOD, who ennobles exalted minds by travels, and has enabled me to visit the holy places; to Him who laid the foundations of the fortresses of legislation, and established them on the groundwork of prophecy and revelation, all praise be given: and may the richest blessings and most excellent benedictions be offered to the most noble and perfect of all creatures, the pattern of prayer, who said, "Pray as you see me pray;" to the infallible guide, Mohammed; because it is in his favour that God, the Lord of empires and Creator of the heavens, made the earth an agreeable residence for the sons of Adam, and created man the most noble of all his creatures. Praise to Him, who directs all events according to His will, without injustice or incongruity! And, after having offered all adoration to God, let every pious aspiration be expressed for the prosperity of his shadow upon earth, the ruler of terrestrial things, the Sultán son of a Sultán, the victorious Prince Murád Khán, fourth son of Sultán Ahmed Khán, and eighth in descent from Sultán Mohammed Khán, the Conqueror, the mercy of God rest upon them all! but most especially on Sultán Murád Ghází, the conqueror of Baghdád, the great Monarch with whose service I was blessed when I began to write an account of my travels.

It was in the time of his illustrious reign, in the year A.H. 1041 (A.D. 1631), that by making excursions on foot in the villages and gardens near Islámbúl (Constantinople), I began to think of extensive travels, and to escape from the power of my father, mother, and brethren. Forming a design of travelling over the whole earth, I entreated God to give me health for my body and faith for my soul; I sought the conversation of dervíshes, and when I had heard a description of the seven climates and of the four quarters of the earth, I became still more anxious to see the world, to visit the Holy Land, Cairo, Damascus, Mecca and Medina, and to prostrate myself on the purified soil of the places where the prophet, the glory of all creatures, was born, and died.

I, a poor, destitute traveller, but a friend of mankind, Evliyà, son of the dervísh Mohammed, being continually engaged in prayer and petitions for divine guidance, meditating upon the holy chapters and mighty verses of the Korán, and looking out for assistance from above, was blessed in the night *'Ashúrá*, in the month of *Moharrem*, while sleeping in my father's house at

Islámbúl, with the following vision: I dreamt that I was in the mosque of Akhí chelebí, near the Yemish iskeleh-sí (fruit-stairs or scale), a mosque built with money lawfully gotten, from which prayers therefore ascend to heaven. The gates were thrown open at once, and the mosque filled with a brilliant crowd who were saying the morning prayers. I was concealed behind the pulpit, and was lost in astonishment on beholding that brilliant assembly. I looked on my neighbour, and said, "May I ask, my lord, who you are, and what is your illustrious name?" He answered, "I am one of the ten evangelists, Sa'd Vakkás, the patron of archers." I kissed his hands, and asked further: "Who are the refulgent multitude on my right hand?" He said, "They are all blessed saints and pure spirits, the spirits of the followers of the Prophet, the Muhájirín, who followed him in his flight from Mecca, and the Ansárí who assisted him on his arrival at Medína, the companions of Saffah and the martyrs of Kerbelá. On the right of the *mihráb* (altar) stand Abú Bekr and 'Omar, and on the left 'Osmán and 'Ali; before it stands Veis; and close to the left wall of the mosque, the first Muezzin, Belál the Habeshí. The man who regulates and ranks the whole assembly is Amru. Observe the host in red garments now advancing with a standard; that is the host of martyrs who fell in the holy wars, with the hero Hamzah at their head." Thus did he point out to me the different companies of that blessed assembly, and each time I looked on one of them, I laid my hand on my breast, and felt my soul refreshed by the sight. "My lord," said I, "what is the reason of the appearance of this assembly in this mosque?" He answered, "The faithful Tátárs being in great danger at Azák (Azof), we are marching to their assistance. The Prophet himself, with his two grandsons Hasan and Hosaïn, the twelve *Imáms* and the ten disciples, will immediately come hither to perform the appointed morning service (*sabáh-namáz*). They will give you a sign to perform your duty as *Muezzin*, which you must do accordingly. You must begin to cry out with a loud voice 'Allah Ekber' (God is great!) and then repeat the verses of the Throne (Súrah II. 259). Belál will repeat the 'Subhánullah' (Glory to God!), and you must answer 'Elhamdu-li-llah' (God be praised!) Belál will answer, 'Allah ekber,' and you must say 'Amín' (Amen), while we all join in the *tevhíd* (i.e. declaration of the divine unity). You shall then, after saying 'Blessed be all the prophets, and praise to God the Lord of both worlds,' get up, and kiss the hand of the prophet, saying 'Yá resúlu-llah' (O Apostle of God!)."

When Sa'd Vakkás had given me these instructions, I saw flashes of lightning burst from the door of the mosque, and the whole building was filled with a refulgent crowd of saints and martyrs all standing up at once. It was the prophet overshadowed by his green banner, covered with his green veil, carrying his staff in his right hand, having his sword girt on his thigh, with the

Imám Hasan on his right hand, and the Imám Hoseïn on his left. As he placed his right foot on the threshold, he cried out *"Bismillah,"* and throwing off his veil, said, *"Es-selám aleik yá ommetí"* (health unto thee, O my people). The whole assembly answered: "Unto thee be health, O prophet of God, lord of the nations!" The prophet advanced towards the *mihráb* and offered up a morning prayer of two inflexions (*rik'ah*). I trembled in every limb; but observed, however, the whole of his sacred figure, and found it exactly agreeing with the description given in the *Hallyehi khákání.* The veil on his face was a white shawl, and his turban was formed of a white sash with twelve folds; his mantle was of camel's hair, in colour inclining to yellow; on his neck he wore a yellow woollen shawl. His boots were yellow, and in his turban was stuck a toothpick. After giving the salutation he looked upon me, and having struck his knees with his right hand, commanded me to stand up and take the lead in the prayer. I began immediately, according to the instruction of Belál, by saying: "The blessing of God be upon our lord Mohammed and his family, and may He grant them peace!" afterwards adding, *"Allah ekber."* The prophet followed by saying the *fátihah* (the 1st chap. of the Korán), and some other verses. I then recited that of *the throne.* Belál pronounced the *Subhánu'llah,* I the *El-hamdulillah,* and Belál the *Allah ekber.* The whole service was closed by a general cry of *"Allah,"* which very nearly awoke me from my sleep. After the prophet had repeated some verses, from the *Suráh yás,* and other chapters of the Korán, Sa'd Vakkás took me by the hand and carried me before him, saying: "Thy loving and faithful servant Evliyà entreats thy intercession." I kissed his hand, pouring forth tears, and instead of crying *"shifá'at* (intercession)," I said, from my confusion, *"siyáhat* (travelling) O apostle of God!" The prophet smiled, and said, *"Shifá'at* and *siyáhat* (*i.e.* intercession and travelling) be granted to thee, with health and peace!" He then again repeated the *fátihah,* in which he was followed by the whole assembly, and I afterwards went round, kissed the hands, and received the blessings of each. Their hands were perfumed with musk, ambergris, spikenard, sweet-basil, violets, and carnations; but that of the prophet himself smelt of nothing but saffron and roses, felt when touched as if it had no bones, and was as soft as cotton. The hands of the other prophets had the odour of quinces; that of Abú-bekr had the fragrance of melons, 'Omar's smelt like ambergris, 'Osmán's like violets, Alí's like jessamine, Hasán's like carnations, and Hoseïn's like white roses. When I had kissed the hands of each, the prophet had again recited the *fátihah,* all his chosen companions had repeated aloud the seven verses of that exordium to the Korán (*saba'u-l mesání*); and the prophet himself had pronounced the parting salutation (*es-selám aleïkom eyyá ikhwánún*) from the *mihráb*; he advanced towards the door, and the whole illustrious assembly giving me various greetings and blessings, went out of the mosque. Sa'd Vakkás at the same time, taking his quiver from his own belt and putting it into mine, said: "Go, be victorious with thy bow and arrow; be in God's keeping, and receive from me the good tidings that thou shalt visit the tombs of all the prophets and holy men whose hands thou hast now kissed. Thou shalt travel through the whole world, and be a marvel among men. Of the countries through which thou shalt pass, of their castles, strong-holds, wonderful antiquities, products, eatables and drinkables, arts and manufacturers, the extent of their provinces, and the length of the days there, draw up a description, which shall be a monument worthy of thee. Use my arms, and never depart, my son, from the ways of God. Be free from fraud and malice, thankful for bread and salt (hospitality), a faithful friend to the good, but no friend to the bad." Having finished his sermon, he kissed my hand, and went out of the mosque. When I awoke, I was in great doubt whether what I had seen were a dream or a reality; and I enjoyed for some time the beatific contemplations which filled my soul. Having afterwards performed my ablutions, and offered up the morning prayer (*saláti fejrí*), I crossed over from Constantinople to the suburb of Kásim-páshá, and consulted the interpreter of dreams, Ibráhím Efendí, about my vision. From him I received the comfortable news that I should become a great traveller, and after making my way through the world, by the intercession of the prophet, should close my career by being admitted into Paradise. I next went to Abdu-llah Dedeh, Sheïkh of the convent of Mevleví Dervíshes in the same suburb (Kásim-páshá), and having kissed his hand, related my vision to him. He interpreted it in the same satisfactory manner, and presenting to me seven historical works, and recommending me to follow Sa'd Vakkás's counsels, dismissed me with prayers for my success. I then retired to my humble abode, applied myself to the study of history, and began a description of my birth-place, Islámbúl, that envy of kings, the celestial haven, and strong-hold of Mákedún (Macedonia, *i.e.* Constantinople).

SECTION I.

Infinite praise and glory be given to that cherisher of worlds, who by his word "BE," called into existence earth and heaven, and all his various creatures; be innumerable encomiums also bestowed on the beloved of God, Mohammed Al-Mustafà, Captain of holy warriors, heir of the kingdom of law and justice, conqueror of Mecca, Bedr, and Honaïn, who, after those glorious victories, encouraged his people by his noble precepts (*hadís*) to conquer Arabia (Yemen), Egypt (Misr), Syria (Shám), and Constantinople (Kostantiniyyeh).

Sayings (hadís) *of the Prophet respecting Constantinople.*

The prophet said: "Verily Constantinople shall be conquered; and excellent is the commander (emír), excellent the army, who shall take it from the opposing people!"

Some thousands of proofs could be brought to shew, that Islámbúl is the largest of all inhabited cities on the face of the earth; but the clearest of those proofs is the following saying of the prophet, handed down by Ebú Hureïreh. The prophet of God said: "Have you heard of a town, one part of it situated on the land, and two parts on the sea?" They answered, "yea! O prophet of God;" he said, "the hour will come when it shall be changed by seventy of the children of Isaac." From (Esau) Aïs, who is here signified by the children of Isaac, the nation of the Greeks is descended, whose possession of Kostantiniyyeh was thus pointed out. There are also seventy more sacred traditions preserved by Mo'áviyyah Khálid ibn Velíd, Iyyúb el-ensárí, and 'Abdu-l-'azíz, to the same effect, *viz.* "Ah! if we were so happy as to be the conquerors of Kostantiniyyeh!" They made, therefore, every possible endeavour to conquer Rúm (the Byzantine empire); and, if it please God, a more detailed account of their different sieges of Kostantiniyyeh shall be given hereafter.

SECTION II.

An Account of the Foundation of the ancient City and Seat of Empire of the Macedonian Greeks (Yúnániyyáni Mákedúniyyah), i.e. the well-guarded Kostantiniyyeh, the envy of all the Kings of the Land of Islám.

It was first built by Solomon, and has been described by some thousands of historians. The date of its capture is contained in those words of the Korán, "The exalted city" (*beldah tayyibeh*), and to it some commentators apply the following text: "Have not the Greeks been vanquished in the lowest parts of the earth?" (Kor. xxx. 1.) and "An excellent city, the like of which hath never been created." All the ancient Greek historians are agreed, that it was first built by Solomon, son of David, 1600 years before the birth of the Prophet; they say he caused a lofty palace to be erected by Genii, on the spot now called Seraglio-Point, in order to please the daughter of Saïdún, sovereign of Ferendún, an island in the Western Ocean (*Okiyúnús*).

The second builder of it was Rehoboam (*Reja'ím*), son of Solomon; and the third Yánkó, son of Mádiyán, the Amalekite, who reigned 4600 years after Adam was driven from Paradise, and 419 years before the birth of Iskender Rúmí (Alexander the Great), and was the first of the Batálisah (Ptolemies?) of the Greeks. There were four universal monarchs, two of whom were Moslims and two Infidels. The two first were Soleïmán (Solomon) and Iskender Zú'l karneïn (the two-horned Alexander), who is also said to have been a prophet; and the two last were Bakhtu-n-nasr, that desolation of the whole face of the earth, and Yánkó ibn Mádiyán, who lived one hundred years in the land of Adím (Edom).

SECTION III.

Concerning the Conquest of the Black Sea.

This sea, according to the opinion of the best mathematicians, is only a relic of Noah's flood. It is eighty fathoms (*kúláj*) deep, and, before the deluge, was not united with the White Sea. At that time the plains of Salániteh (Slankament), Dóbreh-chín (Dobruczin), Kej-kemet (Ketskemet), Kenkús and Busteh, and the vallies of Sirm and Semendereh (Semendria), were all covered with the waters of the Black Sea, and at Dúdushkah, on the shore of the Gulf of Venice, the place where their waters were united may still be seen. Parávádí, in the páshálik of Silistirah (Silistria), a strong fortress now situated on the highest rocks, was then on the sea-shore; and the rings by which the ships were moored to the rocks are still to be seen there. The same circumstance is manifested at Menkúb, a days journey from Bághcheh seráï, in the island of Krim (Crimea). It is a castle built on a lofty rock, and yet it contains stone pillars, to which ships were anciently fastened. At that time the island of Krim (Crimea), the plains of Heïhát (Deshti Kipchák), and the whole country of the Sclavonians (Sakálibah), were covered with the waters of the Black Sea, which extended as far as the Caspian. Having accompanied the army of Islám Giráï Khán in his campaign against the Muscovites (Moskov), in the year——, I myself have passed over the plains of Haïhát; at the encampments of Kertmeh-lí, Bím, and Ashim, in those plains, where it was necessary to dig wells in order to supply the army with water, I found all kinds of marine remains, such as the shells of oysters, crabs, cockles, &c., by which it is evident that this great plain was once a part of the Black Sea. Verily God hath power over every thing!

The fourth builder of Constantinople was Alexander the Great, who is also said to have cut the strait of Sebtah (Ceuta), which unites the White Sea (Mediterranean) with the ocean. Some say the Black Sea extends from Azák (Azof), to the straits of Islámbúl (the canal of Constantinople), the sea of Rúm (Greece), from thence to the straits of Gelíbólí (Gallipoli, *i.e.* the Hellespont), the key of the two seas, where are the two castles built by Sultán Mohammed the Conqueror, and that all below this forms the White Sea. Having often made an excursion in a boat, when the sea was smooth and the sky clear, from the Cape of the Seven Towers (*Yedí kullah búrunú*), near Islámbúl, to the point of Kází Koï (called Kalámish), near Uskudár (Scutari), I have observed in the water a red line, of about a hand's breadth, drawn from one of these points to the other. The sea to the north of the line is the Black Sea; but to the south of it, towards Kizil Adá, and the other (Princes') islands, is called, on account of its azure (*níl*) hue, the White Sea; and the intermixture of the two colours forms, by the command of God, as wonders never fail, a red seam (*ráddeh*), which divides the two seas from each other. This line is always visible, except when strong southerly winds blow from the islands of Mermereh (Marmora), when it disappears, from the roughness of the sea. There is also a difference in the taste of the waters on each side of this line; that towards the Black Sea being less salt and bitter than that towards the White Sea: to the south of the castles (of the Dardanelles), it is still more bitter, but less so than in the ocean. No sea has more delicious fish than the Black Sea, and those caught in the Strait of Islámbúl are excellent. As that strait unites the waters of the Black and White Seas, it is called, by some writers, the confluence of two seas (*mereju'l bahreïn*).

The fifth builder of Constantinople was a king of Ungurús (Hungary), named Púzantín (Byzantinus), son of Yánkó Ibn Mádiyán, in whose time the city was nearly destroyed by a great earthquake, nothing having escaped except a castle built by Solomon, and a temple on the site of Ayá Sófiyyah. From Púzantín, Islámbúl was formerly called Púzenteh (Byzantium).

The sixth builder was one of the Roman emperors; the same as built the cities of Kóniyah, Níkdeh and Kaïsariyyah (Cæsarea). He rebuilt Islámbúl, which, for seventy years, had been a heap of ruins, a nest of serpents, lizards, and owls, 2288 years before its conquest by Sultán Mohammed.

The seventh builder of the city of Mákedún was, by the common consent of all the ancient historians, Vezendún, one of the grandsons of Yánkó Ibn Mádiyán, who, 5052 years after the death of Adam, being universal monarch, forced all the kings of the earth to assist him in rebuilding the walls of Mákedún, which then extended from Seraglio point (*Seráï búrunú*), to Silivrí (*Selymbria*), southwards, and northwards as far as Terkós on the Black Sea, a distance of nine hours' journey.

Both these towns were united by seven long walls, and divided by seven ditches a hundred cubits wide. The remains of these walls, castles, and ditches, are still visible on the way from Silivrí to Terkós; and the kháns, mosques, and other public buildings in the villages on that road, as Fetehkóï, Sázlí-kóï, Arnáúd-kóï, Kuvúk-dereh, 'Azzu-d-din-lí, Kiteh-lí, Báklálí, and Túrk-esheh-lí, are all built of stones taken from these walls; the remains of some of their towers and seven ditches appearing here and there. Chatáljeh, which is now a village in that neighbourhood, was then a fortified market-town close to the fortress of Islámbúl, as its ruins shew. The line of fortifications which then surrounded the city may still be traced, beginning from Terkós on the Black Sea, and passing by the villages of Bórúz, Tarápiyah (*Therapia*), Firándá near Rum-ili hisár, Ortahkóï, Funduklí, to the point of Ghalatah, and from thence to the lead-magazines, St. Johns fountain (*Ayá Yankó áyázmah-sí*), the Ghelabah castle, the old arsenal, the castle of Petrínah, the Arsenal-garden-Point, the castle of Alínah, the village of Súdlíjeh, and the convent of Ja'fer-ábád. All these towns and castles were connected by a wall, the circuit of which was seven days'journey.

Concerning the Canal from the river Dóná (Danube).

King Yánván, wishing to provide water for the great city of Islámbúl, undertook to make a canal to it from the Danube. For that purpose he began to dig in the high road near the castles of Severin and Siverin, not far from the fortress of Fet'h-islám, on the bank of that river; and by those means brought its waters to the place called Azád-lí, in the neighbourhood of Constantinople. He afterwards built, in the bed of the river, a barrier of solid stone, with an iron gate, which is still to be seen, as the writer of these sheets has witnessed three different times, when employed there on the public service. The place is now called the iron gate of the Danube (*Dóná demir kapú-sí*), and is much feared by the boat-men, who sometimes unload their vessels there, as, when lightened of their cargoes, they can pass over it in safety.

He also built another wear or barrier in the Danube, now called Tahtah-lú sedd, upon which many ships perish every year. It was when that river overflowed in the spring, that king Yánván opened the iron gate and the barrier, to allow the stream to pass down to Islámbúl, where it discharges itself into the White Sea, at the gate called Istirdiyah kapú-sí (the Oyster-gate), now Lan-ghah kapú-sí. All this was done by king Yánván during the absence of king Vezendún, who was gone on a pilgrimage to Jerusalem. On his return, his uncle Kójah Yánván went over to Scutari to meet him; and as soon as they met: "Well, my uncle," said Vezendún, have you succeeded in your undertaking with regard to the Danube?"—"I dragged it, O king," said he, "by the hair, like a woman, into Mákedúniyyah (Constantinople), through which it now runs." Scarcely had he uttered this haughty answer, when, by the command of God, the river suddenly returned, deserting its new bed, and bursting forth in a large fountain, at a place called Dóna-degirmánlerí (the Mills of the Danube), between Várnah and Parávádí, where a mighty stream turns a great number of mills, which supply all the people of Dóbrújah with flour. Another branch of the Danube bursts forth near Kirk Kilisá (the Forty Churches), from the rocks of Bunár-hisár (Castle of the Source). A third branch broke out in the lakes of Buyúk and Kuchúk Chekmejeh, whence it unites with the Grecian (Rúmí) sea. The proof that all these streams have their source in the Danube is that they contain fish peculiar to that river, such as tunnies, sturgeons, &c., as I myself have more than once witnessed, when observing what the fishermen caught in the lakes just named. It is also mentioned in the historical work entitled *Tohfet*, that Yilderim Báyazíd (Bajazet) when he conquered Nigehbólí (Nicopolis) and Fet-h-islám, having heard of the ancient course of the Danube, caused straw and charcoal to be passed into it through the iron gate, and that they afterwards appeared again at the above-named lakes Bunár-hisár and Dónah-degirmánlerí. When travelling with the Princess Fatimah, daughter of Sultán Ahmed, and Suleïmán Beg, we stopped at the village of Azád-lí, between Chatáljeh and Islámbúl, where there are evident marks of the ancient channel of the Danube, cut by art through rocks towering to the skies. We penetrated into those caverns on horseback, with lighted torches, and advanced for an hour in a northerly direction; but were obliged to return by bad smells, and a multitude of bats as big as pigeons. If the sultáns of the house of 'Osmán should think it worth their while, they might, at a small expense, again bring the waters of the Danube by Yeníbághcheh and Ak-seráï to Islámbul.

The eighth builder of that city was a king of the name of Yaghfur, son of Vezendún, who placed no less than three hundred and sixty-six talismans (one for every day in the year) near the sea at Seraglio-Point, and as many on the hills by land, to guard the city from all evil, and provide the inhabitants with all sorts of fish.

The ninth builder was Kostantín (Constantine), who conquered the ancient town and gave his name to the new city. He built a famous church on the place where the mosque of Mohamed II. now stands, and a large monastery, dedicated to St. John, on the hill of Zírek-báshí, with the cistern near it; as well as the cisterns of Sultán Selím, Sívásí tekiyeh-sí, near Ma'júnjí Mahal-leh-si, and Kedek-Páshá. He erected the column in the *táúk-bázár* (poultry market), and a great many other talismans.

SECTION IV.

Concerning Constantine, the ninth Builder, who erected the Walls and Castle of Constantinople.

He was the first Roman emperor who destroyed the idols and temples of the Heathens, and he was also the builder of the walls of Islámbúl. 'Isá (Jesus) having appeared to him in a dream, and told him to send his mother Helláneh (Helena) to build a place of worship at his birth-place Beïtu-l-lahm (Bethlehem), and another at the place of his sepulchre in Kudsi Sheríf (Jerusalem), he despatched her with an immense treasure and army to Felestín (Palestine); she reached Yáfah (Jaffa), the port of Jerusalem, in three days and three nights, built the two churches named above, and a large convent in the town of Nábulús.

The Discovery of the true Cross.

By the assistance of a monk called Magháriyús (Macarius), she found the place where the true cross was buried. Three trees in the form of crosses were found in the same grave, and the moment, as the Christians relate, a dead body was touched by them, it came to life again: this day was the 4th of Eïlúl (September), which is therefore celebrated by the Christians as the feast of the Invention of the Cross, and has ever since been held as a great festival by the Greeks. Helláneh also built the convent of the Kamámeh (*i.e.* the church of the holy sepulchre) on the spot where the dead body had been restored to life, spent immense sums of money in repairing and adorning the mosque of Al-aksá built on the site of the temple of Solomon, restored Bethlehem, and did many other charitable and pious works. She then returned to Islámbúl, and presented the wood of the cross to her son Constantine, who received it with the greatest reverence, and carried it in solemn procession to the convent on the summit of Zírek-báshí. The noblest monuments of his power and resolution to surpass all other princes in the strength and durability of his works, are the walls of Constantinople. On the land side of the city, from the Seven Towers at its western extremity to Iyyúb Ansárí, he built two strongly fortified walls. The height of the outer wall is forty-two cubits, and its breadth ten cubits; the inner wall is seventy cubits high and twenty broad. The space between them both is eighty cubits broad, and has been converted into gardens blooming as Irem; and at present, in the space between the Artillery (Tóp-kapú) and Adrianople gates (Edreneh-kapú), are the summer-quarters (*yáïlák*) of the Zagharjíes, or 64th regiment of the Janissaries.

Outside of the exterior wall he built a third, the height of which, measured from the bottom of the ditch, is twenty-five cubits, and its breadth six cubits; the distance between this and the middle wall being forty cubits: and beyond the third wall there is a ditch one hundred cubits broad, into which the sea formerly passed from the Seven Towers as far as the gate of Silivrí; and being admitted on the other side from the gate of Iyyúb Ansárí to the Crooked gate (Egrí-kapú), the town was insulated. This triple row of walls still exists, and is strengthened by 1225 towers, on each of which ten watchful monks were stationed to keep watch, day and night. The form of Islámbúl is triangular, having the land on its western side, and being girt by the sea on the east and north, but guarded there also by a single embattled wall, as strong as the rampart of Gog and Magog. Constantine having, by his knowledge of astrology, foreseen the rise and ascendancy of the Prophet, and dreading the conquest of his city by some all-conquering apostle of the true faith, laid the foundation of these walls under the sign of Cancer, and thus gave rise to the incessant mutinies by which its tranquillity has been disturbed. It is eighteen miles in circuit; and at one of its angles are the Seven Towers pointing to the Kiblah (Meccah). The Seraglio-point (Seráï-búruní) forms its northern, and the gate of Iyyúb its third and north-western angle. Constantine having taking to wife a daughter of the Genoese king (Jenúz Králí), allowed him to build some strong fortifications on the northern side of the harbour, which were called Ghalatah, from the Greek word *ghalah* (γάλα, milk), because Constantine's cow-houses and dairy were situated there.

Names of Constantinople in different Tongues.

Its first name in the Latin tongue was Makdúniyyah (Macedonia); then Yánkóvíchah in the Syrian (Suryání), from its founder Yánkó. Next in the Hebrew ('Ibrí) Alkesándeïrah (Alexandria) from Alexander; afterwards Púzenteh (Byzantium); then for a time, in the language of the Jews, Vezendúniyyeh; then by the Franks Yaghfúriyyeh. When Constantine had rebuilt it the ninth time, it was called Púznátiyám in the language of the Greeks, and Kostantaniyyeh; in German Kostantín-ópól; in the Muscovite tongue Tekúriyyah; in the language of Africa, Ghiránduviyyeh; in Hungarian, Vizendú-vár; in Polish, Kanátúryah; in Bohemian, Aliyáná; in Swedish (Esfaj), Khiraklibán; in Flemish, Isteghániyyeh; in French, Aghrándónah; in Portuguese, Kósatiyah; in Arabic, Kostantínah; in Persian, Kaïsari Zemín; in Indian, Takhti Rúm (the throne of Rome); in Moghól, Hákdúrkán; in Tátár, Sakálibah; in the language of the 'Osmánlús, Islámbúl. Towards the sea it was never defended by a ditch, which is there superfluous, but by a single wall; but to guard the entrance of the Bosporus and Hellespont, and to increase the security of the city, the castles called Kilídu-l-bahreïn (*i.e.* the key of the two seas), were built. It is said to have had three hundred and sixty-six gates in the time of Constantine, who left only twenty-seven open, and walled up the rest, the places of which are still visible.

SECTION V.

Concerning the circumference of Constantinople.

In the year 1044 (1634) when I was first come to years of manhood, and used to walk with my friends all over Islámbúl, at the time that Sultán Murád IV. had marched against (Riván) Eriván, and Kójah Baïrám Páshá was left as Káyim-makám (viceroy), he used to visit my late father; and, in the course of conversation, inquire about the history of Islámbúl. "My lord," said my father, "it has been built nine times, and nine times destroyed; but had never, since it has been in the hands of the house of 'Osmán, fallen into such decay as now, when waggons might be any where driven through the walls." He then suggested to the Páshá, that this city, being the envy of the kings of the earth, and the royal residence of the house of 'Osmán, it would be unworthy him to suffer its walls to remain in that ruinous condition during the period of his government; and that when the Sultán returned victorious from Riván, he would be overjoyed on seeing "the good city," his nest, as brilliant as a pearl, and compensate this service by large remunerations, while the name of the Páshá would also be blessed by future generations for so meritorious a work. All who were present applauded what my father had said, and he concluded by repeating the *Fátihah*. The Mólláhs of Islámbúl, Iyyúb, Ghalatah, and Uskudár (Scutari), the Shehr emíní (superintendent of the town), four chief architects, Seybánbáshí (the third in rank among the officers of the Janissaries), and all other men in office were immediately summoned together, with the Imáms of the 4,700 divisions (mahallah) of the city, for the purpose of giving aid in repairing the fortifications. Many thousands of masons and builders having been assembled, the great work was begun, and happily finished in the space of one year, before the return of the Sultán from his victorious campaign at Riván.

On receiving intelligence of the conquest of that fortress the joy was universal, and the city was illuminated for seven days and seven nights. It was then that a causeway, twenty cubits broad, was formed at the foot of the wall, along the sea-shore, from Seraglio-Point to the Seven Towers; and on it a high road was made for the convenience of the sailors, who drag their vessels by ropes round the point into the harbour. Close to the wall, all the houses, within and without, were purchased by government, and pulled down to make room for the road, and I then was enabled to measure the circumference of the city, by pacing it round as I shall now explain.

Having said a *bismillah* on setting out, and going along the edge of the ditch, from the Seven Towers to Abú Iyyúb Ensárí, I found the distance measured

24

8,810 paces, exclusive of the eight gates. From the little gate of Iyyúb to the Garden-gate (Bághcheh kapú), including the Martyrs gate (Shehíd kapú-sí), a space comprehending fourteen gates, there are 6,500 paces. The new palace (Yení seráï), which is the threshold of the abode of felicity (Asitánehi Dáru-s-se'ádet), beginning from the barley-granary (Arpá-enbárí), which is near the head-lime-burners gate (kirej-chí báshí kapú-sí), has, in its whole circumference, sixteen gates, ten of which are open, and six closed, except on extraordinary occasions. The entire circuit of this new palace, built by Mohammed (II.) the conqueror, is 6,500 paces. The distance from the Stable gate (Akhór-kapú), along the new-made high road to the angle of the Seven Towers, measures 10,000 paces, and comprehends seven gates. According to this calculation, the whole circumference of Islámbúl measures 30,000 paces, having ten towers in every thousand paces, and four hundred towers in the sum total; but, taking into the account those in the triple wall on the land side, there are altogether 1,225 large towers; of which, some are square, some round, some hexagonal. When Baïrám Páshá had undertaken a complete repair of the fortifications, he ordered the walls to be measured by the builders' ell (arshín), and the whole circumference of the city was found to be exactly 87,000 ells or cubits (zirá').

In the time of Kostantín (Constantine), there were five hundred cannons planted on the arsenal (Tóp-khánah) near the lead-magazine, of which the iron gates are still visible; the same number was planted near Seraglio-Point, and a hundred round the foot of the Maiden's Tower (Kiz kulleh-sí, *i.e.* the Tower of Leander). Not a bird could cross without being struck from one of these three batteries, so secure was Islámbúl from any hostile attack. There was then a triple chain drawn from Ghalatah to Yemish Iskeleh-sí, upon which a large bridge was built, affording a passage for comers and goers, and opening when necessary to allow the ships to go through. There were two other bridges also across the sea, from Balát kapú-sí (Palace gate) to the garden of the arsenal (Ters-kháneh-bághcheh-sí), and from Iyyúb to Súdlíjeh. In the time of Yánkó Ibn Mádiyán, also, a triple chain of iron was drawn across the straits of the Black Sea (Karah deniz bóghází), at the foot of the castle called Yórúz (*i.e.* the castle of the Genoese), in order to prevent the passage of the enemy's ships. I have seen fragments of these chains, which are still preserved at Islámbúl in the magazines of the arsenal, each ring of which is as wide across as a man's waist, but they now lie covered with sand and rubbish. Islámbúl was then in so flourishing a state, that the whole shore to Silivrí one way, and to Terkóz on the Black Sea the other, was covered with towns and villages to the number of twelve hundred, surrounded by gardens and vineyards, and following each other in uninterrupted succession. Constantine, having reached the summit of greatness and power, could easily have conquered the world, but he preferred employing the remainder of his life in the embellishment of his capital. On the great festivals, such as the Red-egg-days (Kizil yúmurtah gúnlerí, *i.e.* Easter), Mother Meryem's days (the Feasts of the Virgin), Isvat Nikólah (St. Nicolas), Kásim (St. Demetrius), Khizr Ilyás (St. George), Aúsh-dús, (i.e. the Feast of the Exaltation of the Cross, on the 14th of September), the casting of the crosses into the water (the Epiphany), the days of Karah-kóndjólóz (probably days on which evil spirits were exorcised), and on all Sundays (Bázár gúnlerí, *i.e.* market days), the walls of Constantinople were covered with scarlet cloth, and the emperor himself, having his beard adorned with pearls, and the Kayanian crown of Alexander on his head, walked in solemn procession through the streets of the city.

The number of Paces between each of the twenty-seven Gates.

From the Kóshk (Kiosk) to the gate of the Seven Towers	1,000 paces.
From thence to the Silivrí-gate	2,010
To the Yení-kapú (New-gate)	1,000
To the Tóp-kapú (Cannon-gate)	2,900
To the Adrianople-gate	1,000
To the Egrí-kapú (Crooked-gate)	900

These six gates are all on the west side of the city, looking towards Adrianople.

From thence to the Iyyúb Ensárí-gate	1,000 paces.
To the Balát kapú-sí (the gate of the Palatium)	700
Fánús-kapú-sí (Fanal-gate)	900
To the Petrah-kapú	600
To the Yení-kapú (New-gate)	100
To the Ayà-kapú	300
To the Jubálí-kapú	400
To the Un-kapání-kapú (Flour-market-gate)	400
The Ayázmah-kapú (Fountain-gate)	400
To the Odún-kapú (Timber-gate)	400
To the Zindán-kapú-sí (Prison-gate)	300
To the Báluk-bázárí-kapú (Fish-market-gate)	400
To the Yení jáma'-kapú-sí (New Mosque-gate)	300

This, which is also called the Válideh kapú-sí (Queen Mothers-gate), was erected in order to give access to the new mosque built by that princess.

From thence to Shehíd kapú-sí (Martyr's-gate)   300 paces.

These fourteen gates, from Iyyúb-kapú-sí to Shehíd-kapú-sí, all open to the sea-shore, and face the north. The gates in the circuit of the imperial palace (*seräï humáyún*) are all private, and are, 1. the Kirech-jí (lime-burners); 2. the Oghrún, from which the corpses of criminals executed in the seraglio are thrown into the sea; 3. the Bálukchí (fishmongers); 4. the Ich ákhór (privy stable gate), looking southward; and 5. the gate of Báyazíd khán, which also faces the south, but is not always open. 6. The imperial (Bábi humáyún) or gate of felicity (Bábi Sa'ádet), also open to the south, and within it there are three gates in the same line: one of them is the (7.) Serví-kapú-sí (the cypress gate), by which the Sultán issues when he visits Sancta Sophia, or takes his rounds through the city in disguise; another is (8.) Sultán Ibráhím's gate, also opening to the south, near the cold spring (*sóúk cheshmeh*); a third is (9.) the Sókóllí Mohammed Páshá kapú-sí, a small gate near the Aläï-kóshk, looking to the west; a fourth, also facing westward, is (10.) Suleïmán Khán kapú-sí, a small gate now always shut. (11.) The iron gate (Demir kapú) is a large portal facing the west, and appropriated to the use of the Bóstánjís and imperial favourites (Musáhibler, *i.e.* Ἑταίροι). The above-mentioned eight private gates, from the Akhór kapú to the Demir kapú, all open into the city; but there are nine other private gates opening to the sea on the Seraglio-Point, and facing the north.

The whole circuit of the Seraglio measures	6,500 paces.
From the Privy Stable to the Public Stable-gate (kháss-ú-'ám ákhór kapú-sí), there are	200
From thence to the Chátládí (Broken-gate)	1,300
To the Kúm-kapú (Sand-gate)	1,200
To the Lánkah-gate	1,400
Thence to the gate of Dáúd Páshá	1,600
To the Samátíyah-gate	800
To the Nárlí-gate	1,600
To the gate of the inner castle of the Seven Towers	2,000

Seven of these gates open towards the east, and as the winds blow from the south-east with great violence, the quay built by Baïrám Páshá was soon destroyed, so that when I paced the circuit, as mentioned above, in the reign of Ibráhím Khán, I was obliged to pass between the Stable-gate and the Seven Towers, within the walls. I then found the whole circuit to be 29,810 paces;

but, in Baïrám Páshá's time, when I went outside the walls, it measured exactly 30,000 paces, or 87,000 builders' cubits (*mïmár arshúní*).

SECTION VI.

On the wonderful Talismans within and without Kostantíneh.

First talisman. In the 'Avret-Bázárí (female-slave-market), there is a lofty column (the pillar of Arcadius) of white marble, inside of which there is a winding staircase. On the outside of it, figures of the soldiers of various nations, Hindustánies, Kurdistánies, and Múltánies, whom Yánkó ibn Mádiyán vanquished, were sculptured by his command; and on the summit of it there was anciently a fairy-cheeked female figure of one of the beauties of the age, which once a year gave a sound, on which many hundred thousand kinds of birds, after flying round and round the image, fell down to the earth, and being caught by the people of Rúm (Romelia), provided them with an abundant meal. Afterwards, in the age of Kostantín, the monks placed bells on the top of it, in order to give an alarm on the approach of an enemy; and subsequently, at the birth of the Prophet, there was a great earthquake, by which the statue and all the bells on the top of the pillar were thrown down topsy-turvy, and the column itself broken in pieces: but, having been formed by talismanic art, it could not be entirely destroyed, and part of it remains an extraordinary spectacle to the present day.

Second talisman. In the Táúk-Bázár (poultry-market) there is another needle-like column (the pillar of Theodosius), formed of many pieces of red emery (*súmpáreh*) stone, and a hundred royal cubits (*zirá' melikí*) high. This was also damaged by the earthquake which occurred in the two nights during which the Pride of the World was called into existence; but the builders girt it round with iron hoops, as thick as a man's thigh, in forty places, so that it is still firm and standing. It was erected a hundred and forty years before the era of Iskender; and Kostantín placed a talisman on the top of it in the form of a starling, which once a year clapped his wings, and brought all the birds in the air to the place, each with three olives in his beak and talons, for the same purpose as was related above.

Third talisman. At the head of the Serráj-kháneh (saddlers' bazar), on the summit of a column stretching to the skies (the pillar of Marcian), there is a chest of white marble, in which the unlucky-starred daughter of king Puzentín (Byzantius) lies buried; and to preserve her remains from ants and serpents was this column made a talisman.

Fourth talisman. At the place called Altí Mermer (the six marbles), there are six columns, every one of which was an observatory, made by some of the ancient sages. On one of them, erected by the Hakím Fílikús (Philip), lord of the castle of Kaválah, was the figure of a black fly, made of brass, which, by its incessant humming, drove all flies away from Islámból.

Fifth talisman. On another of the six marble columns, Iflátún (Plato) the divine made the figure of a gnat, and from that time there is no fear of a single gnat's coming into Islámbúl.

Sixth talisman. On another of these columns, the Hakím Bokrát (Hippocrates) placed the figure of a stork, and once a year, when it uttered a cry, all the storks which had built their nests in the city died instantly. To this time, not a stork can come and build its nest within the walls of Islámból, though there are plenty of them in the suburbs of Abú Iyyúb Ensárí.

Seventh talisman. On the top of another of the six marble columns, Sokrát the Hakím (*i.e.* Socrates the sage) placed a brazen cock, which clapped its wings and crowed once in every twenty-four hours, and on hearing it all the cocks of Islámbúl began to crow. And it is a fact, that to this day the cocks there crow earlier than those of other places, setting up their *kú-kirí-kúd* (*i.e.* crowing) at midnight, and thus warning the sleepy and forgetful of the approach of dawn and the hour of prayer.

Eighth talisman. On another of the six columns, Físághórát (Pythagoras the Unitarian), in the days of the prophet Suleïmán (Solomon), placed the figure of a wolf, made of bronze (*túj*), the terror of all other wolves; so that the flocks of the people of Islámból pastured very safely without a shepherd, and walked side by side with untamed wolves very comfortably.

Ninth talisman. On another of these columns were the figures in brass of a youth and his mistress in close embrace; and whenever there was any coolness or quarrelling between man and wife, if either of them went and embraced this column, they were sure that very night to have their afflicted hearts restored by the joys of love, through the power of this talisman, which was moved by the spirit of the sage Aristatálís (Aristotle).

Tenth talisman. Two figures of tin had been placed on another of the six columns by the physician Jálínús (Galen). One was a decrepit old man, bent double; and opposite to it was a camel-lip sour-faced hag, not straighter than her companion: and when man and wife led no happy life together, if either of them embraced this column, a separation was sure to take place. Wonderful talismans were destroyed, they say, in the time of that asylum of apostleship (Mohammed), and are now buried in the earth.

Eleventh talisman. On the site of the baths of Sultán Báyazíd Velí there was a quadrangular column, eighty cubits high, erected by an ancient sage named Kirbáriyá, as a talisman against the plague, which could never prevail in Islámból as long as this column was standing. It was afterwards demolished by that sultán, who erected a heart-rejoicing *hammám* in its place; and on that very day one of his sons died of the plague, in the garden of Dáúd Páshá outside of the Adrianople-gate, and was buried on an elevated platform (*soffah*) without: since which time the plague has prevailed in the city.

Twelfth talisman. In the Tekfúr Seráï, near the Egrí kapú, there was a large solid bust of black stone, on which a man named Muhaydák placed a brazen figure of a demon ('*afrít*), which once a year spit out fire and flames; and whoever caught a spark kept it in his kitchen; and, as long as his health was good, that fire was never extinguished.

Thirteenth talisman. On the skirt of the place called Zírek-báshí there is a cavern dedicated to St. John, and every month, when the piercing cold of winter has set in, several black demons (*kónjólóz*) hide themselves there.

Fourteenth talisman. To the south of Ayá Sófiyah there were four lofty columns of white marble, bearing the statues of the four cherubs (*kerrúblir*), Gabriel (Jebráyíl), Michael (Míkáyíl), Rafael (Isráfíl), and Azrael (Azráyíl), turned towards the north, south, east, and west. Each of them clapped his wings once a year, and foreboded desolation, war, famine, or pestilence. These statues were upset when the Prophet came into existence, but the four columns still remain a public spectacle, near the subterraneous springs (*chukúr cheshmeh*) of Ayá Sófiyah.

Fifteenth talisman. The great work in the Atmeïdán (Hippodrome), called Milyón-pár (Millium?), is a lofty column, measuring a hundred and fifty cubits (*arshún*) of builders measure. It was constructed by order of Kostantín, of various coloured stones, collected from the 300,000 cities of which he was king, and designed to be an eternal monument of his power, and at the same time a talisman. Through the middle of it there ran a thick iron axis, round which the various coloured stones were placed, and they were all kept together by a magnet, as large as the cupola of a bath (*hammám*), fixed on its summit. It still remains a lasting monument; and its builder, the head architect, Ghúrbárín by name, lies buried at the foot of it.

Sixteenth talisman. This is also an obelisk of red coloured stone, covered with various sculptures, and situate in the At-meïdán. The figures on its sides foretell the different fortunes of the city. It was erected in the time of Yánkó ibn Mádiyán, who is represented on it sitting on his throne, and holding a ring in his hand, implying symbolically, 'I have conquered the whole world, and hold it in my hands like this ring.' His face is turned towards the east, and kings stand before him, holding dishes, in the guise of beggars. On another are the figures of three hundred men engaged in erecting the obelisk, with the various machines used for that purpose. Its circumference is such that ten men cannot span it; and its four angles rest on four brazen seats, such that, when one experienced in the builders art has looked at it, he puts his finger on his mouth.

Seventeenth talisman. A sage named Surendeh, who flourished in the days of error, under king Púzentín, set up a brazen image of a triple-headed dragon (*azhderhá*) in the Atmeïdán, in order to destroy all serpents, lizards, scorpions, and such like poisonous reptiles: and not a poisonous beast was there in the whole of Mákedóniyyah. It has now the form of a twisted serpent, measuring ten cubits above and as many below the ground. It remained thus buried in mud and earth from the building of Sultán Ahmed's mosque, but uninjured, till Selím II., surnamed the drunken, passing by on horseback, knocked off with his mace the lower jaw of that head of the dragon which looks to the west. Serpents then made their appearance on the western side of the city, and since that time have become common in every part of it. If, moreover, the remaining heads should be destroyed, Islámból will be completely eaten up with vermin. In short, there were anciently, relating to the land at Islámból, three hundred and sixty-six talismans like those now described, which are all that now remain.

Talismans relating to the Sea.

First talisman. At the Chátládí-kapú, in the side of the palace of an emperor whom the sun never saw, there was the brazen figure of a demon (*dív*) upon a square column, which spit fire, and burnt the ships of the enemy whenever it was they approached from the White Sea (Archipelago).

Second talisman. In the galley-harbour (*kadirghah límání*) there was a brazen ship, in which, once a year, when the cold winter-nights had set in, all the Witches of Islámból used to embark and sail about till morning, to guard the White Sea. It was a part of the spoils captured with the city by Mohammed II. the conqueror.

Third talisman. Another brazen ship, the counterpart of this, was constructed at the Tóp-khánah (cannon-foundery), in which all the wizards and conjurors kept guard towards the Black Sea. It was broken in pieces when Yezíd Ibn Mo'áviyyah conquered Ghalatah.

Fourth talisman. At Seraglo-Point there was a triple-headed brazen dragon, spitting fire, and burning all the enemy's ships and boats whichever way they came.

Fifth talisman. There were also, near the same place, three hundred and sixty-six lofty columns bearing the figures of as many marine creatures; a White sun fish (*khamsín bálighí*) for example, which, when it uttered a cry, left not a fish of that kind in the Black Sea, but brought them all to Makedún, where all the people got a good bellyful of them.

The sixth talisman was, that, during all the forty days of Lent, all kinds of fish were thrown ashore by the sea, and caught without any trouble by the people of Rúm (Turkey).

All these talismans having been overthrown by the great earthquake on the night of the prophets birth, the columns which bore them still lie strewed like a pavement along the Seraglio-Point, from the Selímiyyeh Kóshk, to the castle of Sinán Páshá, and are manifest to those who pass along in boats. Though upset they still retain their talismanic virtues, and every year bring many thousand fishes to the shore.

There were also twenty-four columns round Islámból, each bearing a talisman. All could be visited by a man in one day, provided it was a day of fifteen hours: now the longest day at Islámból, from sun-rise to sun-set, is fifteen hours and a half. That city is situated in the middle of the fifth climate, and therefore enjoys excellent air and water.

SECTION VII.

Concerning the Mines within and without the City of Kostantín.

By God's will there was anciently a great cavern in Islámból, below the Sultán's mosque (Sultán jámi'-sí), filled with sulphur, nitre, and black powder, from which they drew supplies in time of need. Having, by the decree of heaven, been struck by lightning in the time of Kostantín, or, according to our tradition, at the time of the taking of the city by the conqueror, all the large buildings over the cavern were blown up, and fragments of them scattered in every direction; some may still be seen at Uskudár (Scutari), others at Salájak búruní, and Kází kóï (Chalcedon); one large piece, particularly, called the Kabá-tásh, and lying in the sea before the chismehler tekkiyeh, to the north of the village of Funduk-lí, near Tóp-khánah, was probably thrown there when the city was blown up.

In the neighbourhood of the castle of Kúm-búrghaz, half a days journey from the Seven Towers, to the south of Islámból, a fine white sand is found, in great request among the hour-glass makers and goldsmiths of Islámból and Firengistán (Europe).

Near the privy-garden of Dáúd Páshá, outside of the Adrianople-gate, there are seven stone quarries, which appear to be inexhaustible. It is called the stone of Khizr, because it was pointed out by that prophet for the construction of Ayá Sófiyah.

A kind of soft clay (*tín*) like electuary (*ma'jún*), found near the suburb of Abú Iyyúb ansárí, is called tín ansárí; it has a sweet scent like terra sigillata (*tiní makhtúm*), from the island of Alimání (Jezírehi Alimání, i.e. Lemnos); and it is used for the sigillate earth found at Lemnos; making jugs, a draught from which refreshes like a draught of the water of life.

From a pool (*buheïreh*) between the suburbs of Iyyúb Sultán and Khás-kóï, divers bring up a kind of black clay, which is excellent for making jugs, cups, plates, and all kinds of earthenware.

The springs of Jendereh-jí, in the delightful promenade (*mesíreh-gáh*) called Kághid Khánah (Kïahet-haneh, or les eaux douces, *i.e.* fresh-water springs), are famous all over the world. The root of a kind of lign-aloes (*eker*) is found there superior to that of Azák (Assov), the city of Kerdeh, or the canal of the castle of Kanizzhah. One of its wonderful properties is, that when a man eats of it it occasions a thousand eructations; it fattens tortoises marvellously, and the Franks of Ghalatah come and catch them, and use them in all their medicines with great advantage.

At Sárí Yár, north of Kághid Kháneh, a kind of fermented clay is found, which smells like musk, and is used in making jugs and cups, which are much valued, and offered as presents to the great.

At the village of Sári Yár, near the entrance of the strait of the Black Sea, there is a lofty mountain of yellow-coloured earth, covered with gardens and vineyards up to its summit. On its outside, near to the sea-shore, there is a cavern containing a mine of pure gold, free from any alloy of Hungarian (Ungurús) Búndúkání brass. From the time of the infidels till the reign of Sultán Ahmed, it was an imperial domain, farmed out for one thousand yúk of aspers (loads, each equal to 100,000). The Defterdár, Ekmek-ji-zádeh Ahmed Páshá, closed it, as bringing little into the treasury; it is now, therefore, neglected, but if opened again by the Sultán's order would be found a very valuable mine.

From this mountain in the valley of Gók-sú, near the castles (*hisár*) on the Bosphorus, a kind of lime is obtained which is whiter than snow, cotton, or milk, and cannot be matched in the world.

In the same favourite place of resort, the valley of Gók-sú, a kind of red earth is found, of which jugs, plates, and dishes are made; and the doctors say, that pure water drunk out of vessels made of this earth cures the básuri demeví (blood-shot eyes?).

In the mountains near the town of Uskudár (Scutari), is found a kind of fossil whetstone (*kayághán*), which breaks in large slabs, and is much used for tombstones.

Beneath the palace known by the name of Ghalatah-seráï, above the suburb of Tóp-khánah, is an iron mine, called the mine of old Islámból, and the ore extracted from it is known by that name all over the world. Not a soul in the universe knew any thing of it till Khizr pointed it out, in the time of king Ferendú, for the building of Ayá Sófiyah; and all the ironwork of that edifice, as well as the iron hoops round the column in Táúk-bázár [Forum Theodosii], were made of iron from Eskí Stámból. The mine was worked till the time of Sultán Báyazíd Velí, who was much pleased with the air and water of the place, and often spent some time there; and having been admonished in a dream by the Prophet, founded a hospital and college on the spot; and having finally made it a school for pages of the seraglio, the mine was abandoned. The humble writer of this remembers, in the time of his youth, when 'Osmán the Martyr was on the throne, there was there between the lead-magazine (*kúrshúnlí makhzen*) and Tóp-kapú a manufactory of Damascus blades, made from the iron of this mine, where Mohamed the Conqueror, who established it, had most excellent blades made. I myself have seen Mustafá, the head sword-maker of Sultán Murád IV., and master of little David, working in that manufactory. It was a large building, outside of the walls, on the sea-shore. Afterwards, when Sultán Ibráhím ascended the throne, Kara Mustafá Páshá became a martyr, and every thing was thrown into confusion; this building was turned into a house for the Jews, by 'Alí Aghá, superintendant of the custom-house, and neither the name, nor any trace of the mine or the sword manufactory, are to be found.

The thirteenth mine is that mine of men, the Good City, *i.e.* Kostantiniyyeh, which is an ocean of men and beautiful women, such as is to be found no where else. It is said, that if a thousand men die and a thousand and one are born, the race is propagated by that one. But Islámból is so vast a city, that if a thousand die in it, the want of them is not felt in such an ocean of men; and it has therefore been called Káni Insán, a mine of men.

SECTION VIII.

Sieges of Constantinople.

In the forty-third year of the Hijreh (A.D. 663), Mo'áviyyah became Commander of the Faithful; and in the course of his reign sent his commander in chief Moslemah, son of 'Abdu-l-malik, at the head of a hundred thousand men of the Syrian army, with two hundred ships, and two hundred transports laden with provisions, ammunition, &c. from the port of Shám-Tarah-bólús (Tripoli in Syria), and trusting in God, first against the island of Máltah, which at that time was Rodós (Rhodes), and of which they made a conquest almost as soon as they disembarked. They next proceeded to the islands of Istánkóï (Cos), Sákiz (Scio), Medellí (Mitylene), Alimániyah (Lemnos), and Bózjah (Tenedos), which were taken in a few days; and they immediately afterwards laid siege to Kostantaniyyeh, having taken four hundred ships in their passage, and intercepted all vessels laden with provisions coming from the White or Black Sea. The infidels soon sued for peace, on condition of paying the annual tribute of a galley laden with money; and the victorious general returned to Arabia with joy and exultation, carrying with him the impure son of that erring king (*királ*) Herkíl (Heraclius) as a hostage, with treasures to the amount of some millions of piastres.

Second Siege. In the fifty-second year of the Hijrah of the pride of the world (A.D. 671), Ebú Iyyúb Ansárí, the standard-bearer of the Prophet, and 'Abdullah ibn 'Abbás ibn Zeïd, proceeding with some thousands of the illustrious companions of the Prophet, and 50,000 brave men, in two hundred ships, followed by reinforcements under the command of Moslemah, first carried supplies to the warriors of Islám in garrison at Rodós, and then, casting anchor before the Seven Towers and landing their men, laid siege to Islámból by sea and land. Thus, for six months, did this host, which had the fragrance of Paradise, contend day and night with the infidels. By the wise decree of God. Ebú Iyyúb their leader suffered martyrdom in one of these assaults, by an arrow from a cross-bow: but, according to a sure tradition, he was received into mercy (*i.e.* he died) of a disorder in his bowels.

Third Siege. In the year of the Hijrah 91 (A.D. 710), by order of the khalif Suleïmán, son of 'Abdu-llah of the Bení Ummayyah, his nephew 'Omar ibn 'Abdu-l-'azíz marched by land against Islámból with 87,000 men, who ravaged Ghalatah with fire and sword, and having carried off an immense booty, crossed over into Anátólí (Natolia); and after having laid siege to Sínób, which made its peace at a great price, and Kastemúní, the capture of which likewise it did not please God to make easy to him, he returned to Syria

(Shám).

The fourth Siege. In A.H. 97 (A.D. 716), the same khalif again sent his nephew 'Omar ibn 'Abdu-l-'azíz against Islámból, with an army of 120,000 men by land, and 80,000 embarked in three hundred ships at sea. They established their winter-quarters that year in the town of Belkís-Aná, near Aïdinjik (Cyzicus), in the district of Brúsah, and in the following spring they laid siege to Islámból, and reduced the inhabitants to the greatest distress, by laying waste all the surrounding fields and meadows.

The fifth Siege. In the year of the Hijrah——, 'Omar ibn 'Abdu-l-'azíz, having become khalif of Shám (Syria), sent an army of 100,000 men, by land and by sea, against Islámból, and crossing the Strait of the Black Sea at Ghalatah, conquered it, and built the mosque of the lead magazines; and the mosque of the Arabs ('Arab jámi'sí) in that suburb was likewise named from its having been built by him. Having erected a lofty heaven-aspiring tower at Ghalatah, he called it Medíneto-l Kahr (the City of Oppression). He made peace with the Tekkúr of Islámból on condition that Mohammedans should be allowed to settle in that city, from the Crooked (Egrí) and Adrianople gates, and the hill on which the Suleïmániyyah stands, to that of Zírek-báshí, and from thence by the flour-market (ún-kapání) as far as Iyyúb Ensárí. He built the rose-mosque (Gul-jámi'í) in the market of Mustafá Páshá, erected the court of justice near the Sirkehjí-tekiyeh, and formed a new district of the town at the summer-quarters of Kójah Mustafá Páshá, near the Seven Towers. Another condition on which this unilluminated Tekkúr (emperor) obtained peace, was the annual payment of a tribute (kharáj) of 50,000 pieces of gold. 'Omar ibn 'Abdu-l-'azíz fixed his winter-quarters at Ghalatah for that year, having received the tribute due for three hundred years in consequence of a former treaty, departed, leaving Suleïmán ibn 'Abdu-l Malik governor of Ghalatah, and appointing Moselmah his Grand Vizír. His fleet having met near Rodostò one of two hundred sail, sent by the infidels to succour the Tekkúr, a great battle ensued; and just as the infidels were about to be destroyed, a stormy wind sprung up and drove both fleets on shore, notwithstanding all the cherubims in heaven emulated the zeal of the true believers on earth. The Moslims disembarked, laid waste all the villages round about, carried away more than 3,000 horses, asses, and mules, and 23,000 prisoners. The treasures taken from the ships which were sunk, were so great, that God only knows their amount; and the number of the dust-licking infidels passed over the edge of the sword such that their bones lie piled up in heaps in a well known valley, called even now 'Omar Kírdúghí Jórdú, *i.e.* 'the camp broken up by 'Omar.' After gaining another signal victory by sea and land, he returned into Syria (Shám).

The sixth Siege. In the year of the hijrah 160 (A.D. 777) Merván ibnu-l Hakem besieged Islámból with an army of 150,000 Moslims and a fleet of a thousand ships during six months, added three new districts and built a mosque in the Mahommedan part of the city, and compelled Mesendún, son of Herakíl (Heraclius), to pay a yearly tribute of 500,000 golden tekyánúses, (*i.e.* coins called Decianus).

The seventh Siege. Seventy-four years after the peace made with Merván, in the year of the hijrah 239 (A.D. 853-4), after the conquest of Malatíyyah, Islámból was pillaged by the khalif Yahyá son of 'Ali, who returned to Kharrán (Charrhæ) after having smote 20,000 infidels with the edge of the sword.

The eighth Siege. Sixteen years afterwards, A.H. 255 (A.D. 869), I'liyá (Elias) son of Herakíl being king (királ) of Islámból, Harúnu-r-rashíd marched from his paradisiacal abode at the head of 50,000 troops; but finding it difficult to effect the conquest of the city, he made peace on condition of receiving as much ground within the walls as a bulls hide would cover. He therefore cut the hide into strips, so as to enclose space enough in the district of Kójah Mustafá Páshá for building a strong castle, and he fixed the annual tribute at 50,000 fulúrí (florins). He then returned to Baghdád, having levied the tribute (kharáj) due for the last ten years.

About this time the infidels, taking advantage of the dissensions which prevailed among the Muselmáns respecting the khalífat, massacred all those established in Islámból and Ghalatah, not however without great loss on their own side, the king and royal family being all slain; in consequence of which Ghirándó Mihál (Grando Michael), a grandson of Herakíl who had come from Firengistán, was made king; and on that very day Seyyid Bábá Ja'fer, one of the descendants of Imám Hoseïn, and Sheïkh Maksúd, one of the followers of Veïsu-l-Karní, sent by Hárúnu-r-rashíd as ambassadors, entered Islámból. They were attended by three hundred fakírs and three hundred followers, and were received by the new king with innumerable honours. The Sheïkh asked and obtained permission to bury the remains of the many thousand martyrs who had been slain in the late massacre, which lasted seven days and seven nights. He immediately set to work, and with the aid of his own three hundred fakírs and Bábá Ja'fer's three hundred followers, buried those many thousand martyrs in the places where they had died. In the ancient burying ground behind the arsenal, there are large caverns and ancient vaults, where, from the time of 'Omar ibn 'Abdu-l-'azíz, some thousand companions (of the Prophet) had been buried. To that place Sheïkh Maksúd carried some thousand bodies of these martyrs, and buried them there, where, on a hewn stone, there is written in large and legible characters, so that it may be easily read, this inscription, said to be by the Sheïkh's own blessed hand:

These are the men who came and went!

In this frail world (*dári fenà*) what have they done?

They came and went, what have they done?

At last to th' endless world (*dári bakà*) they're gone.

It is to this day celebrated throughout the world as an extraordinary inscription, and is visited by travellers from Rúm (Greece), 'Arab (Arabia), and 'Ajem (Persia). Some of them, who, in the expectation of finding hidden treasures, began to work at these ancient buildings with pickaxes like *Ferhád's*, perished in the attempt, and were also buried there. Some holy men make pilgrimages to this place barefoot on Friday nights, and recite the chapter entitled Tekásur (Korán, chap. 102); for many thousands of illustrious companions (of the Prophet) *Mohájirín*, (who followed him in his flight), and *Ansárs* (auxiliaries) are buried in this place. It has been also attested by some thousands of the pious, that this burial ground has been seen some thousands of times covered with lights on the holy night of *Alkadr* (*i.e.* sixth of *Ramazán*).

In short, Seyyid Bábá Ja'fer, Hárúnu-r rashíd's ambassador, having been enraged, and taking offence at his not having been well received by the king Ghirándó Míhál, reproached him bitterly, and suffered martyrdom by poison in consequence of it. He was buried by Sheïkh Maksúd, who received an order to that effect, in a place within the prison of the infidels, where, to this day, his name is insulted by all the unbelieving malefactors, debtors, murderers, &c. imprisoned there. But when (God be praised!) Islámból was taken, the prison having likewise been captured, the grave of Seyyid Ja'fer Bábá Sultán, in the tower of the prison [the Bagno], became a place of pilgrimage, which is visited by those who have been released from prison, and call down blessings in opposition to the curses of the unbelievers.

The ninth Siege. Three years after that great event related above, Hárúnu-r-rashíd marched from Baghdád with an immense army, to require the blood of the faithful from the infidels of Rúm (Asia Minor and Greece), and having reached Malatiyyah, which was conquered by Ja'fer Ghází, surnamed Seyyid Battál, that hero led the vanguard of the army into Rúm; and Hárún himself brought up the rear with reinforcements. Having taken possession of the straits, they blockaded the city, cut off all its supplies, gave no quarter, slew 300,000 infidels, took 70,000 prisoners, and made an immense booty, which they sent to Haleb (Aleppo) and Iskenderún, and then returned laden with spoils to Baghdád. Yaghfúr (void of light), the king at that time, was taken prisoner and carried before Hárún, who gave him no quarter, but ordered him to be hung in the belfry of Ayá Sófiyyah (Sancta Sophia). Having been from my infancy desirous of seeing the world, and not remaining in ignorance, I learned the Greek and Latin languages of my friend Simyún (Simeon) the goldsmith, to whom I explained the Persian glossary of Sháhidí, and he gave me lessons in the Aleksanderah (Alexandra), *i.e.* the History of Alexander. He also read to me the history of Yanván, from which these extracts are taken. But after the race of the Cæsars (Kayásirah) became extinct in Kanátúr, Kostantiniyyah fell into the hands of various princes, till the house of 'Osmán arose in A.H. 699 (A.D. 1300), and, at the suggestion of 'Aláu-d-dín the Seljúkí, first turned its attention to the conquest of that city.

SECTION IX.

Concerning the Sieges of Constantinople by the Ottoman Emperors.

The first portion of the descendants of Jafeth which set its foot in the country of Rúm (Asia Minor) was the house of the Seljúkians, who, in alliance with the Dánishmendian Emírs, wrested, in A.H. 476 (A.D. 1083), the provinces of Malatiyyah, Kaïsariyyah, 'Aláiyyah, Karamán, and Kóniyah from the hand of the Greek emperors (Kaïsari Rúm Yúnániyán). They first came from Máveráu-n-nehr (Transoxiana). On the extinction of the Seljúkian dynasty, A.H. 600 (A.D. 1204), Suleïmán-sháh, one of the begs (lords) of the town of Máhán in Túrán, and his son Ertoghrul, came into Rúm, to the court of Sultán 'Aláu-d-dín. The latter having been set on his feet as a man (er-toghrílúb), and made a beg by that prince, made many brilliant conquests, and, at the death of 'Aláu-d-dín, was elected sovereign in his stead, by all the great men (a'yán) of the country. He died at the town of Sukúdjuk, and was succeeded by his son 'Osmán, who was the first emperor (pádisháh) of that race. He resided at 'Osmánjik, from whence the dazzling beams of the Mohammedan faith shed their light over Anátólí, Germiyán, and Karamán. In the time of his son and successor, the victorious Órkhán, seventy-seven heroes, friends of God (evliyáu-llah, *i.e.* saints) fought under the banners of the Prophet.

It was in his reign, that the holy (velí) Hájí Begtásh, who had been in Khorasán, one of the followers of our great ancestor, that Túrk of Túrks, Khójah Ahmed Yaseví, came over to his camp with three hundred devout (sáhibi sejjádeh) fakírs carrying drums and standards, and, as soon as they had met Órkhán, Brúsah was taken. From thence he proceeded to the conquest of Constantaniyyeh. His son, Suleïmán Beg, joined by the permission and advice of Begtásh and seventy great saints (evliyà), with forty brave men, such as Karah Mursal, Karah Kójah, Karah Yalavà, Karah Bíghà, Karah Síghlah, in short forty heroes (bahádur) called *Karah* (black), crossed over the sea on rafts, and set foot on the soil of Rúm, shouting Bismillah, the Mohammedan cry of war. Having laid waste the country on all sides of the city, they conquered, on a Friday, the castle of Ip-salà (it is called Ip-salà by a blunder for Ibtidà salà, *i.e.* the commencement prayer), and having offered up the Fridays prayer there, they pushed on to the gates of Adrianople, taking Gelíbólí (Galipoli), Tekir-tághí (Rodosto), and Silivrì (Selymbria) in their way, and returned victorious, laden with spoils and captives, after an absence of seven days, to Kapú-tághí on the Asiatic shore, from whence they marched with their booty into Brúsah. The brain of the whole army of Islám being thus filled with sweetness, the shores of Rúm were many times invaded, all the neighbouring country was laid waste, nor were the infidels (káfirs) able to make any resistance; while the Moslim heroes found means of raising a noble progeny by being tied with the knot of matrimony to the beautiful virgins whom they carried off. Sultán Murád I., who succeeded Órkhán, following the advice formerly given by Aláu-d-dín Sultán and Hájí Begtásh, made himself master of the country round Kostantaniyyeh before he attempted the conquest of the city itself. He therefore first took Edreneh (Adrianople), and filled it with followers of Mohammed coming from Anátólí, while the infidels could not advance a step beyond Islámból. However, they contrived to assemble an army of 700,000 men in the plain of Kós-óvà (Cossova), near the castle of Vechteren in Rúm-ílí (Romelia), where, by the decree of the Creator of the world, they were all put to the sword by the victorious Khudávendikár (Murád); but while walking over the dead bodies in the field of battle, praising God, and surveying the corpses of the infidels doomed to hell (dúzakh), he was slain by a knife from the hand of one Velashko, who lay among the slain. The assassin was instantly cut to pieces, and Murád's son, Yildirim Báyazíd Khán, mounted the throne. In order to avenge his father's death, he fell like a thunderbolt on Káfiristán (the land of the unbelievers), slew multitudes of them, and began the tenth siege of Kostantaniyyeh.

Yildirim Báyazíd wisely made Edreneh (Adrianople) the second seat of empire, and besieged Islámból during seven months with an army of a hundred thousand men, till the infidels cried out that they were ready to make peace on his own terms, offering to pay a yearly tribute (kharáj) of 200,000 pieces of gold. Dissatisfied with this proposal, he demanded that the Mohammedans (ummeti Mohammed) should occupy, as of old in the days of 'Omar ibn 'Abdu-l-'azíz, and Hárúnu-r-Rashíd, one half of Islámból and Ghalatah, and have the tithe of all the gardens and vineyards outside of the city. The Tekkúr king (*i.e.* the Emperor) was compelled of necessity to accept these terms, and twenty thousand Musulmáns having been introduced into the town, were established within their former boundaries. The Gul jámi'í, within the Jebálí kapú-sí, was purified with rose-water from all the pollutions of the infidels, whence it received its name of Gul-jámi'í (*i.e.* Rose mosque). A court of justice was established in the Sirkehjí Tekiyeh in that neighbourhood; Ghalatah was garrisoned with six thousand men, and half of it, as far as the tower, given up to the Mohammedans. Having in this manner conquered one half of Islámból, Báyazíd returned victorious to Edreneh. Soon afterwards Tímúr Leng issuing from the land of Írán with thirty-seven kings at his stirrup, claimed the same submission from Báyazíd, who, with the spirit and courage of an emperor, refused to comply. Tímúr, therefore, advanced and encountered him with a countless army. Twelve thousand men of the Tátár light-horse (eshkinjí), and some thousands of foot soldiers, who, by the bad counsels of the vazír, had received no pay, went over to the enemy; notwithstanding which Báyazíd, urged on by his zeal, pressed forwards with his small force, mounted on a sorry colt, and having entered the throng of Tímúr's army, laid about him with his sword on all sides, so as to pile the Tátárs in heaps all around him. At last, by God's will, his horse that had never seen any action fell under him, and he, not being able to rise again before the Tátárs rushed upon him, was taken prisoner, and carried into Tímúr's presence. Tímúr arose when he was brought in, and treated him with great respect. They then sat down together on the same carpet (sejjádeh) to eat honey and yóghúrt (clotted cream). While thus conversing together, "I thank God," said Tímúr, "for having delivered thee into my hand, and enabled me to eat and discourse with thee on the same table; but if I had fallen into thy hands, what wouldst thou have done?" Yildirim, from the openness of his heart, came to the point at once, and said, "By heaven! if thou hadst fallen into my hand, I would have shut thee up in an iron cage, and would never have taken thee out of it till the day of thy death!" "What thou lovest in thy heart, I love in mine," replied Tímúr, and ordering an iron cage to be brought forthwith, shut Báyazíd up in it, according to the wish he had himself expressed. Tímúr then set out on his return, and left the field open for Chelebí Sultán Mohammed to succeed his father Yildirim. He immediately pursued the conqueror with 70,000 men, and overtaking him at Tashák-óvá-sí, smote his army with such a Mohammedan cleaver, that his own men sheltered themselves from the heat of the sun under awnings made of the hides of the slain, whence that plain received the ludicrous name by which it is still known. But, by God's will, Yildirim died that very night of a burning fever, in the cage in which he was confined. His son Mohammed Chelebí, eager to avenge his father, continued to drive Tímúr forwards, till he reached the castle of Tókát, where he left him closely besieged. He then returned victorious, carrying the illustrious corpse of his father to Brúsah, where it was buried in an oratory in the court before his own mosque. His brothers 'Ísá and Músá disputed his right to the empire; but Mohammed, supported by the people of Rúm, was proclaimed khalífah at Edreneh (Adrianople), where he remained and finished the mosque begun by his father. On hearing of these contentions for the empire, the king (tekkúr) of Islámból danced for joy. He sent round cryers to make proclamation that, on pain of death, not a Muselmán should remain in the city of Kostantín, allowing only a single day for their removal: and he destroyed a great number of them in their flight to Tekirtágh (Rodostó) and Edreneh (Adrianople). The empire, after the demise of Chelebí Mohammed, was held first by Murád II., and then by Mohammed (II.) the conqueror, who during his father's lifetime was governor (hákim) of Maghnísá (Magnesia), and spent his time there in studying history, and in conversing with those excellent men 'Ak-Shemsu-d-dín, Karah-Shemsu-d-dín, and Sívásí, from whom he acquired a perfect knowledge of the commentaries on the Korán and the sacred traditions (hadís). While he was at Maghnísá, having heard that the infidels from Fránsah (France) had landed at 'Akkah (Acri), the port of Jerusalem, on the shore of the White Sea, and in the dominions of Keláún, Sultán of Egypt, and taken possession of 'Askelán and other towns, from which they had carried off much plunder and many prisoners to their own country, he was so much grieved at the thoughts of thousands of Muselmáns being carried into captivity, that he shed tears. "Weep not, my Emperor," said Ak-shemsu-d-dín, "for on the day that thou shalt conquer Islámból, thou shalt eat of the spoils and sweetmeats taken by the unbelievers from the castle of 'Akkah: but remember on that day to be to the faithful an acceptable judge as well as victor (*kúzí ve-ghází rází*), doing justice to all the victorious Moslims." At the same time taking off the shawl twisted round his Turban, he placed it on Mohammed's head, and announced the glad tidings of his being the future conqueror of Islámból. They then read the noble traditions (*hadís*) of what the Prophet foretold relative to Islámból, and observed that he was the person to whom these traditions applied. Mohammed on this, covering his head with Ak-Shemsu-d-din's turban (*'urf*), said: "Affairs are retrieved in their season!" and, recommending all his affairs to the bounty of the Creator, returned to his studies.

On the death of his father Murád II., ambassadors to congratulate him were sent by all monarchs, except Uzún Hasan, Prince (Sháh) of Azerbáïján, of the family of Karah Koyúnlí; against him, therefore, he first turned his arms, and defeated him in the field of Terján.

Account of the Rise of Mohammed II., the Father of Victory.

He mounted the throne on Thursday the 16th Moharrem 855 (A.D. 1451), at the age of twenty-one years. My great grandfather, then his standard-bearer, was with him at the conquest of Islámból. He purchased with the money arising from his share of the booty, the houses within the U'n kapání, on the site of the mosque of Sághirjílar, which he built after the conquest of the city by Mohammed II., together with a hundred shops settled on the mosque as an endowment (*vakf*). The house in which I was born was built at the same time, and with money so acquired. The patents (*baráts*) for the mosques and the shops, however, were made out in the conquerors name, and signed with his cypher (*tughrà*), the administration of the endowment being vested in our family. From the deeds relative to it now in my hands, I am well acquainted with the dates of all the events of his reign. He was a mighty but bloodthirsty monarch. As soon as he had mounted the throne at Adrianople, he caused Hasan, his younger brother by the same mother, to be strangled, and sent his body to Brúsah, to be interred there beside his father. He conquered many castles in the country round Brúsah, built those called the key of the two seas, on the strait of the White Sea, and two likewise on that of the Black Sea, and levied a tribute on Islámból. According to the peace made by Yildirim, a tithe of the produce of all the vineyards round was to be paid to the Sultán, before any infidel could gather a single grape. After the lapse of three years, some grapes having been gathered by the infidels in violation of this article of the treaty, in the vineyards of the Rúmílí hisár (*i.e.* the European castle on the canal of Constantinople), a quarrel ensued, in which some men were killed. Mohammed, when this was reported to him, considered it as a breach of the treaty, and immediately laid siege to Islámból, with an army as numerous as the sand of the sea.

SECTION X.

The last Siege of Kostantaniyyeh by Mohammed II. the Conqueror.

In the year of the Hijrah 857 (A.D. 1453), Sultán Mohammed encamped outside of the Adrianople gate, with an immense army of Unitarians (Muvahhedín); and some thousands of troops from Arebistán, who crossed the Strait of Gelíbólí (Gallipoli), and having joined the army of Islám, took up their quarters before the Seven Towers. All the troops from Tokát, Sívás, Erzrúm, Páï-búrt, and the other countries taken from Uzún Hasan, crossed the strait near Islámból, and encamped on the 'Ok-meïdán in sight of the infidels. Trenches, mines, and guns were got ready, and the city was invested by land on all sides; it was only left open by sea. Seventy-seven distinguished and holy men beloved by God (Evliyáu-llah) followed the camp; among them were Ak-Shemsu-d-dín, Karah-Shemsu-d-dín, Sívásí, Mollá Kúrání, Emír Nejárí, Mollá Fenárí, Jubbeh 'Alí, Ansárí-Dedeh, Mollá Púlád, Ayà Dedeh, Khorósí Dedeh, Hatablí Dedeh, and Sheïkh Zindání. The Sultán made a covenant with them, promising that one-half of the city (devlet) should belong to them, and one-half to the Muselmán conquerors; "and I will build," said he, "for each of you a convent, sepulchral chapel, hospital, school, college, and house of instruction in sacred traditions (Dáru-l-hadís)." The men of learning and piety were then assembled in one place; proclamation was made that all the troops of Islám should renew their ablutions, and offer up a prayer of two inflections. The Mohammedan shout of war (Allah! Allah!) was then thrice uttered, and according to the law of the Prophet, at the moment of their investing the city, Mahmúd Páshá was sent with a letter to the Emperor (Tekkúr) of Constantaniyyeh. When the letter had been read and its contents made known, relying on the strength of the place and the number of his troops, the Emperor proudly sent the ambassador back, saying, "I will neither pay tribute, nor surrender the fortress, nor embrace Islám." On one side, the troops of Islám surrounded the walls like bees, crying out Bismillah, and beginning the assault with the most ardent zeal; on the other, the besieged, who were twice one hundred thousand crafty devils of polytheists, depended on their towers and battlements by land, and feared no danger by sea, the decrees of fate never entering into their thoughts. They had five hundred pieces of ordnance at Seraglio Point, five hundred at the Lead-magazines (on the Ghalatah-side), and one hundred, like a hedge-hog's bristles, inside and outside of the Kíz kulleh-sí (Tower of Leander), so that not a bird could fly across the sea without being struck from these three batteries. The priests (pápás), monks, and patriarchs encouraging those polluted hosts to the battle, promised some useless idols, such as Lát and Menát, to each of the infidels. The 'Osmánlús, in the mean time, began to batter the walls, and received reinforcements and provisions; while the Greeks, who were shut out of the canals of Constantinople and the Dardanelles by the castles built there, could obtain none. After the siege had been carried on for ten days, the Sultan assembled his faithful sheiks, saying, "See to what a condition we are reduced! The capture of this fortress will be very difficult, if the defence of it is thus continued from day to day." Ak-Shemsu-d-dín told him that he must wait for a time, but would infallibly be conqueror: that there was within the city a holy man named Vadúd, and that as long as he lived it could not be taken; but that in fifty days he would die, and then at the appointed hour, minute, and second, the city would be taken. The Sultán therefore ordered Tímúr-tásh Páshá to employ 2,000 soldiers in constructing fifty galleys (kadirghah), in the valley near Kághid kháneh, and some villages were plundered to provide them with planks and other timber for that purpose. Kójah Mustafá Páshá had previously constructed, by the labour of all his Arab troops, fifty galleys and fifty horse-boats (káyik), at a place called Levend-chiftlik, opposite to the Ok-meïdán. The galleys built at Kághid kháneh being also ready on the tenth day, the Sultán went on that day to the Ok-meïdán, with some thousands of chosen men, carrying greased levers and beams to move the said ships. By the command of God, the wind blew very favourably; all sails were unfurled, and amidst the shouts of the Moslims crying *Allah! Allah!* and joyful discharges of muskets and artillery, a hundred and fifty ships slid down from the Ok-meïdán into the harbour. The terrified Káfirs cried out "What can this be?" and this wonderful sight was the talk of the whole city. The place where these ships were launched is still shown, at the back of the gardens of the arsenal (Ters kháneh), at the stairs of Sháh-kulí within the Ok-meïdán.

The millet (dárú, *i.e.* sorghum) which was scattered there under the ships (in order to make them slide down more readily) grew, and is to this day growing in that place. All the victorious Moslims went on board armed cap-à-pie, and waited till the ships built by Tímúr-tásh at Kághid kháneh made their appearance near Iyyúb (at the extremity of the harbour), in full sail, with a favourable wind. They soon joined the fleet from Ok-meïdán, amid the discharge of guns and cannons, and shouts of *Hóï Hóï!* and *Allah! Allah!* When the Káfirs saw the illustrious fleet filled with victorious Moslims approach, they absolutely lost their senses, and began to manifest their impotence and distress. Their condition was aptly expressed in that text (Kor. II, 18): "They put their fingers in their ears, because of the noise of the thunder, for fear of death!" and they then began to talk of surrendering on the twentieth day. Pressed by famine and the besieging army, the inhabitants deserted through the breaches in the walls, to the Moslims, who, comforted by their desertion, received them well. On that day, the chiefs (báïs) of Karamán, Germiyán, Tekkeh-ílí, Aïdin, and Sáríkhán, arrived with 77,000 well-armed men, and gave fresh life to the hearts of the faithful. Tímúr-tásh having passed over with his fleet to the opposite side, landed his troops on the shore of Iyyúb, where he attacked the gates of Iyyúb and Sárí-Sultán; Mulá Pulád, a saint who knew the scripture by heart and worked miracles, attacked that of Pulád; and Sheikh Fanárí took post at the Fener kapú-sí (the Fanal-gate). The Káfirs built a castle there in one night, which would not now be built in a month, and which is actually standing and occupied. A monk named Petro having fled from that castle with three hundred priests, all turned Moslims, and that gate was called from him Petró kapú-sí. Having by God's will conquered the newly-built castle that night, he received a standard and the name of Mohammed Petro. Ayà-dedeh was stationed with three hundred Nakshbendí Fakírs before the gate of Ayá, where he fell a martyr (to the faith), and was buried within the walls, at our old court of justice the Tekiyéh (convent) of Sirkehjí; in the same manner, the gate at which Jubbeh 'Alí was posted, was called the Jebálí gate, in memory of him, Jebálí being erroneously written for Jubbeh 'Alí. He was the sheikh (i.e. spiritual guide) of Keláún, Sultán of Egypt, and having come to Brúsah for the purpose of being present at the taking of Islámból, became a disciple of Zeïnu-d-dín Háfí, and was called Jubbeh 'Alí, from his always wearing a jacket (jubbeh) made of horse-cloth; he was afterwards, when Mohammed marched against Islámból, made chief baker (ekmekchí-báshí), and provided, no creature knows how, from one single oven the whole army, consisting of many hundred thousand servants of God, with bread as white as cotton. He did not embark at the Ok-meïdán, but with three hundred Fakírs, disciples of Zeïnu-d-dín Háfí, who, having spread skins upon the sea near the garden of the arsenal, employed themselves in beating their drums and tambours, and singing hymns in honour of the unity (tevhíd) of God. They then, unfurling the standard of Háfí, passed over the sea clearer than the sun, standing on their skins as on a litter, to the terror of the infidels doomed to hell! Jubbeh 'Alí having taken up his from the sea, was posted at the Jebálí gate. After the conquest he voluntarily fell a martyr, and was interred in the court of the Gul-jámi'í (the rose-mosque), where an assemblage of Fakírs afterwards found a retreat from the world. Khorós dedeh was engaged at the Un-kapání gate, which therefore bears his name; and below it, on the left hand as one enters, there is a figure of a cock (khorós). He was a Fakír, and one of the disciples of my ancestor Ahmed Yeseví. He came from Khurasán, when old and sickly, with Hájí Begtásh, in order to be present at the siege of Islámból, and got the nickname of Khorós-dedeh (father cock), from his continually rousing the faithful, by crying out, "Arise, ye forgetful!" Yáúzún Er, who was a very pious man, built within the Un-kapání a mosque in honour of him; it is now in the Sighirjílar chárshu-sí (beast market), and named afterwards the mosque of Yáúzún Er. Khorós-dedeh died sometime afterwards near the gate called after his name, and was buried near the high-road, outside of the Un-kapání gate, beside my ancestor. A conduit for religious ablutions has been erected near it, and is now visited as a place of pilgrimage. 'Alí Yárík, Bey of Ayázmánd, a nephew of Uzún-Hasan, of the Karákoyúnlí family, attacked the Ayázmah gate. He dug a well there for the purpose of renewing his ablutions; hence the gate received the name Ayázmah (Ἁγίασμα) kapú-sí: the water is pure spring-water, though on the edge of the sea. Sheïkh Zindání was a descendant of Sheïkh Bábá Ja'fer, who having come as ambassador in the time of Hárúnu-r-Rashíd, was poisoned by the king (i.e. emperor), and buried within the Zindán kapú-sí (prison-gate). Sheïkh Zindání visited this place, having come from Edirneh (Adrianople) with "the conqueror," at the head of 3,000 noble Seyyids (descendants of Mohammed), who gave no quarter, soon made the Zindán kapú-sí his castle, and having entered it, made a pilgrimage to his ancestor's tomb, and laid his own green turban on the place where Bábá Ja'fer's head rested. He continued for seventy years after the conquest as Turbehdár (warden of the sepulchre) and built a convent there. The Emperor, as he had made a prison in that place, called it Zindán kapú-sí (the Bagnio), and it was conquered by Zindání. The Sheïkh having appointed in his stead a Sayyid of the same pure race, to take charge of the tomb of Ja'fer Bábá, accompanied Sultán Báyazíd in his expedition against Kilí (Kilia) and Ak-kirmán, in the year 889 (A.D. 1484). He died at Edirneh (Adrianople), after his return with Báyazíd from those conquests, and on that occasion the Sultán caused all the prisoners in the public prison there to be set at liberty for the good of the Sheïkh's soul, and erected a chapel (turbeh) over his tomb, outside of the Zindán Kulleh-sí, having attended his funeral in person. His turbeh is now a great place of pilgrimage, and all his children are buried there. It is called the Ziyáret-gáh of 'Abdu-r-ruuf Samadání. The wardens of the tomb of Bábá Ja'fer at Islámból are still members of his family, and their genealogical tree is as follows: 'Abdu-r-ruuf Samadání (otherwise called Sheïkh Zindání) son of Sheïkh Jemálu-d-dín, son of Bint-Emír Sultán, son of Eshrefu-ddín, son of Táju-d-dín, son of the daughter of Seyyid Sikkín (buried near Ak-Shemsu-d-dín, at Túrbahlí Kóï), son of Ja'fer Bábá (buried at Islámból), the son of Mohammed Hanifí, from whom my ancestor Ahmed Yeseví was also descended; our genealogical trees were therefore well known to me.

Kámkár Beg, of Kútáhiyeh, was one of the Germiyán-óghlú (i.e. the children of Germiyán). He, with three thousand young heroes, assailed the Shehíd kapú-sí (martyrs-gate). As it is near Ayá Sófiyah, the Christians assembled there in great multitudes, opened the gate, and sallying forth with great fury, made all their Muselmán assailants martyrs. In the time of Hárúnu-r-rashíd, also, some of the illustrious auxiliaries of the Prophet (*ansár*) quaffed the cup of martyrdom there, hence it has been named the Martyrs (Shuhúd) gate, though incorrectly called by the vulgar, Jews' (Juhúd) gate. The gates of the royal palace (Khúnkár seráï) sustained no siege; but the gate near the Seven Towers was attacked by Karamán-óghlú with the new reinforcements. The troops from Tekkehbáï were posted before Silivrí-gate; those from Aïdín, before the new gate (Yení kapú); those from Sárúkhán, before the Cannon-gate (Tóp kapú-sí), where they were slain, and replaced by those from Munteshá. The force from Isfendiyár was ordered to besiege the Adrianople-gate (Edirneh kapú-sí), and that from Hamíd, the Crooked-gate (Egrí kapú). So that Islámból was besieged on two sides, and nothing but the Kúm kapú (Sand-gate) on the sea-shore, and the wall from the Seven Towers to Seraglio-Point, remained free from attack. At the Seven Towers, the poet Ahmed Páshá, disregarding the fire of the infidels made several breaches. At the Silivrí-gate, Haïder Páshá's fire gave not a moments respite to the infidels. At the new gate (Yení kapú), Mahmúd Páshá, commander of the troops from Aïdín, stormed the wall which he had battered three times without success. The commander at the Tóp kapú-sí was Nishání, also called Karamání Mohammed Páshá, a disciple of Jellálu-d-dín Rúmí. He had given devilish (*khabelí*) proofs of his valour in the war against Uzún Hasan. While he stood at the Cannon-gate, not a cannon could the Káfirs discharge. At the Edirneh-gate (Adrianople), the commander was Sa'dí Páshá, who having dwelt along with Jem-Sháh in Firengistán, had learned many thousand military arts. Being united heart and soul with the valiant men from Isfendiyár stationed at that gate, they vied with him in their heroic deeds, remembering the prophetic tradition that says "We shall be the conquerors of Kostantaniyyeh" (Constantinople). Seven places are yet shewn near that gate where they battered down the wall. Hersek-Oghlú Ahmed Páshá had the command at the Crooked-gate (Egrí-kapú), where by many straight-forward blows he sidled himself into the midst of the infidels till he reduced them all to a mummy.

In this way Kostantaniyyeh had been besieged for twenty days, without any signs of its being conquered. The Moslem warriors, the seventy Unitarians, and three thousand learned 'Ulemás, favourites of God (Evliyá-llah), masters of the decrees of the four orthodox sects, began to be afflicted by the length of the siege, and with one accord offered up their prayers to the Creator for his aid, when suddenly there was darkness over Islámból, with thunder and lightning; a fire was seen to ascend to the vault of heaven from the Atmeïdán; the strongest buildings flew into the air, and were scattered over sea and land. On that day three thousand infidels fled from the city, through alarm and terror. Some were honoured by the profession of Islám, and admitted into the emperors service; others fled to different countries; but the rest, who would not abandon the faith of the Messiah, set to work to repair the breaches, and continued firm in their resistance. They were much pressed, however, by want of food and ammunition.

On the thirtieth day of the siege, Sultán Mohammed having placed the 'Urf (*i.e.* the judicial turban) on his head, and sky-coloured boots on his feet, mounted a mule which might rival Duldul (Mahomet's steed), made the round of the walls, and distributed largesses among his troops. He then passed over with many thousand men from Iyyúb to Kághid khánah, and crossing the streams of Alí Beg Kóï and Kághid Khánah came to the place called Levend-chiftlik, where forty ships (firkatah) had also been built. These, like the former, they moved on rollers to the Ok-meïdán, and launched them at the Sháh-kúlí stairs into the sea, filled with some thousand scarlet scull-capped Arabs, burning as brandy, and sharp as hawks.

SECTION XI.

There appeared off Seraglio Point ten large admirals' ships and ten frigates, completely armed and equipped, with the cross-bearing ensign flying, drums beating, and music playing; and casting anchor there, they fired their guns with indescribable demonstrations of joy, while the Moslims advanced from the Ok-meïdán in two hundred boats and skiffs, embarked on board their own vessels, rushed on these ten ships like bees swarming upon a hive, and enthralled them, head and stern, with their ropes like a spiders web. The infidels, supposing that they were only come on a parley, stood quietly without stretching out a hand against them. The Moslims, in the mean time, shouting "Allah! Allah!" began to tie their hands behind their backs, and to plunder their ships; when the infidels, speaking in their own language, said *"Chi parlai,"* that is to say, "What do you say?" The Káfirs discovered by the answer who they were, and cried out, "These Turks have entered our ships like a plague, we can make no resistance." On entering the harbour they had fired all their guns as signals of joy, and were now so crowded together that they could not use their arms, they were therefore all taken. The infidels within the town, seeing this sad event, those who were coming to succour them having been thus taken, tore their hair and beards, and began a heavy fire from the batteries at Seraglio Point, the Lead Magazines at Ghalatah, and the Kíz Kulleh-sí (Tower of Leánder). The undaunted Moslims, however, in spite of the enemy's batteries, lowered the cross-bearing flag on the twenty ships which they had taken, put all the prisoners on board of their own vessels, and came to an anchor before the garden of the arsenal, firing their guns repeatedly from joy and exultation. The serden-gechdí (*i.e.* mad caps) immediately disembarking from the vessels, brought the glad tidings to the Sultán and Ak-Shemsu-d-dín, in the garden of the arsenal; when the latter, turning to Mohammed, said: "When your majesty, being then a prince at Maghnísá, heard of the taking of 'Akkà, Saïdá, and Berût (Acrí, Sidon, and Beïrút) in Egypt, by the infidels, and grieved at the thoughts of what the captives, women, and children must suffer, I comforted you by saying, that when you conquered Islámból you would eat of the sweetmeats taken in the plunder of 'Akkà. Lo! those sweetmeats are now presented to you, and my prophetic prayer, that the city might be conquered on the fiftieth day, has been answered!" There were found by the Musulmáns on board the twenty ships, three thousand purses of coins (fulúrí) of Tekiyánús (Decianus), one thousand loads of pure gold, two thousand loads of silver, eight thousand prisoners, twenty captains of ships, a French princess (a kings daughter, a yet unexpanded blossom), a thousand Muselmán damsels, brilliant as the sun, noble and ignoble, and some thousand-times a hundred thousand warlike stores; all of which the Sultán confided to the care of Ak-Shemsu-d-dín, while he himself was entirely engaged in continuing the siege.

The complete account of the affair is this: Kostantín, the late King of Islámból, being betrothed to a daughter of the King of Fránsah, the latter, in order to send her with an escort worthy of her rank, equipped a fleet of six hundred ships, and sent them to ravage the coasts of Arabia ('Arabistán). In that unhappy year they had plundered 'Akkah, Saïdah, Berút, Tarábulus (Tripoli), Ghazzah, and Ramlah, as far as the land of Hásán (Haúrán?), and carried off more than two thousand Húrí-like damsels from 'Arabistán, with spoils to the amount of millions. Of this fleet, ten galeons and ten frigates were dispatched to carry the Princess to Islámbúl. When they reached the straits of the White Sea (the Dardanelles), they discovered that the Túrks had built castles there; but these accursed fellows, by disguising themselves, taking advantage of a fresh southerly breeze, and sending forwards five empty ships to receive the fire from the castles, in two hours got twenty miles beyond them. Having by this stratagem reached Islámból, they were taken, thank God! as has been related. This French princess afterwards gave birth to Yildirím Báyazíd; but other historians tell the story differently, and say that she was taken by the father of Mohammed the Conqueror, and gave birth to him, but he was in truth the son of 'Alímeh Khánum, the daughter of Isfendiyár Oghlú. The correctness of the first account maybe proved thus: My father, who died an old man, was with Sultán Suleïmán at the sieges of Rhodes, Belgrade, and Sigetvár, where that prince died. He used to converse much with men advanced in years: among his most intimate friends there was one who was grey-headed and infirm, but more eloquent than Amrïo-l-kaïs or Abú-l-ma'álí. He was chief secretary to the corps of Janissaries, and his name was Sú-Kemerlí Kójah Mustafà Chelebí. This gentleman was certainly related to this daughter of the King of Fránsah, from whom he continually received presents; and I remember that when I was a boy he gave me some curious pictures which had been given to him by her. During the siege of Sigetvár, before the death of Suleïmán was known to the army, the silihdár (sword-bearer) Kúzú 'Alí Aghá, by the desire of the Grand Vizír Sokól-lí Mohammed Páshá, assembled a council of war, at which the corpse of the Sultán was seated on his throne, and his hands were moved [by some one concealed] behind his ample robe (khil'ah). To this council all the vizírs, vakíls, and senior officers of the army were summoned. Among them were the rikábdár (stirrup-holder) Julábí Aghá, the metbakh emíní (clerk of the kitchen) 'Abdí Efendí, my father, and the abovementioned Sú-kemerli Kójáh Mustafá. He was at that time so old, that when he accompanied the army he was always carried about in a litter (takhti-reván). He had been one of the disciples of the great Muftí Kemál Páshá-zádeh, and was deeply read in divinity and history.

Being one of the servants of Kemál Páshá-zádeh, "I was," he used to say, "when a youth of twenty-five years of age, present at the conquest of Cairo by Sultán Selím I." A.H. 923 (A.D. 1517); and the writer of these pages was lost in astonishment when he heard him give an account of the great battles of Merj Dábik and Kákún, of Sultán Ghaúrí's quaffing the cup of destiny, of his son Mohammed's being deposed by the soldiery on account of his youth, of Túmán-Báï's succeeding him, of his continued war and twenty-three battles with Selím, till at length Caïro was taken. He was a most faithful man, and one whose word could be taken with perfect security; and having heard him relate the story of the abovementioned French princess from beginning to end, I write it down here.

An Explanation of the Relationship between the House of 'Osmán and the King of France.

Sú-Kemer-lí Mustafá Chelebí gave this narrative: "My father was the son of a King of France, named——. When the treaty had been made by which he engaged to give his daughter (my father's sister) to the Tekkúr (the Emperor of Constantinople), a fleet of six hundred vessels was dispatched to ravage the coasts near the castle of 'Akkah, in order to furnish her with a dowry. It returned home laden with an immense booty, and a vast number of captives, male and female, and having reached Párisah, the ancient capital of our country, great rejoicings were made. Among the female captives there was a young Seyyideh (i.e. one of the prophetic race), who was given by the King of France to my father, and from whom I was born. When I was three years old, the king my grandfather sent my father with his sister, and vast treasures, to Islámból, and having been captured at Seraglio Point, we were delivered up to Sultán Mohammed, in the garden of the arsenal. After the city was taken, my father was honoured by admission into Islám (the Mohammedan faith), having been instructed by Ak-Shemsu-d-dín, and all the victorious Moslims having reverently presented his sister the princess to the Sultán, she was also instructed in Islám by the same holy man, but refused to embrace it. The Sultán upon this said, "We will give her an excellent education," and did not trouble himself to insist much on that point. I was then five years old, and being taught the doctrines of Islám by Ak-Shemsu-d-dín, received the honour of Islámism (God be praised!) without any hesitation. My father was made one of the kapújí-báshís (lord-chamberlains), and I was brought up in the seráï kháss (i.e. the Grand Seignor's palace) by my aunt, my father's sister. Mohammed Khán having afterwards formed a close attachment for my aunt, she became the mother of Sultán Báyazíd (II) Velí, and the princes Jem and Núru-d-dín." "When my aunt," he added, "died, as she had never embraced Islám, Sultán Mohammed II. caused a small sepulchre (kubbeh) to be erected beside the sepulchral chapel (turbeh) which he had built for himself, and there she was buried. I myself have often, at morning-prayer, observed that the readers appointed to read lessons from the Korán [in these turbehs] turned their faces towards the bodies of the defunct buried in the other tombs while reading the lessons, but that they all turned their backs upon the coffin of this lady, of whom it was so doubtful whether she departed in the faith of Islám. I have also frequently seen Franks of the Fránsah tribe (*i.e.* French), come by stealth and give a few aspers to the turbeh-dárs (tomb-keepers) to open this chapel for them, as its gate is always kept shut. So that there can be no doubt, according to the account given by Srí Kemer-lí Mustafá Chebebí, that a daughter of the King of France became the wife (khátún) of Mohammed the Conqueror (Abú-l Fat-h), and the mother of Sultán Báyazíd."

An Account of the heroic Deeds and Misfortunes of Jem-Sháh, son of the Emperor Mohammed Abú-l Fat-h (the Conqueror).

When Báyazíd Velí was khalífah, his brother Jem-Sháh (these two being princes of a high spirit) contended with him for the possession of this foul world, and having been worsted in a great battle on the plains of Karamán, fled to Kalávún Sultán of Egypt. From thence as he was going on a pilgrimage to Meccah, he was driven by the buffetting of the sea on the shores of Yemen and 'Aden, whence he visited the tomb of Veïso-l Karní, performed the pilgrimage, and travelling through Hijáz, returned to Egypt, from which country he went by sea to Rhodes and Malta, and from thence to France to visit his grandmother (the Queen of France), one of the most exalted sovereigns of that time, accompanied by 300 Muselmán followers: he spent his time like a prince, in hunting and all sorts of enjoyment. One of his most favoured companions and counsellors was his *defterdár* (secretary) Sivrí Hisárí; another was 'Ashik-Haïder. Seventeen sons of báns (princes) stood before him [as slaves] with their hands crossed upon their breasts [ready to receive and execute his orders]. He was always followed by this suite in all his travels through Káfiristán (the land of the infidels). He composed some thousand penj-beïts mukhammases, and musaddeses (odes), together with kásáyids (elegies), which form a díván (collection of poems), praised by all the world.

A Stanza by Jem-Sháh.

Bird of my soul, be patient of thy cage,

This body, lo! how fast it wastes with age.

The tinkling bells already do I hear

Proclaim the caravans departure near.

Soon shall it reach the land of nothingness,

And thee, from fleshy bonds delivered, bless.

In this kind of elegies he was an incomparable poet. Sultán Báyazíd at length sent an ambassador to the King of France and claimed Jem-Sháh. On this the ill-complexioned Frank caused a sallow-faced fellow to cut his throat while shaving him with a poisoned razor. The corpse of Jem, together with his property, amongst which was an enchanted cup, which became brimful as soon as delivered empty into the cup-bearers hand, a white parrot, a chess-playing monkey, and some thousands of splendid books, were delivered up to Sa'dí Chelebí (Sivrí Hisárí) and Haïder Chelebí, that they might be conveyed to the Sultán. Jem's Sa'dí [*i.e.* Sivrí Hisárí], being a learned and acute man, first dyed the parrot black, and taught him to say, "Verily we belong to God, and to Him shall we return! Long live the Emperor!" He then returned to him with the remains of his master, and delivered over his property to the imperial treasury. But when Báyazíd asked "where is the white parrot?" the bird immediately repeated the above-mentioned text, and added: "Sire, Jem-Sháh having entered into the mercy of his Lord, I have put off the attire of the angel clad in white, and clothed myself in the black of mourning weeds."—"How!" said the Sultán, addressing himself to Sivrí Hisárí, "did they kill my brother Jem?" "By Heaven! O Emperor!" replied he, "though he indulged in wine, yet he never drank it but out of that enchanted cup, nor did he ever mingle with the infidels, but spent all his time in composing poetry; so by God's will there was a certain barber named Yán Oghlí (John's son), who shaved him with a poisoned razor, which made his face and eyes swell, and he was suffocated." Báyazíd ordered the remains of Jem to be buried at Brúsah, beside his grandfather Murád II. While they were digging the grave there was such a thunder-clap and tumult in the sepulchral chapel, that all who were present fled, but not a soul of them was able to pass its threshold till ten days had passed, when this having been represented to the Sultán, the corpse of Jem was buried by his order in his own mausoleum, near to that of his grandfather. Prince Jem Sháh died in A.H. 900, after having spent eleven years in travelling through Egypt, Arabia, Syria, Mesopotamia, and in Firengistán, through Spain and France, and having escaped from his brother's den, and drunk of the cup of Jem, he at last was intoxicated by drinking of the cup of Fate. According to the French account, however, another person was killed by the poisoned razor, and his corpse was sent to Rúm (Turkey) instead of the remains of Jem, who in fact became King of France, and was the forefather of the present sovereign of that country. On enquiring into this report, and hearing what had happened at the tomb, *viz.* that Murád would not allow the corpse to be buried in his mausoleum, he ordered it to be interred elsewhere. After the taking of Uïvár (Raab) in the year 1073 (A.D. 1662-3), Mohammed Páshá was sent as ambassador the following year, 1074 (1663-4), into Germany (Alámán Díarí), in order to conclude a peace with the emperor of that country (Nemseh-Chásárí): having accompanied him I spent three years in visiting, under the protection of a passport (pátentah) written by him, the seven kingdoms of Káfirístán. Having set foot on the land of Dúnkárkeïn (Dunkirk), situated on the shore of the ocean which separates the eastern side of the New World from France, I passed the Ramazán of the year 1075 (March 1665) there, and having an acquaintance with some well-informed priests (pápáslar), I asked them about the history of Jem-Sháh. They answered, that when the order came from the 'Osmánlí (Sultán) to kill Jem, the French king spared him out of pity, as being a relation to the 'Osmánlí (family) and his own sister's son, and that having caused another person who resembled Jem to be poisoned, they sent his corpse to Islámból, saying it was that of Jem: that having been afterwards made king of the country on the borders of France (tísh Fránsah) at the time of the conquest of Egypt by Sultán Selím, he sent him presents with letters of congratulation on his victory. They also confirmed the account of the near relationship between the House of 'Osmán and the Kings of France through the mother of Sultán Báyazíd and the progeny of King Jem. He is buried, they added, in a mausoleum (kubbah) in a garden like Irem, outside of the city of Paris, where all the Musulmáns his companions and slaves have been entombed. It is on account of this relationship between the house of 'Osmán and the French kings, that when the foreign ambassadors are assembled in the díván the Frank ambassadors stand below, because their sovereigns are not Moslems; but the French is placed above the Persian ambassador, below whom the German envoy is seated, so that the ambassador from Persia has an infidel on each side. Murád IV., conqueror of Baghdád, altered this regulation, and gave precedence to the French ambassador over all others, and the Russian (Moskov) then taking the right hand of the Persian; an arrangement which offended the German ambassador, but he was obliged to acquiesce in it. This distinguished honour was granted to France because a French princess was the mother of Sultán Báyazíd.

Let us now return from this digression to the siege of the castle of Kostantín. Sultán Mohammed Khán having taken the daughter of the King of France out of the booty of the captured fleet, and by the advice of the captors, placed the rest in the hands of Ak-Shémsu-d-dín to be divided among the army, continued to encourage the besiegers. At length the fiftieth day came. It was manifest that all was terror and confusion within the city, and these graceless Christian infidels planting a white flag on the ramparts, cried out, "Quarter, O chosen House of 'Osmán! we will deliver up the city." A respite of one day was therefore given to all the unbelievers, to go by land or sea to any country that they would. The Sultán then having the pontifical turban on his head, and sky-blue boots on his feet, mounted on a mule, and bearing the sword of Mohammed in his hand, marched in at the head of 70,000 or 80,000 Muselmán heroes, crying out, "Halt not, conquerors! God be praised! Ye are the vanquishers of Kostantaniyyeh!" He led them directly to the palace of Constantine (Takfúr Seráï), where he found some thousands of infidels assembled and prepared to defend it resolutely. A great battle ensued, and in that contest Kostantín, the king, was slain, and buried with the rest of the faithless (káfirs) in the Water Monastery (Súlú Menastir). The treasures in the king's palace were so great that God only knows their amount. They were amassed by this Kostantín, who was a merchant, and as rapacious as a griffin ('anká), and had rebuilt Islámbúl the ninth time. Mohammed proceeded to the church of Ayá Sófiyah in order to express his thanks by saying a prayer, accompanied by two inclinations of the head (rik'at). Twelve thousand monks who dwelt within and all around it, having closed its doors, threw from the roof, towers, turrets, and belfries, arrows and burning pitch, and naptha on the Moslems. Mohammed having invested the church with the armies of Islám, like a swarm of hornets, for three days and three nights, at length took it on the fifty-third day. He then having slain a few monks, entered the church, bearing the standard of the Prophet of God in his hand, and planting it on the high altar (mihráb), chaunted, for the first time, the Mohammedan ezán (call to prayers). The rest of the Muselmán victors having put the monks to the edge of the sword, Ayá Sófiyah, was deluged with the blood of the idolaters. Mohammed, in order to leave them a memorial of his skill in archery, shot a four-winged arrow into the centre of the cupola, and the trace of his arrow is still shown there. One of the archers of the Sultán's guard having killed an infidel with his left hand, and filled his right with his blood, came into the Sultán's presence, and clapping his hand red with blood on a white marble column, left the impression of a hand and fingers, which is still seen near the turbeh-kapú-sí. It is on the opposite corner as one enters, at the height of five men's stature above the ground.

Eulogium on Yá Vudúd Sultán.

While Sultán Mohammed was going in solemn procession round Ayá Sófiyah a flash of lightning was seen to strike a place called Terlú-direk, and on going thither they found a body lying with its face turned towards the kibleh, and written on its illuminated breast in crimson characters, the name Yá Vudúd (O All-loving). Ak-Shemsu-d-dín, Karah-Shemsu-d-dín, and the other seventy holy men, exclaimed, "This, O Emperor! was the cause of Islámból's falling on the fiftieth day." Having prayed that it might fall in fifty days, on that very day he resigned his soul and bore his prayer to heaven. Then while all those learned, righteous and excellent men were making the necessary preparations for washing that noble corpse, a voice was heard from the corner of the Terlú-direk (the sweating column), saying: "He is washed and received into mercy, now therefore inter him." All were breathless with astonishment: and those venerable sheïkhs having placed the illustrious corpse of Yá Vudúd Sultán on a bier, and intending to bury him near Shehíd-kapú-sí, proceeded to the stairs of Emír Oní, where the bier was put into a boat, which instantly, without an oar plyed or a sail set, flew like lightning, and did not stop till it came near [the tomb of] Abú Iyyúb Ensárí. There the holy man was buried, and the neighbouring landing-place was thence called Yá Vudúd Iskeleh-sí.

Sultán Mohammed Khán, Father of Victory (*i.e.* the Conqueror), a Sultán son of a Sultán of the Islamitic sovereigns of the House of 'Osmán, entered Islámból victoriously on Wednesday the 20th day of Jumázíu-l-ákhir, in the year of the Prophet's flight 867 [1st July, A.D. 1453], as was expressed by the prophetic and descriptive letters of the text *beldetun tayyibetun* (a good city), and in the day, hour, and minute, which had been foretold to the Sultán by Ak-Shemsu-d-dín. Several poets and men of learning have made other lines and technical words containing the date of this victory of victories; but the date found in the exalted Korán is complete, if the last letters are counted as they are pronounced. Sultán Mohammed II. on surveying more closely the church of Ayá Sófiyah, was astonished at the solidity of its construction, the strength of its foundations, the height of its cupola, and the skill of its builder, Aghnádús. He caused this ancient place of worship to be cleared of its idolatrous impurities and purified from the blood of the slain, and having refreshed the brain of the victorious Moslems by fumigating it with amber and lign-aloes, converted it in that very hour into a jámi' (a cathedral), by erecting a contracted mihráb, minber, mahfil, and menáreh, in that place which might rival Paradise. On the following Friday, the faithful were summoned to prayer by the muëzzins, who proclaimed with a loud voice this text (Kor. xxxiii. 56): "Verily, God and his angels bless the Prophet." Ak-Shemsu-d-dín and Karah Shemsu-d-dín then arose, and placing themselves on each side of the Sultán, supported him under his arms; the former placed his own turban on the head of the conqueror, fixing in it a black and white feather of a crane, and putting into his hand a naked sword. Thus conducted to the minber he ascended it, and cried out with a voice as loud as David's, "Praise be to God the Lord of all worlds," (Kor. i. 1.) on which all the victorious Moslems lifted up their hands and uttered a shout of joy. The Sultán then officiating as khatíb pronounced the khutbeh, and descending from the minber, called upon Ak-Shemsu-d-dín to perform the rest of the service as Imám. On that Friday the patriarch and no less than three thousand priests who had been concealed underneath the floor of the church, were honoured by being received into Islám. One of them, who was three hundred years old, they named Bábá Mohammed. This man pointed out a hidden treasure on the right side of the mihráb, saying it was placed there by Suleïmán (Solomon), the first builder of this ancient place of worship. The Sultán having first offered up prayer there for the prosperity and perpetuity of the place, caused the ground to be dug up beneath it, and during a whole week many thousand camel-loads of treasure in coins of Tekiyánús and Okí-yúnus (Decianus and ——), were carried away and deposited in the royal treasury and in the garden of the arsenal.

On the glorious Conquest of the Ok-meïdán (Archery-ground).

When the Sultán had distributed all the booty among the victors, he caused the idols like Vudd, Yághús, Ya'úf, Suvá', and Nesr, which were found set with jewels in Ayá Sófiyah to be carried to the Ok-meïdán, and set up there as marks for all the Muselmán heroes to shoot their arrows at; and from thence an arrow which hits the mark, is to this day called by archers an idol's arrow (púteh ókí). One of those idols was standing till knocked to pieces in the time of Sultán Ahmed Khán. Another was called Azmáïsh, because it stood on the south side, and the arrows hit it when shot with a northerly wind; the spot on which it stood is now called Tóz-kópárán-áyághí (Dust-maker's Foot). Another idol called Hekí, placed near Kháss-kóï, was most easily hit from the north; hence the phrase "a hekí-shot." Another called Písh-rev, placed on the north-west side, and most easily hit from the south-east (kibleh), still gives its name to such a shot. From Pelenk, placed on the west side and hit from the east, the term pelenk is derived. In short, having placed twelve different idols on the four sides of the Ok-meïdán, a grand archery-match was made, and all the old archers, each shewing his skill in taking aim at them, made glad the soul of the illustrious Sa'd Vakkás, and hence arose the custom among the people of Islámból of meeting there on holidays for the purpose of trying their skill in archery. Sultán Mohammed II. having gone thence to the garden of the arsenal, gave a banquet for three days and three nights to all the Moslem conquerors, himself appearing like the cháshnegír báshí (chief butler), with his skirts girt up round his loins and a handkerchief in his girdle, offering them bread and salt, and providing them with a splendid dinner. After the repast he carried round the ewer, and poured out water for the learned and excellent to wash their noble hands; thus for three days and three nights breaking his spirit by performing these services.

Distribution of the Booty.

After this splendid feast, which lasted three days and three nights, the Sultán accompanied by the three imperial defterdárs and all the clerks of the army, proceeded to pile up in the garden of the arsenal, the treasures taken on board of the French fleet, with those pointed out in the Ayá Sófiyah by Mohammed Bábá, and those taken from the seven thousand monasteries, convents, and palaces within the city. The first to whom their share was allotted were the physicians, oculists, surgeons, washers of the dead and grave-diggers serving in the army; next the sherífs (*i.e.* members of the Prophet's family); then the learned and pious 'ulemá and sulehá (*i.e.* doctors of law); then the imáms, khatíbs, and sheïkhs; after them the móllás and kázies (judges); then the serden gechdis (dread-noughts); next the Arab marines who dragged the ships overland, from the village thence called Levend-chiftlik; after them the janissaries; then the sipáhíes, za'íms, tópchís, jebehjís, lághemjís, eshekchís, horsekeepers, and camp-servants, respectively forming together one hundred and seventy thousand men, to whom sixty-three thousand houses were allotted, besides their legal share of the spoils. Out of this the victors paid during their lives the tenth appointed by God's law, to the Sultán, whose own share was three thousand eight hundred captives, twenty thousand purses of gold, coins of Tekiyánús and Yánkó son of Mádiyán, three thousand palaces, two bezestáns, and seven thousand shops. They also gave to the Sultán the mosque of Ayá Sófiyah, with seven great convents, and fixed the rent to be paid by him for the New Seráï at one thousand aspers a day. A Jew, who offered one thousand and one aspers, was put to death. In the karamán-ward of the city three hundred lofty palaces were given to the 'ulemá, one hundred and sixty-two to the janissaries, seventy to the vezírs, seven to each of the seven kubbeh vezírs. In short, all the houses in Islámból were thus distributed among the victors, and the daughter of the French King mentioned above, was given to the Emperor. Thus was every duty which the law required fulfilled. Ak-Shemsu-d-dín then standing up, thus spoke: "Know and understand ye Moslem conquerors, that it is you of whom the last of the prophets, the joy and pride of all creatures, spoke, when he said: 'Verily they shall conquer Kostantaniyyeh; the best of commanders is their commander; the best of armies is that army!' Squander not away then these treasures, but spend them on good and pious foundations in Islámból; be obedient to your Emperor; and as from the days of 'Osmán down to the present time, you called your Emperor Beg, so from henceforth call him Sultán; and as at the feast he girded up his loins, and served you himself, in return for his bounty, call him

Khúnkár." He then fastened to the head of the Sultán a double black and white heron's plume (aigrette), saying: "Thou art now, O Emperor, become the chosen Prince of the House of Osmán, continue to fight valiantly in the path of God!" A shout of victory was then made, and the Muselmán warriors took possession of their new habitations. It was at that time that, with the permission of Ak-Shemsu-d-dín and the other holy men, a coin was first struck bearing this legend: "The Sultán, son of a Sultán, Sultán Mohammed Khán, son of Sultán Murád Khán, be his victory exalted; coined in Kostantaniyyeh in the year 757." On the following day, when the Sultán, as he came out of the harem, received Ak-Shemsu-d-dín in the Arsenal-Garden: "Did you not eat some sweetmeats last night, Sire?" said the latter. "No," replied the Sultán, "we eat none!"—"Do you not remember," replied the holy man, "that when you were so much grieved while governor of Maghnísá, on hearing of the capture of 'Akkah by the Franks, I told you that you would eat some of their sweetmeats when you had taken Islámból? And did you not last night enjoy the society of the French princess? Was not that tasting a sweetmeat won from the Franks? Henceforward let that unexpanded rose be called 'Akídeh (sugar-candy) Khánum, and be thou thyself styled Khúnkár (blood shedder). Let this day be a day of rejoicing, but let it likewise be a day of justice! Of the three thousand blooming Mohammedan virgins who came in the suite of 'Akídeh your spouse (khássekí), let not one be touched, but send to 'Akkah, Ghazzah, Ramlah, Khaúrán, all the countries whence they were taken, a register containing their names, and order their parents, relations, and friends to repair to Islámból, that each of them may, with the consent of their parents, be joined in lawful marriage with one of the Moslem warriors, and the city of Islámból be thus made populous." The counsels of Ak Shemsu-d-dín were followed; and in a short time ten thousand fathers, mothers, relations, and connexions, hastened to the city, and three thousand heroes were made happy by being joined in lawful matrimony to three thousand virgins. Orders were then issued to all the vezírs who were Páshás in Europe and Asia, to send all the sons of Adam from each district to Islámból. Thus the ward of Uskúblí was peopled by the inhabitants of Uskúb; the Yení Mahallah by the people of Yení-shehr; that of Ayá Sófiyah by the people of Sófiyah; that of Tenes by the Urúm (Greeks) from Mórah (the Morea); the neighbourhood of Tekkúr-serái and Shahíd-kapú-si by the Jews of fifty communities brought from Seláník (Thessalonica); Ak-Seráï by the people from Anátólí (Natolia); the ward below the castle by the Syrians and Arabs; the Persians were settled in Khójah-khán near Mahmúd Páshá; the Gypsies (Chingáneh) coming from Balát Shehrí are established in the Balát-mahalleh-sí; the U'luch from 'Akl-bend in the 'Akl-bend ward; the Arnaúts (Albanians) near the Silivrì-gate; the Jews from Safat in Kháss Kóï; the Anatolian Turks at Uskudár (Scutari); the Armenians of Tókát and Sívás near Súlú Monástir; the

Magnesians in the Ma'júnjí ward; the Ekirdir and Ekmidir people at Egrí kapú; the————— in Iyyúb Sultán; the Karamanians in the Buyúk Karamán ward; the inhabitants of Kóniyah in that of Kuchúk Karamán; those of Tirehlí in Vefà; the people of the plain of Chehár-shenbeh in the bázár so called; the inhabitants of Kastemúní in the Kazánjílar (brazier's) ward; the Láz from Tirábuzún (Trebizonde) near the mosque of Sultán Báyazíd; the people of Gelíbólí (Gallipoli) at the Arsenal; those of Izmír (Smyrna) in Great Ghalatah; the Franks in Little Ghalatah (Pera); the inhabitants of Sínób and Sámsún at Tóp-kháneh. In short, the Mohammedan inhabitants of all the large towns in the land of the House of 'Osmán were then brought to people Islámból, called on that account Islámí ból (i.e. ample is its Islám!).

By God's decree, Islámból was taken in the month of Temmúz (July), and the sea was then dyed with the blood of some thousands of martyrs. Now it happens, that for forty days, every year at that season, the sea is still blood-red, from the gate of Iyyúb Ensár to the Martyr's-gate (Shehíd kapú-sí). This is a marvellous thing and one of God's secrets. "Verily God hath power over all things!"

SECTION XII.

Description of the new Seráï, the Threshold of the Abode of Felicity.

The conqueror having thus become possessed of such treasures, observed that the first thing requisite for an Emperor is a permanent habitation. He therefore expended three thousand purses on building the new Seráï. The best of several metrical dates inscribed over the Imperial gate, is that at the bottom in conspicuous gold letters on a white marble tablet, Khalled Allahu azza sáhibihi. May God make the glory of its master eternal! (*i.e.* A.H. 876, A.D. 1471-2). Never hath a more delightful edifice been erected by the art of man; for, placed on the border of the sea, and having the Black Sea on the North, and the White Sea on the East, it is rather a town situated on the confluence of two seas than a palace. Its first builder was that second Solomon, the two-horned Alexander. It was, therefore, erected on the remains of what had been built by former princes, and Mohammed the Conqueror added seventy private, regal, and well-furnished apartments; such as a confectionary, bake-house, hospital, armory, mat-house, wood-house, granary, privy-stables without and within, such that each is like the stable of 'Antar, store-rooms of various kinds round a garden delightful as the garden of Irem, planted with twenty thousand cypresses, planes, weeping-willows, thuyas, pines, and box-trees, and among them many hundred thousands of fruit trees, forming an aviary and tulip-parterre, which to this day may be compared to the garden of the Genii (Jin). In the middle of this garden there is a delightful hill and rising ground, on which he built forty private apartments, wainscoted with Chinese tiles, and a hall of audience (Arz-ódá) within the Port of Felicity, and a fine hippodrome, on the east side of which he erected a bath, near the privy treasury; close to which are the aviary, the pantry, the treasurers chamber, the Sultán's closet, the Imperial mosque, the falconer's chamber, the great and small pages' chamber; the seferlí's and gulkhan's chamber, the mosque of the Buyúk-ódá, and the house of exercise, which joins the bath mentioned above. The privy chambers (kháss-ódá), mentioned before, were occupied by three thousand pages, beautiful as Yúsuf (Joseph), richly attired in shirts fragrant as roses, with embroidered tiaras, and robes drowned in gold and jewels, having each his place in the Imperial service, where he was always ready to attend. There was no harem in this palace; but one was built afterwards, in the time of Sultán Suleïmán, who added a chamber for the black eunuchs (*taváshí aghá-lar*), another for the white eunuchs (*teberdárán khásseh, i.e.* privy halbardiers), a cabinet (*kóshk*) for recreations, and a chamber for the díván, where the seven vezírs assembled four days in the week. Sultán Mohammed, likewise, surrounded this strongly-fortified palace with a wall that had 366 towers, and twelve thousand battlements; its circumference being 6,500 paces, with sixteen gates, great and small. Besides all the other officers before enumerated, there were in this palace twelve thousand Bóstánjís, and, including all, forty thousand souls lodged within its walls.

SECTION XIII.

Description of the Old Seräï.

Sultán Mohammed the Conqueror also determined to place his honourable harem in Islámból. In an airy and elevated position, on the side of the city which overlooks the canal, there was an old convent, built by King Púzantín, and placed in the midst of a delightful grove, full of all sorts of beasts and birds. This convent, in the time of Púzantín and Kostantín, had been occupied by twelve thousand monks and nuns. The occasion of its being built was, that Simon, one of the apostles of Jesus, having engaged in devotion, and in maintaining a friendly intercourse with all sorts of wild animals, dug a pit in the ground in order to supply them with water, on which a spring of truly living water burst forth. Simon afterwards built a small oratory there, which, in process of time, was replaced by the convent which Mohammed destroyed, when he built upon its site the old palace (*Eskí Seräï*) begun in the year 858 (A.D. 1454), and finished in the year 862 (A.D. 1458). The wall has neither towers, battlements, nor ditch; but is very strong, being cased with azure-coloured lead. Its circumference was then twelve thousand arshíns (25,000 feet). It is a solid square building, one side of which stretched from the brazier's (*kazánjílar*) quarter, near the mosque of Sultán Báyazíd, down to the Miskí-sábún (Musk-soap) gate, from whence another extended to the palace of Dellák Mustafá Páshá. Thence a third rested against the wall and cistern of the little bázár. The site of the palaces of the Aghá of the janissaries, and of Siyávush Páshá, now occupies that of the Old Seräï. From thence the fourth side, passing above the quarter of Tahta-l kal'ah, came again to the Brazier's bázár. Within this palace there were many courts, cabinets, cisterns, and fountains; a kitchen like that of Kei-kávus, a private buttery, chambers for three thousand halbardiers (*teberdár*), servants without ringlets, one apartment (*ódá*) for the white, and one for the black Aghá (of the eunuchs), who were both subordinate to the (*Kizlar Aghá*) Aghá of the Porte (*Dáru-s-sa'ádeh*, *i.e.* the house of felicity). Having placed in this all his favourites (*khássekí*), together with the French Princess, he came twice every week from the new palace to the old, and on those nights did justice there.

Eulogium on the living water of the old palace (Eskí Seräï).

Abú-l fat-h Mohammed, being a wise and illustrious Emperor, assembled all his learned men in order to enquire which was the best water in Islámból, and they all unanimously pointed out to him the spring of Shim'ún (Simon), within the Eskí Seráï, as the lightest, most temperate, and copious of all; which was proved by dipping a miskál of cotton in a certain quantity of each different kind of water, then weighing each parcel, and after drying it in the sun, weighing it a second time. The Sultán, therefore, resolved to drink of no other water than this, and to this time it is the favourite source from which all his successors drink. Three men come every day from the Kilárjí-báshí, and three from the Sakká-báshí of the Seráï, and fill six silver flaggons, each containing twenty ounces, with this limpid water, seal the mouths of them in presence of the inspector of water with seals of red wax, and bring them to the Emperor. At present this fountain is in front of the Inspector's-gate (Názir kapú-sí) on the eastern side of the Eskí Seráï, where Sultán Mohammed the Conqueror caused the water to run outside of the palace, and erected the building over it; it is now the most celebrated water in the town, and is known by the name of the fountain of Shim'ún. In the year——, Sultán Suleïmán having enlarged this old palace to the extent of three miles in circumference, built three gates. The Díván kapú-sí towards the east, Sultán Báyazíd kapú-sí to the south, and the Suleïmániyyeh kapú-sí towards the west. On the outside of this gate Sultán Suleïmán built the mosque bearing his name from the booty of the conquest of Belgrade, Malta, and Rhodes; and near it colleges for science, and teaching the traditions and art of reciting the Korán, a school for children, an alms-house, a hospital, a cáravánseráï, a bath, and market for boot-makers, button-makers, and goldsmiths; a palace for the residence of the late Siyávush Páshá, another for the residence of the Aghá of the janissaries, a third for Lálá Mustafá Páshá, a fourth for Pír Mohammed Páshá Karamání, a fifth for Mustafá Páshá, builder of the mosque at Geïbiz, a sixth for his daughter Esmahán Sultán, and a thousand cells, with pensions annexed, for the servants of the mosque. The four sides, however, of the old Seráï, were bordered by the public road, and, to this time, are not contiguous to any house. The abovementioned palaces are all built on the site of the old Seráï, which was erected by Sultán Mohammed Khán, who afterwards constructed barracks for 160 regiments (Bulúks and Jemá'ats) of janissaries, and 160 chambers (ódás) for the Segbáns (Seïmens), a mosque for himself, chambers for the armorers (jebeh-jís), powder magazines at Peïk-khánah, Kalender-khánah, Ters-khánah, Top-khánah, Kághid-khánah, and many other similar public buildings within and without Islámból; the sums thus expended, having been drawn from the treasures amassed in his conquests.

SECTION XIV.

On the Public Officers established at Islámból at the time of the Conquest.

Within three years the city of Islámból became so populous, and contained such a sea of men, that it was impossible to restrain its inhabitants without public authority. The assistants first granted to the Grand Vezír Mahmúd Páshá, were five executioners, a regiment (ódá) of janissaries, with a Muhzir Aghá (colonel), cháúshes (apparitors) of the Tópjís and Jebehjis, a captain (*ódábáshí*) of the Bóstánjís, and a túfenkjí (musketeer), and matarahjí (water-carrier) taken from the janissaries, with whom he took his rounds through the city on the fourth day of every week, in order to punish by the falákah (bastinado) all transgressors of the law. He went first to the Díván-khánah (Court-house) of the tradespeople at the U'n-kapán (flour-market), and held a díván there; he next visited the stairs (*iskeleh*) of the fruit-market, and held a díván to fix the price of fruit; from thence he proceeded to the green-market and shambles (Salkh-khánah), where he settled the rate at which greens and mutton should be sold, and he afterwards returned to the Seráï.

The second public officer was the Segbán Báshí (commander of the Seïmens), to whom the falákah was entrusted, but he had no executioners.

The third was the judge and Móllá of Islámból, who could inflict the bastinado (falákah), and imprison for debt.

The fourth, the Móllá of Iyyúb, who could inflict the same punishments.

The fifth, the Móllá of Ghalatah, and

The sixth, the Móllá of Uskudár, possessing the same power within their respective jurisdictions.

The seventh, the Ayák Náïbí, or superintendant of the markets, who punished all who sold above the legal prices, or used false weights and measures.

The eighth, the Mohtesib Aghá-sí (inspector of shops), by whom all defaulters in buying and selling were punished, according to their offences, with imprisonment and torture; such as covering their heads with the entrails of beasts, or nailing their ears and noses to a plank.

The ninth, the 'Asas-báshí, and

The tenth, the Sú-báshí, two police-officers attended by executioners provided with whips and scourges, but not with rods and stocks (*falákah*). They made domiciliary visits, took up offenders, and attended at the execution of criminals condemned to death.

The eleventh, the Islámból-Aghá-sí, or commandant of Constantinople.

The twelfth, the Bóstánjí-báshí, who constantly, from night till morning, takes the round of all the villages on the sea-shore, punishes all whom he finds transgressing; and if any are deserving of death, throws them into the sea.

The thirteenth, Chórbájís (colonels of the janissaries), who continually go round, from night till morning, with five or six hundred of their soldiers in quest of suspicious persons, whom they send prisoners to the Porte, where they receive their due.

The fourteenth, the forty Judges appointed, according to the law of the Prophet, to preside over the forty Courts of Justice (*mehkemeh*) in Islámból, under the four Móllás mentioned above. They also have power to imprison and inflict punishment.

The fifteenth, the Sheïkho-Islám or Mufti (head of the law). He can only give the legal answer to questions submitted to him, *viz.* "It is," or "It is not." "God knows!" "Yes," or "No."

The sixteenth, the Anátólí Kází-askerí (military judge of Anatolia), has no right to punish, but sits in the díván as chief and president of all the Asiatic judges.

The seventeenth, the Rúm-ílí Kází-'askerí (military judge of Romelia), has likewise no power of punishing, but decides all lawsuits brought into the díván from the country, and is the head of all the European judges. He is likewise appointed, by the canons of Sultán Mohammed the Conqueror, to write all the imperial patents (*beráts*).

The eighteenth, the Commander (Dizdár) of the Seven Towers.

The nineteenth, the chief Architect; if any building be erected in Islámból without his permission it is pulled down, and the builders are punished.

The twentieth, the Kapúdán-Páshá (Lord High Admiral) established in the Arsenal (Ters-khánah); who commands by sea night and day.

The twenty-first, the Kyayà (*ket-khodà*) of the Arsenal (Ters-khánah), who, if any thieves are found by day or night in the district called Kásim Páshá, can inflict the severest punishment, even death, if necessary.

The twenty-second, the Ta'lím-khánehjí Báshí (adjutant-general, commander of the 54th regiment of janissaries), and of the kórújís (invalids), whose barracks are within the boundaries of Ok-meïdán, take their rounds there, and if they meet with any suspicious vagabonds, carry them to their commander, the Atíjí Báshí (Chief of the Archers), who, punishing them according to their deserts, orders them to be suspended from a tree by the string of the bowmen, and assailed by a shower of arrows.

It was ordained by the regulations of Sultán Mohammed the Conqueror, and that ordinance has been renewed by a khatisheríf (imperial rescript) from all his successors, that any offender whom these officers shall apprehend, if he be a soldier, shall receive no mercy, but be hung upon a tree forthwith. In fine, in the districts on both sides of the Strait of the Black Sea, there are thirty-three magistrates, and thirty-five local judges, deputies of the Móllá, in the city. But the town of Bey-kós has a separate jurisdiction, the judge of which is appointed by the Munejjim Báshí (astronomer royal). Besides the judges and magistrates already enumerated, there are also 166 District Judges, subordinate to the four Móllás of Islámból, 360 Subáshís, eighty-seven guards of janissaries, with their commanding officers (serdárs), and forty Subáshís of the free vakfs (charitable foundations). In short, the whole number of Kázís and Súbáshís within the precincts of Islámból, established by the code (kánún) of Mohammed the Conqueror, amounts to twelve hundred. There are also within the same jurisdiction the governors and magistrates of 150 corporations of tradesmen; but these governors have no legal authority to imprison and punish; they can only determine questions respecting the statutes of the corporations over which they preside.

SECTION XV.

On the Imperial Mosques in the Mohammedan City of Kostantaniyyeh.

The first, and most ancient of these places of worship dedicated to the almighty and everlasting God, is that of Ayá Sófiyah, built, as mentioned in the seventh Section, in the year 5052 after the fall of Adam. It was finished by Aghnádús (Ignatius?), a perfect architect, well skilled in geometry, under the direction of the Prophet Khizr; and forty thousand workmen, seven thousand porters, and three thousand builders, were employed in raising its domes and arches on three thousand pillars. Every part of the world was ransacked to find the richest marbles, and the hardest stones for its walls and columns. Stones of various hues, fit for the throne of Belkís, were brought from Ayá Solúgh (Ephesus) and Aïdinjik; marbles of divers colours were removed from Karamán, Shám (Syria), and the island of Kubrus (Cyprus). Some thousands of incomparable columns, wasp and olive-coloured, were imported from the splendid monuments of the skill of Solomon, standing in the neighbourhood of Átineh (Athens). After working at the building for forty years, Khizr and Aghnádús disappeared one night when they had finished half the dome. Seven years afterwards they appeared again and completed it. On its summit they placed a cross of gold an hundred Alexandrian quintals in weight, visible at Brúsah, Keshísh-dágh (Mount Olympus), 'Alem-dághí, and Istránjeh dághí. On the birth-night of the Prophet there was a dreadful earthquake, by which this and many other wonderful domes were thrown down; but it was afterwards restored by the aid of Khizr, and by the advice of the Prophet, to whom the three hundred patriarchs and monks, presiding over the church, were sent by him. As a memorial of the restoration of the dome by the aid of the Prophet and Khizr, Mohammed the Conqueror suspended in the middle of it, by a golden chain, a Golden Globe, which can hold fifty kílahs of grain, Roman measure; it is within reach of a man's hand, and beneath it Khizr performed his service to God. Among the pious, many persons have chosen the same place for offering up their orisons; and several who have persevered in saying the morning prayer there for forty days, have obtained the blessings, temporal and spiritual, for which they prayed: it is, therefore, much frequented by the pious and necessitous for that purpose.

On the Dimensions, Builders, &c. of that ancient place of worship, Ayá Sófiyah.

This mosque is situated on elevated ground at the eastern end of the city, a thousand paces (*ádim*) distant from the Stable-gate (ákhór kapú) near the sea, and a thousand from Seraglio Point. The great cupola which rears its head into the skies is joined by a half-cupola, beneath which is the mihráb (sacred recess), and to the right of it a marble pulpit (*minber*). There are altogether on the whole building no less then 360 gilt cupolas, the largest of which is the great one in the middle; they are ornamented with broad, circular, and crystal glasses, the number of which in the whole mosque amounts to 1,070. The abovementioned cupolas (*kubbehs*) are adorned within by wonderful paintings, representing cherubims and men, the work of Monástir, a painter, skilful as Arzheng. These figures seem even now, to a silent and reflecting observer, to be possessed of life and thought. Besides them, there are, at the four angles supporting the great cupola, four angels, no doubt the four archangels, Jebráyíl (Gabriel), Míkáyíl (Michael), Isráfíl, and 'Azráyíl, standing with their wings extended, each 56 cubits high. Before the birth of the Prophet, these four angels used to speak, and give notice of all dangers which threatened the empire and the city of Islámból; but since his Highness appeared, all talismans have ceased to act. This cupola is supported by four arches (*ták*) that excel the arch of the palace of Kesra (Chosroes) (Táki Kesra), the arch of Khavernak; that of Kaïdafà; that of Káf, and that of Sheddád. The large columns, of the richest colours and most precious marble, are forty Mecca-cubits high; those of the second story are not less beautiful, but are only thirty cubits high. There are two galleries running round three sides of this mosque, and forming upper mosques for the worshippers; there is an ascent to them on both sides, which may be ascended on horseback; it is a royal road paved with white marble. The mosque has altogether 361 doors, of which 101 are large gates, through which large crowds can enter. They are all so bewitched by talismans, that if you count them ever so many times, there always appears to be one more than there was before. They are each twenty cubits high, and are adorned with goldsmith's work and enamel. The middle gate towards the Kiblah, which is the highest of all, is fifty cubits high. It is made of planks from the ark which Noah constructed with his own hand. Over this central southern gate there is a long coffin of yellow brass, which contains the body of Aï Sóf, who caused Ayá Sófiyáh to be built; and though many emperors have tried at different times to open this coffin, an earthquake and a horrible crash immediately heard within the mosque, have always prevented them from compassing their designs.

Above it, in a niche, supported on small columns, stands a picture of Jerusalem (the ancient Kibleh), in marble; within it there are jewels of inestimable value, but it is also talismanic, and cannot be touched by any body. In this place there stood likewise upon a green column an image of Mother Meryem (the Virgin Mary), holding in her hand a carbuncle as big as a pigeons egg, by the blaze of which the mosque was lighted every night. This carbuncle was also removed in the birthnight of the Prophet, to Kizil Almà (Rome), which received its name (Red Apple) from thence. The Spanish infidels were once or twice masters of Islámból, and thence that egg (the carbuncle) came into their hands. The walls of this mosque, as well as the extremities of the columns, are carved like various flowers, with the most exquisite workmanship. The Mihráb and Minber are of white marble highly ornamented.

A Description of the four Minárehs (Minarets).

While Mohammed the Conqueror was residing as Viceroy at Edreneh (Adrianople), there was a great earthquake at Islámból, which made the northern side of Ayá Sófiyah bend, and threatened its ruin. The infidels were much alarmed; but Prince Mohammed, in a friendly manner, sent the old architect, 'Alí Nejjár, who had built the great mosques at Brúsah and Edreneh for Yildirim Báyazíd, and was then living, to the Greek king, in order to repair Ayá Sófiyah. It was he who erected for the support of the building four strong buttresses, every one of which is like the barrier of Yájúj (Gog). The architect having made a staircase of two hundred steps in the buttress on the right side of Ayá Sófiyah, among the shops of the turban-makers (*sárikchí*), the king asked for what purpose this staircase was intended? The architect answered, "For going out upon the leads in case of need?" When the work was completed the king bestowed rich presents on the architect, who returning to Edreneh, said to Sultán Mohammed, "I have secured the cupola of Ayá Sófiyah, O emperor, by four mighty buttresses; to repair it depended on me, to conquer it depends on thee. I have also laid the foundation of a mináreh for thee, where I offered up my prayers." On that very foundation, three years afterwards, by the will of God, Sultán Mohammed built a most beautiful six-sided mináreh. Sultán Selím II. afterwards, in the year——, added another at the corner opposite to the gate of the Imperial palace (Bábi humáyún, the Sublime Porte), which is more ornamented, but a little lower than that of Mohammed the Conqueror. Sultán Murád III. built subsequently two other minárehs on the north and west side, each with only one gallery.

The ensigns ('alems, *i.e.* the crescents) on the top of these four minárehs are each of twenty cubits, and richly gilt; but that on the great dome is fifty cubits long, and the gilding of it required fifty thousand pieces of gold coin. It is visible at the distance of two farasangs by land, and a hundred miles off by sea. Murád III. also brought from the island of Mermereh (Marmora) two princely basons of white marble, each of them resembling the cupola of a bath, and so large that neither Jemshíd nor Dárá ever possessed such an one.

Each of them can contain a thousand kílehs. They stand inside of the mosque, one on the right hand and the other on the left, full of living water, for all the congregation to perform their ablutions and quench their thirst. The same Sultán caused the walls of the mosque to be cleaned and smoothed; he encreased the number of the lamps, and built four raised stone platforms (*mahfil*) for the readers of the Korán, and a lofty pulpit on a slender column for the muëzzins. Sultán Murád IV. the conqueror of Baghdád, raised upon four marble columns a throne (*kursì*) of one piece of marble, for the preacher (*vá'iz*), and appointed eight sheïkhs as preachers of the mosque: the Efendís Kází-zadeh, Uskudárlí Mahmúd, Ibráhím sheïkh to Jerráh Páshá, Sivásí, Kudsí, Terjimán Sheïkhí 'Omar, and the great sheïkh, Emír Ishtíbí, who was so learned and skilful in answering questions and solving difficulties respecting the law, God be praised! We had the happiness and advantage of enjoying the exalted society of all these doctors and hearing their instructions. Sultán Ahmed I. built, on the left of the mihráb, a private recess (*maksúrah*) for the exclusive use of the emperor. In short this mosque, which has no equal on earth, can only be compared to the tabernacle of the seventh heaven, and its dome to the cupola of the ninth. All those who see it, remain lost in astonishment on contemplating its beauties; it is the place where heavenly inspiration descends into the minds of the devout, and which gives a foretaste even here below of the garden of Eden ('Aden). Sultán Murád IV., who took great delight in this incomparable mosque, erected a wooden enclosure in it within the southern door, and when he went to prayers on Fridays, caused cages, containing a great number of singing-birds, and particularly nightingales, to be hung up there, so that their sweet notes, mingled with the tones of the muëzzins' voices, filled the mosque with a harmony approaching to that of Paradise. Every night (in the month of Ramazàn) the two thousand lamps lighted there, and the lanterns, containing wax-tapers perfumed with camphor, pour forth streams of light upon light; and in the centre of the dome a circle of lamps represents in letters, as finely formed as those of Yákút Musta'simí, that text of the Scripture, "God is the light of the heavens and the earth." There are also, on the four sides of the mosque, some thousands of texts in beautiful characters; and there, likewise, by command of Sultan Murád IV., the celebrated writer Etmekjí-zádeh Chelebí wrote the names of the Most High, of the prophet Mohammed and his four companions, in Kara Hisárí hand, so large that each elif measures ten arshíns (10 ells = 23¼ feet), and the rest of the letters are formed in the same proportion. Ayá Sófiyah is the Ka'beh of all Fakírs, and there is no larger mosque in Islámból. It possesses all the spiritual advantages to be obtained in any other, whether it be El Aksà at Kuds (Jerusalem), or the mosque of the Ommaviyyeh (Ommiades), at Shám (Damuscus), or that of El Ez-her at Misr (Cairo). It is always full of holy men, who pass the day there in fasting and the night in

75

prayer. Seventy lectures (on theology) well pleasing to God are delivered there daily, so that to the student it is a mine of knowledge, and it never fails to be frequented by multitudes every day.

The Servants (Khuddám) of the Mosque.

They are the Imáms (reciters of the Form of Prayer); the Khatíbs (reciters of the Khotbah, bidding-prayer on Friday); Sheïkhs (preachers); Devrkhán (Scripture readers); Ders-'ámils (lecturers); Talabah (students); Muëzzins (cryers, who call to prayers from the Minárehs); Ejzá kháns (lesson readers); Na't kháns (reciters of the praises of the prophet and his associates); Bevvábs (door-keepers); and Káyims (sextons): in all full two thousand servants, for the revenues of the mosque settled upon it by pious bequests (evkáf) are very large.

Stations and Places in this Mosque visited as peculiarly fitted for Devotion.

First. Ayá Sófiyah is, in itself, peculiarly the house of God.

Second. The station (Makám) of Moslemah, in a place called U'ch Búják (the three corners), where he, who was commander of the forces in the Khalifate of Mo'áviyyeh, is said to have offered up prayer.

Third. The station of Iyyúb Ansárí, who, after the peace made in the year of the Hijrah 52, entered Ayá Sófiyah and performed a service of two inflections on the spot called Makámi Iyyúb Sultán, south of the Sweating Column. There is now a Mihráb there much frequented at all the five services.

Fourth. The station of 'Omar Ibn 'Abdo-l-'aziz, who being commander at the peace in the year of the Hijrah 97, offered up prayers on the west side of Ayá Sófiyah, at the foot of the green Mihráb. This place goes now by his name.

Fifth. The station of Hárúnu-r-rashíd, who, at his coming a second time to Kostantaniyyeh, in the year of the Hijrah 58, having crucified King Yaghfúr in the belfry of Ayá Sófiyah, offered up prayers within the mosque in the kiblah of the prophet Solomon, on the south-east side, within the gate of the Defunct (Meyyit-kapú-sí).

Sixth. The station of Seyyid Battál Ghází in the sky-smiting belfry of the church.

Seventh. The station of Bábá Ja'fer Sultán, Ambassador of Hárúnu-r-rashíd.

Eighth. The station of Sheïkh Maksúd Sultán, the companion of Bábá Ja'fer. These two, with the king's (*i.e.* the Greek emperor's) permission, both offered up prayers on the eastern side of the mosque, within the sepulchral gate (Turbeh-kapú-sí), at the places now bearing their name.

Eighth. The station of Salomon, who is said to have offered up prayer on the ground where Ayá Sófiyah now stands, at the place called the Green Mihráb, to the right of the Minber.

Ninth. The station of Khizr, beneath the gilt ball in the centre of the cupola, is a place where some thousands of holy men have enjoyed the happiness of discoursing with that great prophet.

Tenth. The station of the forty, to the south of the platform of the Muëzzins, is a place where the ground is paved with forty stones of various colours, and where forty holy men stood when the extraordinary accident which happened to Gulábí Aghá took place.

Narrative of Gulábí Aghá.

Gulábí Aghá, Rikáb dár (stirrup-holder) of Sultán Suleïmán, a pious man, who died at the age of 151 years, relates that in consequence of the great plague in the reign of Sultán Selím II., which at Islámból carried off three thousand souls every day, that prince ordered the prayer Istiská to be proclaimed during three days; and that the mosque being much crowded on the holy night Kadr, in order to hear the sermon of the Sheïkh (*i.e.* Doctor) of the order of Beshiktásh Evliyá Efendí, the Sultán ordered the people present to be numbered. This Sheïkh, who was born at Tareb-afzún (Trapezonde), was a foster-brother of Sultán Suleïmán. The throng to hear his sermon was so great that all the people of Islámból filled the mosque three days before he preached. Sheïkh Yahyá being now in the middle of his sermon, and the whole multitude listening to his admonitions with their utmost attention, Gulábí Aghá, who was in the midst of the crowd, felt himself much distressed by a necessity of withdrawing. His body began to swell like the kettle-drum of Bagdad; he stood up two or three times on tip-toes to see whether there was no possibility of making his way through the multitude, but saw that a man must needs be engulfed in this ocean of men. He was ready to die for shame when he addressed himself to the forty, on the station of whom he was then standing, and begged of them to save him from being disgraced by exposure to the crowd. At that moment he saw a stately man standing near him, in the dress of a Sipáhí (soldier), who said to him, "I will release thee from thy pain;" and thus saying, stretched his sleeve over Gulábí's head, who instantly found himself transported into a meadow on the bank of the stream near Kághid-khánah. His pain and distress were removed forthwith; and in a moment afterwards he was again in the same place in the mosque. When the sermon was finished all the hundred and one gates were shut except the large one at the south side, where the Defterdár Dervísh Chelebí, son of the Sheïkh Bábá Nakkásh, placed himself with his attendants in order to count all those who were then present in the mosque and its three stories of galleries, whose numbers amounted to fifty-seven thousand men. Gulábí Aghá not having the least doubt that the Sípáhí, who had transported him so charitably into the meadows of Kághid Khánah, was no other than the prophet Khizr himself, laid hold of the skirt of his robe, saying, "I am thy slave, O King! and will never again quit thee." The Sipáhí answered him very roughly, "Be gone, man! We are not the man of whom thou speakest." Gulábí Aghá, however, laid hold of him the faster; and the Sipáhí twice boxed his ears, and thus they made their way through the crowd. Gulábí, however, would not lose sight of him, and following him very close, saw him enter a place of retirement near Ayá Sófiyah. Gulábí waited for some time at the door, when, lo! it opened, and there came out a young cook of the Janissaries, elegantly dressed, with his official knife and silver chains. Gulábí instantly laid hold of him; but the Janissary cried out, "Begone, man, thou art mad!" Gulábí, notwithstanding, would not loose his hold; on which the cook of the Janissaries gave him a good thump, and entered a Búzah khánah in the market of Ayá Sófiyah, where he ate some kabábs and bread and drank búzah (a kind of beer), without taking the least notice of Gulábí. The Janissary went out and Gulábí followed him into a narrow street, where finding they were alone, he threw himself down at his feet, and entreated him, saying, "Be gracious to me, O Prophet, and grant me thy love!" The Janissary answered, "O seeker! although thou art a faithful lover, thou art not yet ripe, but wantest much of perfection, and must still undergo many trials; but as, notwithstanding my rebuffs, thou followedst me with unabated zeal, I will now bring thee to an old man, in whose company thou shalt remain forty days without opening thy lips or asking concerning any men or things that shall pass under thine eye." He then, in that solitary place, knocked at a low and dirty gate, which was opened by an old camel-lipped negro, who pushed them both into the house. Gulábí, when he had recovered his senses, found himself in an assembly of men, who saluted him and received his salutations in return. The Janissary changed dress, and took the chief seat, after having kissed the hand of the old man, to whom he related Gulábí's adventures. The Sheïkh said, "If he has renounced the world and all the pleasures of the senses, he is welcome in this assembly of Forty." Gulábí then remained three days and three nights without eating or drinking. His house, family, and relations at U'n-kapání came into his mind; but he put his trust in the Almighty and resigned himself to his will. On the fourth, the old man said, "Now look to the business entrusted to you by God." At the same time the man, who had first assumed the shape of a Sipáhí and then of a Janissary, stood up and brought out from a closet thirty-eight kinds of weapons, one of which he laid before thirty-eight of the men in company, placing before himself a Janissary's basin with water in it. Gulábí being eager to drink, his guide said, "Have patience, we shall this day see whether this place be attainable by thee." Some time afterwards there appeared on the opposite side, a male child; and one of the company, taking his sword, immediately cut off its head. "Friend," said Gulábí, "why did you kill that boy? Did not I say, do not be curious?" replied his companion, the Janissary. Next appeared two men pursued by a lion, who tore one of them to pieces and eat him up, while the other saved himself by taking shelter behind the Sheïkh. Gulábí asking for an explanation, received the same answer. Next came an innocent little child pursued by a wolf. One of the men, sitting on the prayer-carpet (sejjádeh), took his bow and arrow and shot the beast dead; after which the child vanished in a corner. Three men then appeared on the other side, two of whom were hanged by the Sheïkh's permission; and the third was about to be hanged, when Gulábí begun to intercede with the Sheïkh for his life. The Janissary seizing Gulábí by the collar, made him sit down in his place, and said, "Did I not tell you to have patience for forty days?" At that moment the water in the basin before the Janissary began to boil and bubble, and two small ships appeared upon it, one of which, by the Janissary's aid, was saved, but the other perished with all its crew and passengers, except a little boy and girl who escaped to the edge of the basin. The Janissary pushing the innocent boy into the water, he was drowned; but the girl he drew out of the basin. Gulábí crying out, "Why didst thou drown that innocent boy, and why were all those Muselmáns lost in that ship?" The Sheïkh, from his seat as President, said, "Let us give a bit of bread to this man; and come let us offer up a prayer for him in the presence of these Forty." So they all treated him with kindness and gave him a loaf of bread, an akchah, a piece of gold, a bunch of grapes, a date, and an olive; and prayed for him that he might continue in good health till his happy end, be honoured among the angels, preserved from misfortunes, heavenly and earthly, and die, after a long and prosperous life, under the shadow of the banner of the prophet of God. The whole company, at the termination of the prayer, said "Amen!" The Janissary and the negro door-keeper then laying hold of Gulábí's collar, said, "Close thy eyes!" He closed his eyes, and on opening them again, suddenly found himself in one of the taverns at Ghalatah, where a crowd of drunken Janissaries hailed him; saying, "Come, old man, and drink a pot with us!" Gulábí, who had fasted three days, and supposed these Janissaries to be of the same kind as that who had been his guide, removed his hunger by partaking of the food prepared in the tavern. At length, when sunset was near, he took a boat to return to the U'n-kapání. On coming into a narrow street he was assailed by two drunken Janissaries, who stripped him of his turban and his sable robe, and said they would kill him if he did not drink another cup of wine. Whether he would or not, he was compelled to drink it. So he returned home naked, and never afterwards left his house again, having abandoned the world and given himself up to a spiritual life, in which he soon became a great man. He dwelt within the U'n-kapání among the goldsmiths, bestowing great liberalities on all comers and goers, to the astonishment of all men. Having heard the account of these extraordinary events which befel the late Gulábí Aghá (to whom God has granted mercy and pardon) at the station of the Forty, in Ayá Sófiyah, from his own mouth, it appeared proper to insert it here. The proof of it rests with the relater. One of the traditions of the Prophet says, "A liar is he who makes a story out of everything he hears." We now return to our description of the stations in Ayá Sófiyah.

Eleventh. The station of the Apostles on the eastern side of the gallery.

Twelfth. The station of Ak Shemsu-d-dín, near the Sweating Column, which stands on the western side of the South gate. It is a square marble pillar eleven cubits high, and cased to a mans height with brass. It sweats day and night, winter and summer.

Thirteenth. The station of the South-East gate (Kiblah kapú-sí). This gate being made of the wood of Noah's ark, all merchants who travel by sea, and sailors, are accustomed to offer up a prayer, accompanied by two inclinations of the body, and touch the wood with their hands, saying a Fátihah (*i.e.* the first chapter of the Korán) for the rest of Noah's soul before they set sail.

Virtues of the Golden Ball.

If any man have a bad memory which he wishes to improve, he should place himself beneath the Golden Ball suspended in the middle of the cupola, and say the morning prayer seven times; three times repeat the words Allahumma Yá káshifo-l mushkilát Yá 'álimu-s-sir va-l khafiyyát (*i.e.* O God who openest all difficult things and knowest all secret and hidden things), and each time eat seven black grapes, and then whatever he hears will remain fixed in his memory as if engraven on stone. A most noted example of this was Hamdí Chelebí, son of Ak-Shemsu-d-dín, who lived in the village of Turbahlí Góïnuk. He was so foolish and forgetful, that if any one gave him the Selám he was obliged to write the word Selám on a piece of paper and read it before he could comprehend that he ought to answer 'Ve aleïkum es-selám.' No doctors could do him any good, so that at last he was completely a prey to forgetfulness, till he went, by Ak-Shemsu-d-dín's advice, to Ayá Sófiyah, where, after saying the requisite prayers, and eating the grapes as prescribed above, beneath the Golden Ball, he was so completely cured of his stupidity, that he began immediately to compose his poem of Yusuf and Zuleïkhá, which he finished in seven months; after which he wrote his Kiyáfet-námeh (Treatise on Physiognomy), which is known all over the world as a wonderful poem on the nature of the Sons of Adam.

Fourteenth. The station of the cool window, on the south-east side (Kibleh) of Ayá Sófiyah, on the inner side of the Imperial Gate, is a window opening to the north, where fragrant breezes and songs of the nightingales from the garden outside refresh the soul. It is there that Ak-Shemsu-d-dín, immediately after the conquests, delivered his Lectures on Joreïri's Commentary on the Korán; and having prayed that all students who pursued their studies there should be blessed with success, that spot has ever since been a delightful place. It was there also that our instructor, the Sheïkh of Sheïkhs, Evliyá Efendí, that master of the art of reading the Korán, delivered his lectures on that science to some thousands of hearers.

Fifteenth. The station of the Lord Jesus's cradle, in a corner on the eastern side of the upper gallery, is a hollow trough of reddish marble like a cradle, where the Christian women used to place their children when sick in order to obtain their recovery.

Sixteenth. The station of the Washing Place of the Lord Jesus. Near the cradle just mentioned above, there is another square trough of stone, where the Prophet Jesus was washed immediately after he was delivered from the womb of his mother Meryem. Kostantín the Ancient, mentioned above, is said to have brought both the cradle and the font from Beïtu-l-lahm to the south of Kudsi Sheríf, but the humble writer of these lines saw the washing-trough of Jesus at Beïtu-l-lahm. That children who are crooked and sickly, when washed in the trough in Ayá Sófiyah immediately become straight and healthy, as if revived by the breath of Jesus, is known to all the world.

Seventeenth. The station of the Gate of the Seven. On the east side of the upper gallery there is a large door, the folds of which are not of wood, but of white marble adorned with sculpture. It is visited and admired by all travellers and architects as not having its fellow on the face of the earth. It is a favourite place of worship.

The Spectacle of the resplendent Stones.

On the east side of the upper gallery there are five or six smooth flat slabs of various coloured stones, which reflect the rays of the rising sun with so bright a light that the eye of man cannot look stedfastly on them. In short, there are some thousands of holy places of pilgrimage in Ayá Sófiyah, which is a Ka'beh for Fakírs, but the writer of these pages has only described those which he knew. The whole of this mosque is also covered with lead, which has remained uninjured for so many thousand years from its being mixed up with some thousand quintals (kantár) of gold. All architects are lost in astonishment at the solidity of the foundations of this vast building, and no tongue or pen is capable of adequately describing it. We have seen the mosques of all the world; but never one like this. Mohammed the Conqueror, after having repaired this mosque, also repaired that called Little Ayá Sófiyah, near the Kadirghah límání (galley harbour), which had been previously a church built by Elínah, mother of Kostantín.

The Mosque of Zírek Báshí.

This is also a large mosque, built by Kostantín for the benefit of the soul of the Lord Yahyá (St. John), and called, in the time of the Nasárá (Christians) Menastir Sanjovaniyyeh (Monastero San Giovanni). The holy body of that Saint is now at Malta, which is, therefore, called Sanjovanniyyeh (*i.e.* Malta di San Giovanni). It was carried away by the Maltese infidels from a convent in the village of Beït Sabástiyyeh (Σεβαστὴ), near Kudsi Sheríf. His head is still preserved in a golden dish in a cavern in the middle of the mosque of the Bení Ommayyeh in Shám (Damascus). The Maltese having removed the body of St. John from Beït Sabástiyyeh, carried it to 'Akkah, and there enclosing it in a chest adorned with jewels, conveyed it to their own country; having ever since made all their conquests in the name of St. John, whose name and figure they now bear, together with the cross, upon their banners. As St. John was nearly related to Jesus, on his mother the Virgin Marys side, the mother of Constantin built this mosque as a convent to the honour of his spirit. It was enclosed by a very strong wall, had a cistern of its own, and cells for three thousand monks. After the conquest, Mohammed the Conqueror converted it into a mosque, and it has forty-six cupolas great and small, and many beautiful columns. All its cupolas are gilt, and as it stands upon a hill, it is much admired and extremely conspicuous. In short, Mohammed the Conqueror, in the course of his reign, converted no less than 6,670 large monasteries (deïr) into places of worship for Musulmáns. He afterwards began to build a splendid mosque on his own account. He began by building the Irghát hammámí (workmen's bath) in the Karamán chárshú-sí

(Karamanian market), that the workmen might perform their ablutions every day before they began to work at the mosque. This was finished in forty days, and still bears the same name.

Description of the Mosque of Mohammed the Conqueror.

The foundations of it were laid in the year 867 (A.D. 1463), and it was finished A.H. 875 (A.D. 1470). The date of its commencement is expressed by the Arabic words Sheyyed-allahu erkánehá. It is situated on high ground, in the midst of Islámból, on the site of a convent which bore the name of king Vezendún (Byzantium). This convent having been entirely destroyed by an earthquake its site was fixed upon for this new mosque by the conqueror.

Form of this Mosque.

The ascent to it is by a flight of stone steps on the right and left; and its height from the ground to the roof is 87 builders cubits, four cubits being the height from the ground, of the platform on which it stands. It has a large cupola in the centre, and semi-cupolas over the Mihráb. The Mihráb, Mimber, and Mahfils, for the Muëzzins and the Emperor, are of white marble and of ancient workmanship. The cupola has two rows of galleries adorned with lamps. On the left side of the Mihráb stands an ancient banner in long strips, made of Alí's doublet (jubbeh). There is nothing suspended in this mosque except lamps; but it possesses great spiritual advantages, and prayers offered up in it are sure to be answered, because the workmen employed in building it were all Musulmáns; and to this day neither Jews nor Christians are allowed to enter its blessed doors. Its spirituality was secured by the workmen, who never began their work till they had performed their ablutions, and it was built from the wealth obtained in the Conquest.

On issuing from its southern (kiblah) gate, there is seen on the right hand, a square white marble column, on which the following traditional saying of the Prophet is inscribed in blue and gold and in large Jellí characters, by Demirjí Kúlí:—"Verily, Kostantaniyyeh shall be conquered! How excellent a commander is that commander! How excellent a host is that host!" It is approached on the southern side, also, by two stone staircases on the right and left; and on the four sides of its court (harem) there are stone benches (soffahs) and variegated columns, the sculptures on which astonish the beholder. On a needle-like pillar, within the southern gate of the court, there is a figure representing a Mevleví Dervísh, with his cap and fan (mirvahah). In the centre of this court there is a large basin, covered by a leaden cupola, supported by eight columns. Round this basin there are verdant cypresses towering to the sky like minárehs, and each appearing like a green angel. On the right and left of the mosque there are lofty minárehs, with a single gallery. The cloisters round the court are covered with leaden cupolas, and the floor is paved with variegated marble. On the outside border of the windows of the court the Súrah Fátihah (1st chap. of the Korán) is inscribed in white marble letters on a green ground, in the character invented by Yákút Mosta'simí, which is not equalled by any thing of the kind in all Islámból. The architect, to shew his skill in the construction of this basin in the centre of the court, placed over it a brazen cage like a net, which is also itself a masterpiece. The water rushing out, day and night, from the pipes of this basin, affords abundantly wherewith to quench the thirst of the devout, and enable them to perform their ablutions. The great cupola of the mosque seems also to hang without support, like the vault of heaven. Before the Mihráb is the monument of Mohammed the Conqueror and his family. Besides which, on the sides of the mosque there is a great court which has eight gates, and fine gardens on both sides. Outside of it there are the eight celebrated colleges (Semániyyeh), filled with students, on both sides of which are their apartments and stables. There is also a refectory (Dáru-z-ziyáfet), a hospital (Dáru-sh-shifá), a cáravánseraï for guests, an ancient bath, and an A B C school for children. When all these buildings, crowded together, are seen from a height above, they alone appear like a town full of lead-covered domes.

Appeal of the Mi'már Báshí (Head Builder) to the Law of the Prophet against the Conqueror.

Mohammed being, like Jem, a very passionate Emperor, severely rebuked the architect for not having built his mosque of the same height as Ayá Sófiyah, and for having cut down the columns, which were each worth the whole tribute of Rúm (Asia Minor). The architect excused himself by saying, that he had cut down two columns three cubits each on purpose to give his building more solidity and strength against the earthquakes, so common in Islámból, and had thus made the mosque lower than Ayá Sófiyah. The Emperor, not satisfied with this excuse, ordered both the architects hands to be cut off, which was done accordingly. On the following day the architect appeared with his family before the tribunal of the Kází, styled Islámból-Mollá-sí, to lay his complaint against the Emperor and appeal to the sentence of the law. The Judge immediately sent his officer (Kiahyà) to cite the Emperor to appear in court. The Conqueror, on receiving this summons, said, "The command of the Prophet's law must be obeyed!" and immediately putting on his mantle and thrusting a mace into his belt, went into the Court of Law. After having given the selám aleïk, he was about to seat himself in the highest place, when the Kází said, "Sit not down, Prince, but stand on thy feet, together with thine adversary, who has made an appeal to the law. The Mi'már Báshí (head architect) thus made his complaint: "My Lord (Sultánum)! I am a perfect master builder and a skilful mathematician; but this man, because I made his mosque low and cut down two of his columns, has cut off my two hands, has ruined me, and deprived me of the means of supporting my family. It is thy part to pronounce the sentence of the noble law." The Judge then said to the Emperor, "What sayest thou, Prince? Have you caused this man's hands to be cut off innocently?" The Emperor immediately replied, "By heaven! my Lord (Sultánum), this man lowered my mosque; and for having cut down two columns of mine, each of which was worth the tribute from Misr (Egypt), and thus robbed my mosque of all renown, by making it so low, I did cut off his hands: it is for thee to pronounce the sentence of the noble law." The Kází immediately answered: "Prince (Begum), Renown is a misfortune! If a mosque be upon a plain, and low and open, worship in it is not thereby prevented. If thy stone had been a precious stone, its value would have been only that of a stone; but of this man, who has now for these forty years subsisted by his skilful workmanship, you have illegally cut off the hands. He can henceforward do nothing more than cohabit with his wife. The maintenance of him and his numerous family necessarily, by law, falls upon thee. What sayest thou, Prince (Begum)?" Sultán Mahommed answered: "Thou must pronounce the sentence of the law!" "This is the legal sentence," replied the Kází, "that if the architect requires the law to be strictly enforced, your hands be cut off; for if a man do an illegal act which the noble law doth not allow, that law decrees that he shall be requited according to his deeds." The Sultán then offered to grant him a pension from the public treasury of the Musulmáns. "No!" returned the Móllá; "it is not lawful to take this from the public treasury: the offence was yours; my sentence, therefore, is, that from your own private purse you shall allow this maimed man ten aspers (akchahs) a-day." "Let it be twenty aspers a-day," said the Conqueror; "but let the cutting off of his hands be legalized." The architect, in the contentment of his heart, exclaimed, "Be it accounted lawful in this world and the next!" and, having received a patent for his pension, withdrew. Sultán Mohammed also received a certificate of his entire acquittal. The Kází then apologized for having treated him as an ordinary suitor; pleading the rigid impartiality of law, which requires justice to be administered to all without distinction; and entreating the Emperor to seat himself on the sacred carpet (sejjádeh). "Efendí," said the Sultán, somewhat irritated, and drawing out his mace from under the skirt of his robe, "if thou hadst shewn favour to me, saying to thyself, 'This is the Sultán,' and hadst wronged the architect, I would have broken thee in pieces with this mace!" "And if thou, Prince (Begum)," said the Kází, "hadst refused to obey the legal sentence pronounced by me, thou wouldst have fallen a victim to Divine vengeance; for I should have delivered thee up to be destroyed by the dragon beneath this carpet." On saying which he lifted up his carpet, and an enormous dragon put forth its head, vomiting fire from its mouth: "Be still," said the Kází, and again laid the carpet smooth; on which the Sultán kissed his noble hands, wished him good day, and returned to his palace.

Subsequently, Abdál Sinán, when Mi'már Báshí, added some embellishments to this mosque, and, at a later period, 'Alí Kúshjí, the celebrated astronomer, erected a school for the instruction of Muselmán children in the Korán within the precincts (harem) of this mosque, near the Dyer's gate (Bóyájíler kapú-sí) opposite to the great dome. The same astronomer also placed there a sun-dial, which has not its equal in the whole world. It is engraved on a square marble tablet, according to that text of the Korán:—"Dost thou at all know how thy Lord hath extended the shadow?"

After these events, in the reign of Báyazíd Velí, there was a great earthquake at Islámból for seven days and six nights. The castle of Ghalatah was damaged in many places; but it was repaired by the architect, Murád, who recorded the date of the repairs in an inscription engraved in the Jellí character on a square marble tablet. The reparations of the city were finished in sixty days. It is written, that this was the severest earthquake since the time of Yánkó ibn Mádyán. Báyazíd afterwards built a bridge of fourteen arches over the river Sakariyah, at the town of Keïveh, in the Sanják of Izmít (Nicomedia); another of nineteen arches, over the river Kizil Irmák, at the city of 'Osmánjik; and a third of nineteen arches, over the Gedúz (Hermus), in the province of Sárú khán; after which he began to build the mosque that bears his name, near the old palace in Islámból. Its foundations were laid in the year 903 (A.D. 1498), and it was finished in A.H. 911 (1505-6). It is built nearly in the same style as the mosque of his father Mohammed the Conqueror; but its two minarets are contiguous, not to it, but to the two rows of houses built on each side for the accommodation of strangers, which were subsequently added to the mosque.

Description of the Mosque of Sultán Báyazíd II.

It is a square building supporting a large dome, flanked by semi domes on the south-eastern (Kiblah), and opposite sides. On the right and left of the mosque there are two purple columns of porphyry, of which the like are to be found only in the mosque of Sultán Kaláún, in Caïro; and there is suspended from these a double row of lamps. On the right side of the mosque an elevated gallery has been constructed for the use of the Sultáns of the house of 'Osmán at the public service on Fridays. Sultán Ibráhím subsequently enclosed three sides of the gallery with gilt gratings, so that it resembles a beautiful cage, or net-work, or rather a palace of the immortals. The Mihráb, Minber, and Mahfil, though made of marble, are simple and unornamented; and on the first are inscriptions written in beautiful characters. The mosque has five gates, and the outer court (harem) is adorned with stone benches (soffahs), and on each side a cloister, supported by variegated columns; and in the centre there is a large basin, where all the congregation renew their ablutions. A cupola, supported by eight white marble columns, was placed over the basin by Sultán Murád IV., the Conqueror of Baghdád. On different sides of it four lofty cypresses have been planted. When the foundations of this noble mosque were laid, the Mi'már Báshíhaving asked the Sultán where he should place the mihráb, was desired by his Majesty to tread upon his foot; having done which, he immediately had a vision of the noble Ka'bah, and knew, consequently, where to place the mihráb. He, therefore, prostrated himself at the Sultán's feet and began the work, the Sultán having previously offered up a prayer, accompanied by two inclinations of the body, for its happy completion. On the first Friday after it was finished, when there was an assembly of some thousands, the congregation, knowing that the Sultán had never in his life failed to offer up the afternoon ('asr) and evening ('ashà) prayers, insisted on his performing the functions of Imám. The Sultán, being aware that no one present was so well acquainted with those services as himself, consented to perform them. As this mosque was entirely built with lawful money, it has great spiritual advantages; and being situated in the centre of the markets of Islámból, is crowded day and night by thousands of devout Muselmáns, who are offering up their prayers there without ceasing; so that it has often happened that before one party has got through the afternoon ('asr) service, as far as the Ayetu-l Kursí (the verse of the throne, Kor. ii. 256), another coming in prevents the first from finishing. The pipes of the basin in the court are never closed, but pour forth streams of water day and night, because the congregation never fails. This mosque is always illuminated by flashes of light; and before the window of the mihráb there is a garden like that of Irem, adorned with various fruits and flowers, where, beneath a monument of white marble, covered with lead, rest the remains of its founder. Round the inner and outer courts of this mosque there are shops of all kinds of trades, with a public kitchen, a refectory, and hostel for travellers; a school for instructing the poor and rich in the Korán; and a college for lectures on the art of reciting it. This court has six gates; and is adorned, externally, with lofty trees, most of them mulberries, under the shades of which some thousands of people gain a livelihood by selling various kinds of things. Outside of this court there is a large valley, called the Meïdán of Sultán Báyazíd, adorned on its four sides with shops; and on one side by the great college of the same Sultán, which has seventy cupolas. The superintendent (Názir) of this mosque is the Sheïkhu-l Islám (*i.e.* the Muftí);

he also gives the public lectures in this college. He delivers his lectures once a week, and the students receive a monthly stipend, besides an allowance for meat and wax-lights: this is a very well-endowed foundation. This mosque has altogether 2,040 servants; and none has a better salary than the Muvakkit, or Regulator of Time; because all the seamen and mariners in the empire of Islám depend, for the regulation of time, on the Muvakkit of Sultán Báyazíd Khán; and as the mihráb of this mosque was miraculously placed in the true position of Kiblah: all sea-captains regulate their compasses by it; and all the infidel astronomers in Firengistán, as is universally known, correct their watches and compasses by the mosque of Sultán Báyazíd. Besides this mosque, that Emperor built sixty other places of worship in the countries which he conquered. The mosque and convent of Emír Bokhárí, as well as the mosque of Ghalatah-seráï, were built by him. May God reward all his pious works! His conquests are as follows: The castles of Motón and Korón, Arkáriyah, Kalámitah, Kalávertah, Holómích, Tiribólíchah (Tripolizza), Bállí-Bádrah (Palæ Patræ, *i.e.* Patras), and Anávárín (Navarino), in the year 906 (1500-1). All the above castles are in the southern and western parts of the Peninsula (Morea). He also conquered the castle of Ainah-bakhtí (Naupaktus or Lepanto), A.H. 905 (A.D. 1499, 1500). The fortresses of Kilì and Ak-kirmán were taken in the 889 (A.D. 1484). The castles Várnah, Avlóniyah, and in Arnáútluk (Albania) Durráj (Durazzo), were captured, and a tribute imposed upon Karah Boghdán (Moldavia), in the year 918 (A.D. 1512). After having conquered these and many other castles, he was defeated in a second engagement with his son Selím I., at Chórló (Τούρουλος or Τζορλοῦ), where he was deserted by all his servants, who followed Selím to Islámból and proclaimed him Emperor. Báyazíd Khán was immediately ordered to retire to Dímah-tókah (Dymóticho for Didymótichon); but having reached Hávusah, a small town one days journey distant from Edreneh (Adrianople), died there. Various reports were circulated respecting the cause of his death. Some say that he died sighing, and crying out, "O King Jem!" Others, that having been poisoned by his son, he exclaimed, "May thy life be short, but thy victories many!" His corpse was buried within the precincts of his mosque. He reigned thirty-three years, and was succeeded by his son Selím I., who began his victorious course by a signal defeat of Sháh Ismá'íl, King of Írán, on the plains of Cheldir, beneath the castle of Ak hichkah, where 200,000 Kizil-báshes (Persians) were put to the sword. The Sháh himself escaped with difficulty, accompanied by only seven horsemen, and his Queen Tájlí Khánum was taken prisoner, together with three hundred female captives, who were entrusted to the care of the Defterdár Tájir-zádeh Ja'fer Chelebí, and conducted by him to the threshold of Felicity (the Sublime Porte). In this victorious campaign the following castles were conquered:—Kars, Ak-hichkah, Erdehán, Hasan, Erz Rúm, Baïbúd, Iánijah, Kumákh, Karah-Hamíd,

Diyár-Bekr, and forty other castles with their dependencies. Sultán 'Aláu-d-daulah, of the Zúl-kadriyyeh family, Lord of Mer'ash, was also defeated and killed, and his head, together with those of seventy other great chiefs (Bóï Beg), was sent to Ghaurí, Sultán of Egypt, against whom a campaign was immediately commenced: in the course of which Súltán Selím conquered Halebu-sh-shuhbá (the bright), with its twenty, Shám (Damascus), with its forty-two castles; Tarábulu-Shám (Tripoli), with its seventy castles, occupied by the Durúzí (Druzes); Beïtu-l-mokaddas (Jerusalem), Ghazah, and Ramlah, with seventeen castles. In that paradisiacal country, Shám (Syria), he took up his winter-quarters; and in the ensuing year he fought, on the plain of Kákún, the great battle in which Sultán Ghaurí was routed and slain. The wreck of the army of the Cherákis (Circassians) fled to Misr (Caïro), with Selím Khán at their heels; and after one continued battle for a whole month, the province of Misr (Egypt), with its three hundred cities and seven thousand villages, was given up to the conqueror in the year 922 (A.D. 1516). Híreh Beg was appointed Governor of Misr (Caïro); and Kemàl Páshà-zádeh Ahmed Efendí, Military Judge. Possession was taken of Mekkah and Medínah, and Selím assumed the title of Servant of the two noble Mosques, and exalted his victories to the skies. On his returning to Islámból, he laid the foundation of the mosque which bears his name, but did not live to finish it. He was buried in the kubbeh, opposite the Mihráb. He was born in Tarabefzún (for Tarábuzún, *i.e.* Trebizonde), of which he was Governor while a Prince. He reigned nine years, during which the Khotbah was said in his name in one thousand and one mosques. He was succeeded by his son, the determined supporter of the faith, and the breaker of the heads of the people who contemplated rebellion, the tenth of the Sultáns of the house of 'Osmán, Sultán Suleïmán Khán el Ghází, who finished the mosque begun by his father.

Description of the Mosque of Sultán Selím I.

He began it as a monument to the illustrious memory of his father, in the year 927 (A.D. 1521), and finished it in the year 933 (A.D. 1527). It is a lofty mosque, in the interior of Islámból, on the summit of one of the hills which overlook the canal; but it has no fine columns within it like the other mosques. It is only an elevated dome supported by four walls, but such as to raise the admiration of all who are masters in mathematics, and to be pointed at as a proof of the great skill of the old architect Sinán. On examining it, all mathematicians are astonished; for its dome is found, on admeasurement, to be one span wider than that of Ayá Sófiyah. It appears, in truth, to be an azure vault, like the vault of the sky; but is not so high as that of Ayá Sófiyah, since it measures only fifty-eight builder's cubits in height. The cause of its not having been made more lofty, is the elevation of the hill upon which it stands.

On the right side of its precincts (harem) there is a deep cistern, made in the time of the infidels; and on the north side is the ascent called the Forty Stairs, though there are fifty-four steps. The declivity on each side is very steep and precipitous; the architect Sinán, therefore, with a prudent foresight, in order to avoid all risk from earthquakes, gave a very moderate height to the mosque. The platform (mahfíl) for the Muëzzins is placed upon marble columns, adjoining to the wall on the right hand; the Minber and Mihráb are of white marble, in a plain style. On the left side of the mosque there is a gallery supported by columns for the use of the Emperor: this was enclosed like a cage, with a gilt grating, by Sultán Ibráhim. Round the cupola there is a gallery where lamps are lighted on the blessed nights. The mosque is ornamented with some thousand trophies suspended around it, but has no other distinction on the inside. Opposite to the windows on the side of the Mihráb, is the sepulchre of Selím Khán, in a delightful garden, where the sweet notes of nightingales are heard. It is a hexagonal building, surmounted by a cupola. This mosque has three gates, of which that looking towards the Kiblah is always open. On the right and left of the mosque there are hostels for travellers; and there are also, on the right and left side, two minárehs, with one gallery each; but they are not so high as other minárehs. The court of the mosque (harem) is paved with white marble, has three gates, and stone benches (soffahs) all round. There is a basin in the centre of the court, which constantly supplies the Muselmán congregation with fresh and running water for their ablutions. Sultán Murád IV. placed a pointed dome over it, supported by eight columns, and there are four cypresses on the different sides of it. Outside of this court is a large enclosure (harem), planted with trees of various kinds, and entered by three gates. On the south (Kiblah) is the gate of the mausoleum (Turbeh); on the west, that of the market; on the north, that of the Forty Stairs. Below the market, looking towards the Chukúr Bóstán there is a large school for boys, a public refectory (Mehmán-seráï), and lodgings for men of learning and students. The bath (hammám) is three hundred paces beyond this enclosure; but there are no other colleges nor hospitals.

Description of the Fifth Imperial Mosque; that of Sultán Suleïmán.

It was begun in the year 950 (A.D. 1543), and finished in the year——, and is beyond all description beautiful. The learned, who composed the metrical inscriptions, containing the date of its erection, confess that they are not able duly to express its praise; a task which I, the contemptible Evliyà, am now striving to perform as far as my ability will allow. This incomparable mosque was built by Sultán Suleïmán on one-half of the unoccupied half of the summit of the lofty hill on which had been erected, by Mohammed II, the old Seráï. Suleïmán having assembled all the thousands of perfect masters in

90

architecture, building, stone-hewing, and marble-cutting, who were found in the dominions of the house of 'Osmán, three whole years were employed in laying the foundations. The workmen penetrated so far into the earth, that the sound of their pickaxes was heard by the bull that bears up the world at the bottom of the earth. In three more years the foundations reached the face of the earth; but in the ensuing year the building was suspended, and the workmen were employed in sawing and cutting various-coloured stones for the building above the foundations. In the following year the Mihráb was fixed in the same manner as that of Sultán Báyazíd's mosque; and the walls, which reached the vault of heaven, were completed, and on those four solid foundations they placed its lofty dome. This vast structure of azure stone is more circular than the cupola of Ayá Sófiyah, and is seven royal cubits high. Besides the square piers which support it, there are, on the right and left sides, four porphyry columns, each of which is worth ten times the amount of the tribute (Kharáj) from Misr. These columns were brought from the capital of Misr, along the Nile, to Iskanderiyyeh, and there embarked on rafts, by Karinjeh Kapúdán, who in due time landed them at Ún-kapání; and having removed them from thence to the square called Vefà-méïdán, in the neighbourhood of the Suleïmániyyeh, delivered them up to Suleïmán Khán; expressing his wish that they might be received as a tribute from Karinjah (*i.e.* the Ant), just as a gift was graciously received from the Queen of Ants by Solomon. The Emperor, to shew his gratitude, immediately settled upon him the Sanjaks of Yilánlí-jezíreh-sí, and the island of Ródós. God knows, that four such columns of red porphyry, each fifty cubits high, are to be found no where else in the world. On the side next to the Mihráb, and on that opposite to it, the dome is joined by two semi-domes, which do not, however, rest on those columns, as the architect was afraid of overloading them. Sinán opened windows on every side to give light to the mosque. Those over the Mihráb and Minber are filled with coloured glass, the brilliance of whose colours within, and the splendour of the light reflected from them at noon, dazzle the eyes of the beholders, and fill them with astonishment. Each window is adorned with some hundreds of thousands of small pieces of glass, which represent either flowers, or the letters forming the excellent names (*i.e.* the Divine attributes); they are, therefore, celebrated by travellers all over the world. Though the Mihráb, Minber, and Mahfil of the Muëzzins are only formed of plain white marble, yet the last is of such exquisite workmanship, that it seems to be the Mahfil of Paradise; the Minber is also made of plain marble, but is surmounted by a conical tiara-like canopy, the like of which is no where to be found; and the Mihráb is like that of his Majesty Solomon himself. Above it there is engraved in letters of gold, on an azure ground, from the hand-writing of Karah-hisárí, this text of the Korán (iii. 32), "Whenever Zakariyyà (Zacharias) went into the chamber (mihráb) to her." On the right and left of the Mihráb there are spirally-twisted columns, which appear like the work of magic. There are also candlesticks of a mans stature, made of pure brass, and gilt with pure gold, which hold candles of camphorated bees'-wax, each 20 kantárs (quintals) in weight. The ascent to each of them is by a wooden staircase of fifteen steps, and they are lighted every night. In the left corner of the mosque is a gallery (mahfil) raised on columns, for the private use of the Sultán; and it also contains a special Mihráb. Besides this gallery, there are four others, one on each of the large piers, for the readers of the lessons from the Korán. On both sides of the mosque there are benches (soffahs), supported by low columns, and outside of it, parallel with these benches within, galleries, supported on columns, one of which looks upon the sea, and the other on the market. When the mosque is very much crowded, many persons perform their devotions on these benches. There are also, round the cupola, within the mosque, two rows of galleries supported by columns, which, on the blessed nights, are lighted with lamps. The total number of the lamps is 22,000; and there are likewise some thousands of other ornaments suspended from the roof. There are windows on all the four sides of the mosque, through each of which refreshing breezes enter and revive the congregation; so that they seem to be enjoying eternal life in Paradise. This mosque is also, by the will of God, constantly perfumed by an excellent odour, which gives fragrance to the brain of man, but has no resemblance to the odour of earthly flowers. Within the mosque, beside the southern gate (kibleh), there are two piers, from each of which springs a fountain of pure water, in order to quench the thirst of the congregation; and in the upper part of the building there are certain cells for the purpose of keeping treasures, in which the great people of the country and some thousands of travellers keep their money, to an amount which the Great Creator alone knows!

In Praise of the Writing of Karah Hisárí.

There never has been to this day, nor ever will be, any writing which can compare with that of Ahmed Karah Hisárí, outside and inside of this mosque. In the centre of the dome there is this text of the Korán (xxiv. 35): "God is the light of heaven and earth; the similitude of his light is as a niche in a wall wherein a lamp is placed, and the lamp enclosed in a case of glass:" a text justly called the Text of Light, which has been here rendered more luminous by the brilliant hand which inscribed it. The inscription over the semi-dome, above the Mihráb, has been already given. On the opposite side, above the southern gate, there is this text (vi. 79): "I direct my face unto him who hath created the heavens and the earth: I am orthodox." On the four piers are written, "Allah, Mohammed, Abú Bekr, 'Omar, 'Osmán, 'Alí, Hasan, and

92

Hoseïn. Over the window to the right of the Minber: "Verily, places of worship belong to God; therefore, invoke not any one together with God." Besides this, over the upper windows, all the excellent names (of God) are written. These are in the Shikáfí hand; but the large writing in the cupola is in the Guzáfí hand, of which the Láms, Elifs, and Káfs, each measure ten ells; so that they can be read distinctly by those who are below. This mosque has five doors. On the right, the Imám's (Imám kapú-sí); on the left the Vezír's (Vezír kapú-sí), beneath the imperial gallery, and two side doors. Over that on the left is written (Kor. xiii. 24), "Peace be upon you, because ye have endured with patience! How excellent a reward is Paradise!" Over the opposite gate this text: "Peace be upon you! Ye are righteous; enter in and dwell in it for ever!" Beneath this inscription, on the left hand, is added, "This was written by the Fakír Karah Hisárí."

Description of the Court (Harem).

The court of this mosque has three gates, to which there is an ascent and descent by three flights of steps. It is paved with white marble, and is as smooth and level as a carpet. Though very spacious, the body of the mosque is still larger. Round its four sides there are benches (soffahs) of stone, forty feet broad, upon which columns of coloured stones rest, supporting arches of different hues, as various as those of the rainbow. The windows of this court are guarded by iron gratings, the bars of which are as thick as a man's arm, and so finely polished, that even now not an atom of rust is seen upon them, and they shine like steel of Nakhjuván. In the centre of this court there is a beautiful fountain worthy of admiration, but it is not calculated for ablutions, being only designed for the refreshment of the congregation. Its roof is a low, broad, leaden cupola; but the wonderful thing is this, that the water from the basin springs up as though shot from a bow, to the centre of the cupola, and then trickles down its sides like another Selsebíl. It is, indeed, a wonderful spectacle. Over the windows on each side of this court there are texts from the Korán inscribed in white letters on blue tiles. The door opposite to the kibleh (*i.e.* the north door) is the largest of all; it is of white marble, and has not its equal on earth for the beauty and skill with which it is carved and ornamented. It is all built of pure white marble, and the different blocks have been so skilfully joined together by the builders that it is impossible to perceive any crevice between them. Over the sill of the door there are sculptured flowers and festoons of filagree work, interlaced with each other with a skill rivalling the art of Jemshíd. On each side of this gate there are buildings four-stories high, containing chambers for the muvakkits (hour-cryers), porters, and sextons. At the entrance of this gate there is a large circular block of red porphyry, which is unparalleled for its size and the fineness of its polish. It is as large as a Mohammedan simát (*i.e.* dinner-tray). Within the gate, on the right side of the court, there is a square slab of porphyry, on which a cross was sculptured, the traces of which are still visible, though it was erased by the masons. The infidels offered a million of money for it in vain: at length a royal ball was fired from a galleon of the infidels, lying before Ghalatah, purposely at this slab, which was struck; but being on the ground, it received no damage. So that the infidels, with all their rancour, and skill in gunnery, could not break this stone, which had become a threshold of the Suleïmániyyeh; but the mark of the ball still remains, and raises the astonishment of all beholders.

On the pedestals of the columns round the four sides of this court (harem) there are brass plates, on which the dates of memorable events, such as great fires, earthquakes, revolts and tumults, are engraven. This mosque has four minarets, the galleries of which are ten in number, as a record that Sultán Suleïmán Khán was the tenth Sultán of the House of 'Osmán. The two minarets adjoining to the body of the mosque have each three galleries, to which there is an ascent by a staircase of two hundred steps; the two minarets at the inner angles of the court are lower, and have but two galleries each. Of the two lofty minarets which have three galleries, that on the left is called the Jewel Minaret, for the following reason:—Sultán Suleïmán, when building this mosque, in order to allow the foundations to settle, desisted, as has been already observed, for a whole year, during which the workmen were employed on other pious works. Sháh Tahmás Khán, King of 'Ajem (Persia), having heard of this, immediately sent a great Ambassador to Suleïmán, with a mule laden with valuable jewels, through friendship, as he said, for the Sultán, who, from want of money, had not been able to complete this pious work. The Ambassador presented the Sháh's letter to the Sultán while surrounded with the innumerable builders and workmen employed about the mosque; and the latter, incensed on hearing the contents of the letter, immediately, in the Ambassador's presence, distributed the jewels which he had brought to all the Jews in Islámból, saying, "Each Ráfizí, at the awful day of doom changed to an ass, some Jew to hell shall bear! To them, therefore, I give this treasure, that they may have pity on you on that day, and be sparing in the use of their spurs and whips." Then giving another mule laden with jewels to Sinán, the architect, he said, still in the Ambassador's presence, "These jewels, which were sent as being so valuable, have no worth in comparison with the stones of my mosque; yet, take them and mingle them with the rest." Sinán, in obedience to the Sultán's command, used them in building the six-sided basis of this mínaret, which derives its name from thence. Some of the stones still sparkle when the sun's rays fall upon them; but others have lost their brilliance from exposure to excessive heat, snow, and rain. In the centre of the arch, over the Kibla gate, there is a Níshábúrí turquoise (pírúzeh), as large in circumference as a cup. There are on the two sides of this mosque forty different places where ablutions can be renewed.

A Description of the Imperial Mausoleum.

At the distance of a bow-shot from the Mihráb, in the midst of a delightful garden, is the sepulchre of Suleïmán, itself an unparalleled edifice, being crowned by a double cupola, so that one is placed over the other, the smaller below and the larger above. There is not, in the whole civilized world, a building so richly ornamented with wonderful sculptures and carvings in marble as this!

Description of the Outer Court.

The outer court of this mosque is a large sandy level planted with cypresses, planes, willows, limes, and ashes; and surrounding three sides of the building. It has ten gates: two on the Kibla side; *viz.* that of Merá, and that of the old Serái; on the south side, the Mekteb (school gate), chàrshù (market), medreséh (college), and Hakím-Báshi (Head Physicians) gates. On the west, the Imareh (alms-house), Táv-kháneh (hospital), and Aghá's gate (Aghá kapú-sí). On the north side a stone staircase of twenty steps to the gate of the dome of one thousand and one nails, so called because that number of nails was used in constructing it. There is also the Hammám kapú-sí (bath-gate) looking eastwards, whence there is a descent of twenty steps to the bath. On this side the court (harem) is not enclosed by a wall, but merely by a low parapet, that the view of the city of Islámból may not be interrupted. There the congregation remains and enjoys a full view of the imperial palace, Uskudár (Scutari), the castle of the Canal (Bógház Hísárí) Beshik-tásh, Tóp-khaneh, Ghalatah, Kásim Páshá, the Okmeidán, and the harbour (khalíj) and strait (Bogház) traversed by a thousand boats and barges and other kinds of vessels —a spectacle not to be equalled in any other place in the world! The circumference of this outer court (harem) is one thousand paces. There is also a smaller court called the Pehliván Demir meïdání (*i.e.* wrestlers' iron ground) between this mosque and the walls of the old serai. It is a valley where wrestlers from all the convents exercise themselves when afternoon-prayer is over (ba'de-l'asr). To the right and left of this mosque there are four great colleges for the education of lawyers in the four (orthodox) sects, which are now filled with men of the most profound learning. There is likewise a Dár ul-hadís, or school for instruction in the traditional law; a Dár-ul-karrà, or school for instruction in the recitation or chaunting of the Korán; a college for the study of medicine; a school for children; a hospital, a refectory, an alms-house, a hospital for strangers (Táv-kháneh), a karbánserái for comers and goers, a market for goldsmiths and button and boot makers, a bath, with apartments for the students, and thousands of chambers for their servants; so that within the precincts of the mosque there are altogether not less than 1001 cupolas. Seen from Ghalatah the Suleïmániyyeh seems like one vast plain covered with lead. The whole number of servants attached to the mosque is three thousand. They are maintained by secure and liberal endowments, all the islands in the White Sea, as Istankoi (Stanco), Sákiz (Chios), Ródós (Rhodes), &c. having been settled on it by Sultan Suleïmán. Its revenues are collected by five hundred men under the direction of the mutevellí (commissioner). There is no building in the whole empire of Islám stronger or more solid than this Suleïmániyyeh; nor has any cupola ever been seen which can be compared to this. Whether the solidity of its foundation, or the wonderful beauty and perfection of its different parts, be considered, it must be allowed to be, both within and without, the finest and most durable edifice which the world ever beheld. When it was finished, the architect Sinán said to the sultan: "I have built for thee, O emperor, a mosque which will remain on the face of the earth till the day of judgment: and when Halláj Mansúr comes, and rends Mount Demavund from its foundation, he will play at tennis with it and the cupola of this mosque." Such were the terms in which he extolled its strength and durability; and indeed, standing on a lofty hill surrounded and strengthened below by various walls and bulwarks, its foundations are peculiarly solid. First, there is the upper wall of the Tahtu-l kal'ah; then, that of Siyávush Pashá's palace; next, that of the Yenícherí Aghá's; afterwards, that of the cistern in the little market: then those of the Aghá's school, the warm bath, the lead magazine, and hospital. The foundations of all these buildings may be considered as the outworks of the foundation of this mosque. The humble writer of these lines once himself saw ten Franc infidels skilful in geometry and architecture, who, when the door-keeper had changed their shoes for slippers, and had introduced them into the mosque for the purpose of shewing it to them, laid their finger on their mouths, and each bit his finger from astonishment when they saw the minarets; but when they beheld the dome they tossed up their hats and cried Maryah! Maryah! and on observing the four arches which support the dome on which the date A.H. 944 (A.D. 1537) is inscribed, they could not find terms to express their admiration, and the ten, each laying his finger on his mouth, remained a full hour looking with astonishment on those arches. Afterwards, on surveying the exterior, the court, its four minarets, six gates, its columns, arches and cupolas, they again took off their hats and went round the mosque bareheaded, and each of the ten bit his fingers from astonishment, that being their manner of testifying the greatest amazement. I asked their interpreter how they liked it, and one of them who was able to give an answer, said, that nowhere was so much beauty, external and internal, to be found united, and that in the whole of Fringistán there was not a single edifice which could be compared to this. I then asked what they thought of this mosque compared with Ayá Sófiyah; they answered, that Ayá Sófiyah was a fine old building, larger than this, and very strong and solid for the age in which it was erected, but that it could not in any manner vie with the elegance, beauty, and perfection of this mosque, upon which, moreover, a much larger sum of money had been expended than on Ayá Sófiyah. Indeed, it is said, that every ten Miskáls of stone used in this mosque cost a piece of gold (a ducat). The entire sum expended in this building amounted to 890,883 yuks (74,242,500 piastres).

Another of Sultan Suleïmán's monuments at Islámból is the Forty Fountains. Desirous of bringing into the city some sweet water which had been discovered at a considerable distance, he consulted the famous architect Sinán, who replied, that an undertaking so difficult would require enormous sums of money. Suleïmán promised to provide the necessary funds; the work was commenced, and in the course of seven years 3,700 arches were constructed, thus forming an aqueduct, and joining that of Yánkó Mádiyán near the horse-market. By this means the delicious water was circulated throughout the city, and the souls of the thirsty were made glad. In some parts the arches rise two or three stories high.

Suleïmán also commenced the bridge of Chekmejeh, which was completed by Selim II. He also built the mosques of Shehzádeh, Jehángír, and Khásseki; the new arsenal; and the college of Selim I., founded at the Koshk of the Khaljiler, and dedicated to the memory of his father; a mosque at Uskudár, called after his illustrious daughter Mehrebán, and two Kháns. In Rumeïli the monuments of his bounty are almost innumerable: amongst them may be enumerated the fortresses of Segdin, Sigeth, and Ouzi (Oczakow), on the frontiers. At Edreneh (Adrianople) he constructed an aqueduct, a bridge, and a mosque and refectory near the bridge of Mustafa Pasha. In Anátolí he built at Konea, near the tomb of Jelál-ud-dín-Rúmi (may God sanctify his secret state), a splendid mosque with two minárets, a college, a music-room for the Dervíshes, a dining-room for the poor (*imaret*), a refectory, and numerous cells for the poor Dervíshes. At Damascus, an extensive mosque and a college. At Kaf and Iznik (Nice) he converted two churches into mosques; a plan which he put into execution in all the towns and palankas which were conquered during his long and victorious reign. The cupola of the mosque of Solomon's temple was also built by this Emperor, and he adorned the cupola of the sacrificial stone (*sakhra-i-sherif*) with ceilings of carved wood and stone, so that it equals the gallery of Chinese paintings, and resembles paradise. After the conquest of Baghdád, he erected over the tomb of the great Imám, Noamán-ben-Thábet, a castle, and a mosque with a refectory; and over the tomb of the Sheikh, Abdul-káder Jilani, a lofty cupola, a mosque, a refectory and other buildings for pious purposes. For the benefit of the holy cities (Mecca and Medina) he instituted the Surra, a present of 62,000 ducats, which is annually transmitted to those places by the Surrá-Emini; and the annual distribution of wearing apparel. He also repaired the aqueduct built by Hárún-ur-rashíd, adding four fountains to it, and conducting a stream to Mount Arefat. He moreover built at Mecca four colleges in the same style as those of Rumeïli, and endowed them in the same manner. He also rebuilt the cupola of Khadijeh, the Mother of the Faithful, with numerous other pious foundations which we shall have occasion to mention hereafter in the course of our travels: our present object being only to describe those of Islámból. All these pious works were effected by means of the prizes taken at Malta, Rodós, Bodin, Kizil-álma (Rome), Belgrade on the Danube, Baghdád, and other places; the whole amount of which is computed to have been 896,383 fulúrí (florins), which, according to the present value of money, would be 53,782,009 aspres, or 74,666,666 paras, or 1,866,666 piastres. During the reign of Suleimán Khán four aspres weighed one dirhem of pure silver, and one hundred ducats weighed 118 dirhems.

Description of the Mosque of Prince Mohammed.

According to the opinion of all architects and mathematicians, this mosque is situated in the centre of the triangle of Islámból. It ranks as the sixth imperial mosque, and was built by Suleimán Khán for his favourite son Mohammed, who died at Magnesia, and was buried here. Its cupola is an elegant piece of workmanship, and though not so large as that of the Suleïmániyyeh, it rears its head majestically into the skies: it is supported by rectangular pillars and four semi-domes. The mihráb and minber are both of exquisite workmanship. The mahfil is supported by eight columns, and on its left is the Sultán's mahfil, also supported by columns. This mosque has no large columns, but is adorned with a double row of lamps amounting to eight thousand. It is lighted by windows on every side, and has three gates, over one of which, that opposite to the mihráb, is placed the chronogram: "The place of prayer for the Prophet's people, 955" (A.D. 1548), in which year the foundation was laid. This also is of Sinán's architecture. It was commenced on the 1st of Rabi'-ul-avul, 955 (10th April 1548), and was finished in the month of Rajab, 965 (April 1558). It cost 15,000,000 aspres. Facing the mihráb, in a most delightful garden beneath a lofty cupola, is the tomb of Prince Mohammed, and beneath another, that of his brother Jehángír, who died at Halep (Aleppo), and was buried in this place. The court is adorned with numerous columns, and in the centre there is a fountain, beneath a cupola supported by eight columns, which was built by Murád IV. The two minarets, with their double galleries, have not their equal in Islámból, Edreneh, or Brusa, for ornaments and sculptures. The lead-covered roof is a piece of art likewise well worthy of admiration. On three sides it is surrounded by a large plain planted with trees, underneath one of which, on the left-hand side of the mosque, is buried the Sheikh, Ali Tabl, who was drummer in Iyyúbs expedition against Islámból. Round this large court stand the college, refectory, and hospital for strangers (Tav-khaneh); it has neither a bath nor a common hospital.

The mosque at Fundukli, dedicated to the memory of the prince Jehángír, was also built by Suleimán. But this shall be described in its proper place.

Description of the Mosque of the Valideh.

This mosque, which is commonly called Khasseki-evret (the favourite of the women), and is situated near the Evret-bazar, is not so large as other mosques, and has only one mináreh. It has a common kitchen, a refectory, a hospital, a college, and a school for children.

Description of the Mosque of Mehr-máh Sultáneh.

It is a lofty mosque within the Adrianople-gate, and was built by Sultán Suleimán Khán for his daughter Mehr-máh. Its mihráb, minber, and mahfil, are remarkably neat; but there is no royal mahfil. It is surrounded by the apartments of the college, a bath and a market. There is neither refectory nor hospital.

In short, Sultán Suleimán Khán, during a reign of forty-eight years, established order and justice in his dominions; marched victoriously through the seven quarters of the globe, embellished all the countries which were vanquished by his arms, and was successful in all his undertakings; because, mindful of the sacred text, "Take advice in your affairs," he always consulted with his Ulemá.

The Vezirs during his reign were:—

Pír Mohammed Pasha, who was confirmed in his office on the accession of the Sultán.

Ibrahim Pasha, who was educated in the imperial harem, built the seven towers at Cairo, and hanged Ahmed Pasha, the rebellious governor of that city.

Ayás Pasha, a native of Albania, but brought up in the harem.

Lutfí Pasha, also brought up in the harem. He had the Sultán's sister given him in marriage, but was dismissed from office for speaking against a woman who was related to his wife.

Suleimán Pasha, a white eunuch, who took Dív-abád, Ahmed-abád, and several other fortresses from the Portuguese, and gave them to the Raï of India. He also conquered 'Aden, in Yemen (Arabia), and Habesh (Abyssinia), assisted by Oz-demir-beg.

Rustam Pasha, a Khiroad (Croatian) by birth, and an Aristotle in wisdom.

Ahmed Pasha, a judicious, brave, and accomplished minister. He began by being Chamberlain in the Serai, and was gradually promoted to the office of Aghá of the Janissaries, Governor of Rumeïli, and Grand Vezir. He once conducted a night attack against Sháh Tahmas of Persia, and conquered Temesvar.

Kalen Ali Pasha, a native of the village of Parcha, in Hersek (Herzegovina). He was first Chamberlain, then Aghá of the Janissaries, Governor of Egypt, and Grand Vezir. He was a very corpulent man.

So-kolli Khojeh, Ali Pasha, a native of the village Sokol, now called Shahín, in Bosnia, having held various inferior offices, was raised to that of Vezir, which he held for forty years under three monarchs.

The Vezirs of the *kubbeh* (cupola) who did not attain the rank of Grand Vezir were:—Mustafa Pasha, the Bosnian; Ferhád Pasha, the Albanian; Khaïn Ahmed Pasha, a rebellious Albanian who was hanged at Cairo; Gózlujeh Kásím Pasha, who conquered Anabóli (Napoli), in the Morea, and built the mosque bearing his name opposite Islámból; Hájí Mohammed Pasha, poisoned at Bodin (Buda) by a Jew who boasted that he had poisoned no less than forty Moslems; Khosru Pasha, the brother of Khojeh Lála Mustafa Pasha; Khádem Ibrahím Pasha, a man of a brave and generous disposition, who built the mosque bearing his name within the Silivrí-gate; Khádem Heider Pasha, who was chief of the white eunuchs in the harem, but was dismissed on suspicion of having been accessory to the murder of the Prince Mustafa: he was an eloquent and learned man, and died Governor of Hersek (Herzegovina); Balak Mustafa Pasha, a Bosnian, Balak, in the Albanian language, signifying 'old': he was Governor of Egypt and Capudan of the fleet, and was buried at Iyyúb; Dámád Ferhád Pasha,—he was brother-in-law of Prince Mohammed, and was an excellent calligrapher: a copy of the Korán of his penmanship may even now be seen at the mausoleum of Sultán Báyazíd; Mustafa Pasha, who was descended from Khaled, son of Valíd, and younger brother of Shemsi Pasha: he was educated in the imperial harem, made Chakirji-bashi, commanded the expedition against Malta when

Governor of Rumeïli, died on the pilgrimage to Mecca, and was buried by my father.

Begler-begs in the reign of Sultán Suleimán.

Behram Pasha; Davúd Pasha, who died Governor of Egypt; Oveis Pasha, Governor of Shám (Damascus); Dukakin Zádeh Gházi Mohammed Pasha, Governor of Egypt; Oveis Pasha, Governor of Yemen (Arabia), he quaffed the cup of martyrdom at the hand of Pehlevan Hassan, the robber; Oz-demir Pasha, a relation of Ghori, the last Sultán of Egypt, a Circassian by birth, and Conqueror of Habush (Abyssinia); Gházi Omer Pasha, who built a mosque and imaret at Belgrade; Gházi Kásim Pasha, who when Suleimán raised the siege of Pech (Vienna), headed the party which made an excursion into Germany, and came round by Venedik (Venice) to Essek with only three hundred men, the others having fallen martyrs in the expedition: I visited many of their tombs in different places in Germany; Gozlujeh Rustam Pasha, Aga of the Janissaries, and afterwards Governor of Bodin (Buda); Suleimán Pasha, educated in the harem: he died at Astúli (Stuhlweissenburg), of which he was Governor, and was buried before its gate; Othmán Pasha, a Circassian, educated in the Seraï, who was rewarded with the government of Rumeïli for a night attack upon the Persian camp at Nakhchéván; Gházi Hassan Pasha, who was in Arabia and Abyssinia, whence he went to Temeswar, of which he was made Governor; Solak Ferhád Pasha, Governor of Baghdád, where he died; Baltaji Mohammed Pasha, a Bosnian, who was dismissed from the governorship of Baghdád, and died at Islámból; Harem Pasha, a Bosnian; Pír Pasha, of the family of Ramezan; Kobad Pasha, step-brother of the preceding; Músá Pasha, of the family of Isfendiyár,—he was Governor of Erzerúm, and died in the war against the Georgian infidels; Khádem Ali Pasha, who died whilst Governor of Cairo; Arslan Pasha, the son of Sokolli Mohammed Pasha: he built the powder-magazine at Bódin (Buda), and was executed on suspicion of having given up Tátá and Pápá to the infidels; Ayás Pasha, brother of the Grand Vezir, Sinán Pasha: he was beheaded; Behrám Pasha, Governor of Baghdád; Jenáblí Ahmed Pasha, who was twenty years Governor of Anatóli, and built a mulevi (convent) and bath at Angora; Olama Pasha, who was taken prisoner by the Persians, amongst whom he became a Khán, but afterwards deserted them, and returning to Rumeïli obtained the Sanják of Lippova, where he was killed, after having sustained a siege of forty days. Yorksa Pasha, educated in the harem; Shemsí Pasha, of the family of Kuzil Ahmedli, and brother of the Vezir Mustafa Pasha: he was the confidential minister of three Sultáns; Hájí Ahmed Pasha, of the same family; Damád Hassan Pasha, the Sultan's brother-in-law: he was sent as Ambassador to Persia on account of the flight of the Prince Báyazíd, and suffered martyrdom at Sivás: I have visited his tomb; Iskender Pasha, first Bóstánjí báshí, and then Governor of Anatoli; Cherkess Iskender Pasha, for fifteen years Governor of Diárbekr, where he died; Temerrúd Ali Pasha, a native of Bosnia; Kara Mustafa Pasha, he was taken from the chamber of pages; Khizr Pasha, a man of dignified manners, who was educated in the harem; Kara Murád Pasha; Sufi Ali Pasha, who died at Cairo, of which he was Governor; Gulábí Pasha, a man who loved retirement, and conversed much with my father; it was he who related the anecdote of himself, already mentioned in the Description of the Mosque of Ayá Sófiyah: he was indeed a holy man; Mohammed Khán Pasha, who was of the family of Zulkadr, and went over to Sháh Ismaïl, but returning to the Ottomans, was made Governor of Rumeïli and Anatoli, and was distinguished with the title of Jenáb (Excellency).

Capudán Pashas of the Reign of Suleïmán.

Sinán Pasha, from the harem, a great tyrant.

Khairu-d-din Pasha (Barbarossa), born at Medelli (Mitylene), and created Capudán in the year 940 (A.D. 1533). He died A.H. 970 (A.D. 1562), and was buried at Beshiktásh.

Saleh Pasha, a native of Kaz-tagh (Mount Ida), was Pasha of Algiers; and, like his predecessor, a most active Admiral.

Yahia Pasha, Grand Admiral, and died Pasha of Algiers.

Torghúd Pasha, who suffered martyrdom at the siege of Malta.

Mohammed Pasha, who was Pasha of Egypt, and, like Khairu-d-din, extended his devastations even to the islands of Ingleterra (England).

Defterdárs and Nishánjis of the Reign of Sultán Suleïmán.

Defterdár Iskender Chelebi; Hyder Chelebi, of Gallipoli; Lufti Beg, of the harem; Abulfazl Efendí; Abdi Chelebi, son of Jevizádeh'; Mustafa Chelebi, who, though afflicted with palsy, continued to attend the Diván, because he was an excellent penman; Mohammed Chelebi, who was also called Egri Abdi Zádeh; Ibrahím Chelebi, who was the chief Defterdár; Hasan Chelebi; Murád Chelebi, Jemáli Zádeh Mustafa Chelebi, who in his prose and poetical compositions assumed the name of Nishání: he is the author of an historical work, entitled "Tabakátu-l-mamálek," and a statistical one, called "Kanún Námeh;" Ramazán Zádeh Mohammed Chelebi, who was Nishánji, and author of a small historical work.

Begs of Sultán Suleïmán's Reign.

Kochek Báli Beg, son of the Grand Vezir, Yahia; Khosrú Beg, descended from the daughter of Sultán Báyazíd: he built at Seráï, a mosque, a khán, a bath, an imáret, a college, and a school, and achieved some thousands of victories; Kara Othmán Sháh Beg, son of Kara Mustafa Beg by the sister of Sultán Suleïmán: he built at Tarkhaleh a wonderful mosque with a college and an imaret; Ali Beg Ibn Malkoch Beg, who rendered himself famous in Croatia; Núbehar Zádeh, who was a disciple of Jelál Zádeh, and was afterwards made Defterdár; Cherkess Kassim Beg, who was Governor of Kaffa, in the Crimea, but afterwards went on an expedition to Azhderhán (Astrachan) through the desert; Hájí Beg, who, as Governor of Nablús, kept down the Arabs; Kurd Beg; Ján-búlád Beg, of an illustrious Kurd family; Husein Beg, who was distinguished with the title Jenáb (Excellency).

Some of the Illustrious Divines of the Reign of Sultán Suleïmán.

Khairu-d-din Efendí, his Majesty's Khojah; Seidi Chelebi, of Kastemúni; Sheikh Mohammed Jiví-zádeh; Mollah Sheikh Mohammed Ben Kotbu-d-din; Mollah Mohammed Ben Ahmed Ben 'Adíl-pasha, an excellent historian and a good Persian poet; Mollah Abdul-fattáh Ebn Ahmed 'Adíl Pasha, a native of Berdá, in Persia, and an amiable and intelligent man; Sheikh Mohammed, of Tunis, an excellent reader of the Korán, the whole of which he knew by heart; Zehíru-d-din, who came from Tabríz, and was hanged at Cairo with the traitor Ahmed Pasha; Mollah Mohammed, a pupil of Kemál Pasha-zádeh; Mevlená Yakúb, commonly called Ajéh Khaliféh, professor at Magnesia, where he died, A.H. 969 (A.D. 1562); 'Ala'ud-dín Jemáli, Sheikhu-l-Islám (*i.e.* Grand Mufti), which office he held also under Sultan Selím I.; the Sheikhu-l-Islám Kemál Pasha-zadéh Ahmed, who was Kázi-asker of Egypt under Selím I., and is celebrated for his literary productions; the Sheikhu-l-Islam Abú-u-ssaod Efendí, who wrote nearly a thousand treatises, and whose Commentary on the Korán is highly valued: a volume might be written in his praise; Mevlena-Mohíu-d-dín Arab-zédeh, who was drowned on his passage to Egypt; Mevlena Ali, who wrote the Humáyiún Námeh (the Turkish translation of Pilpay's Fables); he was buried at Brusá.

The Kanún-námeh or Statistical Code of the Empire, drawn up by Sultán Suleïmán.

SECTION I.

The Province of Rúmeïli contains 24 Sanjaks, 1,227 Ziámets, 12,377 Timárs.

Bodin	17 Sanjaks,	278	Ziámets,	2,391	Timárs.
Ozi (Oczakov),	6 ditto	188	ditto	1,186	ditto
Bosnia,	7 ditto	150	ditto	1,792	ditto
Temesvar	6 ditto	190	ditto	1,090	ditto
Archipelago	15 ditto	73	ditto	1,884	ditto
Egra	9 ditto	1,081	ditto	4,000	ditto
——	7 ditto	77	ditto	2,007	ditto
Kaffa	9 ditto	(It has neither Ziámets nor Timárs).			
Morea	5 ditto,	but no Ziámets or Timárs.			
Varadin	5 ditto.				

Ardil (Transylvania) pays an annual tribute of 3,000 purses; as do also Aflák (Wallachia), and Bóghdán (Moldavia). The Crimea has no Ziámets or Timárs, but is governed by Kháns. Rodós (Rhodes) has five Sanjaks; Kubrus (Cyprus) seven, and Candia thirteen Sanjaks; making, in all, 167 Sanjaks, 3,306 Ziámets, and 37,379 Timárs.

Anatóli has	14 Sanjaks,	399	Ziámets,	5,589	Timárs.
Karman	7 ditto	68	ditto	2,211	ditto
——	7 ditto	108	ditto	3,699	ditto
Miráish	4 ditto	29	ditto	215	ditto
Shám (Damascus),	2 ditto	138	ditto	1,865	ditto
Trabalós	4 ditto	63	ditto	571	ditto
Seida (Sidon)	4 ditto	94	ditto	995	ditto
Halep (Aleppo), has	5 ditto	99	ditto	833	ditto
Adna	5 ditto	43	ditto	1,659	ditto
Roha	2 ditto	4	ditto	6,026	ditto
Díárbekr	12 ditto	926	ditto	926	ditto
Erzerúm	9 ditto	133	ditto	5,159	ditto
Trebizonde	2 ditto	56	ditto	398	ditto
Gurjístán (Georgia) has no Sanjaks, Ziámets, or Timárs.					
Kars	6 ditto	1	ditto	1,363	ditto
Jíldir	13 ditto	49	ditto	689	ditto
Ván	24 ditto	46	ditto	2,695	ditto
Mosúl	3 ditto	66	ditto	1,004	ditto
Sheherzúl	21 ditto	15	ditto	806	ditto

Baghdád has no ziámet or timár, but is held on an annual lease, as are also

Basrah and Lahsa: Yemen is governed by an Imám; Habesh (Abyssinia) is subject to a tributary Sultán; Mesr (Egypt), Jezäïr (Algiers), Tunis and Trabalos (Tripoli), are held by annual leases. There are in all 151 sanjaks, 1,571 ziámets, 41,286 timárs.

All the land of the Ottoman empire is divided into three parts: the khás humáyún, or crown lands; the lands given to the vezírs and begler-begs; and the lands divided into ziámets and timárs.

SECTION II.

The Khás, or Revenues of the Begler-begs.

Rumeïli, 1,100,000 aspres; Anadolí, 1,000,000; Karamán, 60,671; Shám (Damascus), 1,000,000; Sivás, 900,000; Erzerúm, 1,214,600; Díárbekr, 1,200,600; Ván, 1,132,200; Búdín (Bude), 880,000; the islands of the Archipelago, 885,000; Haleb (Aleppo), 817,760; Mera'ish, 628,450; Bosna, 650,000; Temiswár, 806,790; Kars, 827,170; Jíldir, 925,000; Tarab-afzún (Trebizonde), 734,850; Rika, 681,056; Mosúl, 682,000; Sheherzúl, 1,100,000; Trabalós Shám (Tripoli in Syria), 786,000; Ozí (Oczakov), 988,000; Krím (Crimea), 12,000,000; Kaffa, the revenues of this province are derived from the custom-house; the Páshá receiving 679,000 aspres; Egra(Erla), 800,080; Kanisa, 746,060; the Morea, 656,000; Baghdád, 1,200,200; Basrah, 1,000,000; Lahsa, 888,000; Habesh (Abyssinia), 1,000,080; Egypt, 487 purses of Egypt; the revenues of Tunis, Algiers, Tripoli, Cyprus, and Rhodes, which belong to the Capúdán Páshás, amount to 1,200,700 aspres; Candia yielded 11,990 aspres: this island has since then been entirely conquered, but during the reign of Suleïmán it was allotted with that small sum. According to the constitutional laws of Suleïmán, the gradation of the revenues of the governors followed the chronological order of the conquest; thus the páshás of the provinces first conquered had greater revenues than those conquered at a later period; and the old vezírs at that time received an additional sanjak, under the name of Arpalík (barley-money); thus the sanjak of Adna was given to old Mahmúd Páshá with a revenue of 116,000 aspres. According to the Kánún, the Sultan of Egypt has the privilege of wearing two aigrettes, and the Vezír of Abyssinia is allowed to have two royal tents. The precedence of the vezírs at public festivals, divans, &c. is as follows: The Vezír of Egypt, of Baghdád, Abyssinia, Buda, Anatolí, Mera'ish, and the Kapúdán-Páshá, if the scene is in Anadolí (Asia); but if in Rumeïlí (Europe) it is as follows: the Vezír of Buda, Egypt, Abyssinia, Baghdád, Rumeïlí, and then the other governors according to the chronological order of the conquest. For every 500 aspres of revenue one armed man is to be provided for the field.

SECTION III.

Names of the Sanjaks of each Province.

Rumeïli has two Defterdárs, one of the treasury-office (mál), and of the feudal tenures (tímár) a Kehiyá of Chávushes, an inspector of the Defter (rolls), a Kehiyá of the Defter; an Aláï-beg (colonel of the feudal militia); a Cherí-báshí (lieutenant-colonel); a Voinók-ághá, and seven Yúrúk-begs. The twenty-four sanjaks are: 1. Sofia, the residence of the Páshá. 2. Kústendíl. 3. Skutari. 4. Terkhaleh. 5. Ukhrí. 6. Avlona. 7. Delvina. 8. Yánína. 9. Elbessán. 10. Chermen. 11. Saloník. 12. Askúb (Scopi). 13. Dúkágín. 14. Vídín. 15. Alájeh Hisár. 16. Perzerín. 17. Vejterín. 18. Silistria. 19. Nicopolis. 20. Kirk-kílseh. 21. Bender. 22. Ak-kermán. 23. Ozí (Oczakov). 24. Kílbúrún.

Sanjaks of the Province of Anádólí.

There is a Kehiyá, an Emín (inspector), and Muhásibjí (comptroller of the defter or rolls), an Emín and Kehiyá of the Chávushes, a colonel and captain of the feudal militia, four Begs called Musellim, and eleven Yáyá Begs. 1. Kútáhieh. 2. Saríkhán. 3. Aïdía. 4. Kastamúni. 5. Bólí. 6. Munteshá. 7. Angora. 8. Kara-hisár. 9. Tekkeh. 10. Hamid-sultán. 11. Ogí-karasí.

Sanjaks of the Province of Karamán.

This province has a Defterdár of the treasury, and of the feuds, an Emín of the Defter and of the Chávushes; a Kehiyá of the Defter and of the Chávushes; an Aláï-beg (colonel), and Cherí-báshí (captain). 1. Konia, the residence of the Páshá. 2. Kaiserieh (Cæsarea). 3. Níkdeh. 4. Yení-sheherí. 5. Kír-sheherí. 6. Ak-seráï.

Sanjaks of Sívás.

The Defter (treasury) has a Kehiyá, and Emín, the Chávushes have the same; there is besides a captain and Defterdár of the feuds. 1. Sívás, the seat of the Páshá. 2. Deverbegi. 3. Khúrúm. 4. Keskín. 5. Búzouk. 6. Amasia. 7. Tokát. 8. Zíla. 9. Janík. 10. Arab-gír.

Sanjaks of Bosna.

The officers are, the Defterdár of the treasury, the Kehiyá and Emín of the rolls; the Kehiyá and Emín of the Chávushes, the Aláï-beg and the Cherí-báshí. 1. Seráï, the seat of the Páshá. 2. Hersek. 3. Kilís. 4. Zvorník. 5. Poshega. 6. Záchina. 7. Kírka. 8. Ráhovícha. 9. Banalúka.

The Province of the CapúdánPáshá.

The officers are, the Kehiyá and Emín of the Defter and Chávushes, the Aláï-beg and Cherí-báshí, the Aghás of the Arabs, and the Dáïs of the Yúz-báshís. 1. Gallipoli, the seat of the Pasha. 2. Aghribúz (Negropont). 3. Karlí-eilí (Acarnania). 4. Ainabakht (Naupaktus or Lepanto). 5. Rodós (Rhodes). 6. Mytylini. 7. Kójá-eilí. 8. Bíghá. 9. Izmit (Nicomedia). 10. Izmír (Smyrna).

Sanjaks of the Morea.

Here there is neither Kehiyá nor Emín of the Defter. The Sanjaks are: 1. Misistra. 2. Mania. 3. Corone; Ayá Maura. 4. Napoli di Romania. The sanjaks Sákiz (Chios), Naksha (Naxos), and Mahdia (in Africa), have recently been added to the government of the Capudán-páshá.

Sanjaks of Búdín (Bude).

The number of officers attached to each province in this district is complete, because it always has a grand diván. They are: 1. The Defterdár of the treasury. 2. The defterdár of the Tímárs or feuds. 3. The Kehiyá or deputy of the defter. 4. The Kehiyá of the Chávushes. 5. The Emín or inspector of the defter. 6. The Emín of the Chávushes. 7. The Aláï Beg, or colonel. 8. The Cherí-báshí or lieutenant-colonel of the feudal militia. 9. The Pashá who resides at Bude. The Sanjaks are: 1. Bude. 2. Segdin. 3. Sonluk. 4. Hetwán. 5. Sihún. 6. Germán. 7. Filek. 8. Erla.

Sanjaks of the Province of Kaniza.

This province was separated from the principality of Bude, and there is no Defterdár either of the treasury or of the feudal militia. The sanjaks are: 1. Siget. 2. Kopán. 3. Valiova, 4. Sokolofja.

Sanjaks of Uivár (Neuhausel).

This province was conquered only in the time of Mohammed IV., by Kopreïlí Zádeh Ahmed Páshá. It is a well cultivated district. The sanjaks are: 1. Litova. 2. Novígrád. 3. Húlichk. 4. Boyák. 5. Shaswár.

The Province of Temiswar.

Here the usual offices were established during the reign of Mohammed IV., at the time of its second conquest by Kopreïlí Ahmed Páshá. The fortress of Yanova was then the seat of the Páshá. The sanjaks are: 1. Lipova. 2. Kíánad. 3. Jíulei. 4. Mode. 5. Lugos. 6. Facias Arad. 7. Five churches, the wakf (or pious bequest) of Sokollí Mohammed Páshá.

The Province of Varasdin.

This province was conquered by Kozí Alí Páshá in the time of Mohammed IV. Sanjaks: 1. Slanta. 2. Debrechin. 3. Khalmas. 4. Seus Giorgi. The inhabitants of this country being all infidels, the tribute is collected by Hungarian chiefs who forward it to Constantinople.

Transylvania.

This principality was conquered during the reign of Sultan Mohammed IV. by the arms of the brave Seïdí Ahmed Páshá; and Michael Apasty was made viceroy on condition that he should pay an annual tribute of one thousand purses besides certain presents. The population is composed of native Transylvanians, of Siklev, and of Saxons; the latter have always been disaffected towards the Osmánlí government.

Valachia and Moldavia.

These are also infidel principalities governed by princes appointed by the Ottoman government, and pay an annual tribute of two thousand purses; they are considered as belonging to the province of Silistria.

Oczakov or Silistria.

Here there are no public officers as in the other provinces, having been detached from the government of Rúmeïlí. Its sanjaks are: 1. Nikopolis. 2. Chermen. 3. Viza. 4. Kirk Kilisia (or forty churches). 5. Bender. 6. Akkermán. 7. Oczakov. 8. Kilbúrún. 9. Dúghún. 10. Silistria, which is the seat of the Páshá.

Krim (the Crimea).

This territory is governed by a Khán, who has the privilege of coining, and of having the Khotba read in the mosques, his name being mentioned immediately after that of the Osmánlí Emperor, who has the right of appointing and changing the Kháns. The residence of the Khán is at Baghcheseráï, and that of the Sultan at Ak-mesjid. The subordinate officers are styled Shírín-begs and Másúr-begs; the former are selected from the Nakhcheván family, and the latter from the Manik.

The Province of Kaffa.

Its sanjaks are ruled by Voivodas, immediately appointed by the Osmánlí Sultan and not by the Kháns. These sanjaks are: 1. Bálikláva. 2. Kirej. 3. Támán. 4. Cherkess-shagha. 5. Balisira. 6. Azov. Besides the Defterdár, there are no public officers.

The Province of Cyprus.

There are here, a Defterdár of the treasury and of the feuds; a Kehiyá and Emín of the Defter and Chávushes, an Aláï-beg, and a Cherí-báshí. The sanjaks are: 1. Itshilí. 2. Társús. 3. Aláyí. 4. Sís or Khás. The following have a Sáliáneh, or annual allowance from the treasury: Kerina, Paphos, Tamagusta, and Nicosia. It is a large island, and contains 30,000 Moslem warriors, and 150,000 infidels.

The Province of Candia.

Canea was conquered in the reign of Sultán Ibrahím, by Yúsuf Páshá; and twenty-six years afterwards Candia was taken by Kopreïlí Zádeh the second, after a protracted siege of three years. The sanjaks are: 1. Canea. 2. Retimo. 3. Selina. This island, being so extensive, has the complement of public officers, and maintains a force of 40,000 men.

The Province of Damascus.

Some of the sanjaks of this province are khás (*i.e.* yield a land revenue); and others are Sáliáneh (*i.e.* have an annual allowance from government). Of the former are: 1. Jerusalem. 2. Gaza. 3. Karak. 4. Safet. 5. Náblús. 6. Aajelún. 7. Lejún. 8. Bokoa. Of the latter: Tadmor, Saida, and Bairút.

The Province of Trabalús (Tripoli).

Its sanjaks are: 1. Trabalús (Tripoli) the seat of the Páshá. 2. Hama. 3. Homs.

4. Salamieh. 5. Jebella. 6. Latakia. 7. Husnábád. It has also forty Begs of the Drúzís in the mountains which belong to it.

The Province of Adna.

Having been separated from the government of Haleb, it has no diván officers. The sanjaks are: 1. Sís. 2. Tarsús. 3. Karatásh. 4. Selfekeh. It has also seven Bóï-begs. Being a mountainous country it is very turbulent.

The Province of Haleb (Aleppo).

Two of its sanjaks which receive a stipend, have no ziámet nor tímár. The sanjaks are: 1. Akrád Kilís. 2. Bírejek. 3. Maura. 4. Azir. 5. Bális. 6. Antakia (Antioch). Those which receive the allowance are Massiaf, and the sanjak of the Turkomans, who are very numerous in this province.

The Province of Díúrbeker.

In this province there are nineteen sanjaks, and five hakúmets (or hereditary governments). Eleven of the nineteen sanjaks are the same as the others in the Ottoman provinces, but the remaining eight were, at the time of the conquest, conferred on Kurdish Begs with the patent of family inheritance for ever. Like other sanjaks, they are divided into ziámets and tímárs, the possessors of which are obliged to serve in the field; but if they do not, the ziámet or timár may be transferred to a son or relation, but not to a stranger. The hakúmets have neither ziámets nor timárs. Their governors exercise full authority, and receive not only the land revenues, but also all the other taxes which in the sanjaks are paid to the possessor of the ziámet or timár, such as the taxes for pasturage, marriages, horses, vineyards, and orchards. The Ottoman sanjaks are: 1. Kharpút. 2. Arghání. 3. Siverek. 4. Nissibin. 5. Husunkeïf. 6. Miafarakain. 7. Akchékala'. 8. Khapúr. 9. Sinjár. The Kurdish are: 1. Síghmán. 2. Kúláb. 3. Mehrásí. 4. Aták. 5. Bertek. 6. Chapakchúr. 7. Chermek. 8. Terjíl. The independent governments: 1. Jezíreh. 2. Akíl. 3. Kenj. 4. Palwá. 5. Hezzú. These are extensive provinces, and their governors have the title of Janáb (excellency). The officers of the diván of Díárbeker are: the defterdár of the treasury with a rúz-námjí (journal-writer); a defterdár of the feudal forces, an inspector (Emín), and a lieutenant (Kehiyá) of the defter, and another for the Chávushes; a secretary (Kátib), a colonel, and a lieutenant-colonel of the militia.

The Province of Kars.

Before the conquest this district belonged to Erzrúm, but it was afterwards made a separate province, and had the sanjak of Yásín joined to it. It has a colonel and lieutenant-colonel, but no officers of the defter. Its sanjaks are: 1. Little Erdehán. 2. Hújuján. 3. Zárshád. 4. Kechrán. 5. Kághizmán. 6. Kars, the seat of the Páshá.

The Province of Jíldir or Akhíchkeh.

Of the civil officers of the diván there is here only a defterdár of the treasury; and of the military, there is a colonel and a lieutenant-colonel of the feudal militia. The sanjaks are: 1. Oultí. 2. Harbús. 3. Ardinj. 4. Hajrek. 5. Great Ardehán. 6. Postkhú. 7. Mahjíl. 8. Ijareh-penbek. Besides these there are four hereditary sanjaks: 1. Púrtekrek. 2. Lawaneh. 3. Nusuf Awán. 4. Shúshád. During the reign of Sultán Mohammed Khán, the castle of Kotátis was captured by Kara Mortezá, and was added to this province.

The Province of Gúrjistán or Georgia.

The sanjaks are: 1. Achikbásh. 2. Shúshád. 3. Dádián. 4. Gúríl. The Begs of Megrelistán (Mingrelia) are all infidels; but Murád IV. reduced them, and having placed Sefer Pasha as their governor, made the castle of Akhickha the seat of government. To this day they send the annual presents.

The Province of Tarabafzún (Trebisonde).

1. Gomish-kháneh. 2. Jankha. 3. Wíza. 4. Gúnia. 5. Batúm. Though this province is small it has a defterdár of the Tímárs, a Kehiyá of the defter, an Aláï-beg, and a Cherí-báshí.

The Province of Rika.

The sanjaks of Rika and Rohá are: 1. Jemása. 2. Khárpud. 3. Deïr-rahba. 4. Bení Rebia. 5. Sarúj. 6. Kharán. 7. Rika. 8. Rohá or Urfa, which is the seat of the Páshá; it has no officers.

The Province of Baghdád.

Seven of the eighteen sanjaks of this province are divided, as in other parts of the empire, into ziámets and timárs. They are: 1. Hilla. 2. Zeng-ábád. 3. Javazar. 4. Rúmáhía. 5. Jangula. 6. Kara-tágh. 7.——. The other eleven sanjaks which are called Irák, have neither ziámets nor tímárs. They are: 1.

Terteng. 2. Samwat. 3. Bíát. 4. Derneh. 5. Deh-balád. 6. Evset. 7. Kerneh-deh. 8. Demir-kapú. 9. Karanieh. 10. Kilán. 11. Alsáh. These have no ziámets or tímárs, and are entirely in the power of their possessors.

The Province of Basra.

This was formerly a hereditary government (mulkiat), but was reduced to an ordinary province (eyálet) when conquered by Sultán Mohammed IV. It has a defterdár and Kehiyá of the Chávushes, but neither Aláï-beg nor Cherí-báshí, because there are no ziámets or tímárs; the lands being all rented by the governor.

The Province of Lahsa.

This being a hereditary government, has neither ziámets nor tímárs, but the governor sends a monthly present to the governor of Baghdád. Formerly its governors were installed as Begler-begs, but they now hold their authority without a patent.

The Province of Yemen.

This too, since the time of Mohammed Khán IV., has been unlawfully occupied by the Imáms.

The Province of Abyssinia.

This province is also without ziámets or tímárs. Once in three years an officer is sent from the Sublime Porte, to claim it as a government province (Mulk). There are no private leases (iltizám).

The Province of Mecca.

Mecca is divided between the Sheríf and the Páshá of Jidda. There are no revenues but those derived from the aqueducts.

The Province of Egypt.

Here there are neither ziámets nor tímárs. Its villages are registered either as belonging to the crown (Mír Mál), or to pious foundations (Wakf), or to the Káshif, or as rented by the inhabitants of towns (Iltizám-beledí). There is a defterdár of the treasury, a journal keeper (Rúznámehjí), seven clerks of the leases (Mokata'jí), a comptroller (Mokábelejí) on the part of the Páshá, forty Begs and seven commanders of the seven military bodies. The sanjaks held by Begs are the following: 1. Upper Egypt. 2. Jirja. 3. Ibrim. 4. Alwáhát. (the Oasis). 5. Manfelút. 6. Sharakieh (the eastern part of the Delta). 7. Gharabieh (the western part). 8. Manúfieh. 9. Mansúrieh. 10. Kalúbieh. 11. Bakhair. 12. Damiat (Damietta). These are all governed by Begs. The first in rank of the Begs of Egypt is the Emír-ul-haj, or chief of the caravan to Mecca, who by the Arabs is called Sultán-al-barr, or lord of the continent. His Kehiyá or deputy has the privilege of wearing an aigrette.

As I have not travelled through the kingdoms of Algiers, Tunis, and Tripoli, I do not give any account of them, but it is well known that they are extensive territories.

The Province of Mosul.

This has no officers of the Diván, but a colonel and a lieutenant-colonel. Its sanjaks are: 1. Bájwánlí. 2. Tekrit. 3. Eskí Mosul (Nineveh). 4. Harú.

The Province of Wán.

The officers are, the defterdár of the treasury and of the tímárs, the inspector and deputy of the rolls and Chávushes, a clerk of the Chávushes, a colonel and lieutenant-colonel. Its sanjaks are: 1. Adaljewáz. 2. Arjish. 3. Músh. 4. Bárgerí. 5. Kárkár. 6. Kesání. 7. Zíríkí. 8. Asa'bard. 9. Aghákís. 10. Akrád. 11. Bení-kutúr. 12. Kala' Báyazíd. 13. Burdú'. 15. Khalát. In the governments of Tiflis, Hakkárí, Majmúdí, and Peniánish, there are ziámets and tímárs; the tribute received from them is appropriated to the pay of the garrison of Wán. All other fees and duties are received by the Kháns who hold these governments in hereditary possession.

The Province of Erzerúm.

This has twelve sanjaks; its officers are, a defterdár of the treasury, an inspector and deputy of the rolls and Chávushes, and a clerk of the Chávushes. The sanjaks are: 1. Kara-hisár. 2. Keïfí. 3. Pásín. 4. Ispír. 5. Khanís. 6. Malázgír. 7. Tekmán. 8. Kuzúján. 9. Túrtúm. 10. Lejengerd. 11. Mámar. 12. Erzerúm, the seat of the Páshá.

The Province of Sheherzúl.

This province has the full number of diván officers. Its sanjaks are: 1.

Sarújek. 2. Erbíl. 3. Kesnán. 4. Sheher-bázár. 5. Jengúleh. 6. Jebel-hamrin. 7. Hazár-mardúd. 8. Alhúrán. 9. Merkáreh. 10. Hazír. 11. Rúdín. 12. Tíltárí. 13. Sebeh. 14. Zenjír. 15. Ajúb. 16. Abrúmán. 17. Pák. 18. Pertelí. 19. Bílkás. 20. Aúshní. 21. Kala' Ghází. 22. Sheherzúl, which is the seat of the Páshá. There are some tribes in this province who are not governed by begs invested with a drum and banner; more than one hundred chiefs of such tribes, who hold their lands as ziámets, but by a hereditary right, accompany the Páshá, when required, to the field of battle.

SECTION IV.

Of the ranks of the Sanjak-begs.

According to the constitutional laws of Sultán Soleïmán, the sanjak-begs rank according to their pay, except when there is a deposed grand vezír amongst them, who in such case takes precedence over them all. The pay of a sanjak-beg is at first 200,000 aspres, which is increased in proportion to the period of his service, until he becomes begler-beg, or mír mírán. Should, however, one of the aghás or commanding generals of the military corps at Constantinople be made a sanjak-beg, his pay from the first is more than 200,000 aspres. Thus, the Aghá of the Janissaries, when he is appointed a sanjak-beg, at once receives 500,000 aspres. The nishánjí-báshí (lord privy seal), the mír alem (standard bearer of the empire), the chamberlain, and the grand master of the horse, receive an increase of 100,000 aspres. The cháshní-gír-báshí (comptroller of the kitchen), the mutafarrek-báshí (chief of the couriers), the under-master of the horse, the Aghá of sipáhís and silihdárs, of the ságh-ulúfejíán and sól-ghurebá (two bodies of cavalry), all become sanjak-begs with a salary of 300,000 aspres. The segbán-báshí (a general of the Janissaries), the Kehiyá (deputy) of the defter, the defterdárs of the tímárs and yáyá-begs, and all whose ziámets amount to more than 500,000 aspres, receive an addition of 100,000 aspres, as sanjak-begs. Such begs as distinguish themselves by good conduct are rewarded with vacant tímárs; each sanjak-beg furnishes for every 5,000 aspres of his revenues one armed man. The smallest income of a sanjak-beg being 200,000 aspres, he brings forty armed men into the field; if he has 500,000 aspres he furnishes 500 men, and so on in proportion.

SECTION V.

Of the Khás, or revenue of the Sanjak-begs, the Kehiyás of the Defter and the Defterdárs of Tímárs.

Rumeili.

Khás of the sanjak-begs of the Morea 5,776 aspres; Scutari, 59,200; Avlonia, 39,000; Silistria, 89,660; Nicopolis, 40,000; Okhrí, 35,299; Yanina, 20,260; Terhala, 50,885; Gústendíl 42,400; Elbesán, 1,963; Chermen, 4,000; Víza, 34,465; Delvina, 7,132; Salonik, 80,832; Skopí, 40,000; Dúkagín, 27,500; Widín, 3,000; Alájeh-hisár, 20,399; Weljeterín, 50,000; Perzerín, 28,146; Ziámet of the kehiyá of the defter, 1,426; of the defterdárs, 2,000; of the beg of the Yúrúks (wandering tribes) of Víza, 2,000; of the yúrúk-beg of Rodosto, 60,000; of the yurúk-beg of Yánbolí, 3,470; of the yúrúk-beg of Okchebóli, 3,494; of the yúrúk-beg of Koja, 4,000; of the yúrúk-beg of Salonik, 41,397; of the yúrúk-beg of Naldúkín, 3,500; of the capudán of Cavala, 4,314; of the beg of the Voinoks, 5,052.

Bosnia.

Khás of the beg of Kilís, 42,500; Hersek, 10,515; Zvorník, 35,793; Poshega, 66,230; Zachina, 70,000; Karak, 30,000; Rahovicha, 70,000.

Ziámet of the kehiyá of the defter, 46,000; of the defterdár, 5,530.

The Archipelago.

Khás of the Beg of Negropont, 40,000; Karlíeïlí (Acarnania), 3,000; Einabakht (Lepanto), 30,000; Rodós (Rhodes), 77,004; Mytylini, 40,000; Kojaeïlí, 6,526; Bígha, 13,088; Sighla, 30,000; Misistra, 19,000.

Ziámet of the kehiyá, 8,390; of the defterdár, 22,077.

The Province of Bude.

Khás of Semendria, 40,260; Becheví (Fünf-kirchen or Fife-churches), 40,000; Oustúnbelgrade(Stuhl-weissenburg), 26,000; Osterghún (Gran), 10,000; Segdín, 40,000; Sirem, 25,675; Essek, 20,000; Shamtorna, 40,000; Kopán and Filek, 20,000; Nigisár, 34,000; Novigrád, 33,940; Sonlí, 40,000; Míhaj, 92,000; Siget, 4,230; Segsár, 34,000; Míján, 40,260.

Khás of the Defterdár, 5,520; ziámet of the kehiyá of the defter, 3,240; of the kehiyá of the tímárs, 8,940.

The Province of Temisvár.

Lippova, 10,000; Kiánád, 20,792; Gúla, 28,945; Madava, 60,080; Yánova,

2,420; Ishbesh, 1,945; Ziámet of the defterdár of the treasury, 60,000; of the Kehiyá, 4,880; of the defterdár of the tímárs, 60,000.

The Province of Anatolia.

Khás of the beg of Sárukhán, 40,000; Aïdín, 34,600; Kara Hisár Afíún, 40,299; Angora, 64,300; Brúsa, 18,089; Bolí, 20,122; Kastamúní, 50,000; Muntesha, 40,800; Tekkeh, 28,000; Hamíd, 24,000; Jánkrí, 48,081; Karasí, 3,000; Sultánógí, 5,000.

Ziámet of the kehiyá, 10,912; of the defterdár, 4,596.

The Province of Karamán.

Khás of the beg of Kaisarieh (Cæsarea), 5,000; Begshehrí, 90,000; Akseráí, 35,000; Aksheher, 1,000; Kírsheher, 7,540.

Khás of the defterdár, 5,000; of the kehiyá, 5,000.

The Province of Kubrus (Cyprus).

Khás of Icheïlí, 27,000; Aláíeh, 50,000; Tarsús, 45,260; Sís, 60,299.

Khás of the defterdár of the treasury, 20,000; of the defterdár of the ziámets, 70,000; of the kehiyá, 42,000.

The Province of Tripoli (in Syria).

Khás of Homs, 20,290; Jebellieh, 34,180; Salamieh, 9,000; Hamá, 94,030.

Khás of the defterdár of the treasury, 13,000; of the kehiyá, 64,800; of the defterdár of the timárs, 40,000.

The Province of Haleb (Aleppo).

Khás of the beg of Adna, 95,000; Kilís, 2,827; Bírejek, 5,220; Makra, 30,000; Azíz, 20,000; Balís, 20,000.

Khás of the defterdár of the treasury, 27,826; of the kehiyá, 6,930; of the defterdár of the tímárs, 1,146.

The Province of Zulkadrieh or Mera'ish.

Malatieh, 50,000; Eintáb, 5,130; Mera'ish, 25,300.

The Province of Sivás.

Khás of the beg of Amasia, 30,000; Chorum, 30,000; Búzouk, 300,275; Dívergí, 50,360; Jáník, 7,024; Arabgír, 21,000.

Ziámet of the kehiyá, 80,200; of the defterdár, 2,550.

The Province of Erzerúm.

Khás of the beg of Karahisár Sharakí, 3,000; Keïfí, 3,000; Básín, 94,000; Ispír, 30,000; Khanís, 80,440; Malázgír, 50,000; Turkmán, 4,929; Okúzján, 20,702; Túrtúm, 97,000; Lejengird, 40,000; Mámerván, 3,000.

Khás of the defterdár of the treasury, 42,900; of the defterdár of the tímárs, 20,200.

The Province of Kars.

Khás of Erdehán Kúchuk, 9,030; Hújú-ján, 2,500; Rúshád, 40,000; Kázmaghán, 2,000; Kecherán, 2,000.

The Province of Childer or Akhichka.

Khás of Oultí, 2,017; Pertek, 2,190; Erdenúh, 70,000; Erdehán Buzúrg, 2,000; Shúshád, 56,000; Livána (two hereditary sanjaks), 65,000; Kharbús, 2,500; Sahrek, 65,000; Pústúkh, 6,500; Mánjíl, 3,229; Penbek, 40,000.

The Province of Trebisonde.

Ziámet of the kehiyá of Bátúm, 3,000 apres; ziámet of the defterdár of the tímárs, 42,290.

The Province of Díárbeker.

Khás of Kharpút, 9,999; Arghaní, 20,515; Súrek, 3,043; Aták, 47,200; Nesíbín, 30,000; Terjíl, 45,200; Jermík, 3,140; Husn-keïf, 2,955; Akíl, 9,675; Chapík-júd, 7,000; Jemishgezek, 4,223; Samsád, 9,057; Sha'ir, 3772; Akchakala', 20,000; Sinjár, 1,517; Mufarakín, 20,000; Lisán and Búzbán, 6,000; Khákenj, 7,834.

Khás of the defterdár, 40,395; ziámet of the kehiyá of the defter, 10,924; khás of the defterdár of the timárs, 8,000.

The Province of Rakka.

Khás of Jemáseh, 5,122; Dair Rahba, 8,000; Kápúr, 10,000; Así Rabia', 40,000; Sarúj, 20,000; Ana, 82,215.

The Province of Baghdád.

Khás of Zangábád, 70,000; Helleh, 51,000; Javázer, 20,000; Rúmnáhieh, 45,000; Jengúleh, 20,000; Kara (an hereditary government), 4,287; Derteng, 20,000; Samvát, 55,000; Derneh, 6,931; Dehbálá, 60,000; Váset, 20,000; Kerend, 29,260; Tapúr, 20,000; Karanieh, 20,000; Kílán, 20,000; Al Ságh, 200,000; Ziámet of the kehiyá of the defter, 10,000; of the defterdár of the tímárs, 80,000.

The Province of Wán.

Khás of Adeljaván, 50,346; Arjís, 30,000; Músh, 1,000; Bárgerí, 20,000; Kárkár, 20,000; Keshán, 25,000; Ispághird, 20,000; Aghákís, 50,000; Akrád, 90,000; Wádí Bení Kutúr, 70,000; Kala' Báyazíd, 1,044; Bardú', 20,000; Wáwjik, 95,000.

Ziámet of the kehiyá of the defter, 60,999; of the defterdár of the tímárs, 3,870.

The Province of Mosul.

Khás of Bájuvánlí, 15,000; Tekrít, 7,284; Harún, 20,000; Bána, 30,000.

Section VI.

Statement of the number of swords or men brought into the field by the Possessors of Tímárs and Ziámets.

The Province of Rumeili.

The number of its swords or armed men is 9,274, of which 914 are ziámets, the rest tímárs, with and without tezkerehs (commissions). The Zái'ms, or possessors of the ziámets, for every 5,000 aspres of their revenues provide one armed man. Tímárís, or possessors of the tímárs, of from 10,000 to 20,000, find three men. Thus the militia of Rúmeïlí consists of Zái'ms,

Tímárs, and Jebellís, or guards, amounting in all to 20,200 men. The sanjak-beg, the kehiyá of the defter, and the defterdár of the timárs, for every 5,000 aspres of their revenues provide one man: the number of men found by these being 2,500, the troops of Rúmeïlí amount to 33,000 men; and, including the servants, to 40,000 men.

SECTION VII

Number of Ziámets and Tímárs in each of the Sanjaks in Rúmeïlí.

Sofia, the seat of the Páshá, has 7,821 ziámets and tímárs; Kustandíl 48 ziámets, 1,018 tímárs; Terkhaleh 32 ziámets, 539 tímárs; Yánina 62 ziámets, 34 tímárs; Uskúb 57 ziámets, 340 tímárs; Ohrí 20 ziámets, 529 tímárs; Avlonia 38 ziámets, 489 tímárs; Morea 200 ziámets; Eskenderieh 75 ziámets, 422 tímárs; Nicopolis 20 ziámets, 244 tímárs; Chermen 20 ziámets, 130 tímárs; Elbesán 18 ziámets, 138 tímárs; Víza 30 ziámets, 79 tímárs; Delvina 34 ziámets, 1,155 tímárs; Saláník (Salonica) 36 ziámets, 762 tímárs; Kirk-kilisá 18 tímárs; Dúkagín 10 ziámets, 52 tímárs; Widín 12 ziámets, 25 tímárs; Alaja-hisár 27 ziámets, 509 tímárs; Wejterín, 10 ziámets, 17 tímárs; Perzerín 17 ziámets, 225 tímárs; Akchebólí, an Oják of the Yúrúks or wandering tribes, 188; of the Yúrúks of Teker Tághí or Rodosto 324; of the Yúrúks of Saláník 128; of Koják 400; of Na'ldúkín 314; of the Mussulmans of Rúmeïlí 400; of the Mussulmans of Kuziljeh 300; of the Mussulmans of Chermen 301; of Chinganeh (Gypsies or Bohemians) 198; of Víza 178;—in all 1,019 hereditary ojáks or families. In the government registers thirty persons of these Yúrúks or Mussulmans are called an *oják*, or family. In the time of war these Yúrúks and Mussulmans constitute the flying troops (ishkenjí), and in their turn twenty-five of these perform the duties of yamáks, or servants, to the other five. During war the Yamáks are obliged to pay 55 aspres per head in lieu of all diván duties, but in time of peace they are exempt from all taxes. The ishkenjí or flying-troops (voltigeurs) pay no farm-taxes when they go to war; but should they become sipáhís or feudatory tenants, they are not exempt from the duties of Yúrúks. To the Mussulmans a portion of land is allotted, which is registered as a tímár, and of which they pay no tithes. Their duties are to drag the artillery in the time of war, to clear the roads, and to carry the necessary provisions for the army.

SECTION VIII.

Number of Ziámets and Timárs in Anatolia.

There are 7,313 swords, of which 195 are ziámets and the other tímárs; they provide 9,700 jebellí or armed men, and others, amounting in all to 17,000 men. Their annual revenue amounts to 37,317,730 aspres. The ziámets and tímárs are as follows: Kútáhieh 79 ziámets, 939 tímárs; Sarúkhán 41 ziámets, 674 tímárs; Aídín 19 ziámets, 572 tímárs; Karahisár, 15 ziámets, 616 tímárs; Angora 10 ziámets, 257 tímárs; Brúsa 30 ziámets, 1,005 tímárs; Bolí 14 ziámets, 551 tímárs; Kostamúní 24 ziámets, 587 tímárs; Munteshá 52 ziámets, 381 tímárs; Tekkeh 7 ziámets, 392 tímárs; Hamíd 9 ziámets, 585 tímárs; Karasí 7 ziámets 381 tímárs; Sultán-ogí 7 ziámets, 182 tímárs. In Anatolia there are also Musselmans (freemen) and Píádeh or Yáyá (pioneers), who to the number of 900 men go to war; these with the Yamáks amount to 26,500 men; their duties are to drag the guns, clear the roads, and carry provisions. They have lands (chiftlik) like the Yúrúks of Rúmeïlí, which are registered as tímárs. This was the establishment in the reign of Sultán Soleïmán, but at present they are all enrolled as rayás, and the possessors of these tímárs are obliged to accompany the Kapúdán Páshá when he goes to sea. Formerly there were in this province 1,280 volunteering Arabs, who, for every ten men providing one armed-man, sent 128 men into the field. They are now disbanded.

The Province of the Kapúdán Páshá, or the islands of the Archipelago.

This formerly provided 1,618 swords; but Ja'fer Páshá, who was formerly Bóstánjí Báshí, during the reign of Murád IV. increased their number to 9,900: of these 106 were ziámets and the rest were tímárs; adding to them the jebellís the entire number was 12,067 men. The Arabs, the volunteers of the Arsenal, and the men of sixty galleys, also formed a body of 10,000 men. The annual revenue of their ziámets and tímárs amounted to 1,800,000 aspres. The following are the ziámets and tímárs: Negropont 12 ziámets, 188 tímárs; Einabakht (Lepanto) 13 ziámets, 287 tímárs; Mytylini 83 tímárs; Kojaeïlí 25 ziámets, 187 tímárs; Sighla 32 ziámets, 225 tímárs; Kárlieïlí 11 ziámets, 19 tímárs; Gallipolí 14 ziámets, 132 tímárs; Ródós (Rhodes) 5 ziámets, 785 tímárs; Bíghá 6 ziámets, 136 tímárs; Misistra 10 ziámets, 91 tímárs.

The Province of Karamán.

This province supplies 1,620 men, 110 of which are ziámets, the rest tímárs; with the jebellís they amount to 4,600 men. Their annual revenue is 1,500,000 aspres. Konia has 13 ziámets, 515 sanjaks; Kaisaria (Cæsarea) 12 ziámets, 200 tímárs; Níkdeh 13 ziámets, 255 tímárs; Begshehrí 12 ziámets, 244 tímárs; Akshehrí 9 ziámets, 22 tímárs; Kirkshehrí 4 ziámets, 13 tímárs; Akseráï 12 ziámets, 228 tímárs.

The Province of Rúm or Sivás.

This has 3,130 swords or men, of which 109 are ziámets, the rest tímárs. The begs, záims, and tímariots with their jebellís amount to 9,000 men. Their annual revenue amounts to 3,087,327 aspres. Sivás has 48 ziámets, 928 tímárs.

The Province of Mara'ish.

2,169 swords, of which 29 are ziámets, and the rest tímárs. The begs, záims, tímariots, and jebellís amount to 55,000 men. Their annual revenue amounts to 9,423,017 aspres. Mara'ish has 3 ziámets, 1,120 tímárs; Kars 2 ziámets, 656 tímárs; Eintáb 2 ziámets, 656 tímárs; Malatea 8 ziámets, 276 tímárs.

The Province of Haleb (Aleppo).

933 swords, of which 104 are ziámets, the rest tímárs; the whole number of troops with the jebellís is 2,500 men. Haleb 18 ziámets, 1,295 tímárs; Adna 11 ziámets, 190 tímárs; Kilís 17 ziámets, 295 tímárs; Ma'kra 9 ziámets, 890 tímárs; Azíz 2 ziámets, 190 tímárs; Balís 6 ziámets, 57 tímárs.

The Province of Shám (Damascus).

996 swords, of which 28 are ziámets and the rest tímárs; it has with the jebellís 1,600 men. Kuds-Sheríf (Jerusalem) 9 ziámets, 16 tímárs; Aajelún 4 ziámets, 21 tímárs; Lajún 9 ziámets, 26 tímárs; Safed 5 ziámets, 133 tímárs; Gaza 7 ziámets, 108 tímárs; Náblús 7 ziámets, 124 tímárs.

The Province of Cyprus.

1,667 swords, of which 40 are ziámets, and the rest tímárs. The begs, záims, tímariots and jebellís amount to 4,500 men. Cyprus 9 ziámets, 38 tímárs; Aláïeh 9 ziámets, 152 tímárs; Tarsús 13 ziámets, 418 tímárs; Sís 2 ziámets, 52 tímárs; Ich-eïlí 16 ziámets, 602 tímárs.

The Province of Tripoli (in Syria).

614 swords, with the jebellís, 1,400 men. Tripoli 12 ziámets, 875 tímárs; Homs 9 ziámets, 91 tímárs; Jebellieh 9 ziámets, 91 tímárs; Salamieh 54 ziámets, 52 tímárs; Hama 27 ziámets, 171 tímárs.

The Province of Rakka.

654 swords, with their jebellís, 1,400 men. Rakka 3 ziámets, 132 tímárs; Roha 9 ziámets, 291 tímárs; Birehjík 15 ziámets, 109 tímárs; A'na 6 ziámets, 129 tímárs.

The Province of Trebizonde.

454 swords, with their jebellís, 8,150 men. Trebizonde 43 ziámets, 226 tímárs; Batúm 5 ziámets, 72 tímárs.

The Province of Díárbekr.

730 swords, with their jebellís, 1,800 men. In the reign of Sultán Murád IV. this province provided 9,000 men. Amed has 9 ziámets, 1,129 tímárs; Kharpút 7 ziámets, 123 tímárs; Argháneh 9 ziámets, 123 tímárs; Sívrek 4 ziámets, 123 tímárs; Nesíben, 15 ziámets and tímárs; Berehjík 4 ziámets, 123 tímárs; Chermik 6 ziámets, 13 tímárs; Husnkeïf 45 ziámets and tímárs; Chabákchúr 5 ziámets, 30 tímárs; Jemeshgezek 2 ziámets, 7 tímárs; Sinjár 6 ziámets, 21 tímárs.

The Province of Erzerúm.

5,279 swords, with the jebellís 8,000 men. Erzerúm 5 ziámets, 2,215 tímárs; Túrtúm 5 ziámets, 49 tímárs; Bámerwán 4 ziámets, 92 tímárs; Keïfí 8 ziámets, 229 tímárs; Malázgír 9 ziámets, 281 tímárs; Khanís 2 ziámets, 425 tímárs; Tekmán 1 ziámet, 253 tímárs; Kara-hisár 4 ziámets, 94 tímárs.

The Province of Childer.

650 swords, with the jebellís, 8,000 men. Oultí 3 ziámets, 132 tímárs; Erdehán 8 ziámets, 45 tímárs; Ezerbúj 4 ziámets, 49 tímárs; Hajrek 2 ziámets, 12 tímárs; Kharnús 13 ziámets, 35 tímárs; Pústú 1 ziámet, 18 tímárs; Benek 8 ziámets, 54 tímárs; Básín 9 ziámets, 14 tímárs; Alúrí 9 ziámets, 10 tímárs; Oustjeh 8 ziámets, 17 tímárs; Cháklik 33 tímárs; Jetla 13 ziámets, 14 tímárs; Ispír 1 ziámet, 4 tímárs; Petek 3 ziámets, 98 tímárs.

The Province of Wán.

Regulars and jebellís 1,300 men. Wán has 48 ziámets, 45 tímárs; Shevergír 47 ziámets, 33 tímárs; Júbánlú 2 ziámets, 26 tímárs; Wedáleh 7 ziámets, 21 tímárs; Kala' Báyazíd 4 ziámets, 125 tímárs; Arjísh 14 ziámets, 86 tímárs; Aduljeváz 9 ziámets, 101 tímárs; Kúrládek 7 ziámets, 67 tímárs.

In the reign of Sultán Soleïmán the feudal force of Rúmeïlí amounted to 91,600 men. On so firm a foundation had he established the Ottoman empire, that when he made war in Europe he required not the troops of Asia; and when he took the field in Asia, he had no occasion for the forces of Europe. His victorious wars in Germany and Persia, were carried on solely with his regular troops. His whole army having been numbered amounted to 500,000 men. Of these there were 40,000 janissaries and 20,000 cavalry or sipáhís, who with their servants amounted to 40,000 men. After the conquest of Yánova, Mohammed IV. increased the army by 3,000 men, and after the conquest of Uivár by 8,000 men. Keríd (Candia) also, having been conquered and divided into ziámets and timárs, gave 100,000 rayás and 20,000 troops.

In the year 1060 (A.D. 1649) during the reign of Sultán Mohammed IV. my noble lord Melek Ahmed Páshá being grand vezír, a royal firmán was issued to review the whole of the Ottoman army. Every soul receiving pay in the seven climates was registered, and the result was 566,000 serving men, the annual pay of whom amounted to 43,700 purses, and with the pay of the troops in Egypt to 90,040 purses (45,020,000 piastres): thus the army far exceeded that of Soleïmán's time.

SECTION X.

The order of the Diván.

Before the time of Sultán Soleïmán there was no regular diván. He held a grand diván on four days during the week, composed of the seven vezírs of the cupola, the two judges of the army, the Aghá of the Janissaries and of the six bodies of cavalry. The Chávush-báshí (marshal of the court); and the Kapíjílár Kehiyásí (chief chamberlain) were required to attend on such days with their silver staffs of office. The grand vezír gave judgment on all lawsuits; and the Kapúdán Páshá, seated without the cupola, decided all matters relating to the navy. On Wednesdays the chief of the eunuchs decided causes relating to Mecca and Medina. It was Sultán Soleïmán who established the regular dress of the diván. The vezírs and the Kapúdán Páshá wore the turban called the *selímí*, and so did the Aghá of the Janissaries provided he were a vezír. The Chávúsh-báshí (marshal), the Kapíjílár Ketkhodásí (the chief chamberlain), the Mir-alem (the standard-bearer of the state), the Chakirjí-báshí (superintendent of the household), the Mír Akhor (master of the horse), the Cháshnígír-báshí (comptroller of the kitchen), and the Mutaferrika-báshí (chief of the couriers) wore the *mujavera*, or high round turban, and Kháláts of atlas or satin called *oust*. The generals of the Janissaries and Sipáhís, the Chávushes of the diván, and the seventy heads of the offices of the treasury, all stood in their places dressed in their *mujavera* and *oust* ready to transact business. On these days the Janissaries were served by the Aghá with 3,000 dishes of wheat broth, which if they would not touch, the emperor at once knew that they were dissatisfied. On such occasions he repaired to the Adálet Koshkí (kiosk of equity), where he in person decided some of their most important questions. In the evening they all sat down to a sumptuous repast, which was served by the Zulflí-báltají to the vezírs, and by the tent-pitchers to the rest of the company. After the repast the seven vezírs, the Kapúdán Páshá and the Aghá of the Janissaries with the two great judges were introduced by the gate of the Harem, to the presence of the emperor. They then returned to the diván, where the Chávush-báshí taking the seal of the grand vezír, sealed the treasure, and then returned it to the vezír.

The conquests and victories of Soleïmán.

His first conquest was the defeat of the Circassian governor of Syria, Ján Yazdí Ghazálí Khán, whose rebellious head Ferhád Páshá severed from its body, and sent to the Sublime Porte in 927 (A.D. 1520). The conquest of Yemen and death of Iskender the rebel 927 (1520). The reduction of Belgrade and Tekúrlen, of Slankement and Kópanik in the same year. The conquest of Rodos (Rhodes) in 928 (1521); of the fortresses of Iskaradín, Helka, Eiligí, the island of Injírlí, the fortress of Takhtalú, Istankoi (Cos), Bodrúm (Halicarnassus), in the same year. The victory of Mohacz, followed by the fall of Waradin, Oïlúk, Koprik, Eïlúk, Dimúrjeh, Irek, Gargofja, Lúkán, Sútan, Lakwár, Wárdúd, Rácheh, Essek, Bude and Pest, in the year 932 (1525). The siege of Kizil Alma (the Red Apple or the capital of Germany), and in the following year the release of Yánush (John Zapolia) by Yehiyá Páshá Zádeh. The conquest of Sokolofja, Kapúlieh, Shíla, Balwár, Lotofjí, Túsh, Zákán, Kaniza, Kaporník, Balashka Chopanija, Shárwár, Nimetogur, Kemendwár, Egersek, Moshter, and Moshtí in 939 (1532). Conquest of the eastern provinces of Irák, Kazwín, Karákán, Baghdád, Eriván, Sultánieh, Tabríz, and Hamadán, in 941 (1534). Wán, Adeljúváz, Arjísh, Akhlát, Bárgerí, Amik, Khúsháb, Sultán, Sabádán, Jerem-bidkár, Rúsíní, Hella, and Tenúr, in 941 (1534), Tabríz in the same year. An expedition into Georgia and Appulia; with the conquest of Kilís in Bosnia, in the year 943 (1536). The conquest of Uivárin, Nadín, Sín, Kádín, Oporja, and the expedition against Korfuz (Corfu) in the same year. The conquest of Poshega, and the defeat of Sorkújí John near Essek in 944 (1537). The expedition into Moldavia, the conquest of Yássí, Bassra, and Bosnia, in 945 (1538). The relief of Nureh in Hersek, the conquest of Yemen and Aden, the naval expedition against India and Díú; and the conquest of Abyssinia in the same year, by the Eunuch Soleïmán Páshá. Bude twice before besieged was now reduced, and Gházi Soleïmán Páshá made governor, and Khair-ad-dín Efendí first judge. The conquest of Stuhlweissenburg, Lippova, Grán, Tátá, Pápá, Vesperim, Poláta, and Chargha in 950 (1543).

The death of the prince Mohammed happened in the same year. The capture of Vishegráde near Grán, Khutwán, Shamtorna, Walifa in Bosnia, and of the castle of Cerigo in 951 (1544). In 954 (1547) Alkás Mirzá, the governor of Shírván and brother of Sháh Thamás took refuge at the court of Soleïmán; and in the following year the towns of Kóm, Káshán and Ispahán, were sacked by the emperors expedition. The conquest of Pechevi (Five Churches) Pechkerek, Arát, Jenád (Cianad) Temesvár; the battle of Khádem Alí Páshá in the plains of Segedin. Temesvár was conquered in 959 (1551) by the second vezír, Ahmed Páshá; the conquest of Solnuk; and the siege of Erla raised in the same year. The expedition against Nakhcheván; the death of the prince Jehángír whilst in winter quarters at Haleb (Aleppo) in 960 (1552). The conquest of Sheherzúl and Zálim, with the castles belonging to it. The conquest of Kapúshwár, Farúbeneh, and the Crimea. The victory of Malkúch Beg at Kilís in Bosnia in 961 (1553). The contest between the princes Selím and Báyazíd in the plains of Kóníya, in which Báyazíd was defeated and took refuge with the Sháh of Persia, who gave him up, after which he was put to death with his children at Sivás, 966 (1558). Expedition against Siget, during the siege of which Pertev Páshá conquered, on the Transylvanian side, the castles of Gúla, Yanova, and Dilághosh. Ten days previous to these victories the Emperor Soleïmán bade farewell to his transitory kingdom and removed to his never fading dominions. This event happened during the siege of Siget, but the vezír Asif concealed his illness and death so well for seventy days that even the pages of the Khás óda were ignorant of it. On this account it is said that Soleïmán conquered the towns of Siget, Gúla, and Kómár after his death. Thus died Soleïmán after a reign of forty-eight years, having attained the highest glory. His conquests extended over all the seven climates; and he had the Khotba read for him in 2,060 different mosques. His first victory was in Syria over the Circassian Khán Yezdí Ghazálí, and his last that at Siget: he died seven days before the reduction of this fortress. His death, which happened at nine o'clock on Wednesday the 22d of Sefer, was kept concealed till the arrival of his son Selím from Magnesia. His body was carried to Constantinople and buried before the Mihráb of the mosque which bears his name.

The Reign of Sultán Selím II.

Sultán Selím the son of Sultán Soleïmán Khán was born in 931, and ascended the throne in 974 (1566). He was an amiable monarch, took much delight in the conversation of poets and learned men, and indulged in pleasure and gaiety. His vezírs were,—the grand vezírs Sokollí Mohammed Páshá, Ahmed Páshá (the conqueror of Temisvár), Piáleh Páshá, (the Kapúdán Páshá), Zál Mahmúd Páshá, Láleh Mustafá Páshá, and Tútúnsez Husain Páshá. These were vezírs endowed with the wisdom of Aristotle.

The Mír-mírán, or Begler-begs, who adorned his reign were,—Kapúdán Alí Páshá, Súfi Alí Páshá, Yetúr Husain Páshá, Mahmúd Páshá, Mohammed Páshá the son of Láleh Mustafa Páshá, Abd-ur-rahmán Páshá, Dávud Páshá, Rús Hasan Páshá, Murád Pashá, Khádem Ja'fer Páshá, Dervísh Alí Páshá, Arab Ahmed Páshá.

Defterdárs and Nishánjís.

Murád Chelebí, Dervísh Chelebí the son of Bábá the painter, Lálá-zádeh, Mohammed Chelebí, Memí Chelebí, Abd-ul-ghafúr Chelebí, Moharrem Chelebi: Fírúz-beg the Nishánjí (lord privy seal), Mohammed Chelebí, nephew of the late Nishánjí Jelál-zádeh Beg.

The most distinguished of the Ulemá in his reign were,—Yehíá Efendí from Beshiktásh; Mevlena Mohammed Ben Abd-ul-waháb; Mevlena Musalih-ud-din; Mevlena Ja'fer Efendí; Mevlená Ata-allah Efendí; Mevlena Mohammed Chelebí; Ahmed Chelebí; Abd-ul-kerím Ben Mohammed, the son of the Shaikh-ul-Islám (grand muftí) Abú-sa'úd.

Physicians.

Mevlená Hakím Sinán, Hakím Othmán Efendí, Mevlená Hakím Isá, Hakím Is'hák, Hakím Bder-ud-dín Mohammed Ben Mohammed Kásúní, Tabíb Ahmed Chelebí.

Mesháiekh or Learned Men.

The Sheïkh Ala-ud-dín (may God sanctify his secret state!) was of Akseráï in Karamánia, and celebrated for his proficiency in the Ilm Jefer, or cabalistic art, Sheikh Abd ul Kerím, Sheikh Arif billah Mahmúd Chelebí, Sheikh Abú Sa'íd, Sheikh Hakím Chelebí, Sheikh Ya'kúb Kermání, Serkhosh Bálí Efendí, Sheikh Ramazán Efendí, surnamed Beheshtí, and Sheikh Mohammed Bergeví, who died in 981 (1573).

Conquests &c. in the reign of Sultán Selím II.

The tribe of Alián of Basra having rebelled was subjugated in 975 (1567). The expedition to Azhderhán (Astrachan) in 977 (1569). The conquest of Dasht Kipchák in 976 (1568). The conquest of Yemen and Aden, a second time, by Sinán in 977. Arrival of the Moors banished from Spain 978 (1570). Conquest of Cyprus with all its fortresses by Lálá Kara Mustafa Páshá, in the same year. Of Tunis and the African coast, by Kilij Alí Páshá in 977 (1569). Defeat of the grand imperial fleet at Lepanto in 979 (1571). Flight of Tátár Khán to Moscow. Renovation of Mekka in the same year. The recovery of Bosnia from the infidels in 982 (1574).

Sultán Selím died on the 18th of Sha'bán 982. He left many monuments of his grandeur, but none of them can be compared to the mosque which he erected at Adrianople: in truth there is not one equal to it even in Islámbol. He was succeeded by his own son Sultán Murád III., who ascended the throne in 982 (1574). His sons were the princes,—Mustafa, Osmán, Báyazíd, Selím, Jehángír, Abdullah, Abd-ur-rahmán, Hasan, Ahmed, Ya'kúb, A'lem-sháh, Yúsuf, Husain, Korkúd, Alí, Is'hak, Omar, Ala-ad-dín Dávud Khán. He had also twenty-four fair daughters, in all one hundred and twenty-seven children, who were killed after his death and buried beside him at Ayá Sofía. May God have mercy upon them all! Sultán Murád built the Koshk called Sinán Páshá's Koshk in 992 (1584).

Conquests &c. in the Reign of Murád.

Lálá Kara Mustafa Páshá's grand battle on the plain of Childer, 983 (1575), followed by the fall of the fortresses of Childer, Tomek, Khartín, Dákhil, Tiflís, Shebkí, Demir Kapú or Derbend, and the reduction of the province of Shirván, which was given to Ozdemir Zádeh Osmán Páshá. All these conquests were achieved in 991 (1583). The first royal expedition was in 990. The defeat of Imám Kúlí Khán in 991. In the same year the government of Magnesia was given to the Prince Mahmúd Khán, and in the following year Mohammed Gheráï, Khán of the Crimea, was deposed and put to death. In 992 the castle of Tabríz was rebuilt, the fortress of Ganja was taken, and the expedition against Baghdád under Jeghálah Zádeh. The conquest of Despúl, Nahávund, and Guhardán, in 995 (1586). The grand battle of Khádem Ja'fer Páshá, in the neighbourhood of Tabríz, 997 (1586). A peace concluded with the Sháh (of Persia), who sent one of his sons as a hostage, 1000 (1591). Capture of Bihka, and a new fortress built upon the Save in the same year; also the defeat of the grand army in Bosnia, and the conquest of Besperin and Polata. Defeat of the Mussulmán army near Istúlíní (Stuhlweissenburg).

Conquest of Tátá and Set-Martín (Saint Martin). Commencement of the siege of Raab (which was reduced some time after by Sinán Páshá), in 1003 (1594), when Sultán Mohammed Khán III. ascended the throne (being on a Friday the 16th of Jemází ul evvel). In 1002 Sultán Murád Khán, resigned the reins of government and joined the divine clemency. May God have mercy upon him!

Sultán Mohammed Khán son of Sultán Murád Khán was born at Magnesia in 976. The principal events and conquests of his reign are the following: In 1004 (1595) the Tátár Khán arrived in Walachia and subdued the rayás. In the same year Ja'fer Páshá delivered Temisvár from the infidels. In the following year Egra (Erla) was taken, and the army of the infidels routed in the plain of Shatúsh near Erla. In 1006 the infidels recover Yánuk (Raab). Wárad besieged by Satúrjí Hasan Páshá in 1007 (1698). Yemishjí Páshá was deposed and killed, and Jeghál eh Zádeh died after having been defeated by the Persians in 1011 (1602). In the following year the Persians took possession of Ganja and Shirwán; and Mohammed died on the 18th of Rajab. He built a mausoleum for himself in Islámból, and left numerous monuments in other towns of the empire, particularly at Mecca and Medina. The sending of two ship-loads of corn from Egypt to Mecca and Medina annually originated with him.

Sultán Ahmed Khán I., was born at Magnesia in 998 (1589). He was a fair child of four years, when he ascended the throne on the 18th of Rajab 1012 (1603). I, the humble writer of these pages, Evliya the son of Dervísh Mohammed, was born in the reign of this Sultán on the 10th of Moharrem 1020 (1611). Six years after my birth, the building of the new mosque (of Ahmed) was commenced, and in the same year the Sultán undertook the expedition to Adrianople: God be praised that I came into the world during the reign of so illustrious a monarch.

Sons of Sultán Ahmed.

Othmán; Mohammed, who was murdered by his brother Othmán, in the expedition to Hotín. Othmán was however unsuccessful and was also slain; thus was verified the sacred text, "as you give so shall you receive". Murád, afterwards the fourth Sultán of that name; Báyazíd, Soleïmán; these two were both strangled whilst Sultán Murád IV. was engaged in the expedition to Eriván. Ibrahím was the youngest son of Sultán Ahmed. May God extend his mercy to them all!

Grand Vezírs of Sultán Ahmed.

Yávuz Alí Páshá, was promoted from the government of Egypt to the rank of grand vezír. Mohammed Páshá, called also Sháhín Oghlí. Dervísh Páshá. Ghází Khoajeh Páshá; who exterminated the rebels in Anadolí. Nasúh Páshá. Dámád Mohammed Páshá was twice grand vezír, as was also Khalíl Páshá.

Vezírs of the Kubba (Cupola).

Káïmmakám Kásim Páshá. Khádem Ahmed Páshá. Háfiz Sárikjí Mustafá Páshá. Súfí Sinán Páshá. Khezr Páshá. Gúrjí Khádem Mohammed Páshá, who was made grand vezír in the time of Sultán Mustafa. Etmekjí Zádeh Ahmed Páshá. Kúrd Páshá. Gúzeljeh Mahmúd Páshá. Jegháleh Zádeh Sinán Páshá. Jegháleh Zádeh Mahmúd Páshá, son of Sinán Páshá.

Celebrated Divines.

Mollá Mustafa Efendí, was Shaikh ul Islám, when the Sultán ascended the throne. Mollá Sana'allah Efendí. Mollá Mohammed Efendí, son of Sa'd-ud-dín Efendí, known by the name of Chelebí Muftí. Mollá Shaikh ul Islám Asa'd Efendí. Mollá Mustafa Efendí, tutor to the Sultán. Mollá Káf Zádeh Efendí. Mollá Yehíá Efendí. Mollá Dámád Efendí. Mollá Kemál Efendí, better known by the name of Tásh Koprí Zádeh. Mollá Kehiyá Mustafá Efendí. Mollá Bostán Zádeh Mohammed Efendí. Mollá Husain Efendí. Mollá Ghaní Zádeh Mohammed Efendí.

Masháiekh or Learned Men.

Mahmúd of Uskudár (Scutari). Abdulmajíd of Sívás. Omar, known better by the name of Tarjumán Shaikh (interpreter). Shaikh Emír Ishtipí. Ibrahím, otherwise Jerráh Páshá, a disciple of the last-mentioned; Mussaleh ud-dín Nakshbendí, the Imám or chaplain of the Sultán.

Conquests &c. of the reign of Sultán Ahmed.

The grand vezír dies at Belgrade, and Bochkái appears in Hungary in the year 1012 (1604). Conquest of Osterghún (Gran); and Bochkái and Serkhúsh Ibrahim Páshá extend their depredations to the very walls of Vienna. Engagement between the rebels in Anadólí and Nasúh Páshá; the Káïm-makám Mustafa Páshá is executed. The grand vezír Súfí Sinán Páshá is deposed, 1014 (1605). Nasúh Páshá is appointed to conduct the expedition against Aleppo; Koja Mohammed Páshá is appointed to lead the expedition against the Persians and is afterwards created grand vezír. Murád Páshá, Dervísh Páshá, Bostánjí Ferhád Páshá, and Jelálí Murád Páshá, are all alternately made vezírs; and the execution of Dervísh Páshá, in 1015 (1606). Kapújí Murád Páshá is appointed commander of the forces sent to Haleb against Jánpúlád Zádeh; the country about Brúsa is laid waste by the rebel Kalender Oghlí; capture of Haleb by Murád Páshá; defeat of Kalender Oghlí; and the appearance of the rebel Múmjí, 1016 (1607). Yúsuf Páshá killed at Uskudár (Scutari) by the rebels; and the grand vezír sacks Tabríz and seventy other Persian towns 1019 (1610). Death of Murád Páshá at Chulenk near Díárbekr; Nasúh Páshá is made commander-in-chief in 1021 (1612). Betlen is installed king of Transylvania, which country is taken possession of, and 200,000 prisoners are carried off, besides immense plunder. In the same year the illustrious emperor undertook a journey to Adrianople. The cossacks of the black sea plunder and burn Sinope, and Nasúh Páshá being suspected is put to death, 1023 (1614). Mahmúd Páshá, his successor, returns without success from the siege of Eriván, in 1024 (1616). In 1026 (1616) Khalíl Páshá is created grand vezír, and the illustrious Sultán Ahmed dies in the month of Zilkadeh. During his auspicious reign Islámból enjoyed the greatest tranquility. One of his grandest monuments is the mosque which he built in the At-maidán (Hipodrome), which we are now about to describe and thus resume the description of the imperial mosques with which we commenced. It is situated on an elevated spot, its Kibla side being near the Chateldí gate, and commanding a view of the sea. Sultán Ahmed purchased five vezírs' palaces which stood on this spot, pulled them down, and with the blessed Mahmúd Efendí, of Scutari, and our teacher Evliya Efendí, laid the foundations of this mosque. The Sultán himself took a quantity of earth, and threw it upon the foundation. Evliya Efendí performed the functions of the Imám of the foundation-ceremony; Mahmúd Efendí those of the Kází (judge); Kalender Páshá those of the Mo'tamid (counsellor); and Kemán-kesh Alí Páshá those of the Názir (inspector). In three years they commenced the dome.

Description of the Mosque of Sultán Ahmed.

The cupola is seventy feet high and is supported by four massive pillars, and four demi cupolas. It has no large columns within like those of Ayá Sofíá and the Soleïmánieh. Along three sides of it runs a gallery (tabaka) for the congregation, supported by small columns, and over that a second gallery, from which is suspended a treble row of lamps reaching half way to the first gallery. The mahfil of the Moazzíns is supported by small pillars like the mahfil of the emperor. The minber, or pulpit, is of variegated marble and sculptured in the most tasteful manner. On the top of it is a most magnificent crown, and over that is suspended a golden banner. The pen fails in attempting to describe the beauty of the mehráb, on both sides of which are candlesticks, containing lighted candles each weighing twenty quintals. On the left side of the mehráb between two windows there is a fine view of a most extraordinary square rock, which is certainly one of the wonders of creation. All the windows are ornamented with painted glass; and behind the two pillars, as in the Soleïmánieh, there are fountains of ever-flowing water, where the faithful may perform their ablutions or satisfy their thirst. The mosque has five gates. On the right-hand corner is the gate of the Khatíb (or reader of the Khotba). On the left-hand corner, beneath the mehráb of the Sultán, is the gate of the Imám. Two lofty gates open on both sides of the building. The ascent to these four gates is by a flight of marble steps. The fifth and largest gate is that of the Kibla, facing the mehráb. No mosque can boast of such precious hanging ornaments as those of this, which by the learned in jewels are valued at one hundred treasuries of Egypt; for Sultán Ahmed being a prince of the greatest generosity and the finest taste, used all his jewels, and the presents which he received from foreign sovereigns, in ornamenting the mosque. The most extraordinary ornaments are the six emerald candelabra which are suspended in the emperor's mehráb, and which were sent as a present by Ja'fer Páshá, the governor of Abyssinia. The sockets, each of which weighs eight *okkas*, are suspended by golden chains, and terminate in golden feet with green enamel. The experienced and learned have estimated the value of each of these candelabra equal to one year's tribute of Rúmeïlí. In short, it is a most wonderful and costly mosque, and to describe it baffles the eloquence of any tongue. Some hundred copies of the Korán lying near the mehráb, on gilt desks inlaid with mother-o'-pearl, are presents from sultáns and vezírs. The library consists of 9,000 volumes marked with the toghra of the Sultán, the care of which is entrusted to the Mutavellí (curator) of the mosque. On the outside, facing the mehráb, is a most delightful garden, where the sweet notes of a thousand nightingales give life to the dead-hearted, and the fragrant odour of its flowers and fruits gratifies the senses of the faithful assembled to prayer. The size of the mosque is the same as that of the princes of Soleïmán. The court is a square paved with marble, and has stone benches running along the four sides. The windows are guarded with brass gratings: in the centre of the square plays a fountain of the purest water, for the use of the faithful: it is however only used for drinking, not for ablutions. The court has three gates. The kibla gate, facing the chief entrance and mehráb of the mosque, is a masterpiece of art, being of solid brass, twelve feet high, and the astonishment of all who behold it. On the brass plates which form this gate are carved oranges and arabesques, intermingled with flowers of pure silver and with precious stones, and ornamented with rings, locks, and bars of silver. It is indeed a most wonderful gate. Some say that it was brought from Osterghún (Grán), where it adorned the Roman church; but this is a mistake, for the famous gate at Osterghún was carried off when the infidels retook that city, and it now adorns, as the chief-door, the church of St. Stephen at Vienna.

The gate of this mosque was made under the superintendence of my father, Dervísh Mohammed, at the time when he was chief of the goldsmiths. The two inscriptions on brass were engraved by his own hand. On the outside of the windows of the court there are several covered porches supported by small columns, in which, when the assembly within is too great, many of the faithful perform their devotions; and the Hindú fakírs find shelter. The six lofty minárs of this mosque are divided into sixteen stories, because it is the sixteenth royal mosque of Islámból, and the founder of it, Sultán Ahmed, was the sixteenth of the Ottoman emperors. Two minárs rise on the right and left of the mehráb, two others on the north and south gates of the court, each three stories high, which make in all twelve stories. The roofs and gilded crescents, which are twenty cubits high, dazzle the eye with their splendour. The two minárs on the corners of the court are lower and have only two stories; their roofs are covered with lead. On the sacred nights these six minárs are lighted up with 12,000 lamps, so that they resemble as many fiery cypresses. The cupolas are all covered with lead. This mosque being richly founded, has seven hundred and fifty attendants attached to it. The tribute of Ghalata and many other pious bequests (wakf) constitute its revenue. The outside of the court is a large sandy level planted with trees, and surrounded by a wall which has eight gates. On the north is the gate of the college, and near it is the mausoleum of Sultán Ahmed. Three gates open towards the At-maidán (Hippodrome). All these gates are made of iron like those of a fortress. On the south-east of the At-maidán are the pious establishments belonging to the mosque, the kitchen for the poor (imáret), the dining-hall (dár-uz-ziáfat), the hospital (tímár-kháneh), and the fountain-house (sebíl-kháneh).

Sultán Ahmed died before the outer court, the mausoleum, and the college were completed. They were finished by his brother and successor Sultán Mustafá, who, however, being very weak-minded, was soon compelled to abdicate the throne in favour of his nephew Othmán Khán, the eldest of Sultán Ahmed's sons. He ascended the throne in the year 1027 (1617). In the same year Mohammed Gheráï Khán of the Crimea effected his escape from the Seven Towers, and fled to Právádí, where however he was retaken. The Moslem army marched to Eriván, and a peace was concluded with the Persians. In 1028 (1618) Súfí Mohammed Páshá became grand vezír, and in the following year he was succeeded by Kapúdán Alí Páshá. In the year 1030 the Bosphorus was frozen over; Othmán killed his brother; and Husain Páshá was made grand vezír.

The Imperial Expedition against Hotín.

Sultán Othmán having in 1030 (1620) failed in his attempt to reduce the fortress of Hotín, returned to Islámból, and in the following year he ordered the banners to be raised at Uskudár, as a sign of his marching to the southern provinces of the empire, to Syria and to Egypt. This caused a revolt amongst the troops, and the emperor finding no support, either in the seráï (palace) or in the barracks of the Janissaries, was thrust into a cart by the wrestler Bunyán and strangled within the walls of the Seven Towers. The Jebbehjí-báshí cut off one of his ears and carried it with the news of his murder to Dávud Páshá. His body was buried in the At-maidán in the mausoleum of Sultán Ahmed Khán. He was cut off by fate before he could leave any monument of his reign.

Sultán Mustafá now ascended the throne a second time, and commenced his reign by executing all those who had taken any share in the murder of Sultán Othmán. Khoaja Omar Efendí, the chief of the rebels, the Kizlar-ághá Soleïmán Aghá, the vezír Diláver Páshá, the Káïm-makám Ahmed Páshá, the defterdár Bákí Páshá, the segbán-báshí Nasúh Aghá, and the general of the Janissaries Alí Aghá, were cut to pieces. Dávud Páshá was created grand vezír because he was the son of Sultán Mustafá's sister. He was afterwards killed by Murád IV. In the same night the white eunuchs also cut their ághá into pieces, threw the body out, and afterwards suspended it by the feet on the serpent-column in the At-maidán.

The most distinguished divines during the reign of Sultán Othmán were: The Shaikh al Islám Asa'd Efendí; the Nakíb ul Ashraf or head of the Emírs Ghobárí Efendí; Zekeriá Zádeh Yahíá Efendí; and Arzí Zádeh Háletí Efendí.

The Mesháiekh, or learned men, were: Omar Efendí; Sívásí Efendí, and Dervísh Efendí.

Dávud Páshá was nominated grand vezír, but was instantly deposed because that on the very day of his appointment the rebels plundered some thousands of respectable houses. Lefkelí Mustafá Páshá received the seals, and kept them two months and eighteen days, he was subsequently appointed to the governments of Kastamúní and Nicomedia. He was of a gentle disposition, and unable to check the rebellious spirit of the times. The office of grand vezír was next conferred upon Kara Husain Páshá. This vezír assembled a diván of all the Mollás in the mosque of Mohammed II., but they were all murdered by the rebellious populace, and their bodies thrown into the wells in the court of the mosque. The rebellion increased every day, and every one disregarded the laws. Abáza Páshá also raised the standard of rebellion at Erzerúm; and the vezír Mahmúd Páshá was sent against him. The Persians took possession of Baghdád and Mosúl. Háfiz Ahmed Páshá returned without succeeding in taking Baghdád from the Persians. The Arabian tribe of Táï plundered the Persian camp. Kara Husain Páshá had the seals of office taken from him: they were transferred to Kemán-kesh Alí Páshá in 1032 (1622). After a reign of one year and four months, Sultán Mustafá was deposed a second time, and was succeeded by Sultán Murád IV. He was tall and corpulent, round-faced, with a black beard, open eye-brows, and grey eyes. He had large shoulders and a thin waist, strong arms, and a hand like the paw of a lion. No monarch of the Ottomans was ever so powerful in subduing rebels, maintaining armies, and in dealing justice. Being aware that the vezír Kemán-kesh Alí Páshá secretly favoured the rebels, he slew him without mercy. This vezír was a native of Hamíd, and left the royal harem when he was appointed governor of Baghdád and Díárbekr, whence he returned as successor to Kara Husain the grand vezír. He fell a victim to his own avarice, and was succeeded by Cherkess Mohammed Páshá, who died at Tokát in 1034 (1624). After him Háfiz Ahmed Páshá was made grand vezír. The Georgian Beg Máúro killed the Persian Khán Kárcheghäï, and subdued Georgia. Háfiz Ahmed Páshá besieged Baghdád, but to no purpose, in 1035 (1625). Khalíl Páshá received the seals of office a second time, and was appointed commander-in-chief against Abáza. Díshlenk Husain, who had marched against Kars to rescue it from the infidels, fell a martyr, and his whole army was put to rout. Khosrau Páshá was next made grand vezír, and took Erzerúm from the rebel Abáza, and Akhiska from the Persians. He brought Abáza before Sultán Murád in 1038 (1628), and obtained the royal pardon for him. He then marched to Sheherzúl, built the castle of Erkek Hamíd on the frontiers of Sheherzúl, reduced Mehrebán, plundered the Persian provinces and twenty castles near Báerján, and laid waste the suburbs of Hamadán and Dergezín in the year 1039 (1629). The year after, Khosrau Páshá succeeded in opening the trenches before Baghdád, but it being the middle of winter, he was obliged to raise the siege and to retreat to Hella and Mosúl. He was then deposed, and his office was given a second time to Háfiz Ahmed Páshá, whilst he himself was executed at Tokút. Rajab Páshá was made grand vezír; and the defterdár Mustafá Páshá was hanged with his head downwards in the At-maidán. Háfiz Ahmed Páshá was stabbed in the Sultán's presence, and cut to pieces. The Aghá of the Janissaries, Hasan Khalifeh, and Músá Chelebí the emperor's favourite, were both put to death. Yassí Mohammed Páshá was created a vezír in 1041 (1631). Sultán Murád had a dream in which he received a sword from the hand of Omar, with which he slew the Shaikh al Islám Husain, and then with a bismillah (in the name of God) fell upon the rebels and killed them all. In 1044 Sultán Murád marched to Eriván, and took Tabríz and the town of Eriván in seven days; he left Murtezá Páshá with a garrison of 40,000 men, and returned to Islámbol. His entrance was celebrated in 1045 (1634) by a festival of seven days. The ill-favoured Sháh (of Persia) however returned and laid siege to Eriván, which being left without sufficient strength, after a siege of seven months fell into the hands of the infidels, who put the whole of the garrison to the sword. Sultán Murád, on receiving the melancholy news, took the seals from Mohammed Páshá and appointed him governor of Silistria. The seals were transferred to Bairám Páshá, who however died soon after, and was succeeded by Tayyár Páshá. To him was entrusted all the necessary preparations for the expedition against Baghdád, which was undertaken by the emperor in person. Tayyár Páshá was killed during the siege, which lasted forty days. He was succeeded by the Kapúdán Kara Mustafá Páshá. Melek Ahmed Páshá, late salihdár, or sword-bearer of the Sultán, was appointed to the command of Díárbekr, and Kúchúk Hasan Páshá to that of Baghdád, with a garrison of 40,000 men. By the decree of God, when after the fall of Baghdád a great number of Kizilbáshes (red-heads or Persians) had assembled and were preparing to make an attack at one of the gates, a large powder magazine exploded, and thus the blood of the true believers which had been shed at Eriván was fully avenged. Kara Mustafá Páshá the grand vezír, and my lord Melek Ahmed Páshá, were sent to Derneh and Derteng, to conclude the treaty with the Persians, and to fix the boundary lines. Sultán Murád Khán, next went to Díárbekr, where in one day he put to death the daughter of Kímájí Ma'án Oghlí, and the Shaikh of Rúmieh. He then returned to the Porte of Felicity (Constantinople), on which occasion seven days were spent in general festivity. About this time Sultán Murád, having repented of his wine-drinking propensity, by way of expiation, resolved upon an expedition against the infidels of Malta, and ordered five hundred galleys, two large máonas, and one admiral's ship (báshtirda) to be built. This same year the grand vezír Mustafá Páshá returned to Constantinople, and the emperor, forgetting his vows of repentance, again fell into the vice of drunkenness, and his royal constitution being thoroughly weakened, he died after having been lord of the carpet (*i.e.* confined to bed) fourteen days. May God have mercy upon him! He was buried in the mausoleum of his illustrious grandfather Sultán Ahmed, in the At-maidán. Several chronograms of his death are inscribed by Júrí, on the walls of the inner apartments in the seráï. He had thirty-two children, of whom only one, the Sultána Esmahán Kíá, remained alive at his death. She too died after her marriage with Melek Ahmed Páshá, and was buried at Ayá Sofía between Sultán Ibráhím and Sultán Mustafá. Sultán Murád's reign having been extremely turbulent, and being constantly engaged in warlike preparations in every quarter, he had no opportunity of raising to himself any monument of importance in Islámbol. The only public work executed in his reign was the repairing of the walls of Islámbol, which was undertaken by his express orders during his absence at the siege of Eriván by the Káïm-makám Bairám Páshá. He repaired the castles of Mosúl, Sheherzúl, Chengí-ahmed, Tenedos, and of the Bosphorus, and at Islámból the Gul-jámi' (rose-mosque).

Description of the Gul-Jámi'.

This is a very ancient mosque, and was known in the times of Harún-ur-rashíd, Omar ben 'Abdu-l-'azíz, Moslemah, Sultán Yelderím Báyazíd, and Sultán Mohammed the conqueror. In the reign of Sultán Murád Khán a great earthquake so shook it that its foundations were completely destroyed, and the emperor immediately undertook to repair it. Several thousand workmen were employed upon it, and in seven years it was completed. Several small cupolas were added to the principal one, whence it assumed the appearance of a rose, and thence its name. It was also washed with an hundred measures of rose-water. The mehráb and minber are extremely plain. There are no granite columns in it as in the other mosques. On account of the great antiquity of this mosque, prayers in distress for rain and on extraordinary occasions are offered up in it. On both sides of the gate of the Kibla (facing the mehráb) there are benches. There is no court-yard. The mosque has only one minár of but one story high; for the original building having been destroyed by an earthquake, they were afraid to erect any lofty building upon the spot.

Besides the above mosque, Murád built two new castles on the Bosphorus, near the entrance to the Black Sea, with an arsenal and a mosque proportionate to their size. At Kandillí-bághcheh he built a large koshk, another at Istávros, and one in the gardens of Uskudár (Scutari), which was called the koshk of Eriván.

Chronological account of the principal Events during the Reign of Sultán Murád IV.

Sultán Mustafá Khán ascended the throne on the deposition of his brother the unfortunate Othmán, who though he was considered weak-minded, was rather an intelligent prince, but unfortunately had not sufficient strength to extinguish the fire of sedition which had been kindled in his time, nor to subdue the revolutionary spirit of his troops. The Janissaries at the instigation of one of their ághás, Kara Mazák, gave the seals to Dávud Páshá, afterwards to Kara Husain Páshá, and then to Lefkelí Mustafa Páshá. The latter having also failed in quelling the riots, was deposed after having been seventy-eight days in office: and the rebels then transferred the seals to Gúrjí Mohammed Páshá. But as he was detected in making an improper use of the public money, the seals were returned to Kara Husain Páshá. This person was a great tyrant, and having in a royal diván, in the presence of the two great judges, ordered two hundred lashes of the bastinado to be inflicted upon a Mollá, the whole body of the Ulemá, with the Shaikh-al-Islám, assembled in the mosque of Sultán Mohammed II. The mufti, however, made his escape, under the pretence that he was going to remonstrate with the grand vezír, who in the mean time having heard of this assemblage, ordered his own servants, those of the treasury, and some troops, to assail the assembled Ulemá. The result was that many hundreds of the Ulemá were slain, and the wells in the court of the mosque of Sultán Mohammed were filled with dead bodies. These affairs having become known in the provinces, Abáza Páshá rebelled at Erzerúm, and Háfiz Ahmed Páshá at Díárbekr. It having been rumoured that, in order to avenge the innocent blood of Sultán Othmán, Abáza had killed all the Janissaries at Erzerúm, Jegháleh Zádeh was appointed commander against Abáza, and Kara Mazák ághá of the Janissaries; but they proceeded no farther than Brúsa, fearing they had not sufficient strength to meet the rebel. The Persians taking advantage of these favourable opportunities, made an inroad with 30,000 men, and with the assistance of Chopúr Bekirzádeh took possession of Baghdád and Mosúl, in the year 1033 (1623). Kemán-kesh Alí Páshá was raised to the rank of grand vezír. He had been one of the lower officers of the Janissaries, and had raised himself to the honour of an alliance with one of the daughters of Sultán Ahmed. The Janissaries and Sipáhís now united, and Kemán-kesh was made the tool of their bloody designs. The principal inhabitants, however, of the city, the Ulemá, and the people of the seráï, were afraid to appear either at the mosques or at the baths. At last the chiefs of the troops began to meditate the change of their emperor; but as the public treasury had been exhausted by three general donations to the troops since the time of Sultán Ahmed's reign, they swore amongst themselves to dispense with the usual largess, and raised Sultán Murád to the throne, on the 14th of Zilka'deh 1032. A new aspect was now given to the capital, and old and young rejoiced in the auspicious event. On the following day Sultán Murád repaired to the mosque of Ayiúb, where two swords were girded on him; one being that of Sultán Selím, and the other that of the blessed Prophet (on whom be the peace of God!): no monarch was ever girt in this manner. On his return he entered by the Adrianople gate, and in passing he saluted the people who had assembled in crowds on his right and left, and received him with loud acclamations. He then proceeded to the seráï, in the inner apartment of which he saluted the Khirka-sheríf, or cloak of the Prophet; placed on his head the turban of Yúsúf or Joseph, (on whom be peace!) which had been brought to Islámbol from the treasure of the Egyptian Sultán Ghúrí; he then offered up a prayer of two inclinations, in which he prayed that he might be acceptable to God and the people, and be enabled to perform important services to religion and to the state. Though young in years (being only four years), he was remarkable for prudence and intelligence. The Khás-oda-báshí (master of the inner chamber), the Khazíneh-dár-báshí (chief treasurer), the Khazíneh Kátibí (secretary of the treasury), and the Khazíneh Kehiyásí (deputy of the treasurer) now approached his presence, and invited him, as is usual on such occasions, to visit the treasury. Dervísh Mohammed Zelellí, the father of the humble author, happening to be present at the time, entered the treasury with them. There were no golden vessels to be seen, and besides a quantity of lumber, there were found only six purses of money (30,000 piastres), a bag of coral, and a chest of china-ware. On seeing this, Sultán Murád filled the empty treasury with his tears, and having made two prostrations in prayer, he said "Inshallah, please God! I will replenish this treasury with the property of those who have spoiled it, and establish fifty treasuries in addition." He contrived, however, the same day to raise 3,040 purses for the usual largess, which was distributed amongst the troops notwithstanding their oath not to accept of it. That same night Sultán Murád had a dream, in which he saw Omar, who girt a sword about him, and unsheathing it, put it into his hand, and said: "Fear not Murád!" On awakening from his sleep, he banished his uncle Sultán Mustafá to Eskí Seráï, telling him at the same time to pray for his (Murád's) prosperity. Sultán Murád made many excursions in disguise throughout the city, accompanied by Melek Ahmed Aghá his sword-bearer, and Vujúd the Bostánjí Báshí, on which occasions many riotous persons and robbers were executed and their heads stuck upon poles. Murád was the most bloody of the Ottoman Sultáns. He prohibited all the coffee, wine, and búza-houses, and every day some hundreds of men were executed for transgressing this order.

In Anatolia, Abáza Páshá reduced the strength of the disaffected Janissaries and Sipáhís by numerous executions. The remainder of the rebels desiring to be enrolled amongst the troops, were sent into the provinces, where they gradually disappeared: some having been executed, others became students, porters or dervíshes, and others migrated. In the year 1033 (1623) the Shaikh ul Islám Yehiyá Efendí was degraded at the instigation of the grand vezír Kemán Kesh Alí Páshá, and Ahmed Efendí was appointed to succeed him. The vezírs Khalíl and Gúrjí Mohammed were imprisoned in the same year, but were liberated on the Sultán's being convinced that they were not concerned in the rebellion of Abáza Páshá. But Kemán Kesh, presuming upon his having been the means of raising the Sultán to the throne, lost sight of the respect due to his sovereign, and engaged in many disputes with him: he was therefore imprisoned in a part of the palace, called the Sircheh-seráï, and afterwards put to death. Cherkess Mohammed Páshá was named commander-in-chief against Abáza Páshá, and marched towards Wán. He was a most faithful and amiable man, and was unequalled by any vezír. The same year he gave battle to Abáza Páshá near Cæsarea, and forced him to retreat to Erzerúm, where he took up his residence. Cherkess Mohammed died in 1034, and was buried at Márdín. His successor, Háfiz Ahmed Páshá, appointed Khosrau Páshá Aghá of the Janissaries. In the same year Karchaghái Khán was routed by the prince of Georgia, and brought before Háfiz Ahmed Páshá, then at Díárbekr, whence he was sent, with all the drums and standards which had been taken, to Sultán Murád. Mauro, the prince of Georgia, was invested with a robe of honour.

The siege of Baghdád having commenced, the Moslem troops had the city before them, and behind, the camp of the prince I'ísá, the son of the Persian Sháh. The latter found means to throw twenty thousand Mazanderání rotops into the castle, and made a night attack upon the Moslems. The Ottoman army being thus between two fires, suffering from the greatest scarcity of provisions, and surrounded by deserts, was glad to avail itself of an opportunity to make a safe retreat to Díárbekr. The Sultán being highly displeased at this movement, dismissed Háfiz Páshá, and gave the seals a second time to Khalíl Páshá. Whilst the troops were in winter quarters at Tokát, intelligence was received that Akhiska had fallen into the hands of the enemy. Khalíl Páshá immediately despatched Díshlen Husain Páshá with ten thousand chosen men, and wrote at the same time by the express orders of the emperor to Abáza Páshá, directing him to march with Husain Páshá to relieve Akhiska. Abáza, however, fearing the whole was a plot, and supposing that Husain was sent against him, invited him to a feast in the castle, where he murdered him, and attacked his troops, many thousands of whom quaffed the cup of martyrdom, and the remainder fled naked and in the greatest distress to Tokát. The news having reached Constantinople, and Abáza's rebellion being evident, an imperial order was issued to all the vezírs and Páshás to besiege Abáza Páshá in Erzerúm, under the direction of the grand vezír Khalíl Páshá. As, however, they had not much artillery, the Ottoman army suffered great inconvenience from the frequent attacks of Abáza from the city, and many thousands of the Janissaries fell. In this state, a tremendous storm of snow buried the tents, and a general disaffection arising among the troops, the siege was raised, and they retreated, pursued by Abáza's men. At Habs and Mámákhátún they were overtaken by the enemy, who cut off the hands and feet of many thousands of the Ottomans, and threw them into a well, which to this day is called the well of hands and feet (Cláh Dast ú Pá). This well is near the tomb of Mámákhátún. Sultán Murád was greatly displeased with this news, and in 1038 (1628) transferred the seals of office to Khosrau Páshá the Bosnian. Abáza Páshá (not the rebel, but the salihdár or sword-bearer of the Sultán) was named ághá of the Janissaries, and sent against Abáza the rebel, to demand the evacuation of Akhiska. He stopped before Erzerúm to prevent any communication, and to guard the trenches, lest Abáza, when hard pressed, should evince any inclination to deliver the fortress to the Persians. Forty thousand brave warriors were employed in attacking it, with seven batteries of heavy guns. Many of the garrison now began to come over to the Ottoman camp, where they were received with great kindness. This kind treatment had so good an effect, that the whole garrison surrendered, and claimed the powerful protection of the Osmánlís. The ulemá and all the inhabitants now came out of the city and implored Khosrau Páshá to spare them, according to the saying, "Pardon is the choicest flower of victory." On the 9th of Moharrem the victorious army entered the city, and before winter set in they repaired all the walls. Kana'án Páshá was left to keep it with a garrison of fifty thousand men. By the assistance of Mauro Khán the fortress of Akhiska was also reduced; and the government of Childer was given to Sefer Páshá.

When the news of these splendid victories reached the imperial ear, orders were given to bring the rebel Abáza Páshá before the imperial stirrup. It was on the day of a grand diván, when many thousands were assembled before their august emperor. The emperor said: "O thou infidel! wherefore hast thou for so many years cruelly oppressed the faithful, and by thy obstinacy and rebellion caused the destruction of so many thousands of brave men?" Abáza Páshá kissed the ground three times, and said: "My emperor! for the sake of the holy prophet, and by the souls of thy illustrious ancestors, I beseech thee to show favour to me, and pardon me whilst I lay before thee the grief of my heart." The emperor having graciously granted this request, Abáza proceeded as follows: "My emperor! at the time your brave brother Othmán of glorious memory, actuated by a zeal for the true faith, undertook the campaign of Hotín, in order to be avenged on his enemies, he saw that the Janissaries, though few in number, were well paid. He wished to review them, but they would not consent. Afterwards, when with a thousand difficulties the emperor opened the trenches, the Janissaries made it as plain as day that they were the enemies of the faith, inasmuch as they constantly associated with the infidels, to whom they sent food, and received wine in return. The governor of Bude, Kara Kásh Páshá, was killed, and his army dispersed, without their offering the least assistance; and they even sent to the Tátár Khán, who was coming to the assistance of the imperial army, requesting him to slacken his march instead of accelerating it. Some of the vezírs seized several spies who were paid by the Janissaries, brought them into the presence of your brother Othmán, and killed them before his eyes. It was in this manner that the siege of so small a fortress as Hotín was abandoned by their taking to flight. Seven thousand purses, and many hundred thousands of Ottoman subjects were lost, together with the glory of the Sultán, against whom they rebelled on his return to Islámbol. When Sultán Othmán went to their mosque, the Orta-jáme', he was assailed with the most abusive language; and when he held by one of the windows on the left side of the mehráb, whilst he earnestly appealed for assistance from the people of Mohammed, an abject wretch, worse than an infidel, and of the ignominious name of Pehleván, thus insulted him: 'Othmán

Chelebí! you are a fine boy; come along with us to Yúsuf Sháh's coffee-house or to our barracks.' Othmán Khán not accepting this impudent invitation, the audacious fellow struck the arm with which the emperor held the window a blow which broke it. From the mosque they carried him in a cart to the Seven Towers, where he was barbarously treated, and at last most cruelly put to death by Pehleván. Whilst his sacred body was exposed upon an old mat, the Jebbehjí-báshí, Káfir Aghá cut off his right ear, and a Janissary one of his fingers, for the sake of the ring upon it. The former brought the ear and the finger to Dávud Páshá, who rewarded the bearer of such acceptable news with a purse of money. The Jebbehjí-báshí said to Dávud Páshá: 'My lord, may your name be everlasting in the world, and may the family of the Dávuds always be in power. For this wish he was rewarded with the place of ághá of the Janissaries, and actually entered into a plan to raise his own son, Soleïmán Beg, to the throne of the Ottomans; and promised the Janissaries that, instead of the blue cloth of Salonik, they should wear fine scarlet cloth. This story having circulated throughout the city, it raised the indignation and excited the greatest grief in the hearts of all true believers and faithful subjects. A mob of Ajem-oghláns and Janissaries assembled at the mosque of Sultán Mohammed II., and there killed many thousands of the learned and worthy divines, and threw their bodies into the wells: the houses also of many honest men were entirely pillaged. On hearing of these dreadful events, I endeavoured to alleviate the grief of my heart, caused by the martyrdom of such a monarch as Sultán Othmán. It was then that a zeal to show I was deserving of his bread and salt, took possession of your lálá (tutor) Abáza, and I instantly resolved upon avenging the innocent blood of Sultán Othmán. Having at that time been appointed governor of Erzerúm by your uncle Sultán Mustafá, I was in the habit of offering up my daily prayers in the mosque of the late Láleh Páshá. I heard the rebellious Janissaries saying, 'Abáza Láleh, you go to the kilísíá (church) of your nearest relation Láleh.' Thus they dared to call that noble mosque a church! When I went through the city, they cried out 'oush! oush!' as if they were speaking to barking dogs; but it was intended for me. I pretended, however, to take no notice of it, and continued to show them many favours. Still, my emperor, I was insulted in a thousand ways. They brought kabáb (roast meat) and wine to the diván, and said, 'Abáza, we are come to your play-house to make a feast, to dance and sing to your music.' I suffered even this profanation of the imperial diván, and provided them with refreshments. They then began to plunder the houses and shops of the wealthy, and I have, my emperor, the legal attestations of the depredations they committed in this way." Here Abáza handed over to the Sultán the legal documents. "My emperor," he continued, "this mutinous state of the Janissaries did not escape the notice of the Persian sháh, who taking advantage of it, besieged the fortress of Akhiska. I immediately resolved to relieve it: but not a single Janissary would move from the wine tavern, or the buzá-house; and the consequence was, that the Persians took possession of this noble fortress, which had been so gloriously taken by Sultán Selím. My beglerbegs being like myself disgusted with the dastardly conduct of the Janissaries, united themselves with me by solemn oath to avenge the blood of Sultán Othmán, and each swore to subdue the Janissaries under him. On an appointed day I fulfilled my oath, took possession of the interior fortress of Erzerúm, subdued the Janissaries, and became their master. In the mean time the begs and vezírs, who had taken the same obligation, deserted me. From that hour my affairs have every day become worse. This, my emperor, is a true statement of my conduct. Whatever I have done has been from a pure zeal, for the best interests of the Sublime Porte. Your servant Abáza, a poor slave bought for seventy piastres, is not ambitious to obtain dominion in the world through rebellion."

Thus did Abáza, without fear, boldly detail all the particulars of his conduct, in the presence of the emperor and many thousand spectators. He then kissed the ground, crossed his hands over his breast, bowed his head, and was silent. The emperor listened to his discourse with the greatest attention, and when reminded of the melancholy martyrdom of Sultán Othmán he shed tears of blood, and sighed so deeply, that all who were present lost their senses. The Sultán proceeded to ask him: "But after the battle with my lálá Cherkess Mohammed Páshá at Cæsarea, when I not only pardoned you, but gave you the government of Erzerúm, why did you kill so many excellent men that were sent with Díshlen Husain Páshá? why did you make war against my lálá, Khalíl Páshá? and why did you not give up the castle, and come to rub your forehead on my stirrup? Abáza replied: "My Sultán! not one of those generals who were sent against me, knew how to keep their troops in proper discipline. They plundered wherever they went, like the notorious rebels, Yázíjí Kalender Oghlí and Sa'íd Arab; they crowded every day round the tent of their general with some new claims; they were all a seditious set, to whom I was afraid to trust myself; and instead of devoting myself to a rebellious multitude, who knew no law, I thought it much safer to oppose them as open enemies. When, however, I heard that Lálá Khosrau Páshá was coming from Tokát with an imperial commission, and my spies unanimously bearing witness to his justice, and his determined opposition to the villains, I knew that he was a perfect man, and I was overawed by his power and dignity. He came to Erzerúm like a wolf against a sheep, opened the trenches, and attacked the fortress with seven batteries. Night and day I kept my eyes on the trenches, but never saw a single man leave them to go to plunder the villages, the camp being abundantly supplied with provisions by the peasants in the surrounding villages. I saw none of the villages on fire; but every evening the fátihat (the first chapter of the Korán) was read in every tent, and the prayers were offered up at the five appointed hours. Former commanders never maintained any discipline in their camp; the neighbouring villages were destroyed by fire; and when after three months they effected an entrance into the trenches, they fired a few guns and returned to riot in their tents, from which were heard, night and day, the sound of musical instruments, and the shouts of Armenian women and boys. Observing this state of affairs, I made numerous nocturnal excursions, from which I generally returned with plenty of plunder, and a great number of Janissaries heads with which I adorned the towers of the castle. As winter came on they deserted their commander, and returned to their homes. When, however, I saw the just and upright character of Khosrau Páshá, I said, "Here is a commander who justly deserves the name!" and I hastened to his camp to offer my obeisance. Praise be to God, I was not mistaken in my good opinion of him, for after so long a stay in the midst of an army numerous as the waves of the sea, I have been conducted in safety to the presence of my emperor, whose commands I now wait. "Behold what my zeal for your glory has urged me to do! The sword hangs over my neck: I have come from Erzerúm as your devoted victim!" Saying this, he knelt down with his face directed towards the kibla, and began to recite the confession of faith. When the whole court, the vezírs, the ulemá, the muftí Yahia, and the grand vezír Khosrau Páshá, perceived that the emperor was pleased with Abáza's humble submission, and that his anger had subsided, they threw themselves at the foot of the throne, beseeching pardon for Abáza. This intercession had the desired effect: the emperor not only pardoned Abáza, but appointed him governor of Bosnia. The vezírs, emírs, and senior officers of the army that had undertaken the expedition against Abáza, were rewarded with robes of honour. Abáza was soon after removed from the government of Bosnia, to that of Silistria. After an unsuccessful expedition against Kamienik he was recalled to Islámból, where he soon became the most confidential adviser of the Sultán. One day when the Janissaries were dissatisfied with the Sultán and would not eat their soup, Abáza said, "Give me leave, my emperor, and I will make them eat not only their soup, but even the dishes." Sultán Murád having given him permission, he appeared in the diván; on which a murmur was heard from the ranks of the Janissaries, who began to eat their soup with such avidity as if they would have swallowed the very dishes: so great was the awe which his appearance and name excited amongst the Janissaries. When an expedition against Erzerúm was proposed, a report was spread amongst the Janissaries that Abáza was kept only to ruin them. "If the emperor wishes to conquer Erzerúm," said they, "let him do so with Abáza." This mutinous spirit of the Janissaries at last forced the Sultán to submit to them, and to give up Abáza, who was one morning dressed in a white shirt and delivered over to the Bostánjí Báshí, by whom he was put to death. His body was publicly interred near the mosque of Sultán Báyazíd, not far from the ink-makers' row in the district of Murád Páshá. Thus he received according to his actions. May God have mercy upon him!

A curious Anecdote.

In the year 1056 (1646), when Soleïmán Páshá was governor of Erzerúm, and I, the humble Evliyá, was with him, Abáza Páshá again made his appearance on his return from Persia. Soleïmán Páshá immediately assigned him an allowance, and reported the case to the Sublime Porte. Abáza began to find out his old acquaintances, and soon became the chief of a party to whom he related all his remarkable adventures. According to his account, Sultán Murád being obliged to yield to the Janissaries, who refused to march to Erzerúm so long as Abáza was in the camp, took another man, whom he dressed in a white shirt, and had him executed instead of Abáza, by the Oják Bostánjí-báshí. Abáza himself was taken in a galley to Gallipolí, whence he sailed on board an Algerine ship-of-war. He soon afterwards obtained the command of that ship, and for seven years was a formidable pirate in the Archipelago. On the very day on which Sultán Murád died, he was beaten at the Cape of Temenis by a Danish ship, and remained seven years a prisoner amongst the Danes. He was then sold to the Portuguese, with whom for three years he sailed about in the Indian ocean, and touched at the Abyssynian coast, where he lost his ship. He thence went to India, China, the country of the Calmucks, Khorásán, Balkh, Bokhárá, Isfahán, and Erzerúm, to the governor of which town he related the whole of his adventures, in a manner which excited my greatest astonishment. Soleïmán Páshá's report having reached the emperor Sultán Ibrahím, he asked the Oják Bostánjí Báshí (the chief executioner) whether he recollected having executed Abáza in the time of Sultán Murád. The executioner replied that he had executed a person in a white shirt whose name was said to be Abáza, that the usual ablutions after his death were performed by the imám of the imperial garden, and that the body was interred at the monument of Murád Páshá. A thousand strange reports having been raised by this story, a Kapíjí-báshí was immediately dispatched with a khat-sheríf (imperial warrant); and on his arrival at Erzerúm, he seized Abáza at the gate of the music chamber of the lower diván, severed his head from his body, and carried it to Constantinople. Soleïmán Páshá was removed from Erzerúm, and his government was given to Mohammed Páshá, the son of Mustafá Páshá, who was hanged. Derzí Mustafá Aghá came in his stead as Musallim, and he appointed me the inspector of the charcoal to a caravan proceeding to Eriván, for which place I set out. Farewell.

Abáza Páshá having been subdued in the year 1038 (1628), the grand vezír

Khosrau Páshá marched with an immense army to plunder the provinces of Persia, and never even thought of Baghdád. Whilst he was on his way, and had even resolved upon attacking Isfahán, he received an imperial order to the following effect: "Shouldst thou bring the Sháh himself in chains to my imperial stirrup, I should not be satisfied; if thou considerest thy head necessary to thee, conquer Baghdád, the ancient seat of the Khalifat, and deliver from the hands of the despicable Persians, the tombs of No'amán ben Thábet, the great imám and founder of our sect, and of the Shaikh Abdul Kádir Jílání." On account of this imperial command, the trenches of Baghdád were opened on the 17th of Sefer 1040 (1630); and the siege was continued for forty days. The winter however having set in, the Ottoman army was obliged to raise the siege, and to retire to Hella, Mosúl, and Márdín. In the beginning of spring, whilst Khosrau Páshá was on his march to Eriván, he received an imperial firmán recalling him to Constantinople, and Murtezá Páshá was appointed governor of Díárbekr. Khosrau Páshá fell sick on his arrival at Tokát, and was murdered whilst in bed by Murtezá Páshá, in the month of Sha'bán 1041 (1631). On the 18th of Rajab in the same year, Háfiz Páshá was again appointed grand vezír. In the same month the Janissaries mutinied at Islámból, and attacked the grand vezír Háfiz Páshá within the imperial gate near the hospital. He retreated into the hospital, the gate of which he closed, and thence fled to the imperial garden, took the turban and robes of ceremony of the Bostánjí-báshí, and appeared before the Sultán, to whom he stated that some villains had attacked him, but that by urging his horse against them, he had dispersed them all. Next day, however the rebellion assumed a more serious aspect; the Janissaries began by taking Háfiz Páshá from the emperor's presence, and in order to avenge the death of Khosrau Páshá, they stabbed him in the cheek with a dagger, and then tore him into a thousand pieces. In the month of Rajab 1040 (1630) Rajab Páshá was made grand vezír; and Husain Efendí, Shaikh-ul-Islám or muftí. Rajab Páshá was a Bosnian by birth, had been created Bostánjí-báshí with the rank of vezír, and afterwards Kapúdán Páshá. He took three large English ships in the Mediterranean, and attacked three hundred Cossack boats in the black sea, and upsetting the crosses, brought all the boats to Islámbol. When Khalíl Páshá, the grand vezír, was appointed commander of the expedition against Abáza, Rajab was Káïm-makám of Constantinople, and Hasan Páshá performed the duties of Kapúdán Páshá. He built a castle near the mouth of the river Ouzí (Dneiper), and added a square fort to the castle of Oczakov. He was also Káïm-makám during the vezírship of Khosrau Páshá, and was the cause of Háfiz Páshás being killed by the Janissaries. Músá Chelebí, one of the Sultán's favourites, was also attacked at his instigation by the rebels; he was killed and his body thrown out on the At-maidán in 1041 (1631). Hasan Chelebí, the Aghá of the Janissaries, having been found concealed in a corner, was put to death by the imperial executioner. In the beginning of Ramazán the rebels discovered the place where the defterdár Borák Mustafá Páshá was concealed, killed him, and hanged him on a tree in the At-maidán. It being evident that Rajab Páshá was a traitor, having taken the part of the rebels who killed Músá Chelebí, he was therefore hanged on his entering the diván. On that day I, the poor Evliya, was present with my father. The office of grand vezír was given to Tabání Yassí Mohammed Páshá, who had just returned from Egypt. He was an Albanian by birth, and a dependant of Mustafá Aghá, the chief eunuch of Sultán Othmán. He left the imperial harem to go as governor of Egypt, whence he was recalled to receive the seals, and was at last killed whilst grand vezír, because he had not hastened to the relief of Eriván, and had been found concerned in the disturbances of Moldavia and Valachia. He was buried near the monument of Eyyúb. Bairám Páshá was made grand vezír in his place. He had been brought up as a Janissary at Constantinople. During the vezírship of Tabání Yassí Mohammed Páshá, Sultán Murád, following the custom of his ancestors, went to Adrianople, to enquire into the state of the provinces, and to receive the renewed treaty of peace with the emperor of Germany. When Tabání Yassí Mohammed Páshá received his appointment as commander in the expedition to Eriván, Bairám Páshá was Káïm-makám. On this occasion the Sultán himself repaired to Uskudár (Scutari), and began to reign with the wisdom of Solomon. My father, an old and experienced man, who had been present at the siege of Siget, received the imperial command to join the army, and I, the humble Evliya, accompanied him. Besides my father there were several other old men, who had witnessed the victories of Sultán Soleïmán; such as Gulábí Aghá, who lived in the Unkapáni (flour-market), and whose story has been related above in the description of the mosque of Ayá Sofiá; Abdí Efendí, the inspector of the kitchen, who lived in the house of Brinjí Zádeh at Zírek Básh; Kozú Alí Aghá; and Isá Aghá. Aged and respectable men like these were carried in litters, and were consulted during the march on all important questions. The army marched from Konia to Kaisería (Cæsarea), and thence to Sívás, where the feast of the Korbán (sacrifice) was celebrated. Here Mustafá Páshá, the emperor's favourite, was promoted to the rank of second vezír, and called into the diván. The army then continued its march to Erzerúm. Besides the guns provided by the commander-in-chief, there were forty large guns dragged by two thousand pairs of buffaloes. The army entered the castle of Kázmaghán, and halted under the walls of Eriván in the year 1044 (1634). The trenches were opened the same day on seven sides; the batteries were raised against the place called Mahánat Báïrí, and for seven days not a moment's rest was given either to the camp or fortress. This was most successful, and filled the hearts of the faithful army with joy. By the favour of God, the victory was certain: the khán of Eriván Emírgúneh Oghlí, surrendered by capitulation, and was appointed as a vezír of two tails to the government of Haleb (Aleppo). The breaches in the walls were repaired, and Murtezá Páshá was left in garrison with 40,000 men. Khoaja Kana'án was appointed commander against Akhiska, which was reduced in the same month; and the Sultán left Eriván to plunder the Persian provinces. On the sixth day he entered the beautiful city of Tabríz, where the Tátárs of the Ottoman army caused terrible havock, making the inhabitants slaves, and levelling the houses with the ground so that not a stone was left upon another. The lowest servants of the Ottoman army, such as the muleteers, camel-drivers, grooms, tent-pitchers, flambeau-bearers, and water-carriers, became rich as Afrásíáb with the public and private treasures. Sultán Murád visited the beautiful gardens and koshks of Tabríz, particularly the garden celebrated by the name of Khíábání. By his orders the army entered this garden, and in a moment brought to the ground all its houses and koshks, not leaving a single atom upon the page of existence; they also cut down all the trees as if they had been armed with the hatchet of Ferhád or the battle-axe of Moslem. The beautiful valley was changed into a desert, in which not the smallest vestige of cultivation could be seen, as if it had remained a barren wilderness ever since the descent of Adam upon the earth.

From Tabríz the Sultán returned, and laid waste the countries to the right and left of Azerbáïján, such as Khóí, Manand, Tesú, Barúd, Dúmbolí, Rúmieh, and after a few days arrived safe and sound at the castle of Kotúr. This castle, one of the strongest belonging to the Persians, though fiercely attacked, did not surrender, and as winter was approaching they abandoned it. Hence the army entered the country of the Mahmúdí Kurds, where they had a slight fall of snow. They then passed through Amik, Bárgerí, Arjísh, Adaljuváz, Akhlát, Khántakht, and lastly Ván. All these fortresses are situated on the borders of the lake of Ván. Thence the army marched to Tiflís, Kefender, Huzzú, Míáfarakaïn, Díárbekr, Malátieh, Sívás, Tokát, Amásia, Othmánjik, Túsieh, Bólí, and on the sixth day reached Izmít (Nicomedia). On the 19th of Rajab 1045 (1635) the illustrious emperor made his entry into Constantinople with a splendour and magnificence which no tongue can describe nor pen illustrate. The populace who poured out of the city to meet the emperor had been dissatisfied with the Káïm-makám Bairám Páshá, but, gratified by the sight of their emperor, they became animated by a new spirit. The windows and roofs of the houses in every direction were crowded with people, who exclaimed, "The blessing of God be upon thee O conqueror! Welcome, Murád! May thy victories be fortunate!" In short, they recovered their spirits, and joy was manifest in every countenance. The Sultán was dressed in steel armour, and had a threefold aigrette in his turban, stuck obliquely on one side in the Persian manner: he was mounted on a Noghäï steed, followed by seven led horses of the Arab breed, decked out in embroidered trappings set with jewels. Emírgúneh, the khán of Eriván, Yúsuf Khán, and other Persian kháns walked on foot before him, whilst the bands with cymbals, flutes, drums, and fifes, played the airs of Afrásíáb. The emperor looked with dignity on both sides of him, like a lion who has seized his prey, and saluted the people as he went on, followed by three thousand pages clad in armour. The people shouted "God be praised!" as he passed, and threw themselves on their faces to the ground. The merchants and tradesmen had raised on both sides of the way pavilions of satin, cloth of gold, velvet, fine linen, and other rich stuffs, which were afterwards distributed amongst the Soláks, Peiks, and other servants of the Sultán. The old Solák báshí told me that his guards alone had carried home silk tents to the value of 7,000 piastres. During this triumphant procession to the seráï all the ships at Seraglio-point, at Kizkala' (Leander's tower), and at Topkháneh, fired salutes, so that the sea seemed in a blaze. The public criers announced that seven days and nights were to be devoted to festivity and rejoicing. During this festival such a quantity of rich presents were brought to the Sultán that not only the treasury but even the koshk-kháneh (garden house) was filled with them. The next day being Friday, the Sultán repaired to the mosque of Eyyúb, and was much gratified to see the new buildings as he went along the harbour, and on his return by the Adrianople gate. Pleased with the improvements which he saw, he pardoned the Káïm-makám Páshá the discontent which he had occasioned among the people, and bestowed upon him a robe of honour. On his arrival at the mosque of the conqueror he offered up a prayer of two inclinations, and being pleased with the manner in which the mosque was illuminated, he conferred a second robe of honour on the Káïm-makám. He then visited the tomb of the conqueror, the mosque of the princes, and their monument, the mosque and mausoleum of Sultán Báyazíd, and the mosque and mausoleum of his own father. Observing the good repair in which these mosques were kept, he expressed his satisfaction, and returned to the palace. In this month very unfavourable reports were received from the grand vezír Tabání Yassí Mohammed Páshá. The Sháh had taken Eriván, and owing to the severity of the winter it was impossible to send it any relief. The seals were therefore immediately given to Baïrám Páshá, and an expedition to Baghdád was resolved upon. All the necessary arrangements were completed, and the imperial firmáns were issued to summon troops from every quarter to the number of one hundred thousand men, to be ready by spring for the imperial expedition. Kapújí-báshís, Khásekís, and Musáhibs were despatched in every direction with imperial orders, and an army numerous as the waves of the ocean began to assemble.

Account of the humble Evliyá's admission into the imperial harem of Sultán Murád, and of some pleasant conversation which he enjoyed with the Emperor, in 1045 (1635).

It was in this year that I completed, under my tutor Evliyá Efendí, the study of the Korán, according to the seven various readings by Shátebí, and commenced a course according to the ten readings. By the advice of my father, Dervísh Mohammed Aghá, on the sacred night of Kadr, when several thousand individuals were assembled in the mosque of Ayá Sofia, I took my place on the seat of the Moazzins, and after the prayer Teravih, began to repeat from memory the whole of the Korán. When I had finished the Súra Ena'ám, Guzbegjí Mohammed Aghá and the Salihdár Melek Ahmed, came up to the seat, and putting on my head, in the presence of thousands, a túrban wrought with gold, informed me that the emperor desired to see me. They then took me by the hand and led me into the mahfil of the emperor. On beholding the dignified countenance of Sultán Murád I bowed and kissed the ground. The emperor received me very graciously, and after the salutations, asked me in how many hours I could repeat the whole of the Korán. I said, if it please God, if I proceed at a quick rate I can repeat it in seven hours, but if I do it moderately, without much variation of the voice, I can accomplish it in eight hours. The Sultán then said, "Please God! he may be admitted into the number of my intimate associates in the room of the deceased Músá." He then gave me two or three handfuls of gold, which altogether amounted to 623 pieces. Though I was then only a youth of twenty-five, I was sufficiently well educated, and my manners were polished, having been accustomed to associate with vezírs and muftís, in whose presence I had more than once repeated the As'har and the Na't of the sacred volume. Murád left the mosque in the usual style with flambeaux and lanterns. I mounted a horse, and entered the imperial seráï by the cypress gate. The emperor next repaired to the Khás oda, and recommending me to the chief, directed him to invest me with the kaftán, in the chamber of the Kílárjí báshí. He then retired to the inner harem. Next morning he surrendered me to the Kílárjí báshí Safíd Aghá, and a room was assigned to me in the apartments of the Kílár. The Túrshíjí báshí was appointed my governor (lálá). My masters were: of writing, the Gógúm báshí; of music, Dervísh Omar; of grammar, Gejí Mohammed Efendí; and of reading the Korán, my old master Evliyá Efendí. Khorús Imám was my companion in the reciting of the Korán, and Táyeh Zádeh Khandán, Ferrokh Oghlí Asaf Beg, Mo'án Oghlí, Gejejí Soleïmán, and Amber Mustafá were my fellow Mu'azzíns. A great part of my time was spent in the Meshk-kháneh or gymnasium, near the private bath, in practising music. One day they invested me with an embroidered dress, put an amber-scented tuft of artificial hair upon my head, and wishing me a thousand blessings, told me I had the crown of happiness on my head. Sometimes also they put on me a fur cap like that worn by my companions. The Salihdár Melek Ahmed Páshá never lost sight of me, and as I was related to him on my mother's side, he made me many presents. He, the Rúznámehjí Ibrahím Efendí, and the calligrapher Hasan Páshá, were the means of my obtaining an introduction into the seráï. On the day I was dressed as above related, with the splendid turban, two mutes came, and with many curious motions led me into the Khás oda (inner chamber), to Melek Ahmed Aghá and his predecessor Mustafá. These greatly encouraged me and taught me several expressions and ceremonies, which I was to observe in the presence of the emperor. I now found myself in the Khás oda, and had an opportunity of examining it. It is a large room with a cupola; in each corner there are raised seats or thrones; numerous windows and balconies; fountains and water-basins, and the floor is paved with stone of various colours, like a Chinese gallery of pictures. The emperor now made his appearance, like the rising sun, by the door leading to the inner harem. He saluted the forty pages of the inner chamber and all the Musáhib (associates), who returned the salutation with prayers for his prosperity. The emperor having with great dignity seated himself on one of the thrones, I kissed the ground before it, and trembled all over. The next moment, however, I complimented him with some verses that most fortunately came into my mind. He then desired me to read something. I said, "I am versed in seventy-two sciences, does your majesty wish to hear something of Persian, Arabic, Romaic, Hebrew, Syriac, Greek, or Turkish? Something of the different tunes of music, or poetry in various measures?" The emperor said, "What a boasting fellow this is! Is he a Reváni (a prattling fellow), and is this all mere nonsense, or is he capable to perform all that he says?" I replied, "If your majesty will please to grant me permission to speak freely as a Nadím (familiar companion), I think I shall be able to amuse you." The emperor asked what the office of a Nadím was: "A Nadím," said I, "is a gentleman who converses in a pleasing manner: but if he is permitted to drink with the emperor, he is called Nadím náb, or companion of the glass. Nadím is derived from Monadamat, and by a transposition of letters we have Mudám, which in Arabic signifies pure wine. If such a Nadím is permitted to enjoy the company of the emperor, he is called Musáhíb (intimate companion)." "Bravo! said the Sultán, "he understands his business and is no Reváni." "Reváni indeed!" replied I, looking at the same time towards Yúsuf Páshá, the late Khán of Revan (Eriván). The emperor struck his knees with his hand, and burst out in such a fit of laughter that his face became quite red; then addressing Emírgúneh, his favourite musician, he said: "What do you think of this devil of a boy?" Yúsuf Páshá said, "Mark this youth, he will very soon astonish all Irán and Túrán, for his eyes are constantly dancing." "Yes," said I, "the eyes of Turkish boys dance in order to excite mirth in strangers." I alluded to Emírgúneh, who, when he was in a good humour frequently danced and played. The emperor laughed and said, "The boy has ready answers," and being full of good humour, he ordered some chákír to be brought. Chákír in his metaphorical language signified wine. He drank a glass, and said, "Evliyá, thou art now initiated into my secrets; take care not to divulge them. I replied by the following verses.

"Deep in thy breast be love's sweet secret hid—

Forbid thy soul to feel its presence there,—

And when death hovers o'er thy dark'ning lid,

Still in that knowledge let no other share!"

I also quoted the saying, "He who keeps silence escapes many misfortunes;" and added, "my emperor, he who is admitted to your secrets ought to be a magazine of secrecy."—"Evliyá," said the Sultán, "having spoken so much of science, let us now hear some of your performances in music." I enumerated all the different tunes, and having made many allusions to the taste of Emírgúneh for wine, the Sultán was so much pleased with my ready wit that he said, "Now, Evliyá, I shall no more call thee to account, or ask thee any reason for what thou sayest: I appoint thee a Musáhib;" and he then ordered me to be dressed in a fur robe. Seeing that it was too long for me, he said, "Send it to thy father that he may remember me in his prayers;" and he directed that another should be given to me. He next with his own hands put on my head a sable-fur kalpak. Before this I had only a plain Tátár kalpak. He then desired me to sing a wársikí. At one time my music-master was a Dervísh Omar, a disciple of the famous Sheikh Gulshaní, with whom he became acquainted in the reign of Sultán Soleïmán, and with whom he passed seventeen years in Egypt, performing all manner of menial services, such as valet, groom, cook, &c. One day Gulshaní, perceiving the worth that was concealed under the garb of this poor Dervísh, advised him to repair to Turkey, where he was wanted by Sultán Soleïmán. On his departure Gulshaní gave him his own carpet, and on this carpet Dervísh Omar had the honour to associate with all the Sultáns, from Soleïmán to Murád. Having arrived in Turkey with seventy followers, he was present at the siege of Siget, and at the death of Soleïmán. From that time he enjoyed the confidence and patronage of all the Sultáns. He was well skilled in the science of music, in which he gave me lessons. In obedience to the Sultán's orders, I took up a *dáyara* (tambourine) and kissed the ground before the Sultán. On looking at the dáyara, he observed that it was set with jewels, and said, "I make thee a present of this dáyara, but take care thou dost not go beyond this circle."[5] I leaped in a sprightly manner, kissed the foot of the throne, prayed for a blessing on Dervísh Omar, and said, "If it please God, I shall never be debarred from this circle of the Ottoman court, for I know my limits too well to overstep them.

"It is very necessary for every one to know his bounds,

Whether he be poor, or whether he be rich."

I then seated myself on my heels as is usual, offered up a short prayer for assistance from God, and after several symphonies, I exclaimed, "O thou Sheikh Gulshaní, tutor of my tutor Dervísh Omar Raushaní, hail!" I now began to sing and dance, turning round in the manner of the Dervíshes, and accompanying with the dáyara, the following wársikí (mystic song) composed by Dervísh Omar for the late Músá, whose situation I had just entered; with a low and plaintive voice I sang:

"I went out to meet my beloved Músá; he tarried and came not.

Perhaps I have missed him in the way; he tarried and came not."

On hearing this plaintive song, the Sultán took up his pocket handkerchief, and when I approached him, he turned round and said: "The boy has brought to life the spirit of Músá Chelebí! Now tell me the truth instantly; who told thee to sing this song, which I have forbidden to be sung in my presence, and who taught thee it?" I replied, "My emperor, may your life be prolonged! My father had two slaves who learnt the song from the writings of Irmaghán Mohammed Efendí, who died during the late plague, and from them I learnt it. I have heard it from no one else, nor did any one tell me to sing it in the presence of my emperor." The Sultán said, "The boy is very ingenious; he quotes the authority of dead men, that he may not compromise the living." He then said, "Mayest thou live long," and desired me proceed with my performance. I accordingly put my hand on the dáyara and sang:

"The mouth of my beloved betrays the hidden secret,

When he speaks he utters magic spells;

Should he look in anger, even Rustam would be overcome,

For his eyebrows resemble the bow, and his lashes the arrows."

I then stood silent, and having kissed the ground before the emperor, he praised me highly, and gave me several pieces of gold. The emperor then addressing Emírgúneh, said: "The first verses sung by Evliyá were composed by myself, on the death of my favourite companion Músá, whom I had sent on a message to Rajab Páshá, when he was assaulted by the rebels, who threw his murdered body into the At-maidán. O! Emírgúneh, hadst thou but known what an amiable and intelligent youth that was! I have hitherto found no servant like him; and that innocent boy died a martyr!" "My emperor," replied

Emírgúneh, "have you not opened the life-veins of those who shed his innocent blood?" "Yes," said the Sultán, "it is to avenge the murder of my favourite, and the violent death of my brother Othmán, that I have made the heads of 307,000 rebels to roll in the dust." "May God prosper all your undertakings," replied Emírgúneh; "the 307,000 heads did not indeed belong to men, but to so many rebels, who sprung from the ground like mushrooms. Your armies however, in avenging the blood of their companions, did so sufficiently in taking the fortress of Eriván out of my hands, and cutting up the root and branch of the Persian army." The Sultán, pleased with this reply, called for wine and drank a glass. In the evening he ordered me to read a tenth of the Korán; I commenced where I had left off on the holy night of Kadr at Ayá Sofiá, that is, at the Súra Aa'ráf, and read two hundred and four verses, divided into two *mákam*, twenty-four *sha'ba*, and forty-eight *tarkíb*. I then repeated the names of the Sultáns Ahmed, Othmán, and all their illustrious ancestors, to whom I transferred any merit I might have from this reading of the Korán, and concluded with the Fatihat (first chapter of the Korán). The Sultán then presented me with a fish-bone belt set with jewels, which he had in his hand; and asked Emírgúneh whether they read the Korán so well in Persia. Emírgúneh replied that the Persians cared little to conform their actions to the Korán, and much less to read it properly. "It is only to the piety of your majesty, that we are indebted for such reading, which reminds us of the assemblies of Husain Bhikará." At this moment the Mu'azzins began to call to prayers at the head of the staircase, which looks toward the court-yard of the palace. The emperor ordered me to assist them; I flew like a peacock to the top of the staircase, and began to exclaim, "*Hai a'la'-as-saláh! i.e.* Ho! to good works!" Before the commencement of prayers, I was observed by my good master Evliyá Efendí, the imperial Imám, who meeting the emperor in the oratory, outside of the imperial mosque, close to the Khás-oda, thus addressed him: "My gracious emperor, this boy, the darling of my heart, has not attended my lectures since the sacred night of Kadr, when you took him to the Harem. He has already learnt by heart the whole of the Korán, according to the seven readings; he is thoroughly acquainted with the Shátabíeh treatise on that subject, and was beginning the study of the ten different readings; allow him, then, to perfect himself in these studies, after which he may return to your majesty's service." The emperor, not in the least regarding these requests, said, "Efendí! do you suppose that our palace is a tavern, or a den of robbers? Three thousand pages are here devoted night and day to the study of the sciences, besides attending to the seven general lectures, and the two which your reverence delivers twice a week. He may attend your lectures as before; but I cannot leave him to your disposal, for he is a lively and intelligent youth, and must remain with me as my son. His father, the chief of the goldsmiths, is my father; but he may come as often as he pleases to see his son." Evliyá Efendí seeing there was no hope of obtaining what he wished, said: "Well, my gracious sovereign, allow him at least the books that are necessary for his education." The Sultán immediately called for pen and ink, directed the treasurer to be in attendance, and with his own hand he wrote the following imperial order: "Thou, chief of the treasury, shalt immediately supply Evliyá with the following works: the Káfiah, the commentary of Jámí, the Tafsír Kází, the Misbáh, the Díbácheh, the Sahíh Moslem, the Bokhárí, the Multeka-al-Abhar, the Kadúrí, the Gulistán and Bostán, the Nisáb-sabiyán, and the Loghat Akhtarí." The kehiyá or deputy treasurer immediately brought me these valuable works, which had been written for the use of sovereigns, and the Sultán presented me with a copy of the Korán, in the hand-writing of Yákút Musta'samí, which he was in the habit of reading himself; also a silver inkstand set with jewels, and a writing-board inlaid with mother-o'-pearl. At the same time he gave instructions to the Kílárjí-báshí respecting my accommodation. Thus three times a week I read the Korán with Evliyá Efendí, and also had lessons in Arabic, Persian, and writing. In this manner it was but seldom I could attend in the service of the emperor, but whenever I came into his presence he was always delighted, and treated me so graciously, that I never failed to shew my wit and pleasantry. I should never have been tempted to repeat any of my witty sayings, but for the express commands of the Sultán. Kara Hisárí, the great calligrapher my writing-master, and many other witnesses are still living, who can attest that, versed as I then was in every branch of science, I enjoyed the greatest favour of the Sultán, who liked a joke or a laugh as well as any plain dervísh.[6] I had frequently the honour of conversing familiarly with this great monarch, and were I to relate all the conversation that passed between us I should fill a volume. In short, Sultán Murád was a man who had the nature of a Dervísh, but he was brave and intelligent. His fingers were thick, but well proportioned, and the strongest wrestler could not open his closed fist. He generally dressed in blue coloured silk, and liked to ride very fast. Neither the Ottoman nor any other dynasty of Moslem princes ever produced a prince so athletic, so well-made, so despotic, so much feared by his enemies, or so dignified as Sultán Murád. Though so cruel and bloodthirsty, he conversed with the rich and poor without any mediator, made his rounds in disguise night and day to be informed of the state of the poor, and to ascertain the price of provisions, for which purpose he frequently went into cookshops and dined incognito. No monarch, however, was guilty of so many violent deeds. On the march to Baghdád, when he left Cæsarea, a wild goat was started in the mountains of Develí Kara Hisár. The emperor immediately gave it chase, struck it with his spear, followed it up amongst the rocks, and divided his prey amongst his vezírs. The whole army was surprised to see him dismount and climb up the craggy mountain in pursuit of his game. On another occasion I saw him seize his Salihdárs Melek Ahmed and Músá Aghá, both remarkably stout men, take them by their belts, lift them over his head, and fling them one to the right and the other to the left. Ahmed Páshá, Hasan Páshá the calligrapher, Delí Husain Páshá, and Pehleván Díshlenk Soleïmán, were all athletic men who were fond of playing and wrestling. The Sultán frequently stripped himself and wrestled with these men, on a spot of the seráï called Chemen-sofa. It was I who on such occasions read the usual prayer of the wrestlers. It is as follows: "Allah! Allah! For the sake of the Lord of all created beings—Mohammed Mustafá, for the sake of Mohammed Bokhárá of Sárí Sáltik, for the sake of our Sheikh Mohammed who laid hold of the garments and the limbs, let there be a setting-to of hand upon hand, back upon back, and breast upon breast! And for the love of Alí the Lion of God, grant assistance O Lord!" After this prayer the Sultán began to wrestle either with Melek Ahmed or Delí Husain. They met according to the rules of wrestling, laying hold of each other, and entwining themselves like serpents. But when the emperor grew angry he knelt down upon one knee, and endeavouring to master his opponent from beneath, it was difficult to resist him. He generally succeeded in bringing his antagonist to the ground. All the early heroes of Islamism, such as Ma'di Karb, Okail Ben Abú Táleb, Sohail Rúmí, Sa'íd, Kháled Ben Walíd, Asa'd Ben Mokdád, Haddád, Omar, Alí, Hamza, and Malek, used to wrestle in the presence of the Prophet, who was himself a great wrestler, and at different times vanquished his enemies, the cursed Abúlahab and Abújahal. Thus wrestling became one of the favourite exercises of the Moslems; and Pír Mahmúd became the patron saint of the art, which was made to consist of forty arts, seventy rounds, and one hundred and forty tricks, and with all of which a good wrestler must be thoroughly acquainted. Wrestlers are forbidden to engage in karakosh, boghma, and jeríd, because wrestling is an exercise on foot, and not a contest with an enemy. If in battle an enemy lays hold on another to wrestle, he may take advantage of the karakosh, boghma, or jeríd. He may even cut off the head of his adversary. Murád, when a stout young man, was never satisfied until he brought his antagonist to the ground. One day he came out covered with perspiration from the hammám (bath) in the Khás-oda, saluted those present, and said, "Now I have had a bath." "May it be to your health," was the general reply. I said, "My emperor, you are now clean and comfortable, do not therefore oil yourself for wrestling to-day, especially as you have already exerted yourself with others, and your strength must be considerably reduced." "Have I no strength left?" said he, "let us see;" upon which he seized me as an eagle, by my belt, raised me over his head, and whirled me about as children do a top. I exclaimed, "Do not let me fall, my emperor, hold me fast!" He said, "Hold fast yourself," and continued to swing me round, until I cried out, "For God's sake, my emperor, cease, for I am quite giddy." He then began to laugh, released me, and gave me forty-eight pieces of gold for the amusement I had afforded him. Sometimes he would take his two sword-bearers, Melek Ahmed and Músá, both stout men, and carrying them in his hands would make the circuit of the Chemen-sofa several times. He was a man who ate much, and indeed he was a hero surpassing Sám, Zál, Narímán, Afrásíáb and Rustam. One day he pierced with a jeríd the shield of an Albanian, which was composed of seven layers of the root of the fig-tree, and sent it to Cairo, where it is suspended in the díván of Sultán Ghúrí. Hasan the calligrapher wrote the toghra of the Sultán in gold and purple on Chinese paper five cubits square. This is also preserved in the díván of Ghúrí. When I was there, I inscribed underneath it the names of the four associates of the prophet (Abúbekr, Omar, Othmán and Alí), also in the manner of a toghra (monogram), imploring the blessing of God upon them.

On another occasion Murád, in the presence of the German and Dutch ambassadors, pierced some shields composed of ten camel-hides, which they had brought with them as presents. He returned these shields, and the spear with which he had pierced them, as presents to the emperor of Germany. I saw them suspended in the archway of the inner gate at Vienna. Ten other shields, sent as presents by the emperor of Germany, he pierced in the same manner, and sent them to Músá Páshá when governor of Bude, where I saw them suspended. When he was at Halep (Aleppo) he threw a jeríd from the castle, which passing over the ditch and a considerable space beyond, fell in the market-place of the stirrup-makers, where a column inscribed with a chronogram marks the spot where it fell.

One day while he was exercising himself in the old palace, he saw a crow on the crescent of the left minareh of Sultán Báyazíd. He immediately rode to the At-maidán, and throwing his jeríd to the height of the mosque, struck the crow, which fell dead at his feet. The At-maidán of the old palace is distant one mile from the minareh of Sultán Báyazíd. If the jeríd had not hit the raven, but had pursued its course, it would certainly have fallen in the poultry-market. On the spot where the crow fell there now stands a white marble column of the height of a man, with a chronogram by Júrí inscribed with letters in gold. A similar monument of the extraordinary distance to which a jeríd was thrown stands in the garden of Beykos, also inscribed with a chronogram by Júrí.

Sultán Murád was taught the science of archery by Pehleván Hájí Soleïmán and Sárí Solák. There is still to be seen in the Ok-maidán near the Tekieh of the archers, a marble column indicating the spot where an arrow shot by Sultán Murád fell. This shot surpassed that of all the former Pehleváns excepting Túzkoparán, and left far behind the aims of Karalandha, Báyazíd

Khán, Khattát Sheikh, Demirdilisí and Meserlí Dúndár. In the gardens of Tokát, Sultán Murád once cut an ass in two with one stroke of his sword. In the game of the mace (gúrz) he could wield with the greatest ease a mace weighing two hundred okkas, and perform all the tricks of the art. And so did he distinguish himself in the exercises of wrestling and boxing. Our master in these exercises, Dervísh Omar, on hearing several slang expressions of the art, such as, "Cut not! strike not! hold not!" used by Sultán Murád, exclaimed, "Look at that master-butcher!" in reference to his cruel disposition, which was never satisfied without shedding blood. The Sultán was pleased with the joke, and smiled at it. He was also expert in the game of matrak, in which balls are struck with clubs, and which has no less than one hundred and sixty *band* or tricks. He used to strike the ball with such force that it struck the head of his partner. His master in this game was Toslák Kapúdán, the juggler of the admiral's galley, who was an expert marine (levend), and whose name is recorded in the elegy composed by Júrí Chelebi Sheikh in twelve languages. This Toslák Kapúdán, though considered one of the most skilful in this play, did not equal Sultán Murád.

Finally, the emperor was a good poet, equal to Nafa'í and Júrí; and his diván or collection of odes, consists of three hundred leaves; but it wants the odes ending in the letters Ta and A'in. These were to have been supplied by Vahabí Othmán Chelebí, but he died before he could complete them.

During the winter he regulated his assemblies as follows: On Friday evening he assembled all the divines, Sheiks, and the readers of the korán, and with them he disputed till morning on scientific subjects. Saturday evening was devoted to the singers who sang the Iláhí, the Na't, and other spiritual tunes. Sunday evening was appropriated to the poets and reciters of romances, such as Nafa'í, Júrí, Nadímí, Arzí, Nathárí, Beyání, Izzetí, &c. On Monday evening he had the dancing boys, Sárí Chelebí, Chakmak Chelebí, and Semerjí-zádeh; and the Egyptian musicians Dabágh Oghlí, Parpúr Kúlí, Osmán Kúlí, Názlí Kúlí, Ahmed Kúlí, and Sheher Oghlání. This assembly sat till daybreak, and resembled the musical feast of Husain Bhikará. On Tuesday evening he received the old experienced men who were upwards of seventy years, and with whom he used to converse in the most familiar manner. On Wednesdays he gave audience to the pious saints; and on Thursdays to the Dervíshes. In the mornings he attended to the affairs of the Moslems. In such a manner did he watch over the Ottoman states, that not even a bird could fly over them without his knowledge. But were we to describe all his excellent qualities we should fill another volume.

Praise be to Allah, that my father was the chief of the goldsmiths from the time of Sultán Soleïmán till that of Sultán Ibrahím; and I was honoured with the society of so glorious a monarch as Sultán Murád IV. Previously to his Majesty's undertaking the expedition to Baghdád I left the imperial Harem, and was appointed a Sipáhí, with an allowance of forty aspres per day.

List of the Kapúdán Páshás during the Reign of Sultán Murád IV.

The first was Rajab Páshá, who, as we have before related, captured three hundred Cossack boats in the Black Sea, and brought them to Constantinople. His successor, Khalíl Páshá, an Albanian by birth, took near the rocks of Flúra in the Mediterranean, a famous ship of the infidels which was called Kara-jehennem (black-hell), and which had a large mill within it, and a garden on the quarter-deck.

Hasan Páshá, the son of a Janissary of Tahtáljeh, near Constantinople. In the year 1035 (1625) he built two castles on the Dneiper. He was afterwards degraded, and died suddenly at Yenísheher in 1041 (1631).

Vezír Jánpúlád Zádeh Mustafá Páshá, married Fatima the sister of Sultán Murád, and was made Kapúdán Páshá in 1041. His name spread terror over the whole of the Mediterranean even as far as the straits of Gibraltar; he built a castle at Athens; and even before that was finished he was appointed governor of Rúmeïlí. In this capacity he was ordered to undertake the expedition against Eriván, and so many troops did he assemble, that the suburbs of Constantinople were filled with them; and three months were required to have them passed over the Bosphorus to Scutari on flat-bottomed boats.

Ja'fer Páshá resigned the office of Bostánjí Báshí for that of Kapúdán Páshá in 1043 (1633). He spread terror amongst the infidels. That same year, on the Feast of Victims, he met three English men-of-war in the Mediterranean, between the castles of Kesendreh and Kolúz. The English being fire-worshippers, according to the sacred text, "They were burnt and the men drowned;" they set fire to two of the vessels. The third, with two hundred guns, was taken before they could set fire to it, and was brought with immense booty to Sultán Murád.

After Ja'fer Páshá, Delí Husain Páshá was made Kapúdán Páshá, in which capacity he took the field against Eriván. He was afterwards appointed governor of Egypt.

His successor was Kara Mustafá Páshá, an Albanian by birth, and educated a Janissary. During the siege of Baghdád, he was the deputy of Píáleh at the Ters-kháneh (arsenal), and cruised in the Black Sea with two hundred ships of the imperial fleet. In this expedition he encountered two hundred Cossack boats, of which he captured seventy, with the hetman. The rest made their escape during the night, and secured themselves, in the reeds and marshes of the river Kúbán. Píáleh Páshá pursued them, and closed the entrance of the river; but the infidels carried their boats overland, whilst Píáleh waited for their appearance in vain. At last he was informed by Khoajeh Kana'án Páshá, the governor of Oczakov, and by the khán of the Tátárs, of the scheme of the infidels; upon which he weighed anchor, came round to the island of Tamán, and shut up the channel by which the Cossacks had intended making their escape. Being now surrounded on land by Khoajeh Páshá, and the Tátár Khán, the Cossacks made a camp with their boats in the mouth of the river, and defended themselves for seven days and nights. This battle is even now memorable by the name of Adakhún. Finally, not one of their boats escaped, but they were all carried in triumph to Constantinople, with the crosses of their flags turned downwards, and the whole fleet anchored opposite the arsenal. The news of this victory gave fresh courage to the troops engaged at the siege of Baghdád.

The other Kapúdán Páshás were, Salihdár Mustafá Páshá, and Síávush Páshá. The latter was an Abází by birth, and being a man of the strictest honour, he was disliked by the people of the arsenal, and was consequently dismissed from office.

The Muftís and Ulemá during the Reign of Sultán Murád.

Yehiyá, the son of Zekeríá, was Sheikh al Islám when Sultán Murád ascended the throne; in the year 1034, he was succeeded by Khoajeh Zádeh Isa'd Efendí, and in 1041 by Husain Efendí, who was slain in the rebellion and thrown into the sea. Yehiyá was then made Sheikh al Islám a third time. I was then the first Mu'azzin at the mosque of the eunuch Mohammed Aghá, when he appointed me his reader of the Na'át, in which capacity I attended him every Friday.

The chief judges of Constantinople were, Kehiyá Mustafa Efendí; Bostan-zádeh Efendí, and his brother; Azmí Zádeh Efendí; Sáleh Efendí; Cheshmí Mahmúd Efendí; Hasan Efendí; and Cheshmí Efendí, a third time.

Chief Judges of Rúmeïlí.

Abdul-ghaní Mohammed Efendí; Sheríf Mohammed Efendí; Kara Chelebí Zádeh Efendí; Husain Efendí in the year 1037; Azmí Zádeh Mustafá Efendí 1038; Hasan Efendí 1039; Bostánjí Zádeh Yehiyá Efendí 1039; Abú Sa'íd Efendí 1039; Husain Efendí, a third time chief judge of Rúmeïli; Cheshmí Efendí; Husain Efendí, a fourth time judge of Rúmeïlí; Kara Chelebí Zádeh

Mohammed Efendí, a third time 1042; Abdullah Efendí 1042.

Chief Judges of Anatolia.

Azmí-zádeh Efendí 1032; Sheríf Mohammed Efendí, a second time, and his son Chelebí Zádeh Abdullah, 1037; Abú Sa'íd Efendí, 1039; Abú Sa'úd Zádeh Efendí, 1040; Cheshmí Mohammed Efendí, 1041; Ahmed Efendí Zádeh; Núh Efendí.

Defterdárs during the Reign of Sultán Murád.

Cheshmí Mohammed Efendí, 1032; Sáleh Efendí; Hedáyet-allah Efendí, 1033; Osháki Zádeh Efendí, 1035; Abú Isa'd Efendí, 1035; Otlokjí Hasan Efendí, 1035; Abú Sa'úd Zádeh Efendí, 1036; Abu Sa'íd Efendí; Núh Efendí, 1039; Rajab Efendí, 1040; Músá Efendí, 1041; Jeví-zádeh Efendí 1042; Makhdúm Husain Efendí 1043; Azíz Efendí Kara Chelebí Zádeh 1043.

Aghás of the Janissaries during the Reign of Sultán Murád.

Cheshlejí Alí Aghá; Kara Mustafá Aghá; Bairám Aghá; Khosrau Aghá; Mohammed Kehiyá Aghá; Alí Aghá; Khalíl Aghá; Soleïmán Aghá; Hasan Aghá; Hasan Khalífeh Aghá; Mustafá Aghá; Kosseh Mohammed Aghá; Mohammed Aghá.

Sultán Murád's Expedition against Malta.

When Sultán Murád had returned from Baghdád crowned with victory, he was obliged to undertake an expedition in person against Malta, an island in the Mediterranean. The causes which led him to this determination are as follows. Complaints were made by the Musulmáns in every direction of the depredations committed by the Maltese Christians in every port of the Mediterranean, particularly on the African coast. Trade of every sort was at a stand, and the pilgrims to the holy cities were molested in their passage. But above all, the Mainotes had become very troublesome in the Archipelago. These had been subdued in the time of Sultán Mohammed II., and at the time of this rebellion they amounted to fifty thousand men. They had about one hundred vessels with which they plundered the islands, intercepted the ships of merchants and pilgrims, and every year took thousands of prisoners. Since the time that the Kapúdán Púlád-zádeh had scoured the coast of Sicily, Corsica, and Sardinia no imperial fleet had made its appearance in those quarters, the infidels raised their heads, their audacity knew no bounds, and they plundered on the shores of the Ottoman empire.

These complaints were at length laid before the Sultán in a report by Kara Mustafá Páshá. A council was immediately held consisting of the grand vezír Kara Mustafá Páshá, the Kapudán Síávush Páshá, the Kehiyá of the arsenal Píáleh, and seventy begs of the sea (captains of war-ships), and the most experienced officers of the arsenal; the result of which was that the building of a *báshtirdeh* (admirals ship) and of twenty galleys, each eighty cubits long, was immediately commenced by the express order of the emperor. Two thousand purses (one million of piastres) were allotted to the Kapúdán Páshá, to the Kehiyá, and to the inspector of the arsenal. Five docks near the arsenal were pulled down, and three new ones were built in their stead each as large as a caravanserai; and in them a báshtirdeh for the emperor, and two green *máonas* were constructed in the space of three months. The máonas had seventy benches and one hundred and forty oars, each of which was moved by eight men. At the stern and bow of each there was a large gun, weighing from forty to fifty okkas, besides hundreds of guns on each side. They were indeed such vessels that even Noah might have considered himself secure in them. In short, on the return of spring, two hundred ships of war, consisting of báshtirdehs, galleys, and others were ready for sea, with arms, men, and provisions three times the quantity required. The galleys of all the islands of the Archipelago of Egypt and of the Morea, amounted to five hundred, which were followed by the same number of transport ships. They had besides some huge vessels called *Káruváns* because they made a voyage to Egypt only once a-year, requiring six months to load and six months to discharge. Each of these carried fifteen hundred serving men and two thousand troops. Besides these, there were five hundred smaller vessels of every description; *viz.* Barja (barges), Kalíún (galleys), Perk, Porton, Shika, and Kara-mursál which were hired by government. In short the whole fleet amounted to eleven thousand seven hundred vessels, which being prepared for sailing, were moored in the harbour of Constantinople.

Account of the Death of Sultán Murád.

The *Togh* (tails) and *Seráperdeh* (tents) were already raised at Dávud Páshá preparatory to a new expedition, when the emperor enfeebled by sickness found it impracticable to set out. According to the Arabic text: "Every one must perish," and the Persian verse: "If any person could remain for ever upon the earth, Mohammed would have remained; if beauty could secure immortality, Yúsuf (Joseph) would not have died," no one is exempt from destiny. And Sultán Murád being obedient to the call, "Return to thy lord," bade farewell to this perishable world and entered on his journey to the

161

everlasting kingdom. The whole of the Mohammedan nation were thrown into the deepest affliction, and lamented his loss. Horses hung with black were let loose in the At-Maidán, where his Majesty was buried close to Sultán Ahmed.

The new emperor, Sultán Ibráhím, gave the seals to Kara Mustafá Páshá. Kara Hasan Páshá was made Defterdár; Abd-ur-rahím Efendí, Shaikh-ul-Islám; and in order that the fleet prepared by Sultán Murád against Malta should not lie useless, it was sent to the Mediterranean, where a máona was lost, nothing of consequence effected, and the whole fleet with its troops returned to Islámbol after the autumnal equinox. One of the máonas was moored off the arsenal and painted black to represent the mourning for the death of Sultán Murád, an event which gave the Maltese infidels an opportunity of recommencing their hostilities. "Man proposes, but God disposes." I have since heard from the pearl-shedding lips of my worthy lord, Kara Mustafá, that had God spared Murád but six months longer, the whole of the infidels would have been reduced to the capitation tax. The Ragusians came forward as mediators for the infidels of Malta and Spain, stipulating on the part of the former to give up the island of Malta, and on the part of the latter, the Red-apple (Rome). But fate had otherwise decreed.

Ibráhím, the youngest of Sultán Ahmed's seven sons, ascended the throne in the year 1049 (1639). He was then twenty-five years old; but not very intelligent.

Vezírs of Sultán Ibráhím.

Kara Mustafá Páshá was vezír when Ibráhím came to the throne, and was confirmed in his office. Fearing he should fall a victim to the rebels, he fled from the garden of the Seráï to his own palace, and changed his dress, but he was shot by a bústánjí opposite the palace of Músá Páshá. He was buried in his own mausoleum at the Pármak-kapú. He was followed by Juván Kapújí-báshí, who died at the siege of Candia. Sáleh Páshá, a Bosnian by birth, from the village of Lúbin in Herzegovina, was put to death by the intrigues of Tezkerehjí Ahmed Páshá. Ahmed Páshá succeeded him, but he too was intimidated by the rebels, which being discovered by Mohammed Páshá, he was strangled, his body thrown into the At-Maidán, and instantly torn to pieces by the rebels. The same day Pezavenk, and the emperor's mosáhib, Khoajeh Jenjí, were also torn to pieces by the permission of the Ulemá.

The Vezír who rebelled against Sultán Ibráhím.

Várvár Alí Páshá, the governor of Sívás, having refused to give to Mavrúl for Sultán Ibráhím, his daughter, the wife of Ibshír Páshá, on the ground that such a demand was contrary to law, he was dismissed from his office; after which he placed himself at the head of a party of troops to maintain his cause against the order issued for his death. Kopreilí Mohammed Páshá took the field against him; but he vanquished Kopreilí, and on his arrival at Cherkesh, he was assailed and put to death by Ibshír Páshá, on whose account he had rebelled.

Ibráhím built several koshks in the New Seráï, on which many chronograms were composed.

Conquests, &c. during the reign of Sultán Ibráhím.

Nasúh Páshá Zádeh was defeated in the plains of Scutari by Kara Mustafá Páshá. The Cossacks became masters of Azov, the khán of the Tatars having been tardy in affording it the necessary succours; in consequence of which, seven hundred vessels were sent to besiege Azov. The siege continued two months, during which time the Moslems reduced the walls of the fortress to dust; but the infidels held out, by subterraneous trenches, a month longer, when, on account of the approach of winter, the brave army of Moslems was obliged to return without victory. In the following year Juván Kapújí Báshí equipped three hundred ships, and filling them with Moslem warriors, renewed the siege of Azov. The Cossacks, being much alarmed, left the castle without the least attempt to defend it; and hence the well-known proverb, "Husain Páshá gave battle, but Mohammed Páshá conquered without battle." Mohammed Páshá kept the whole army of Moldavia, Valachia, Circassia, and the Ottoman troops, in order to rebuild the fortress, which was effected in the space of seven months. I, the humble Evliyá, saw it in the fourth campaign when I remained in the Crimea, and the Tátár Khán wintered with his army in Azov. The grand vezír at the same time returned with the imperial fleet to the Sublime Porte.

The second conquest of Sultán Ibráhím is that of Valachia and Moldavia by the khán of the Tátárs. Mátí Voivode, the prince of Valachia, and Lipúl, the prince of Moldavia, having reigned twenty years and acquired the wealth of Kárún (Crœsus), they cherished a deadly enmity against each other. Lipúl gave one of his daughters in marriage to the Hettman of the Cossacks, Prince Khmelentski, who assisted him with 20,000 Cossacks; whilst Mátí Voivode collected an army of 100,000 men at Bucharest. The accounts of this quarrel having reached Constantinople, the troops of Rúmeilí and of the Tátár Khán were ordered out to prevent their coming to battle. The armies of the two infidels, however, met at Fokshán, on the frontiers of Moldavia and Valachia. Lipúl was beaten, and upwards of 70,000 men were killed on both sides. The Ottoman army and the Tátár troops availed themselves of this opportunity to make numerous inroads into the countries of Moldavia and Valachia, whence they carried off more than 100,000 prisoners, besides many thousands of cattle. They, moreover, wasted the country, reduced the towns to ruins, and carried the Voivode Lipúl to Constantinople, where he was imprisoned in the Seven Towers. The Voivode of Valachia was pardoned for the sum of two thousand purses (a million of piastres), and confirmed in his principality. Heaven be praised that I was in the Tátár army at the time of this splendid victory; and after sharing plentifully in the plunder, returned to the Crimea.

The third conquest is that of Canea in the island of Candia, by Salihdár Yúsuf Páshá. This glorious victory must be ascribed to the piety of Sultán Ahmed Khán, who prayed that he might obtain that island from the Venetians, with the view of appropriating its revenues to the endowment of two mosques. Another cause, however, of the conquest was, that a large caravella, carrying 3,000 pilgrims, with the late chief of the eunuchs Sunbul Aghá, to Egypt, was attacked off Degirmenlik by six Maltese vessels. After a fierce battle of two days, in which Sunbul Aghá, and the master of the caravella were killed, the Maltese became masters of it, and carried it to Canea in Candia, where they anchored; although this was contrary to the treaty entered into by Khair-ud-dín Páshá, according to which the infidels were not allowed to shelter in their harbour any vessels taken by the enemies of the Ottoman empire. The Venetians however favoured the Maltese, and even allowed all the horses and property of the deceased chief of the eunuchs to be sold at Canea. Sultán Ibráhím, displeased with this proceeding, feigned an expedition against Malta, and appointed Salihdár Yúsuf Páshá to the command of seven hundred ships. These first sailed as far as Navarino, where they took in water, left twenty of the slowest sailing vessels behind, filled the others with troops, and sailed directly for the castle of San Todors on Candia, which immediately surrendered. They then laid siege to Canea, which was the sixth conquest, and shall be described shortly. Thank God! I was present at this sixth conquest, being on board the frigate of Dúrák-beg, who plundered the islands of Cerigo and Cerigotto. Yúsuf Páshá, the conqueror of Canea, having returned to Constantinople, as a reward for his services, was killed at the instigation of Jinjí Khoájeh.

The fourth victory was that over Várvár by Ibshír Páshá the traitor. Várvár Alí preferred losing his place to giving up his daughter, the wife of Ibshír Páshá, to Sultán Ibráhím. The infamous traitor Ibshír joined his father-in-law at Tokát, and persuading him that he would accompany him to Constantinople, there to seek redress for the outrage committed on their family, lulled him into a sleep of security; and on arriving at a place called Cherkess, attacked him suddenly, sent his head to Constantinople, and as a reward, received the government of Síwás.

Defeat of Tekelí Mustafá Pashá.

The Venetians having ravaged the native country of Yúsuf Páshá, the conqueror of Canea, who was a Croatian by birth, and having brought over to their interests the Uskoks, the inhabitants of those countries, Tekelí Páshá was nominated commander, and besieged the castle of Sebenico in the Adriatic sea for forty days. On the fortieth day they were driven from the trenches by a dreadful storm, after which they assembled in the plain of Vanul near Sebenico. The next morning they found themselves surrounded by many thousands of banners bearing the cross, and a bloody engagement ensued, in which 22,000 Moslems were slain, 18,000 made prisoners, and the whole camp fell into the hands of the infidels. I, the humble Evliyá, was present at this unfortunate battle, being in one of the regiments of Janissaries; and in order to save myself, I fled on horseback towards the mountains of Ghulámúj, where I left my horse, entered a thick forest, and remained concealed seven days and nights, living upon roots and herbs. The infidels then advanced to Kilisa, where they pitched the Ottoman tents, and the commander-in-chief even put on the turban of Tekelí Mustafá Páshá. The garrison, deceived by this stratagem, came out without fear to meet the diván, whilst the infidels rushed in, and thus became masters of that strong hold. Such misfortunes never befel the Ottoman empire as those which followed the defeat at Sebenico. The ships with pilgrims were captured by the Venetians, as was also the imperial fleet on its annual cruise in the Mediterranean; and the whole were carried to Venice.

Character of Sultán Ibráhím.

Kara Mustafá Páshá, the brave and sagacious vezír, being put to death, the Sultán fell into the hands of all the favourites and associates of the harem, the dwarfs, the mutes, the eunuchs, the women, particularly Jinjí Khoájeh, and the vezír Ahmed Hazár-pára Páshá, who corrupted him to such a degree that he received bribes from his own vezírs. He lavished the treasures of Egypt on his favourite women Políeh, Sheker Pára, Tellí, and Sájbághlí Khásekí; and squandered his revenues in circumcision feasts, building koshks lined with sable, and in presents to his favourite Jinjí Khoájeh, who at last, with the vezír Ahmed, fell under the displeasure of the public. So loud was the cry for vengeance, that the vezír was obliged to call to his assistance the Ottoman troops who had served in Candia under the command of Delí Husain Páshá. Jinjí Khoájeh, the favourite, was constantly about the person of the Sultán, the vezír, or the válideh; and whenever the latter went out in the carriage or the chair, he always accompanied her. When any gave good advice he laughed in their faces, and by his flattering conversation, he kept the Sultán in a state of constant lethargy: in short, he knew nothing of state affairs. He was originally called Shaikh-zádeh, and attended with me at the college of Hámid Efendí. I was then reading the Káfiyeh with Jámí's commentary, under my worthy tutor Akhfash Efendí, when this boy was taken from his grammar into the presence of the Sultán, whose favour he obtained by reading several tales, and lulled him into the sleep of carelessness. He then received the name of Jinjí Khoájeh. As I was well acquainted with him, I knew that he had no taste for the secret sciences; and that the rise of his brilliant star would only tend to his own misfortune and that of the empire.

At length Murád Aghá arrived from Candia to the assistance of the Sultán; but the latter having demanded of him a present of one thousand purses, seventy sable skins, and two female slaves, he put himself at the head of the Sipáhís and Janissaries, who turned out in the At-maidán in open rebellion. Sultán Ibráhím was confined in a part of the palace called Sircheh-seráï, and his son Mohammed IV. was proclaimed emperor. The divines and vezírs made obeisance to him; Dervísh Mohammed was named grand vezír, and Murád, ághá of the Janissaries. The day after, Ahmed Páshá, the late vezír, who had concealed himself, was discovered and torn to pieces by the populace, as were also Yani Sireh and Jinjí, and their bodies were thrown out upon the At-maidán. The rest of the favourites were either killed or exiled. Of the favourite women, Sheker-pára was banished to Ibrím, the rest were confined in the old Seráï, or distributed amongst the vezírs. On the morning of the 25th of Rajab, Sultán Mohammed proceeded in state to the mosque of Eyúb, to be invested with the sword. On his return, he visited the tomb of his ancestor Mohammed II. and then took his seat in the Khás-ódá. In the mean time a report was circulated through the city that Sultán Ibráhím had escaped from his confinement, and that he was supported by a party of the Bóstánjís. In consequence of this report, many thousands were in an uproar, and proceeded armed to the At-maidán, where they received a *fetvá*, or warrant for the execution of Ibráhím Abdu-r-rahmán Efendí. The grand vezír, Murád, Emír-Páshá, and some of the first officers of government, also assembled in the Sircheh Seráï. The vezír, with many blows, obliged Kara Alí, the executioner, to enter the Sircheh Seráï and do his work. Ibráhím asked: "Master Alí, wherefore art thou come?" He replied, "My emperor, to perform your funeral service." To this, Ibráhím replied, "We shall see." Alí then fell upon him; and whilst they were struggling, one of Alí's assistants came in, and Ibráhím was finally strangled with a garter. This happened in 1058 (1648). Kara Alí received a reward of five hundred ducats, and was urged to remain no longer at Constantinople, but to proceed on a pilgrimage to Mecca. The corpse of the emperor was washed before the Khás-ódá, and the last prayers were read under the cypresses before the Díván-Kháneh, in the presence of all the vezírs, and of Sultán Mohammed himself, the Shaikh-ul-Islám acting as Imám. The vezírs wore black veils, and horses covered with black were led before the coffin, which was deposited in the mausoleum of Sultán Mustafá I., the uncle of Sultán Ibráhím.

Reign of Sultán Mohammed IV., which may God perpetuate!

This emperor ascended the throne on Saturday the 18th of Rajab 1058(1648), being then seven years old. Not a single *falús* was found in the treasury, and it was evidently necessary to collect some money by executing those who had squandered it away in the time of Sultán Murád, to make the usual largess to the troops. From the property of Jinjí were realized 3,000 purses; from that of the late vezír, 5,000; and from that of Sheker-pára, 1,000; so that on Tuesday the 5th of Sha'bán, 3,700 purses were distributed as presents, and 7,000 purses as arrears of pay. Three thousand Janissaries, who had been proscribed and ordered to march to Baghdád, and the same number of Sepáhís destined for Candia, although they had no claim to the largess, received 1,000 purses; and the whole army were highly satisfied. On the 11th of Sha'bán, the largess was distributed amongst the servants of the Seráí. The cooks and confectioners, not having received any thing, rebelled, on which account the Kilárjí-báshí was disgraced.

Personal description of Sultán Mohammed.

Though very weak when he mounted the throne, he acquired strength when, at the age of twenty, he took to field sports. He had broad shoulders, stout limbs, a tall figure, like his father Ibráhím; a powerful fist, like his uncle Murád, open forehead, grey eyes, a ruddy countenance, and an agreeable voice, and his carriage was princely, in short, that of an emperor. The astrologers had predicted to Sultán Ibráhím that he should have a son called Yúsuf (Joseph), and possessing the beauty of a Joseph, who would subdue the nations from the east to the west, and quell all external and internal commotions. When his mother was near her time, Ibráhím took an oath, that if it were a male child, he would name him after the person who should first bring him the good news. By the decree of God, he received the intelligence from Yúsuf, the Imám of the palace, who at the same time read the confession of faith over the young prince, calling him Yúsuf, which name he had only seven hours; the favourites and women of the palace having insinuated that Yúsuf was a slave's name, and that Mohammed would sound much better, he was accordingly named Mohammed, though in truth he grew up beautiful as Yúsuf. He had a small beard, large mustaches, and was much devoted to field

167

sports.

History of the Vezírs.

Mevleví Khoájeh Dervísh Mohammed Páshá retired from the office of defterdár with the rank of a Páshá of three tails, and resided in a monastery of Mevlevís. He was appointed grand vezír when Sultán Mohammed IV. came to the throne; but having made immense confiscation of property in order to raise funds for the payment of the troops, he was obliged to retire to Malagra, where he was strangled. He was a just and valuable servant of the state. His successor was Kara Murád Páshá, who was born in Albania, and was brought up as a Janissary. Like his predecessor, he was dismissed from office for having spent too much money in organizing the imperial navy and army. He was succeeded by my lord Melek Ahmed Páshá, who was born at Constantinople; but at the age of three years was sent to the country of Abáza, where he was educated till he was fifteen. He was then, along with my mother, sent as a present to Sultan Ahmed. He was consigned to the pages in the harem, and my mother was given to my father, shortly after which union, the humble writer was born. Melek Ahmed's father was the kehiyá of the kapújís of Ozdemir-oghlí Osmán Páshá; and having been present in the battles of Shírwán, Ganjeh, and Derbend, died at the age of one hundred and forty years. Melek then became the sword-bearer and confidential attendant of Sultán Murád IV., and on the day of the conquest of Baghdád, he received the government of Diárbekr. He subsequently enjoyed all the high offices in the state; and having held the governments of Cairo and Budin, and become an old and experienced statesman, he was at last raised to the rank of grand vezír. He sent 3,000 Sipáhís to aid Delí Husain Páshá in Candia, and a togh (tail) to Biklí Mustafá Páshá. By this assistance, Delí Husain was enabled to take the castles of Selina and Retimo. The following year Hasám Oghlí Alí Páshá was made Kapúdán Páshá, and sailed to the Mediterranean with a fleet of 300 vessels, equal to the famous fleet of Kílí Alí Páshá. After an engagement with the infidels, in which the latter were defeated, the fleet anchored in the harbour of Kara Khoájehler, and the troops having carelessly gone on shore, the infidels came upon them and set fire to forty galleys and eleven galeons. When the news of this calamity reached the vezír, he offered to give up the seals, but the emperor would not accept his resignation, and thus he remained in office with a salary of 700 purses.

The cause of his fall.

The garrison at Azov having mutinied for want of pay, and murdered some of their officers, three hundred purses of money were changed into ducats, and were sent off by messengers on horseback, it being impossible to forward them by sea in the winter season. These three hundred purses were levied upon the merchants and tradesmen of Constantinople, to whom the Defterdár Emír Páshá, Kadda Kehiyá, and the inspector of the customs Hasan Chelebí, distributed linen, red and blue Morocco leather, and drugs, the confiscated property of many Musulmáns. One morning all the guilds of Constantinople assembled in arms on the At-Maidán, and with cries of "Alláh! Alláh!" proceeded to the royal Seráï to make their complaints against the three officers above mentioned. The Sultán sent three times for Melek Ahmed, who, fearing the violence of the mob, refused to come. At last the kapújílar kehiyásí (chief chamberlain), and the khás oda báshí (chief of the pages), came and insisted that he should either come to the presence or give up the seals. With the latter proposal he at once complied, and was afterwards appointed governor of Silistria, though he continued to reside some time at a house called the Topjílar Seráï in the vicinity of Constantinople.

The grand vezír who succeeded him was Síávush Páshá, an Abáza by birth. He was first chokadár to Sultán Murád IV., then Kapúdán Páshá, and passed through all the offices in Egypt. The kizlar-ághá, Dív Soleïmán Aghá, having strangled the mother of Sultán Murád, Kosem Sultáneh, with her own hair, and killed the ághá of the Janissaries, their lieutenant-general and their secretary, was one day boasting of his feats, when he suddenly gave Síávush a blow on the face, and taking the seals from him, gave them to Gúrjí Mohammed Páshá. Gúrjí had formerly obtained some repute as jebbehjí báshí (chief of the armoury) in the war of Hotín. He succeeded in raising a large fleet, and sent two thousand Janissaries and three thousand Sipáhís to Candia; but was dismissed from office on the pretext of being imbecile. His successor Tarkhúnjí Ahmed Páshá had been kehiyá to the vezírs Músá and Hazár-páreh Ahmed Páshá. He was subsequently made grand vezír of Egypt and of the Cupola; and though he raised the means of supporting the navy and army, and kept both in an excellent state, he was put to death on the plea of being a traitor.

Kapúdán Bíklí Dervísh Mohammed Páshá was a slave of Mustafá, the kizlar-ághá of Sultán Othmán, and a native of Circassia. He was a man possessed of great ability, and took a great interest in the affairs of state; but by the decree of God, he was attacked by a paralytic stroke, which confined him six months. During this period, the business of his office was transacted by Melek Ahmed Páshá, as káïm-makám or lieutenant. His disease proved fatal, and the seals were consigned a second time to Melek Ahmed Páshá; but after a consultation of all the Ulemá, which lasted for seven hours, on the suggestion of Melek Ahmed himself, it was resolved that the seals should be sent to Ibshír Páshá, a relation of the famous rebel Abáza Páshá, then governor of Haleb, and already noticed for the treacherous manner in which he killed his father-in-law, Várvár Páshá. He accepted the office; but not wishing to come to Constantinople, he excused himself by pleading the necessity of quelling some disturbances on the Persian frontier, whither he marched with a hundred thousand men. After repeated invitations, and having been presented with Aisha Sultáneh, the widow of Voinok Ahmed Páshá, as his wife, he at last, after a march of seven months, arrived at Scutari, but would not enter Constantinople. The kizlar ághá, and Sheikh-ul-Islám, then waited upon him at his palace at Scutari; and, presenting him with a sable pelisse and a dagger set with jewels, invited him in the name of the emperor to visit Constantinople, proposing at the same time to leave several páshás and Ulemá as hostages in his camp. To this he consented, and had an audience with the emperor; but the day after he was on the point of returning, and it was with great difficulty that he was prevailed upon to make a public entry into Constantinople at the head of his army of eighty thousand men. His first measure was to insist upon the necessity of sending the káïm-makám, Ahmed Páshá, to Ván, on the Persian frontier, on account of the disturbances in that quarter. The emperor remonstrated that it was not a proper province for so old and meritorious a vezír; but Ibshír replied, that it was a fine province of twenty-seven sanjaks and an annual revenue of a hundred thousand piastres. The diploma of the Páshá was therefore instantly made out and sent to Melek Ahmed by a chamberlain and ten chávushes, who pressed his immediate departure. Melek Ahmed, on ascertaining the object of their visit, raised the firmán, without kissing it, to his head, and presented three purses with a sable pelisse to the chamberlain, and fifty piastres to each of the chávushes. He however remained five days longer in making the necessary arrangements for his journey. On the fifth day, Ibshír complained to the emperor of Melek's delay, and urged the emperor to put him to death for his disobedience. The day after, the emperor sent a chamberlain to call Melek, and on his appearing was asked why he delayed going to so desirable a province as Ván, which, according to the account of Ibshír, had an income of a hundred thousand piastres. Melek boldly declared that what Ibshír stated was false; that Ibshír had no means of knowing, having never been admitted into the citadel by the mutinous garrison, and that the revenue scarcely amounted to seven thousand piastres. The emperor immediately called for pen and ink, and with his own hand wrote a khatisheríf, by which the power of appointing all the governors from Scutari to Egypt and Baghdád, together with the title of governor general, was conferred upon Melek Ahmed. Besides that, five hundred purses of gold, one hundred strings of mules, as many camels, an imperial tent, and two sable pelisses were given to him; and the emperor addressing him said: "Proceed now, my Lálá, and, if it please God, I propose some day to visit that country." At this Ibshír became pale as death, whilst Melek, after having offered up prayers for his Majesty's prosperity, went out, and, escorted by the bostánjí-báshí, he and his retinue passed over to Scutari in one hundred and fifty boats. Here he remained a week in the palace of Kíá-Sultáneh, making preparations for his journey. After a march of one hundred and seventeen days he entered Ván; and on the same day a messenger, named Yeldrim (lightning), having travelled with the speed of lightning, arrived bringing the news of the murder of Ibshír at Constantinople.

Murád Páshá was made grand vezír a second time; but the troops not being satisfied with him, he was dismissed from office; and dying shortly after in the palace of Arnáúd Páshá, he was buried in the tomb which the latter had built for himself. It is related as a well known story that, that when Murád Páshá, heard that Arnáúd Páshá was building a tomb for himself, he said: "Please God! he shall not have the satisfaction of being buried in it, but I will bury a black hog in it." The event was, that he himself was buried in it.

Silihdár Soleïmán Páshá was appointed governor of Rumeïlí, after having been for some time sword-bearer to the emperor. He was born at Malátieh and educated in the imperial harem, and was an amiable and worthy vezír. He was dismissed on some slight pretext, and was succeeded by Zúrnázen Mustafá Páshá, an Albanian by birth, and educated in the imperial harem. He was defterdár during the vezírat of Melek Ahmed Páshá, but was degraded on account of his great avarice, and filled several inferior offices. The seals were conferred upon him merely to tantalize him, for he had to return them one hour after he received them: thus he had the pleasure of enjoying only a faint shadow of the dignity of grand vezír. The seals were then sent by the khásekí, Sipáhí Mohammed, to Delí Husain, who was engaged in the siege of Candia. But the khásekí, having been delayed by contrary winds on his passage from Menkesheh to Candia, was overtaken by another messenger, who brought back the seals. They were then sent to Síávush, the governor of Ouzí (Oczakov), who became grand vezír a second time. At this time Melek Ahmed Páshá, having been recalled from the government of Ván, was delayed at Erzerúm, by the winter, on his return to Constantinople. Here he received the news of the death of the vezír Síávush, and of Defterdár Zádeh, who was strangled under the false accusation of having been concerned in the death of Síávush. Boiní Egrí Mohammed Páshá was next nominated grand vezír, and in his absence his duties were performed by Haider Aghá-Zádeh, as káïm-makám. Boiní Egrí, however, immediately sent to Melek Ahmed, inviting him to return to Constantinople, whilst Haider Aghá-Zádeh was appointed governor of Oczakov. On the very day that Melek Ahmed took his seat amongst the vezírs of the Cupola, Haider, who was setting out for Silivria from Silistria, was murdered, and his province was conferred upon Melek

Ahmed Páshá. Boiní Egrí Páshá having through his avarice lost his office, Kopreïlí Válí Mohammed Páshá was appointed his successor. This man being invested with absolute power, and being ambitious to bring glory to the Ottoman power, killed in Anatolia four hundred thousand rebels, seventeen vezírs, forty-one beglerbegs, seventy sanják begs, three mollahs, and a moghrebín sheikh. He proportioned the expenditure of the empire to its revenues, which he considerably enlarged by several conquests. The astrologers and cabalists call this Kopreïlí *Sáhib Kharúj, i.e.* Expenditor. He is buried in the mausoleum, near the poultry-market (Táúk-bázár). He was an Albanian by birth, but most zealous and active in the cause of the true faith. He was educated in the imperial harem, and when Khosrau Páshá left it with the rank of Aghá of the Janissaries, Kopreïlí was promoted to the office of Khazíneh-dár. After him his son, Fázil Ahmed Páshá, was named grand vezír. He was not of a blood-thirsty disposition like his father, but shewed himself a virtuous, upright, prudent, and honourable governor. He was born in the village of Koprí in the province of Sivás, and at first devoted himself to the study of the law, but was afterwards appointed governor of Erzerúm, then káïm-makám, and lastly grand vezír. He was the first instance of a son's holding the seals in succession from the father. Of the castles which he reduced, may be mentioned those of Kamenick and Candia. He died between Adrianople and Rodosto, on the *chiftlik* (estate) of Kara Bovir, and was buried beside his father.

His successor was Kara Mustafá Páshá, who was also educated in the harem of the Kopreïlís, and at different periods held the offices of chief master of the horse, governor of Silistria, kapúdán páshá, káïm-makám, and lastly, grand vezír. He was the son of a Sipáhí of Merzífún, and was a most excellent and prudent minister.

Vezírs of Provinces in the time of Sultán Mohammed IV.

During the rebellion in which Sultán Mohammed was raised to the throne, when the Janissaries were beaten by the Sipáhís, and loads of dead bodies were thrown into the sea, when Haider-Aghá-Zádeh, unable to make Seraglio-point, lost a great number of his gallies, on that same day, Murtezá Páshá was appointed governor of Damascus; Melek Ahmed Páshá was transferred from Díárbeker to Baghdád; Zilelí-Chávush-Zádeh Mohammed Páshá made governor of Jerusalem; Emír Páshá, governor of Egypt; Noghái Oghlí, governor of Haleb (Aleppo); Hamálí Arnáúd Mohammed Páshá, of Tripoli; and Afrásíáb Oghlí, of Basra.

Prince of Sultán Mohammed IV.

The Prince Mustafá was born in the year 1071 (A.D. 1660).

Monuments of Sultán Mohammed IV.

He built a mosque at Cairo, on the spot called Ibráhím Páshá Kadam-áltí. Over the gate there is a chronograph by Zekí Chelebí, in the Talík hand. He also built the koshks of Jámlíjeh, Kara Aghach, Ak-bikár, and the Adálet, which was rebuilt after the fire in the imperial palace; all in the year 1071 (1660).

Victories and Conquests, at which Sultán Mohammed IV. was present in person.

The first was the execution of the rebels in the At-maidán. In the same month the rebel Haider Oghlí was defeated in Anatolia, and carried prisoner to Constantinople by the Aghá of the Turcomans, Kara Abáza. The vezír, Khoajeh Mevleví, seeing that his thigh-bone was broken by a musket-ball, and that there was no hope of his recovery, ordered him to be executed immediately. He was therefore hanged at the gate called Parmak-kapú, where his body remained three days, and was afterwards thrown into the sea. In the same year, Emír Páshá defeated twenty thousand rebellious Arabs off Algiers;

and Gúrjí Ibní and Katerjí-oghlí were defeated by the vezír, Kara Mustafá Páshá. The first of these, at the head of eighty thousand men, had ravaged Anatolia as far as Scutari, and had taken up his position on the heights opposite Constantinople, called Bolghúrlí Jámlíjeh. He demanded seventy heads, and the government of Haleb (Aleppo). Defterdár-zádeh Mohammed Páshá led out his troops against him, and a battle was fought at Ziljámlíjeh. Murád Páshá arriving in person to the aid of the imperial troops; the rebels were completely routed.

Defeat of the Druses in Syria by Murtezá Páshá.

Yúváshjí Mohammed Aghá and Na'lband Alí Aghá, the commanders of Safet, owed one thousand purses which were to be paid by the Druses; but as the payment was delayed, Murtezá Páshá took the field against them with seventy banners. A great battle took place at Nákúra, where the Druses were beaten; and instead of one thousand purses, were now obliged to pay three thousand. I, the humble writer, had this year (1059) made the pilgrimage to Mecca by way of Egypt, and on my return to Syria was present at this battle, which I commemorated by a chronograph.

Conquest of Selina and Retimo in Candia.

In the same year Dashnik and Hainafí, two rebels who were offended with Melek Ahmed Páshá because they had not received the appointment of Aghás of the Turcomans, assembled a number of troops at Scutari, ravaged Anatolia, pillaged a caravan, and pitched their camp between Lefkeh and Súgúd. Melek Páshá, with the troops of some other Páshás, attacked them in this place, reduced their strength, and chased the greater part of them into the mountains. Dashnik Emerza and Hainafi Khalífeh were made prisoners, and on their way to Constantinople, were met at Jisrí (or Koprí) by the Bostánjí Báshí, who carried an imperial *firmán* for their execution. They were accordingly beheaded, and their heads were thrown down before the imperial gate. By the divine permission a stream of light rested that night on the head of Hainafí Khalífeh, which was witnessed by several hundreds of persons. Seventeen days after this, a rebellion broke out, by which Ahmed Páshá was obliged to resign the seals and retire to the government of Ouzí (Oczakov).

Defeat of the Infidel Fleet by Kapudán Chávush Zádeh.

This Kapudán brought to Constantinople three gallies and a gallion, which he had taken from the fleet of the despicable infidels.

Attack on the Cossacks, by Mohammed Gheräï Khán, at Oczakov.

The result of this expedition by this brave Tátár, was the capture of one hundred and fifty thousand prisoners. In the same year, Kalghá Sultán made an inroad upon Moldavia, penetrating as far as Yassy, Fokshan, and Hotín, and carrying off one hundred and fifty thousand prisoners, and one hundred thousand head of cattle of various kinds. The Cossacks were also defeated near Varna by Melek Ahmed Páshá, who, attacking their boats which had been left upon the shore, took twenty of them, but the rest escaped. Of the men who were on shore, seven hundred were made prisoners and a thousand killed. This took place in the year 1064 (1650). The castle Gúnieh, on the mouth of the river Júrúgh on the Black Sea, was delivered by Ketánjí-zádeh Mohammed Páshá in the year 1065. In the same year the Khán of Betlís, Abdál Khán, was subdued by Melek Ahmed Páshá, who also, in the following year, delivered the castle of Oczakov from the Cossacks. The castle of Tenedos was delivered from the Venetians by Kopreïlí Mohammed Páshá.

Defeat of Rakoczy.

Rakoczy, who had been named King of Poland by the grand vezír Boyúní, Egrí, but was not acknowledged as such by his successor Kopreïlí, assembled two hundred thousand men, in order to support his claim against the Poles, who had sent an envoy to request the assistance of the Ottoman arms. In consequence of this application, the Tátár Khán, Melek Mohammed Gheräï, and Melek Ahmed Páshá, the governor of Oczakov, took the field against Rakoczy, who was defeated, and fled with three hundred horsemen to the mountains of Szeklers in Transylvania. In the engagement, forty thousand infidels were slain, and seventeen princes, with Rakoczy's minister, taken prisoners, after which, the armies of the Tátár Khán, and Melek Ahmed Páshá, marched victoriously to Ak-kermán. I, the humble Evliyá, who composed a chronograph for this occasion, received seventeen prisoners, twenty horses, ten sable pelisses, a pair of silver stirrups, and other silver articles, as my share of the booty. The Hungarians seeing the defeat of Rakoczy, assembled an immense army composed of various nations, with which they attacked Temisvar, Lippa, Cianad, Gulia, and Fecsat. Complaints from these places having reached the Porte, the governor of Buda, Kana'án Páshá, received orders to march against the invading enemy. On the banks of the Maros, between Lippa and Arád, the Páshá encountered eighty thousand of the hostile army and was routed, but saved himself and some thousands of his cavalry by a flight to Slankament. In this defeat the Ottoman army lost no less than eleven thousand men. Kana'án Páshá was in consequence removed from Buda, and the government was given to Seidí Ahmed Páshá of Bosnia;

whilst the government of Bosnia was conferred upon Melek Ahmed Páshá. In the same year, Seidí Ahmed Páshá, with twelve thousand brave horsemen, entered the province of Transylvania by Demir-kapú (the Iron Gate), gave battle to the detested Rakoczy's army, who defended the castle of Koljovar, and defeated them, with the assistance of Husain Páshá, the brother of the governor of Temisvar, Síávush Páshá. The white bodies of the infidels were strewed upon the white snow; and the carriages, cannon, and tents were sent to Constantinople; where, however, no thanks were voted to Seidí Páshá for the victory, nor was even a "well done" said on the occasion, although it was a victory not less brilliant than that of Erla by Mohammed III.; for Seidí Páshá had no more than eleven thousand men opposed to a hundred and sixty thousand infidels, now inhabitants of hell. The vile Rakoczy escaped to the castle of Koljovar, where he began to collect a new army.

The emperor having heard of the depredations committed by the infidels in Bosnia, appointed Melek Ahmed to the command of an army against Zara. The Páshá assembled his troops under the walls of this fortress, but not being able to reduce it, he plundered the neighbouring country, attacked the castle of Rinjisi, which he took after a storm of seven hours, and carried off the inhabitants.

In the same year Rakoczy having refused to pay the tribute due by Transylvania, and having encamped with two hundred thousand men under Koljovar, was attacked a second time by Seidí Páshá with forty thousand chosen troops of Buda, Erla, Temisvar, and Kanisa. Rakoczy was beaten, wounded, and obliged to fly to Kalova, where he expired, calling out, "Receive me, O Jesus!" Jesus however would not receive him, but he was seized by the angel Azraïl. Seidí Páshá carried an immense booty, with several thousand heads to Constantinople; but even by this signal exploit he could not gain the emperor's favour.

The fortresses of Lippa, Jeno, and Lugos were conquered by Kopreïlí Mohammed Páshá, who also repaired the fortifications of Arad and Jeno, and was on the eve of undertaking an expedition against the Transylvanian fortresses, when he received repeated imperial rescripts, intimating that it was not the emperors wish to continue the war any longer in that country, and that should the Páshá even bring the king of Transylvania or the emperor of Germany prisoners to Constantinople, it would not meet his Majesty's approbation; but he was desired to proceed with all possible speed to the Porte, because Kara Husain Páshá in Anatolia, Sárí Kana'án Páshá, Sayár Mohammed Páshá, and forty rebellious Begs were marching against Brúsa. Kopreïlí, on receiving this *khatisheríf*, exclaimed, "Well done, Kara Husain, to come at this moment to the aid of the Hungarian infidel; may the result be fortunate!" Preparations for departure were immediately commenced, and it was proclaimed that all who valued their bread and honour should repair to Constantinople in order to engage in the religious war (*ghazá*). Sinán Páshá and Seidí Páshá were left to protect the castle of Jeno, whilst Kopreïlí marched with the greatest possible haste towards Constantinople, in the vicinity of which, at Kiaght-Kháneh, he encamped. The troops were daily paid, and three thousand Sipáhís and seven thousand Janissaries, who were absent from the review, had their names struck off the lists. The emperor of the seven climates then moved his camp to Scutari; fetvás of the muftis of the four orthodox sects were circulated throughout Anatolia, and firmáns were sent to Kara Murtezá Páshá, the governor of Díárbekr, to Gúrjí Mustafá Páshá, governor of Erzerúm; and to Tútsák Alí Páshá, governor of Haleb (Aleppo), who were all summoned to march against Abáza Kara Hasan Páshá. The latter in the same year defeated Murtezá Páshá, the governor of Díárbekr, in the field of Ulghún, and obliged him to fly to Haleb. He then collected his Segbáns and Saríjehs, and excited such a terror in the four vezírs, who were, besides, much distressed by a scarcity of provisions, that they sent messengers to Constantinople to obtain pardon for the rebels, who, at the same time, had taken possession of Aleppo.

In the same year Melek Ahmed Páshá of Bosnia sent seven thousand heads to the Porte, and announced the reduction of the fortresses of Kámín, Kirád, and Rinja. Alí Páshá, who had the government of the Dardanelles, was removed, and sent against the castle of Arad, which surrendered.

The rebellion of Mehneh Beg in Valachia being evident, Fazlí Páshá, Ján Arslán Páshá, and several Begs were sent against him. The two armies met at Gurgivo, and the Ottoman army was defeated. At the same time the prince of Moldavia, Búrúnsiz Kostantin (Constantine without a nose) erected the standard of rebellion at Yassy, began to coin new *zolotas* (money), and took possession of Moldavia. The Tátár Khán of the Crimea, and the Tátárs of Búják, were ordered against him; whilst young Stefano, son of Lipul, the late prince of Moldavia, a prisoner in the Seven Towers, was nominated prince. On this occasion Kemán-kesh Ahmed Aghá was appointed *Iskemla-Aghá* (aghá of the chair), and Siláhshúr Ahmed Aghá, the Sanjak-ághá (ághá of the banner.[7]) The army reached Yassy on a severe winter day, when a battle ensued, the result of which was the flight of Búrúnsiz Kostantin, the loss of ten thousand men on the part of the infidels, and the establishment of prince Stefano. The flying Moldavians were pursued by the Tátárs as far as Valachia, and the whole country was ravaged by fire. Fazlí Páshá and Ján Arslán Páshá, who at this time were shut up in the fortress of Gurjivo, were in the greatest distress, and had already resolved to drown themselves, when the infidels being afraid of the Tátárs, left the trenches and fled to Bucharest. The

Ottomans pursued them, and took a great number of prisoners and immense booty. The Tátárs, also, continued their pursuit after the infidels as far as the mountains of Prashova (Kronstadt) on Irshova (Orsova), and took prisoners twenty thousand Valachians and sixty-seven thousand Moldavians. Thus, God be praised! in twenty days Valachia and Moldavia were reduced; and I, the humble writer, who was present, received as my share the value of twenty prisoners. Young Stefano presented me with a purse of gold, six saddle-horses, and a robe; and Ghazá-Zádeh, the Aghá of the Sanjak, gave me a purse, one horse, and a fine boy. On the forty-second day we entered Adrianople. God be praised that I was in this brilliant expedition! I then proceeded to join my lord, Melek Ahmed Páshá, whom I found at Háluna. Were I, however, to describe the Bosnian victories, my list would be extended to an inconvenient length. To be brief, my lord, Melek Ahmed Páshá, was removed from the government of Bosnia, and on a Monday, the 12th of Rabiul-evvel 1071 (1660), was promoted to the government of Rúmeïlí. The province of Bosnia was given to Alí Páshá, the conqueror of Arad, who, in the year 1072 (1661) was also appointed commander of the army against Kemeny, in Transylvania. Seventy sanjaks, twenty odas of Janissaries and artillerymen, and four Búlúks, altogether amounting to eighty-seven thousand men, assembled on the plains of Temesvar, and headed, after the death of Alí Páshá, by Seidí Páshá, entered Transylvania by the Demir-kapú, and encamped on the plain of Hájak. On the twentieth day they were joined by Sháh Púlád Aghá, with forty thousand Tátárs, who had been sent to distress Kemeny, and had obtained useful information of the movements of the enemy, and taken several thousands of prisoners. The Vezír of Bude, Ismail Páshá, had the command of the vanguard, and Transylvania was ravaged for eight months, as far as the Teiss, which Husain Páshá, the brother of Síávush Páshá was ordered to pass. He advanced with his chosen troops as far as Kasha and Hasswar, and proposed the son of Zulúmí as king of Transylvania. The people, however, having declared that they would have no other king but Kemeny, with whom they were satisfied, Husain, after encountering a thousand difficulties, repassed the Teiss. Ismail Páshá having been appointed commander against the Szeklers, returned to the imperial camp with seventeen thousand prisoners. He then moved his camp to Odvarhel, where he proclaimed the infidel, Apasty Michel, king, and collected two thousand purses (a million of piastres), being the arrears of tribute which had been due for three years. This year (1071), during our stay near the castle of Sázmajár, at Sibín, we received intelligence of the death of Kopreïlí Mohammed, and of the promotion of his son to the vazírat. A great battle, also, on a severe winters day, was fought at Forgrash: the army returned by the Demir kapú, with forty thousand waggons and a hundred thousand prisoners, and were sent into winter quarters. My lord, Melek Ahmed Páshá, took up his winter quarters at Belgrade, whence, by the express command of the emperor, he repaired to Constantinople, to be present at the marriage of Fátima, the daughter of Sultán Ahmed. My lord had been a vezír of the cupola for three months when he died, and was buried in the burial-ground of Eyúb, at the feet of his late master, Kechí Mohammed Efendí. Thus the unfortunate Evliya was left without a patron; but God is merciful!

The following castles were also conquered: Uivár, Litra, Novígrád, Lowa, Sikíán, Kermán, Deregil, Holáúk, and Boyák, and many thousands of prisoners were taken. But forty-seven days earlier the famous victory of Gran was won, which might be compared to the victories of Erla and Moháj. It was followed by the fall of the castles of Kiskúivár, Kemenvár, Egervád, Egerzek, Balashka, Washún, and forty others, which were all burnt. All these belonged to Zerín Oghlí (Zriny). Before Kiskúivár was conquered, it was necessary to deliver from the hands of the infidels the castles of Essek, Lippova, Siklos, Beks, Kapushvár, Kopen, Nadas, Berebisinj, Siget, and Kaniza, which were all besieged by the German Electors. When, however, they heard of the arrival of the grand vezír, they raised the siege of Kanisa, and fled to the new castle (Kiskúivár), which was also subsequently conquered. Croatia was ravaged, thirty-six castles were burnt, and the inhabitants carried away captives.

Elated with such success, the Moslem army advanced to the river Raab, where, after the conquest of Kiskúivár, it was defeated by the mismanagement of the grand vezír, Ismail Páshá, and Gurjí Mohammed Páshá. Many thousands of Moslems were drowned in the Raab; the Sipahís were deceived by a retrograde motion of the Janissaries, and these, seeing the retreat of the Sipahís, also took to flight, in consequence of which the bridge broke down, and an immense number of men were drowned. The vezír defended himself bravely for twenty-four hours longer, but at last retreated to Stuhlweissenburg, whence he sent proposals of peace. He then took up his winter quarters at Belgrade, and an envoy having been sent from the German emperor, Kara Mohammed Páshá was dispatched as ambassador to Vienna, and the humble author received orders to accompany him in the embassy. The peace being concluded at Vienna, I travelled, with the emperor's patent, through Germany to Dunkirk, thence to Denmark, Holland (where I saw Amsterdam), Sweden, and Cracovie, in Poland, making, in three years and a half, the tour of the countries of the seven infidel kings (the seven Electors). In the year 1668, on the night of the Prophets ascension, I found myself on the Ottoman frontier, at the castle of Toghan-kechid, on the Dneister. Conducted by my guides, who were Kozaks, I saw lights in the minaret, and, for the first time, after so long an absence, I heard the sound of the Mohammedan call to prayer. As the gates of the castle are closed after sunset, I spent the night in one of the Búza houses outside, and in the morning crossed the river to Sháhín Germán, whence in three days I reached the Crimea, and continued my journey through Dághistán to Russia. Here, God be praised, I completed my travels through the seven climates. I then travelled seventy days with the Russian envoy, and joining Ak Mohammed Páshá and his deputy, I returned to the Crimea. Here I received presents from the Tátár Khán, Chobán Gheráï Oghlí, and travelling with Ak Mohammed Páshá, who had been deprived of his governorship, I reached Constantinople in eighty days. Thence I proceeded to Adrianople, and afterwards to Candia, which surrendered to Kopreïlí Zádeh Fázil Ahmed Páshá in 1080 (1669), after a struggle of three years. This was followed by the conquest of Maina, and the building of the castle of Zarenta in 1081 (1670). In the same year Kamienik, in Poland, one of the strongest fortresses of the infidels, was reduced, and mosques were erected in it. For this, and several other places, the King of Poland paid tribute to the Porte. The victorious sultan then proceeded to his second capital, Adrianople, and fixed his winter quarters at Hájí Oghlí Pasání, whilst the grand vezír remained at Bábátághí. The sultan subsequently removed to Yassi, and the vezír remained where he was.

All the fortresses and castles conquered were adorned with mosques, wherein divine worship was performed according to the true faith, and in the name of Sultan Mohammed IV., whose reign may God perpetuate.

Here I conclude my historical account of the sultáns, and their vezírs and muftís, from Mohammed II. to Murád IV., who are all buried at Constantinople.

Having digressed a little, by giving an account of the statistics and principal historical events, I shall now resume my description of the imperial mosques of Constantinople.

Description of the Mosque of the Válideh.

This building was undertaken, at an immense expense, by the Sultáneh Válideh, the mother of Mohammed II.; but at her death it remained unfinished, and fell into decay. It was then called *zulmíeh* (the dark); but, when the Válideh was travelling in the country, after the burning of Constantinople, the foundations were cleared of the rubbish, and the sultán, devoting five thousand purses from his own treasury, ordered the building to be completed. It was then called *a'dlíeh* (the just). It is now the tenth of the imperial mosques of Constantinople, and is situated between the Shahíd Kapú-sí (gate of martyrs) and the Bálik Bázár (fish market), in the quarter of the Jews, whose houses, by the divine permission, being burnt down, themselves were banished from the spot, and the ground occupied by their houses was added to the court and market of the mosque, which was completed in ten years, and was properly called a'dlíeh instead of zulmíeh. The north of the building looks towards the walls of the city, and on the south is the great court (haram). The cupola, from its base to the top, measures no less than seventy yards. The whole is built upon an elevated pavement, which is ascended on four sides by flights of steps. The mosque is built in the same style as the mosque of the Princes, and that of Sultán Ahmed I. in the At-maidán; four small semi-cupolas support the centre one, which is besides supported by four large columns. The mahfil of the moazzíns is elevated by small columns; and the mahfil of the emperor is on the left hand, made of the most exquisite marble-work. One of its columns occasioned the death of Yúsuf Páshá, the conqueror of Egypt. Some informers accused him of having in his possession a pillar of pure gold, which, however, upon examination was found to be only of yellow stone; but this discovery was made when it was too late; and this valuable column, which shines brighter than gold, was put under the emperors mahfil. The building is well lighted by a great number of windows, and at night by lamps. The mehráb (recess) and mimber (pulpit) are of fine variegated stone. The gates are five in number; two side gates, one for the imám, one for the khatíb, and the fifth facing the mehráb. The rich trappings and ornaments suspended in the mosque are unequalled, not only in any mosque in Constantinople, but throughout the dominions of the Islám. The doors and window-shutters are all inlaid with mother-o'-pearl; and the Persian and Egyptian carpets, with which the floor is covered, give the mosque the appearance of a Chinese picture gallery. No where else is there to be seen so great a number of beautiful inscriptions. Over every window are verses from the sacred word, inscribed by Teknéjí-Zádeh Mustafá Chelebí, in the Karahisárí hand. The sheikhs of this place were the celebrated preachers Vaní, and Isperí Efendí. In the time of Sultán Mohammed IV. it was the resort of the most renowned doctors, professors, and readers of the Korán. The great gate is ornamented with a beautiful chronograph in golden letters, expressing the date 1074. The large court-yard, which lies before the principal gate, is paved with marble and surrounded by stone benches. The cupolas are covered with lead, and the windows are of glass. In the centre of the yard are a fountain and basin. The harem or court-yard has two side gates and one grand gate, which opens into a second or outer court, planted with different sorts of trees. On the kibla side is a mausoleum intended for the Sultáneh Válideh, to whom may God grant long life! In the garden before the harem Sultán Mohammed built, on the bulwark called Komliklí Kalla', a koshk resembling those in Paradise. On the south and west sides of the great court are built about a thousand shops of stone (the Egyptian market). This grand court has four gates, and two lofty minárehs, the tops of which being covered with bronze, dazzle the eyes of the beholders by their brightness. They are both of three stories.

Description of the Mosque of Abul-vafá.

The eleventh imperial mosque is that of the sheikh Abul-vafá, built by Sultán Mohammed, on a small scale, but eminent on account of its age and sanctity. It has one mináreh, a court, a school, and a bath.

Description of the Mosque of Emír Najárí.

This, like the former, is a small mosque, built by Sultán Mohammed the Conqueror. It has a mináreh and an imáret (refectory).

The Fat'híeh Mosque.

This mosque was formerly a large convent, and was converted into a mosque by Sultán Mohammed the Conqueror, who also built the Orta-jámi', or the mosque of the Janissaries, in the middle of their barracks. It was destroyed by fire, but rebuilt by Soleïmán Kehiyá.

The above are the imperial mosques within the walls of Constantinople; the most remarkable of those in the suburbs are the following: The mosque of Eyúb; the mosque of Jehángír at Top-kháneh; the mosque of Mohammed II. in the castle of Rúmeïlí; the mosque of Murád IV. in the upper castle of Rúmeïlí, called Kawák, near Búyúkdereh; the mosque of the same sultán in the castle opposite, Kawák Anadoli, or Majár; the mosque of the conqueror in the delightful valley of Kok-sú (the Aretas); the mosque of Sultáneh Mehrmáh, the daughter of Sultán Soleïmán, in the harbour of Scutari; and a second mosque at Scutari, of the Válideh of Sultán Murád IV., Kosem Sultáneh.

These are the imperial mosques in the suburbs of Constantinople; but there are many more in the villages on the shores of the Bosphorus, which, if it please God, shall be described in their proper place.

SECTION XVI.

Of the Mosques of the Vezírs at Constantinople.

The most ancient of these is the mosque of Mahmúd Páshá, near the new bezestán, as large as an imperial mosque. It has three cupolas, three gates, and a spacious court. Over the principal gate there is written in Arabic: "May God sanctify this good place to us," which is a chronograph.

The second is the mosque of Mollá Khair-ad-dín within the Corn-market, and, like the former, was built in the time of Sultán Mohammed II. When Khair-ad-dín was building it, he was one day disturbed in his meditations by the noise of a stork; he exclaimed, "Begone ye noisy birds; fly without the town;" and since that time no stork has ever been seen within the walls of Constantinople, though numbers of them are to be found in the suburbs and neighbouring villages.

The mosque Kahríeh, near the Adrianople gate, was originally a church. Khoajeh Mustafá Páshá, the vezír of Sultáns Mohammed and Báyazíd II., built the large mosque near the Selivrí gate in the year 950 (1548). It is surrounded by a yard, in which, it is said, are buried all the heroes who fell during the siege of Constantinople by Hárún-ar-rashíd. It is a mosque of great sanctity. The chained fig-tree (zinjírlí injír), which stands in the court, was so called, because, when nearly split and decayed, it was chained up by a pious man. The imáret, convent, and college of this mosque, are well attended.

The mosque of Fírúz-ághá near the At-maidán, has one cupola, and is also well attended.

In the Chehár-shenbeh bázár (Wednesday market) is the mosque of Mohammed, the ághá of Sultán Murád IV.

In the Uzún-chárshí (long market) is the mosque of Ibráhím Páshá, the cupola of which is constructed of wood.

The mosque of Yúnus Beg Terjimán is near the Fat'híeh, and has a chronograph, giving the date of its erection and the name of its founder.

The Ouch Básh (three heads), near Zinjírlí Kapú, is so called because it was built by a barber who shaved three heads for one small piece of money, and, notwithstanding, grew so rich that he was enabled to build this mosque. It is a small but peculiarly sanctified mosque; the inscription expresses the date 929 (A.D. 1522).

The mosque of Sana'allah Efendí, near the Kirk-chesmeh (forty fountains), was destroyed by fire, but was restored in 1013 (1662).

The mosque of Kúrekjí-báshí, near the Silivrí gate, has, in the south-east corner, a dial (míkát) which points out the time with the greatest exactness both in summer and winter.

The Balát-jámi' (of the palace), within the Balát Kapú, was built in the time of Sultán Suleïmán, by Farrukh Kehiyá, Sinán being the architect. On the exterior of the south-east wall, an able artist has painted all the difficult passes and stations on the road from Jerusalem to Egypt, and thence to Mecca and Medina.

Near the mosque of Sultán Selím is that of the convent of Sívársí Efendí. It has a cistern supported by six columns, but having no water it is now used by the silk spinners.

The Ak-shems-ad-dín, near the custom-house, on the land side, is a mosque in which the prayers offered up are always accepted by Heaven; it is on that account frequented day and night.

The mosque of the Azabs, within the Corn-market, was built by Elwán Chelebí, in the time of the Conqueror. It is commonly called the Shiftálú Jámi' (peach mosque), because a peach tree grew out of the south-east wall, which was afterwards destroyed by fire.

The mosque of A'áshik Páshá is also much frequented.

The Altí-boghácheh Jámi' (six cakes mosque), near the hammám of the muftí, was built by the chief baker of Mohammed II., Jibbeh Alí, who used to supply the emperor, as he did Sultán Báyazíd, with six cakes daily.

The mosque of Kara Pír Páshá, near the Zírek-báshí, on an elevated spot: this has a cistern, supported by three hundred columns, and containing water delicious as that of Paradise.

The mosque near the At-bázár (horse-market) was that in which, during the reign of Mohammed II., the twelve Janissary colonels, who every night patroled the city, assembled for evening prayers.

The mosque of the mír-ákhor (master of the horse), near the Seven Towers and the Súlúmonástir, was also formerly a convent, built by the architect Sinán.

The mosque of Khádim Ibráhím, the grand vezír of Suleïmán, within the Selivrí gate. The court is full of trees. It is a fine mosque.

The mosque of Dávud Páshá, near the Altí-marmar (six marbles), was built by one of the vezírs of Sultán Báyazíd II. It has a spacious court, and a hall of justice attached to it.

The mosque of Jerráh Mohammed Páshá, with six minárehs, was built by one of the vezírs of Sultán Ahmed I., near the Evret-bázár (women market).

The mosque of Khosrou Páshá, near the Ak-seráï, is a neat mosque.

The mosque of old Alí Páshá, near the column of Táúk-bázár (the poultry), is very commodious.

The mosque of Nishánjí Páshá is situate near the Kúm-kapú (sandgate).

The mosque of Ahmed Páshá, the grand vezír of Sultáns Selim and Suleïmán, is very large, like an imperial one, and is built upon a small hill within the Top-kapú (cannon-gate).

The mosque of Bairám Páshá, the vezír of Sultán Murád IV., is on an elevated spot, near that of the conqueror, and ascended by a flight of steps.

The mosque of the great Nishánjí Páshá, near Keskíndedeh, is built in an elegant style like those of the Sultáns. The founder is buried in an adjoining vault.

The mosque of Háfez Páshá, near that of Mohammed II. The founder of this mosque had a dream, in which the conqueror appeared to him, and demanded of him how he dared to erect a mosque so near his own, thus taking away the people who attended it? The conqueror was then about to kill him, when Háfez Ahmed awoke. He died seventy days after this dream, and, as he was carried to the tomb, a stone fell upon him from the mosque of Sultán Mohammed, and cut his head as if it had been severed by the sword.

The mosque of Khalíl Páshá is also near that of Sultán Mohammed II.

The mosque of TaváSh Mesíh Páshá is also near the above, in the market of Alí Páshá. Its founder was taken from the chamber of cellar-pages (kílár), in the time of Murád III., and made governor of Egypt, and afterwards grand vezír.

The mosque of Bálí Páshá is a lofty building, near the mosque of Emír Najárí, and was built by Sinán.

The mosque of Rustam Páshá, the vezír of Soleïmán, in that part of the town called Takht-ul-kala', is ornamented with glazed tiles. It is beautiful beyond the powers of description. On all sides it is surrounded with shops.

The mosque of Yavursár, in the corn-market, has one cupola, but no chronograph. It was built by my grandfather.

The mosque of the corn-market was built by the lieutenant of police in the time of Sultán Soleïmán. It is situate without the corn-market, on the sea-shore, and was built by Sinán. Being decayed, it was repaired by Kara

185

Chelebí Zádeh. It stands on an elevated spot, has a lofty cupola, six shops, several warehouses, and a minaret, which in point of elegance surpasses all others in Constantinople.

The mosque of the Válideh of Sultán Othmán II. is near the Ak-seráï, and was built by the famous architect Khoajeh Sinán.

The mosque of the famous architect himself is near that of Sultán Báyazíd.

The mosque of the Kádhí Asker Abdu-r-rahmán Efendí, by Sinán.

The mosque of Hájí Evhad Allah, at the Seven Towers, by the same architect.

The mosque of Khádim Mahmúd Aghá, the kapú ághá, or chief of the white eunuchs, is near the Akhor-kapú (stable-gate). He was the ághá of Sultáns Soleïmán and Selím II.

The mosque of Khoajeh Khosrou Beg, is near that of Khoajeh Mustafá Páshá, and was built by Sinán.

The Khátún-jámi' (mosque of the lady) is near the Hammám of Súlí Monástir; also the work of Sinán.

Near the fountain Oskoplí, at the place where seven streets meet (which is not the case in any other part of Constantinople), stands the square built mosque of Defterdár Soleïmán Chelebí.

The mosque of Harem Chávush, near the new garden, built by Sinán; who also built the mosque near the Kádhí-cheshmeh (fountain of the judge), and called it after his own name.

The mosque of Akhí-chelebí is in the fruit market, and was built by Sinán.

The Old Mesjids, or small Mosques of Constantinople.

Sultán Mohammed II. alone consecrated one hundred and seventy mesjids at Constantinople.

The mesjid of the Crimea, near the old barracks; that of Mohí-ad-dín, near the mosque of Mohammed II.; Khárájí Beg, near the corn-market, over the door of which the architect has formed most ingeniously, with red and white bricks, "There is no god but God; Mohammed is his Prophet." The mesjid of Sáleh Páshá, near the corn-market; of Haider Páshá, in the same neighbourhood; of Hájí Hasan, near the last, built by Sinán; of Demír Khán, near the cold-well; of Hámid Efendí, with a chronograph expressing 985; the Arabajílar, near the corn-market; of Pápás Oghlí, within the corn-market; the Bárhisár, within the gate Jebbeh Alí; the Reváni, near the Forty Fountains.

The mesjids built by Sinán are: the Rustam Páshá, at Yení-bághcheh; the Sinán Páshá, in the same place; the Muftí Cheví Zádeh, at the Cannon-gate; that of his own name, at Yení-bághcheh; that of Emír Alí, near the custom-house, on the land side; the Uch-básh (three heads), near the above; the Defterdár Sheríf Zádeh; the Sirmákesh, at the top of Yení-bághcheh, near Lutfí Páshá; the Khoajehgí Zádeh, near Mohammed II.; the Takíájí Ahmed Chelebí, near the Selivrí-gate; the Dabbágh Hájí Hamza, at the Aghá's meadow; the mesjid of the lady of Ibrahim Páshá, near the Kúm-kapú; the mesjids of the goldsmiths; of the tailors; of the Aghá, at St. Sophia; of Sheikh Ferhád, near Lanka-bostán; of Kurekjí Báshí, without the Kúm-Kapú; of Yáyá Báshí, within the Fener-gate; of Abd-sú Báshí, near the mosque of Selím I.; of Husain Chelebí; of Hájí Eliás; of La'l Zádeh Dámád Chelebí; of Dokhání-Zádeh, near old Mustafá Páshá's mosque; of Kádhí-Zádeh, near Chokúr-hammám; of the gun factory, in the corn-market; of the Seráï Aghásí, without the Adrianople-gate; of Eliás-Zádeh, without the Cannon-gate; of the Sarráf-Zádeh, in the same quarter; and of Hamdullah Hamídí Chelebí, at Súlí Monástir. All these mesjids were built by the famous architect, old Sinán, the builder of the mosque of Sultán Soleïmán, who erected no fewer than three thousand and sixty buildings, consisting of kháns, mosques, imárets, colleges, schools, palaces, &c. It was he who built the round cupola, entirely of marble, for his monument, near the mosque of Sultán Soleïmán, in the corner of the palace of the ághá of the Janissaries, adjoining the Fountain-house. He died one hundred and seventy years old. On the stone placed at his head is an inscription in letters of gold, in the Kara-hisárí Hasán Chelebí hand, which is a most exquisite performance.

There are many other mosques and mesjids in Constantinople, but those which we have described are the most remarkable for their architecture.

SECTION XVII.

Of the Medresehs or Colleges.

The first college founded at Constantinople after its conquest by Sultán Mohammed was that of Ayá Sofía; the next was the foundation of the eight colleges on the right and left, that is, on the north and south of Sultán Mohammed's mosque; these eight colleges may be compared to eight regions of Paradise. The Sultán also founded a school for the reading of the Korán on a spot adjoining the college, and on the east a hospital for the poor. This hospital is a model for all such foundations. On the north and south of the eight colleges are the cells of the students (*sokhté*), three hundred and sixty-six in number, each inhabited by three or four students, who receive their provisions and candles from the trust (*wakf*). There is also a conservatory (*dár-uz-ziáfat*), and a kitchen lighted by seventy cupolas, which may be compared to the kitchen of Kaikáús, where the poor are fed twice a day. Near this refectory there is a cárávanseráï, and a large stable capable of holding three thousand horses and mules.

The medreseh of Sultán Báyazíd is situate on the south side of the grand court of his mosque. The Sheikh-ul-Islám is the chief lecturer, and superintends its affairs.

The medreseh of Sultán Selím, near Yení-bághcheh, at the Koshk of Khaljílar, was built by Sultán Soleïmán, but dedicated to the memory of his father. Its revenue was derived from the Yení-bághcheh (new garden), which originally was one mile long and half a mile broad. On this very spot Sultán Selím pitched his camp when he came to the empire, and received the act of obeisance.

The medreseh of Sultán Soleïmán, on the north and south of this mosque, consists of four schools, one for the traditions (*dár-ul-hadíth*), one for reading the Korán (*dár-ul-kiráa't*); a separate one for medicine, with an hospital and an asylum for the insane, numerous baths, a cárávánseráï, a stable, and a boys' school.

The college of the Prince Mohammed was built by Sinán, and is famous for its learning.

The college of Sultán Ahmed I. adjoins the mosque of the same name.

The college of Kara Mustafá Páshá is near Parmák-kapú (finger-gate).

The college of Mo'íd Efendí is near the Kádhí Cheshmeh.

The college of Hámid Efendí, at the Fílyúkúshí (Elephant's hill).

The college of Hasan Páshá, near the palace of Jánpúlád Zádeh, is a fine lofty building, and the lower part of it is ornamented with shops.

The college of Esmakhán Sultán, is within the Adrianople gate.

The colleges of Kadhí Mahmúd Efendí; of Murád Páshá; of Dávud Páshá; of old Alí Páshá; of Mesíh Páshá; of Rustam Páshá; of Chevízádeh; of Kapenkejí; of Báshjí Ibrahím Beg; of Altí-marmar; of Nishánjí Mohammed Beg; of Kúrekjí-báshí; of Kara Pírí Páshá, near Soúk-koyú; of Afzal Zádeh; of Mardumíeh, near the Kizil Maslak; of Mollá Kúrání, the khoájeh of Sultán Mohammed II.: being offended with the Sultán he left him and went to Egypt, but subsequently returned at the Sultán's request, and was present at the siege of Constantinople; the college of Revání, an eloquent man of the time of Sultáns Selím I. and Soleïmán, a native of Adrianople, and was buried near the Kirk Cheshmeh (Forty Fountains) before his own mosque; the college of Etmekjí Zádeh Ahmed Páshá, the Defterdár of Sultán Ahmed I.; of Sunnat Khatún; of Fatima Sultáneh; of Uch Básh (three heads); of Núr-ad-dín Hafr, within the Adrianople gate, built by Sinán; of Farrúkh Kehiyá; of Mená; of Ak-hesám-ad-dín, near the bath of Sultán Selím; of old Ibrahím Páshá; of Khásekí Sultán; of Kahriéh, built by Sinán; of Khásekí, in the women-market, also built by Sinán, at the expense of Sultán Soleïmán; of the Válideh of Sultán Othmán II. near the Ak-seráï; of Makbúl Ahmed Páshá; of Iskender Páshá; of Súfí Mohammed Páshá; of Ibrahím Páshá, near the Isá-kapú (gate of Jesus); of Ja'far Aghá; of the Treasurer, Ahmed Aghá; of Moavil Emír; of Omm-valad; of the Kádhí Asker Dervísh Efendí; of Khoajehkí Zádeh, near the Sultán Mohammed II.; of Aghá Zádeh; of Defterdár Abd us-salám Beg; of Túti Kádhí; of Sháh Kúlí Hakím Mohammed Chelebí; of Husain Chelebí; of Emír Sinán Chelebí; of Daraghán Yúnus; of Kárjí Soleïmán; of Hárjí Khatún; of Defterdár Sherífeh Zádeh; of Kádhi Hakím Chelebí; of Bábá Chelebí; of Germástí Zádeh; of Segbán Alí; of Bezestán Kehiyásí; of Kowájilar; of Imám Zádeh; and of Kor Ahmed Páshá. Fifty of these colleges were built in the time of Sultáns Selím I. and Soleïmán, by the famous architect Sinán.

SECTION XVIII.

Of the Dár-ul-kirá of Constantinople.

Each grand mosque has a *dár-ul-kirá*, or school for the reading of the Korán, the most remarkable of which is the *dár-ul-kirá* of Sultán Soleïmán. Those of Khosrou Kehiyá, near the mosque of Etmekjí Zádeh Ahmed Páshá; of Sa'dí Chelebí; of Muftí Zádeh; and of Bosnalí Ahmed Páshá, were all built by the celebrated architect Sinán.

SECTION XIX.

Of the Mekteb, or Boys' Schools.

Each imperial mosque has a school attached to it. There are besides these, the schools of Kara Mustafá Páshá, opposite the monument of the same name: it is a large establishment; the school of Khosrou Páshá, near the Yeníbághcheh; of Aghá Kapú-sí, near the mosque of Sultán Soleïmán, which is attended by three or four hundred boys; of Pápás Oghlí, near the corn-market; of Aáshik Páshá; of Alí Jemálí, at Zírek; and of Mohammed Páshá, in the quarter of Khoájeh Páshá.

SECTION XX.

Of the Dár-ul-hadíth, or Tradition Schools.

The traditions are read at all the Imperial mosques according to the principles of *Moslem* and *Bokhárí*. The schools built especially for that object are: the dár-ul-hadíth of Hasan Efendí, near Keskindeh; of Mollá Is'hák Chelebí, built A.H. 926; and of Dámád Mohammed Efendí, near the mosque of Sinán.

SECTION XXI.

Of the Tekíeh, or Convents of Dervíshes.

The most ancient of these is the one founded by Mohammed II., within the grand gate of Ayá Sófíya, and is called Sirkejí Tekíeh. It was founded when Moslema and Eyúb besieged Constantinople, and was afterwards turned into a nunnery; but on Mohammed's conquering Constantinople he again made it a convent. Its first Sheikh was Oveis, who had the charge of seventy-four disciples. He was buried at Damascus, near Belál the Abyssinian: may God sanctify his secret state! The other tekíehs are those of Ak-shems-ud-dín, near Alí Páshá; of Emír Najárí; of Sofílar; of Khoájeh Mustafá Páshá; of Umm-sinán; of Sívásí; of Táváshí Mohammed Aghá, near Ayá Sófiya; of Erdebílí; of Sunbul Efendí; and of Gulshení at Ak-Seráï.

SECTION XXII.

Of the Imáret, or Refectories.

Praise be to God! who, according to the sacred text of the Korán: "There is no beast on the earth for which God hath not made a provision," has provided a plentiful supply for the poor by the foundation of Sultán Mohammed II. at the new palace, in which food is distributed to them three times a day; at the Imáret of Sultán Báyazíd twice; the same at the imárets of Sultán Selím I.; Soleïmán; Prince Mohammed; Ahmed; Eyúb; Khasekí Sultán, near the women-market; Vafá Sultán; Prince Jehángír, near the Top-kháneh; Mehrmáh Sultán, at Scutari; Válideh of Murád IV.; Ibráhím Khán; and of Othmán Khán. May God extend His mercy to them all! Besides these there are some hundreds of kitchens attached to the various convents; but the above are the old establishments of the Sultáns and Princes, where the poor receive a loaf of bread and a dish of soup every day. I, the humble Evliyá, who during a period of fifty-one years have visited the dominions of eighteen different monarchs, have no where seen such establishments.

SECTION XXIII.

Of the Tímáristán and Moristán, or Hospitals.

The Tímár-kháneh of Mohammed II., which consists of seventy rooms, covered with eighty cupolas, is attended by two hundred servants, a physician-general, and a surgeon. All travellers who fall sick are received into this hospital, and are well attended to. They have excellent food twice a day; even pheasants, partridges, and other delicate birds are supplied. If such are not at hand in the hospital, it is provided by the charter of foundation that they shall be furnished from the imárets of Sultán Soleïmán, his son Prince Mohammed, Sultán Ahmed I., Khásekí Sultán, Vafá Sultán, Eyúb Sultán, Prince Jehángír, Mehrmáh Sultáneh, and of the Válideh's mosque at Scutari. There are musicians and singers who are employed to amuse the sick and insane, and thus to cure their madness. There is also a separate hospital for infidels. The hospital of Sultán Soleïmán is an establishment so excellent, that the sick are generally cured within three days after their admission, it being provided with most able physicians and surgeons. The mosques of Báyazíd and Selím have no hospitals attached to them. The hospital of Sultán Ahmed is chiefly for the reception of insane persons, on account of the purity of its air. The attendants are remarkable for their patience and good-nature, the reason of which is, that they are under the immediate inspection of the Kizlar-ághásí, who himself attends to inquire into the state of the sick. The hospital of the Khásekí, near the women-market, is also an excellentinstitution.

SECTION XXIV.

Of the principal Palaces of Constantinople.

One of the grandest of these is that of Ibráhím Páshá, the Vezír of Sultán Soleïmán, on the At-maidán, in which two thousand pages of the seráï were formerly educated. It is next in point of magnitude to the imperial seráï. The Seráï of Mehrmáh, near the mosque of Sultán Báyazíd, consists of seven hundred separate apartments. But even larger than this is the seráï of Siyávush Páshá, to the north of the mosque of Sultán Soleïmán, which has three hundred rooms, seven baths, fifty shops, and stables more extensive than those of the imperial palace. The others are: the seráï of the ághá of the Janissaries, near the mosque of Sultán Soleïmán; the seráï of Tekelí Mustafá Páshá; of Dallák Mustafá Páshá; of the Defterdár (who was hanged) Mustafá Páshá, near the Soleïmániyeh; of Pertev Páshá at the Vafá; of Sevgelún Moslí Sultáneh, within the corn-market; of Perinjí Zádeh, at Zírekbáshí; of Korshúnlí Sultáneh, in the same place; of Moralí Mustafá Páshá, near the place of the Ajemoghláns; of Kapújí Murád Páshá, near the ink-makers' row; of Silihdár Mustafá Páshá, near the mosque of Soleïmán; of Khoájeh Vezír Mohammed Páshá, near the mosque of the Sháhzádeh; of Kana'án Páshá, near the old Seráï; of Músá Páshá, near Khoájeh Páshá; of Kara Mustáfá Páshá, near Ak-Seráï; of Sokollí Mohammed Páshá, near the Aláï Koshk; of Melek Ahmed Páshá, near Ayá-Sófiya, with three baths and two hundred apartments; of Reís Ismáíl, near Mahmúd Páshá; of Khán Zádeh Sultán, or Bairám Páshá, near Ayá-Sófiya; of Wárwár Alí Páshá, near Sultán Ahmed's mosque; of Emírgúneh Zádeh Yúsuf Páshá, near the stable-gate; of Mokábilijí Hasan Efendí; of the Kapúdán Hasan Páshá, near Ayá-Sófiya; of Aísha Sultáneh, near Ak-Seráï; of Ján Pulád Zádeh Husain Páshá; of Juván Kapijí the Vezír, otherwise the Seráï of Rustam Páshá, near the convent of Khoájeh Ahmed Sultán; of Ankabút Ahmed Páshá; of Khoájeh Ibrahím, better known by the name of Jinjí Khoájeh; of Sáleh Páshá, near Mahmúd Páshá; of Kapúdán Síávush Páshá, near the harbour of galleys; of Ak-Mohammed Páshá, near the Jinjí Maidán; of Balátlí Solák Chelebí; of Husain Aghá, near the mosque of Sultán Selím; the barracks of the Janissaries, near the Orta Jámi'; the palace of Ibrahím, the inspector of the arsenal, near the Vafá, for which the humble writer composed a chronograph.

The following palaces were built by the architect Sinán during the reigns of Sultáns Selím I. and Soleïmán: The imperial palace of Sultán Mohammed II. having been burnt down, it was rebuilt by Sultán Soleïmán, who also restored the Galata Seráï, which was built by Sultán Báyazíd. Sinán also built the palace of Yení-kapú; of Mohammed Páshá, in the galley-harbour; of Mohammed Páshá, at Ayá Sófíya; of Rustam Páshá, Vezír of Sultán Soleïmán; of Kojeh Alí Páshá; in the place of Gúzel Ahmed Páshá's palace, in the Hippodrome, was built the mosque of Sultán Ahmed I.; the seráï of Ferhád Páshá, near Sultán Báyazíd; of Pertev Páshá, on the Vafá; of Kojeh Sinán Páshá, at the Hasán place; of Súfí Mohammed Páshá, near Khoájeh Páshá; of Mohammed Aghá, near Yení-bághcheh; of Sháh Khúbán, near the fountain of Kásim Páshá.

SECTION XXV.

Of the Grand Kháns for Merchants.

The first is the Khoájeh Khán, near the Mahmúd Páshá, in which all the great Persian merchants have their establishments. It has seventy rooms. The khán of Mahmúd Páshá has one hundred and twenty rooms; the Kebejílar Khán one hundred rooms: this is the residence of the rich Bulgarian merchants; the khán of Pírí Páshá, eighty rooms; Eskí Khán, two hundred rooms: it was built by Bairám Páshá, the Vezír of Sultán Murád IV., and is called the khán of the captives (*asír*), because all captives are bought and sold here: it has seventy apartments, and an office for receiving the *penjek* or slave duty, a fifth of the value; the khán of Angora, for the dealers in woollen goods (*súf*), one hundred rooms; the khán of Pertev Páshá, two hundred rooms; the khán of Ferhád Páshá, near the Bezestán, two hundred rooms; Kilíd Khán, two hundred rooms; the khán of the Valídeh Kosím, mother of Murád IV., was originally the palace of Jarráh Mohammed Páshá, but having fallen into decay it was rebuilt by the Válideh, and consists of three hundred warehouses, so that this khán, and that of Mahmúd Páshá, are the largest in Constantinople. In one corner is a koshk, which raises its head to the skies, and commands a magnificent view: its stables are capable of holding one thousand horses and mules: it has a mosque in the centre; the Kiaghid Khán, near Mahmúd Páshá; Kátir Khán, near Takht-ul-kala'; the khán of the honeymarket, inhabited by Egyptian merchants; Ketán Khán; Katá Khán; the khán of Rustam Páshá; the khán of old Yúsuf Páshá; the khán of the Muftí; Chokúr Khán; Súlú Khán; the khán of the tallow-market; and the khán of the Zendán-kapú. All these kháns are in that quarter of the town called Takht-ul-kala': they are extensive buildings, and are covered with lead. The Juván Kapújí Khán is in the centre of the raisin-market. The new khán of Kara Mustafá Páshá, Grand Vezír to Sultán Mohammed IV., near Khoájeh Páshá, is a small but strong building. The khán of Kopreilí Mohammed Páshá, Grand Vezír to Mohammed IV., though, like the last mentioned, a new building, near the poultry-market, is not inferior, as regards solidity, to the Válideh Khán. It has upwards of two hundred and twenty apartments.

SECTION XXVI.

Of the Cárávánseráis.

The Elchí Khán (Ambassador's Khán), even in the time of the infidels, was a khán for strangers, but it was endowed after the conquest by Ikbál Páshá; the cárávánserái of Mohammed II.; of Báyazíd II.; of Selím I.; of Soleïmán; of Khásekí Sultáneh; of Ahmed I.; of the Kapújílar, near Ayá-Sófiya, where two great kháns stand opposite to each other; of Kojeh Mohammed Páshá; of the Vafá; of the At-Maidán; of Sinán Páshá; Báklálí Khán, near the palace of Melek Ahmed Páshá; and of Alí Páshá, near the Bít-bázár (louse-market). These were all built by Sinán Páshá.

SECTION XXVII.

Of the Barracks (Bekár oda).

The most extensive barracks are those called *Yolgechen*, which consist of four hundred rooms, and, in case of necessity, can hold one thousand armed men. The odas of Sultán Murád IV. are eight in number, and, like the former, have their officers and inspectors. Sultán Soleïmán one day being offended with the Janissaries, said to them: "Be silent, or I will subdue you by the shoe-makers at Merján-chárshu (the coral-market). This threat having spread, forty thousand Janissaries assembled instantly, armed with clubs and bludgeons, and with cries of "Allah! Allah!" entered the imperial court. The Emperor, roused by these shouts, came out, and said, "Well, my brave fellows, what is the matter?" They replied, "You have this day declared your intention of putting down the Janissaries by the shoe-makers, and we now wait for your orders. We have on the instant assembled forty thousand men, but if you will wait till to-morrow we shall have forty thousand more." Pleased with their bravery, the emperor told them they might ask for a favour. They, therefore, asked that the price of a pair of *pápújes* and *mests* (slippers and leather-socks) should be fixed at between one and two hundred akcha, which was immediately granted.

The odas of the armoury are near the Mahmúd Páshá; those of Pertev Páshá and Hiláljí, near the Soleïmáníeh; forty odas for unmarried men on the At-maidán; forty at Búyúk Karamán; the odas of Yedek Páshá; and seven odas of Gharíbs, near the corn-market. Each of these barracks can contain from one to two thousand men.

SECTION XXVIII.

Of the Fountains ornamented with Chronographs.

In the times of the infidels there was no other fountain except that called Kirk-chesmeh (supplied by the aqueduct of Valens). In other parts of the town they collected the water in cisterns, five of which were filled partly with rain-water, and partly from the aqueduct. Sultán Mohammed II., having finished his mosque, built two hundred fountains; Báyazíd built seventy, and Soleïmán seven hundred. Their number was shortly increased to thousands by the vezírs. Sultán Soleïmán repaired the aqueduct, and increased the quantity of water carried to Constantinople. The principal fountains are the following: the fountain of Haider Páshá, near the bath of the same name; that of the Beglerbegs, beyond the ditch between the Aderneh-kapú and the Top-kapú; of the Imáms, erected to the memory of Hasan and Husain, who died of thirst in the plain of Kerbelá; the fountain of Skander Beg, without the gate leading to Eyúb; of Sultán Murád III., without the gate of Eyúb, on the sea-shore, beneath the *sháhneshín* (projecting window) of the palace of Fátima Sultána; the Souk-chesmeh (cold fountain), near the Alái koshk; the fountain of Kara Mustafá Páshá, near his sepulchral monument; of Hasan Beg, the son of Fátima Sultána, near the Okjílar Báshí; of the Kehiyá of the Janissaries, Soleïmán Aghá, near the Sernáj Khán; of Alí Páshá, near the custom-house on the land side; of Kátib Husain, near the convent of Oghlán Sheikh at Ak-seráï; of Hájí Mansúr, near the monument of Aáshik Páshá; of the Válideh Kosum, near the Yení-kapú; of Ibrahím Páshá, near the mosque of the princes; of Hasan Páshá, near the palace of Jánpúlád Zádeh; of Kharájí Mohí-ad-dín, before his mosque, near that of Sultán Mohammed II.; of Mahmúd Páshá, near the new Bezestán; of Mesíh Páshá, near the market of Alí Páshá; and of Hasan Aghá, the chief of the Khás-oda, within the corn-market, in the quarter of the Arabajílar.[8]

SECTION XXIX.

Of the Sebíl-khánehs, or Water Houses.

The Sebíl-khánehs were built to the memory of Hasan and Husain, who suffered martyrdom from thirst on the plain of Kerbelá. They are all adorned with chronographs. The Sebíl of Músá Páshá, near the Aláï Koshk; the Sebíl of Kana'án Aghá, opposite the grand gate of Ayá Sófiyah; of A'áishá Sultána, at the Okjílar-báshí; of Mustafá Aghá, the chief of the treasury, near the mosque of Ayá Sófiyah; of Erdebílí, near Ayá Sófiyah; of Kapúdán Kosse Alí Páshá, in the corn-market; of Abbás, the Kizlar Aghá, near the fountain of Lálalí; of Ibrahím Páshá, the Kehiyá of Kopreïlí Zádeh, near the Vafá; and the Sinán Páshá, the conqueror of Yemen, near the factory of the Sirma-kesh (gold-wire).

SECTION XXX.

Of the Principal Baths.

The bath is a legal establishment of the Islám, founded on the text of the Korán: "If you are polluted, purify yourselves." The two baths which existed in Constantinople before the conquest were those of the Azabs and the Takhtáb. The first bath built after the conquest was that at the mosque of Sultán Mohammed II., for the use of the workmen employed in the building of the mosque. Afterwards the bath of the Azabs was converted to the use of the Moslems. The baths next built were those of Vafá, Eyúb, and Chokúr. All these baths are still kept up and repaired by the endowment (*wakf*) of Sultán Mohammed. I have preferred assigning each of the principal baths to a certain class of men in the following amusing way: For the sick, the bath of Ayúb Sultán; for the Sheikhs, that of Ayá Sófiyah; for the Súfís, that called by the same name; for strangers, that called the bath of strangers (*gharíb*); for the Bostánjís, the garden-bath (*bóstán*); for the market-people, that called the Friday-market (Juma' bázár); for debauchees, the Chokúr (the pit); for painters, the Chínlí (Chinese); for the women, the khátún (lady); for sportsmen, the Kojeh Mohammed Páshá; for the Janissaries, the bath of the new barracks (yení oda); for the workmen, that so called (irghát); for the surgeons, the Jerráh (surgeon) Alí Páshá; for the men of the Seráï, that of the Ak-seráï; for the black Arabs, that called the mice (Sichánlí); for the saints, that of Sultán Báyazíd II., the saint; for the insane, the variegated bath (Alájeh); for cruel tyrants, that of Zinjírlí-kapú (chained-gate); for the oppressed, that of Sultán Selím the Just; for the porters, the Sort-hammám; for poets, that of Sultán Suleïmán; for Dervíshes, that of Haider Páshá; for the children of the Arabs, the Takht-ul-kala'; for the favourites, that of the Khásekí; for astronomers, the Yeldiz-hammám (star bath); for merchants, that of Mahmúd Páshá; for mothers, that of the Válideh; for horsemen (*jinjí*), that in the Hippodrome; for Muftís, that of the Muftí; for the Zaims, that of Gedek Páshá; for the armourers, that of Dávud Páshá; for Khoajas, that of the same name; for Sultáns, the bath so called; for Mollás, the bath of Mollá Ko400ní; for the Greeks, the Fener bath (in their quarter); for singers, the Balát (Palatium) bath; for villains, the Khanjarlí (armed with a dagger); for musicians, the Lúnja (or parade); for sailors, the bath of the port of galleys (kádirga límán); for the *imáms*, or chiefs of the baths, that of Little Ayá Sófiyah; for the members of the Díván, the bath of Bairám Páshá; for the eunuchs (*khádim*), that of the eunuch Mohammed Aghá; for the vezírs, that of Alí Páshá; for the generous, that of Lutfí Páshá; for the gardeners, that of

Yení-bághcheh (new garden); for the Albanians, that of the Adrianople-gate; for the Mevlevís, that of the Yení-kapú (new-gate); for the stone-masons, that of the Silivrí-gate; for the magicians, that of the Seven Towers; for beggars, that of Chár-ták; for clerks, that of Nishánjí Páshá; for the Drogománs, the bath so called; for invalids, that of Lanka; for miners, that of Sárígurz; for doctors, the Majúnjí-hammam (medicine-makers); for the Kádíaskers, the bath of the same name; for the Persians, the bath of the Ajem-oghláns; for the sellers of weights and scales, that of the Veznejilár (weighers); for the Shátirs (foot-guards), that of Pertev Páshá; for gamblers, the painted bath (Tesvírlí-hammám); for the Sháfeís, that of the mint (Dharab-kháneh); for lovers, that of the cage (kafeslí); for the Aghás, that of the Little Aghá; for the barley-merchants, that of the Arpa-amíní (the inspector of barley); for the Seids (descendants of the Prophet), that of Abbás Aghá; for women, that of the women-market (Evret-bázár); for the Jews, that of the Jehúd-kapú (Jews-gate); for grooms, that of the Akhor-kapú (stable-gate); for the infirm (Maatúh), that of Koja Mohammed Páshá; for buffoons, that of Shengel; for Kapudáns, the Deníz-hammám (sea-bath); for the Ehl-touhíd (unitarians), the bath of Koja Mustafá Páshá; for dwarfs, that of the Little Aghá; for the elegant, that of the Chelebí (*petit maître*).

In the same manner we allotted the baths in the suburbs, which, with those within, amount to one hundred and fifty-one, all of which I have visited. Seventeen more were built during my travels, but these I have not seen. The most elegant and commodious is the Chokúr-hammám, built by Mohammed II. It is paved with granite, and can accommodate five thousand men. Next in rank may be noticed the baths of Mahmúd Páshá, of Takht-ul-kala', of Báyazíd, and of Koja Páshá; the best lighted up are those of Haider Páshá, the Suleïmáníeh, and the Válideh; the cleanest, those of Ayá Sófiyah, of the Súfis, of Abbás Aghá, and of Mohammed Páshá, in the Chehár Shemba-bázár.

When I was received into the haram of Sultán Murád IV., on the night that I read the Korán, I had the good fortune to see the imperial bath, with which no other in the world can be compared. The four sides of it are assigned to the use of the pages, and in the centre there is an inclosed bath for the emperor. Water rushes in on all sides from fountains and basins, through pipes of gold and silver; and the basins which receive the water are inlaid with the same metals. Into some of these basins, hot and cold water run from the same pipe. The pavement is a beautiful mosaic of variegated stones which dazzle the eye. The walls are scented with roses, musk, and amber; and aloes is kept constantly burning in censors. The light is increased by the splendour and brilliancy of the windows. The walls are dry, the air temperate, and all the basins of fine white marble. The dressing rooms are furnished with seats of gold and silver. The great cupola of the first dressing-room, all of bright marble, may be equalled by that at Cairo only. As this bath stands upon a rising ground it towers to the heavens: its windows all look towards the sea, to Scutari, and Kází-koi. On the right of the door of the dressing-room is the room for the musicians (motrib-khán) and on the left, the cupola of the inner treasury (khazáneh khás). I have no where seen so splendid a bath, except that of Abdál, the Khán of Tiflís, in the province of Ván.

Most of the above baths are adorned with chronographs; and they are all double (chifteh), that is, consist of two rooms, except that of Mohammed Páshá, in the Little-market. In the afternoon women are admitted. If to the great public baths we add the smaller ones, the number would exceed three hundred; and if the private ones are reckoned, they will amount to the number of four thousand five hundred and thirty-six.

END OF PART I.